The Mysteries of Wolf

By: Rev. John Riggs

Order this book online at www.trafford.com
or email orders@trafford.com

Most Trafford titles are also available at major online book retailers.

Note for Librarians: A cataloguing record for this book is available from Library
and Archives Canada at www.collectionscanada.ca/amicus/index-e.html

Printed in Victoria, BC, Canada.

ISBN: 978-1-4269-0441-7

Our mission is to efficiently provide the world's finest, most comprehensive
book publishing service, enabling every author to experience success.
To find out how to publish your book, your way, and have it available
worldwide, visit us online at www.trafford.com

Trafford rev: 8/11/2009

 www.trafford.com

North America & international
toll-free: 1 888 232 4444 (USA & Canada)
phone: 250 383 6864 ♦ fax: 812 355 4082

FOREWORD
By: Rev. John Riggs

In 2005, I published a book entitled **Keyhole Cave**. That book was the result of an actual dream I had one night. Upon waking, I grabbed a notebook and started writing. For several months, I invested every spare minute in capturing that story. Many people read the draft. Without exception, the two comments that I received from the reviewers were "What happened to the Indian boys?" and "What happened to the modern boys?" To be honest, I had been so focused on the story itself; I had not given any thought to those two loose ends. This book expands that original book and supplies the answers to those two questions.

Essentially, the original book is all still within this one and can be found in Chapter 1 and resumes in Chapters 14 through 30. The question of what happened to the Indian boys is found in Chapters 2 through 13. The conclusion of the story is found in Chapters 31 through 46. There is a glossary at the end of the story that includes some terms and phrases which may not be familiar to younger readers. Throughout the story, any word that is included in the glossary will be italicized within the text of the story. A character list is also included at the beginning of the story to aid the reader in keeping track of the many key people who will be introduced during the course of the story.

Throughout my life, friends and family, young and old, have slipped through the fragile veil of life. When I was in the first grade, my best friend, Buddy, died from a bee sting. When I was a senior in high school, my best friend, George, died in an automobile accident. There have been far too many others to list. I don't know why God takes some and leaves others, but I do know that – someday – everyone will make that journey. Whatever you choose to believe will be tested against the real truth, and eternity is a very long time to just "hope" you chose correctly. My earnest prayer is that you will honestly seek to know the real truth before you die and find out for sure.

%%%%%%%

Cover design by: Creston Shrum

Character List

Wolf: An excellent hunter and renowned for his skills.

Deer: Second best hunter of the Indian boys. Survival skills were in place, but his mind was prone to wander.

Rock: Had a talent for fashioning raw stones into highly functional tools. The hunting party relied on him to make the tools that were needed as well as to repair and resharpen the weapons that they had.

Arrow: Arrow's skill was in woodworking and he had the talent to make valuable tools from the natural plant materials that grew abundantly in nature.

Jim Flagstone, Sam Jefferson, Bill Perkins, and Dustin Rogers: Four friends living in the rural area near Huntsville in northwest Arkansas.

Sarah Jackson: Jim Flagstone's girlfriend in high school and then wife

Martha Jefferson: Sam Jefferson's older sister; Archeologist and Professor at the University

Dr. Jerry Smith: Professor of Archeology at the University

Ted Wilson: Landowner and Museum benefactor

Dr. Hodges: Chairman of the Archeology Department

PART 1

Chapter 1

The campfire provided some light as the hunting party sat quietly under the majestic full moon that had risen above the ridgeline. The days were growing longer and the first hints of spring were beginning to emerge. They spoke in low tones about the day's events. Wolf, Deer, Arrow, and Rock were young braves from the Osage tribe.

Not being the most experienced hunters, the four young men had grown up together on the banks of the Big River. The harsh winter had forced most of the able-bodied men and women to forage farther from home than usual in search of food. However, unbeknownst to them, they had traveled, in their youthful zeal, over fifty miles to the south. Now finding themselves well beyond their tribe's normal territory, and gone for almost a month, they quite literally did not know exactly how to get back.

Somewhat to their relief and dismay, they had not encountered any other people; however, the land they were now exploring was clearly rich in wildlife as well as edible plants and nuts. The downside was the rugged terrain. It was clearly not conducive to the more sedentary lifestyle of farming in which they had been raised. Nevertheless, the four friends could not quench their seemingly irresistible curiosity to know what lay beyond the next ridge or around the next bend.

"The turkeys will begin to gobble soon," said Arrow.

"Winter is almost gone. The trees are budding," Wolf added.

"I wonder how far we are from home – as a matter of fact, where is home?" Rock mused more to himself than to anyone else. Deer just sat there, staring at the flickering fire. None of them would admit it, but they were homesick. What started as a big adventure by four young men, each about fifteen summers old, was turning into an endurance test. They knew that they were supposed to be home by now. Before they left home, Deer and Rock had overheard their fathers talking about selecting wives for their respective sons from the neighboring village up the Big River. Both of them could hardly think about anything else despite the beauty and tranquility of the land surrounding their makeshift campsite. They had chosen this overnight locale at the mouth of this previously unexplored hollow. In the morning they would start heading north in hopes of finding their way home.

Deer awoke and noticed that the fire had almost burned out. He tossed a few sticks on the dying coals to keep it going. Far up the hollow was the familiar sound of a tom turkey gobbling in the predawn night. Deer roused Wolf and shared the news. They always hunted in pairs for safety as well as effectiveness.

It was a technique that his father had always insisted on and with their current situation, he fully understood why. Deer knew that the tom would not fly down until sunrise, but their best chance to kill it was to shoot it off its roost using the moonlight to find the wary bird.

They slipped quietly up the hollow and in a few moments were deep into the forest. The full moon provided them with just enough light to see the major obstacles, but the smaller items eluded their fervent scanning. To the boys it sounded like they might as well have been beating a war drum. The tom had sounded off a few times and they knew they were not within bow range yet, but they felt like they were close. One side of the hollow was bounded by a steep solid rock wall. They were glad when they realized that the turkey was not on that hill side. They eased up the hollow for a short distance more and sat down on a log to wait for some sign of the turkey, fearful that they had made too much noise getting this close.

GOBBLE, GOBBLE, GOBBLE!!!!!!

Deer jumped and nearly fell off the log backwards. The tom was just a short distance up the hill from where they were sitting. They decided to use the moon to their best advantage and try to silhouette the bird for a sure shot. Having crossed the narrow valley, they started up the hill. In a few minutes Wolf stopped and pointed to a dark mass that was sitting about halfway up the leafless oak tree. He raised his bow, aimed, and shot. The arrow ricocheted off a limb about half way to the big bird and fell harmlessly to the ground. With clear concentration, he *nocked* a second arrow, adjusted his footing to avoid the previously unseen limb, and launched the second projectile.

True to his skill, Wolf's arrow struck the bird just below the lead edge of the wing and exited through the opposite wing. Impaled by the cedar shaft, rendering both wings immobile, the startled tom came crashing to the ground. Deer was already moving when he heard the arrow hit its mark. By the time the bird bounced twice on the rock-strewn hillside, Deer was on it. Knowing that the big gobbler would probably not be dead, despite the mortal wound that he had sustained, Deer whacked the bird on the head with the staff that he had been carrying as a walking stick. The big spurs of a mature gobbler are nothing that a person wants to tangle with.

Wolf was searching for his first arrow when Deer came back down the hill carrying the bird to where Wolf was standing. The two boys shared quick congratulations and decided to come back after sunrise to find the first arrow. Deer handed the bird to Wolf and they headed back to camp.

As they exited the big woods, they could see two blanket wrapped lumps still sleeping by the smoldering embers of last night's fire. Deer grabbed some small

6

twigs and began to stoke up the coals. The noise and activity roused Arrow and Rock. They both stretched and yawned, looking in disbelief at the large gobbler that was lying at their feet. The first rays of the sun were just breaking the horizon and a day's worth of food for the foursome was ready to be prepared.

Wolf looked at Arrow and Rock, grinned, and said, "I killed it, you two clean and cook it." Knowing that was the deal that they had agreed upon when they left home, Arrow picked up the bird and headed down to the creek. Rock got his stone knives from his tool kit and followed close behind. They weren't really excited about butchering another dead animal that Wolf had killed, especially this early in the morning, but the thought of fresh turkey meat for breakfast made the task tolerable.

The two boys made quick work of the job and returned to camp, where Deer had a perfect fire already going. The morning temperature was still cool enough to see their breath, but it was better than it had been during the past few months. Wolf and Deer related the tale of the hunt to Rock and Arrow as the bird roasted over the open fire.

After the sun rose, Wolf and Deer headed back up the hollow while Rock and Arrow tended the fire and breakfast. The forest certainly looked more open than it did before sunrise and they quickly arrived at the location of the shot. In a few minutes, the first arrow was retrieved but the delicate stone arrow point was missing. Wolf inspected the arrow and decided that the tip as well as the accompanying shaft was probably embedded in the bottom of the limb that he hit. He collected the feathered end of the arrow and the duo headed back toward camp.

They had not walked far when they noticed steam wafting out of the face of the bluff. Wolf took the lead and began to pick his way up the bluff face until he reached the small opening. He peered inside, but could see nothing. He checked for any animal signs to determine if there might be some current occupant inside, but the tiny cave mouth yielded no indication. However, the modest flow of air escaping from the opening suggested that the cave was quite extensive and he longed for a way to explore the pitch-black bowels of the mountain.

"It's a neat little cave. We should take a look before we head for home," Wolf reported down to Deer. Deer nodded in agreement although he was not altogether sure it was a good idea. He figured that Wolf probably meant that he would squirm into the tight shaft and then report back to the other three if there was anything worth seeing.

By the time Wolf and Deer got back to camp, the turkey was almost cooked. Arrow and Rock had each taken a wing for a sample, sure that the cook should taste-test the fare before declaring it ready. It seemed like a good idea, since Wolf was not around to claim his first share. Besides, the wings were flopping through the fire and were clearly done even if the remainder was not.

Seeing the wingless carcass suspended above the fire did not upset Wolf. He knew that the large bird would supply ample meat for all of them. He dropped the slightly shortened arrow into his quiver and sat down next to the fire. To be honest, his mind was reeling with thoughts of the little cave and he began to talk to the others about exploring its dark recesses.

The boys talked about the lore that surrounded caves and they wondered aloud what they would find. The turkey meat quickly disappeared, but their attention was not really focused on it or what a rare treat it was. Their normal diet had consisted mostly of sucker fish they had gigged in the bountiful, clear streams they always camped by.

Arrow fashioned a torch from a bundle of dry river cane that stood nearby, since he was the most resourceful of the four. The fat was scraped from the turkey skin and smeared on the tightly bound head of the primary torch. A piece of tree bark was trimmed down to make a scoop, which they used to scoop up a heaping pile of coals from the dwindling fire. With their gear and the usable remains of the morning's meal stashed under a nearby log, they set out on the third trip up the hollow.

Standing below the tiny cave opening, Arrow and Rock suddenly understood why Deer thought the idea was not well advised. However, Wolf insisted that he would go alone if he had to. They rekindled a fire from the transported coals and Deer and Arrow volunteered to tend the fire. Wolf and Rock started up the bluff. While the path was not simple, it was certainly not treacherous either. As Wolf entered the cave, the torch flickered violently from the rushing air, but stayed lit. As Wolf cleared the opening, Rock followed close behind carrying the four reserve torches and a bag of tinder and kindling, just in case of an emergency.

Neither boy had ever been in such a confined space, but the glow of the torch that seemed to lead the way helped reduce their apprehension. They had slithered just beyond where the light from the opening extended when the cave opened up dramatically into a large, open room. The sound of squeaking bats could be heard but the light of the torch was not strong enough to actually see them. As they entered the room, Wolf suggested that he would stay close to the wall and that Rock should stay at the virtually invisible black hole that was their doorway back to the sunshine. Rock readily agreed, knowing that even without a light he could grope around and find his way out. He also figured he could signal his position in the absolute dark by sparking his flint rock fire starter so Wolf could find him. It seemed like a "safe" plan.

Wolf started to the right, but soon came to a drop off. His torch did not show the bottom and the small rock he dropped over the edge did not give him any reassurance either. He turned around and backtracked to Rock and continued to the left instead. The large room soon bent farther to the left and Rock could see the flickering light, but only indirectly. He hollered at Wolf, "What are you seeing?"

"This room looks like it goes on forever," was Wolf's astonished reply.

Soon Rock was sitting in pitch-black darkness and utter silence except for the squeaks of the bats. It was very unsettling and he began to feel trapped. He rehearsed his escape plan in his mind, but truly wondered what he would do if something happened to Wolf. Besides being his friend, he had provided the bulk of the food they had eaten since they left the village.

After what seemed like a long time, the faint flicker of the torchlight began to dance from around the corner. It was moving quickly. As Wolf rounded the corner, Rock exclaimed, "Well, what did you find?"

A big-eyed Wolf declared, "A huge pile of bat dung!" He continued, "I was quite a ways down the cavernous room and I turned to see if I could see you. Well, I couldn't. I had decided that I should turn back, when I saw a small opening in the wall. I stepped through the opening into the next room and lost my footing. I slid down the side of a huge pile of manure! It was the nastiest stuff I have ever encountered! I managed to keep the torch lit as I clawed my way back up the heap, then I headed out. I recommend that you lead the way – you don't want to follow me!"

Trying to suppress a laugh, Rock quickly turned and headed back into the tiny shaft that led to the exit. In his haste, he left the unused torches lying on the floor of the large room where he had been sitting and waiting. Wolf dropped his exhausted torch and followed close behind. Both boys were thrilled to see the growing daylight near the exit.

Rock emerged and could not help but grin. Wolf emerged immediately behind him but his face was declaring his relief. The two explorers scampered down the bluff and reunited with Arrow and Deer, where the three sat and listened as Wolf related all of the details of the less than spectacular adventure. Rock, Arrow, and Deer headed back down the hollow to retrieve their gear while Wolf headed for the creek. The water was cold but he had to get cleaned up. The cleaner he got, the less he figured it was necessary, until he finally rationalized that the smell would be a good cover scent for tomorrow's hunting. He soon descended the hollow and joined the other boys at their overnight campsite.

The next few days progressed fairly normally, except that Wolf complained about being tired. Wolf had never complained about being tired. Something was wrong. Deer picked up the slack. They made concerted efforts to head north. They soon moved far enough to the north to notice that the trees were not budded. They did not hear any turkeys either. Happily the days were getting warmer but more importantly the nights were not so cold.

Ten days into their journey, Wolf was too sick to keep up. Fortunately, the evening before, they had wandered into a village. It was not an Osage village, but the people were eager to hear the tales of these young adventurers and share some food with them. The boys told about the bountiful land to the south and regaled especially the young women with stories of their travels, including Wolf's most exciting discovery in the cave. Despite his obvious embarrassment, he managed to defend himself by pointing out that the others were not brave enough to even go that far.

During the night, Wolf had a dream that he was playing in a game of chunky. He had seen the game played in his village by the older braves when there was leisure time or when there was a contest of strength and physical prowess. In his dream, he realized that he was dreaming, but everything seemed so real. The next morning Wolf was too weak to travel. Rock, Arrow, and Deer consulted with the elders and got basic directions for finding their way home. Unfortunately, it was still too far for Wolf to travel in his degenerating condition. The elders vowed to take care of him and try to return him to his former health. The boys vowed to go home and then return for Wolf later if he did not return home on his own soon.

Chapter 2

Deer had tossed and turned all night, barely able to rest. He missed Wolf very much. This realization had only fully surfaced since his return home without his good friend. Returning home had indeed been good, especially after the grand adventure that the foursome had undertaken, but he knew it was his duty to bring help and get Wolf back home also. Rock and Arrow had not rested much better. When the sun finally began to rise, it was a relief to just go ahead and get up.

Wolf's father was already sitting alone by a small campfire at the center of the village. The others knew he was meditating and praying to the ancestors for guidance and help. However, at the emergence of the three boys from their respective homes, he rose from the fireside and quietly began to take final inventory of the supplies and gifts he had assembled the evening before. The boys approached him carrying their own packs. He glanced up briefly and smiled at each of them to silently acknowledge their presence, but more so to affirm the common mission they were about to embark upon.

Chief Long Feather soon appeared from the surrounding twilight and joined the entourage. It was thought that it would be a sign of good faith if Wolf's chief were to lead the journey to the distant village where Wolf had remained due to his illness. Wolf's father suspended his rummaging and turned to face the chief.

"Chief Long Feather, it is very kind of you to join us on this journey. I know it will be such a beneficial gesture in building a relationship with these distant people," Running Bear said.

"I too believe this is not only a necessary diplomatic measure, but I personally desire to find our missing brave. I have watched Wolf grow up and have truly admired the skills that he has mastered at such a young age. He will grow to be a leader of our people. I want to do everything possible to see that that comes to pass," the Chief replied.

Wolf's three friends stood nearby and listened as the two men continued talking. Deer had supplied the most accurate description of the distant village and how to relocate it. Everything was ready. It was time to leave. As the small band of travelers set out, there was a level of anxiety within the boys that bounced back and forth between the feelings of foreboding and exhilaration.

Chief Long Feather and Bear walked side by side through the expansive forest, talking in low, hushed tones. The three boys followed quietly behind them, making observations of things like the occasional rock outcrop and the different kinds of flowers which were beginning to bloom. Gray squirrels

11

would periodically scamper across the path or sit on an overhead limb and bark as the travelers passed by. Spring was certainly in full swing. The pleasant temperatures that existed that morning were steadily rising. The sun continued to climb and was now directly overhead. The boys were beginning to wonder if the two men were planning to take a rest break anytime soon. The boys had spent four days traveling from the distant village to their home, but they had taken their time along the way. This trip should only take a couple of days at the pace they were traveling.

Arrow reached into his pack and got a handful of parched nuts and popped them into his mouth. Rock and Deer then followed suit and took a snack from their packs as well. Apparently, the crunching from the rear of the group did not go unnoticed because the chief turned and said, "Let's take a break and rest by this stream for a few minutes. There is no need to walk all the way without stopping."

They had been making their way along the south edge of the Big River *floodplain*. The trail was well worn and very familiar to the men. They had walked through several small camps and had simply waved to the residents as they passed by. It was not uncommon to have people pass through the area without stopping to visit. After all, these camps were part of the same tribe as their own, and the news of the upcoming journey had already preceded their arrival. Everyone was aware of the mission. No one wanted to delay them until they were returning with Wolf in their midst.

The travelers got a drink from the cool stream and then chose a resting place nearby where a large tree had fallen beside the trail. The log made a nice bench where they could all sit down for a few moments. The boys waited until the two men had settled down before they chose their respective places. Since they had already eaten some of the food they carried, they each decided they would save the rest for later. After Chief Long Feather and Bear had eaten a portion of food, they arose and resumed the journey. The boys grabbed their packs, thankful for the brief rest, and quickly took their place at the rear of the solemn parade.

They steadily walked eastward until mid-afternoon, then turned south, following a large creek that the boys had followed on their way home several days before. This creek was a major stream leading out of the mountains and would eventually lead them back to the village where they left Wolf. They had passed the last village of their own tribe some time before and had not seen any other settlements since. The trail had also deteriorated significantly, forcing the travelers to walk single file. Occasionally fallen trees blocked the dim path, forcing momentary detours around the obstructions. Although Bear still lead the way, Deer was now walking immediately behind him relaying his recollection of various details to Bear, thus assuring everyone that they were indeed on the correct path. As the sun reached the horizon, it was clear that further progress would not be possible today. They moved away from the trail a short distance and climbed onto a knoll where they could settle down for the night.

The boys gathered a couple of armloads of dead limbs and enough kindling to get a fire started. They had seen abundant evidence that black bears and mountain lions were common in this relatively uninhabited area. It was agreed that a fire would discourage any wild predators and hopefully keep them at bay. With the fire going, they each dug into their own packs and pulled out a few morsels of food that they had brought for this meal. Neither Chief Long Feather nor Bear had ever ventured into this area.

Deer looked at his two friends and said, "If we cover as much distance tomorrow as we did today, we should arrive at our destination tomorrow afternoon." They nodded in agreement. The two elders had judged that the destination should be reachable in two days, but it was reassuring to hear that the boys thought so, too.

Each of them pulled a blanket from their pack and then raked up a pile of leaves to make a bed. It was not as good as home, but after the distant march, they each quickly drifted off to sleep.

The first morning light was barely visible through the treetops when the small band of travelers roused and began to prepare for the next day's leg of the journey. When it was light enough to see, they began moving south once again.

The farther they walked, the steeper the terrain around them became. While their path had become more akin to a game trail, they determined to maintain a southward direction and to stay along the main creek channel that they had chosen to follow.

After a brief stop to rest and eat a midday meal, they were back on the journey. As the valley progressively narrowed, the amount of water flowing in the stream diminished as well. Deer said, "We should reach a clearing soon. There was an abandoned farm there. I remember it because there was a flock of hen turkeys feeding there when we passed through this area last time."

Almost before Deer finished speaking, an opening in the forest could be seen in the distance. "There it is!" Rock exclaimed. A sense of renewed assurance could be seen in each of their weary faces. Deer glanced at Arrow and received a confident smile. They were almost there.

No wildlife was present when the travelers arrived this time. However, they were most eager to find the trail that led up and over the ridge. It was easily found near the partially collapsed hut.

"If we follow this trail, it will take us to the village where Wolf is," Deer declared.

Bear nodded and guided the group onto the path, and with a sense of accomplishment they began to ascend. The path was clear enough, but the higher they hiked, the rockier it became. At one point, the trail reached the base of a bluff just below the summit. The view was spectacular. Since they were well above the tops of the trees that were growing on the slopes below them, they could see for many miles back down the valley they had just hiked up and even further beyond.

While a refreshing breeze was a welcome relief when they were down in the valley, it was even more appreciated with the strenuous climb up the steep ridge. Despite the very slow progress, it was unanimously agreed that this was a perfect place for a break.

Apparently they were not the first ones to think so. Several walking sticks were leaned up against a large rock that was lying just inside the overhanging bluff. Chief Long Feather walked over and selected one. "This may be useful for getting an old man down the other side," he quipped to himself.

The boys looked at each other, exchanging grins and nods of agreement. Respect for the elders of the tribe demanded that they keep whatever was racing around their individual minds more or less to themselves. Bear had heard the chief's comment as well but showed no reaction to it. He more fully understood the physical limitations of getting older. After all, he was not as young as he once was either.

The trail continued for a short distance before arriving at a low saddle on the ridge top. Thankfully, there was no need to climb any higher. The trail down the south side of the ridge was not as steep and they were able to navigate it much more easily. Smoke from a campfire wafted up the mountain from the village somewhere below. Their destination would soon be at hand and the anxiety of what they would discover weighed on their minds like a cold winter rain.

Chapter 3

Well before the party of travelers arrived at the village nestled in the valley far below, news of their approach was circulating amongst the people. The watchmen had spotted them shortly after they crossed the ridge top and began their careful descent down the zigzagging path. Near the base of the ridge a few huts were located along the trail leading to the main part of town. The women and children who lived in them had already taken their places nearby to watch the strangers pass. While traders and hunting parties from other tribes occasionally traversed the mountain trail for one reason or another, no one could remember ever seeing a chief from a distant village coming to town. This was indeed a rare and exciting event.

The boys were trying to absorb every sight and sound as they walked past. The local residents smiled and waved politely from doorways or other places where they were busy with their daily tasks. The overall mood was quite positive, and it encouraged the travelers to think that Wolf was there and would soon be headed back home. Some of the young girls recognized the three boys and whispered and pointed before ducking back into the shadows behind open doorways. The boys glanced at each other, smiled, and occasionally offered a timid wave to a girl who seemed especially intrigued by their passing. It was a very encouraging initial reception, to say the least.

After passing several grass-thatched huts and seeing only women and children, Bear spotted an old man sitting on a log beside the trail not too much farther ahead. As Bear approached, the man stood up and stepped toward the trail. Chief Long Feather and Bear smiled at the stoop-shouldered, elderly man, and each raised his right hand in a traditional greeting. "Good afternoon, sir," Chief Long Feather began. "I am Chief Long Feather and this is Running Bear. We are looking for your tribal chief."

The old man mustered a gentle, yet toothless, smile then simply pointed down the trail and shuffled back to his log-perch. The travelers stepped back onto the trail and continued walking south. There was a faint sound of voices and general activity ahead, but the vegetation obscured their line of sight.

"Everyone seems very pleasant and friendly," Bear observed.

"The boys said that these people were very helpful to them when they were here before," Chief Long Feather added. "I know that they have taken good care of Wolf."

As they rounded the last bend in the trail, a large opening in the forest appeared. There were dozens of grass-thatched huts scattered around the perimeter with several larger communal buildings in the center. A general flurry of activity could be seen in and around most of the homes. Men, women, and children seemed to be hurriedly attending to some last-minute details, but it was not altogether clear to the travelers just what they were doing.

A trail of smoke was rising from the main building near the center of the numerous structures. A quick glance between the two men surmised that this was where the chief would be found. At virtually the same moment, two young men stepped out of the huts on either side of the trail and approached the band of travelers. Chief Long Feather and Running Bear once again raised their right hand in the traditional greeting as the chief said, "I am Chief Long Feather and this is Running Bear. We are looking for your tribal chief."

"Welcome to our town, sir. It is very nice to have you here. Our chief, Red Eagle, is in the council house and has been anticipating your arrival. We are all pleased to meet you."

Bear remained silent and dropped in line behind Chief Long Feather as the two men led them to the council house. While he certainly understood the formal pleasantries and the protocol of this meeting, he was really more interested in being reunited with his missing son. He consoled himself with the thought that in just a few moments he would have his answer. However, the fact that Wolf was not there to greet them had certainly darkened his *countenance* and sent his mind racing.

As they approached the council house, one of the young men slipped inside while the other stopped at the door. The travelers also stopped and waited for their invitation to enter. Almost by the time they stopped, the first man returned with a big smile and motioned everyone to come inside.

It was not customary for young boys to be invited into the council house, but as guests in the company of a visiting chief it would have been rude to exclude them. The three boys knew they were to be on their best behavior and to remain invisible, if possible.

Knowing that there was a rather awkward situation with the young boys being present, Bear motioned for them to sit down along the wall just inside the door. They gladly complied. Chief Long Feather and Bear crossed the small space and approached Chief Red Eagle, who was standing beside the small fire. Once again, Chief Long Feather made the introductions with all of the traditional words and gestures befitting the meeting of two leaders. Chief Red Eagle returned the greetings and invited them to join him by the fire. The two young men who had brought the travelers to the council house took their places just slightly farther back from the fire to signify their reduced status to

16

those at the inner circle, but still closer than the three wide-eyed boys sitting quietly against the wall.

As their eyes adjusted to the dim light emanating from the fire, they could see the walls of the council house were made of mud that had been packed over a standard framework of saplings and small sticks. It was the same design that was used in their own village. However, the amazing thing was that the inside walls were painted with all kinds of figures and scenes depicting hunting successes, military victories, and even a section which looked like a map with villages arranged along a stream. Along the top of the wall, above the various drawings, was a narrow shelf that encompassed the room. On the shelf, the boys could barely make out what appeared to be gourds but they had a different shape than any gourd with which they were familiar.

Arrow leaned over close to Rock's ear and asked, "What are those things on the shelf? They look like gourds with holes in them." It was a question that all three were thinking. They really wanted to take a closer look, but did not dare to move.

Chief Red Eagle picked up a stick and stirred the fire, causing the flames to increase slightly, casting just enough light to help the boys identify the objects on the shelves.

"HEADS!" Rock blurted out loudly before he could stop himself and then clamped both hands over his mouth as he realized that he was not supposed to make a sound.

Chief Red Eagle had heard the quiet question regarding the objects on the shelves and when he heard Rock's shocked announcement, he could not help laughing heartily. Chief Long Feather and Bear both whipped their heads around and glared at the boys, who were each wishing they had waited outside.

"Those are the skulls of our honored dead ancestors," Chief Red Eagle began to explain. "We keep them here so that they can listen in on our council meetings and help us to make the right decisions."

"We have much the same kind of wall of honor in our council house, too," Chief Long Feather interjected, not wanting Chief Red Eagle to be offended. "These boys have never been in the council house before, though. I am sorry for any unintended disrespect."

"No offense taken, Chief Long Feather. I would expect much the same reaction from anyone who was unfamiliar with this custom," Chief Red Eagle replied.

After a few more minutes of general conversation, Chief Long Feather said, "I am sure you are aware of the reason for our visit. Running Bear is the father of Wolf, one of our young men who was left here many days ago when he fell ill during an exploring adventure with these three boys," gesturing over his shoulder to Arrow, Rock and Deer. "I am very grateful for your hospitality and care. We have come to take him back home."

Red Eagle looked up from the fire with a perplexed scowl on his face and said, "Did he not return home a few days ago? He seemed to have gotten well enough to travel and he set out for home about five days ago. One of our young men led him to the top of the ridge and watched him descend the other side until he was out of sight. I just assumed that your visit today was to establish friendly relations between our towns. Oh, I had no idea..." His words trailed off as his mind raced to rearrange the new facts and formulate the proper response. However, silence filled the room as everyone came to grips with the fact that Wolf was gone. Not just gone from this village; he was probably gone forever.

Bear had been sitting completely still through much of this time, just listening. He leaned forward slightly and spoke with all the control that he could muster, "Chief Red Eagle, I truly appreciate what your people did, taking care of my son during his time here. Can you share any details with me – things he said, things he did? I would greatly appreciate knowing." As he finished, he leaned back once again and waited.

Chief Red Eagle sat motionless for a moment, pondering the request. "I will take you to meet the woman who actually took care of your son. She will be more able to give you the information you seek." As he finished speaking, he rose to his feet. Chief Long Feather and Bear rose as well. The two young men were already moving toward the door. The boys stood also but did not move until all of the elders had exited the room.

Chief Red Eagle was taller, more muscular, and somewhat younger than Chief Long Feather, but older than Bear. He quickly walked across the open courtyard and proceeded toward one of the huts along the perimeter. The men from the council house followed closely behind him, each in the order of his corresponding social status. Bear noticed that the general din of activity had stopped as everyone watched the parade of men leave the council house. It was obvious to all of those standing around that something important was afoot.

The hut was nothing special on the outside, but Chief Red Eagle stopped at the door, bowed his head, and uttered a brief prayer. When he lifted his head, a shriveled old woman no taller than a young girl was standing in the doorway. Her long, straight, black ponytail was pulled over her left shoulder and hung in an elegant flow down her chest. The buckskin robe she wore was highly decorated with beads, shells, and painted symbols. She was obviously the Medicine Woman, and from the respect the chief had demonstrated, she was very powerful.

Chief Red Eagle smiled and began the introductions of the extensive line of men who were standing behind him. When he got to Bear, he added, "This is Wolf's father."

The mere mention of Wolf's name drew a broad smile across her face and she stepped forward to greet him first. She was so old and grizzled that she felt no need to greet strangers in any particular order based on social status or any other criteria. She could do what she wanted in any way that she wanted to do it.

"It is an honor to meet you, sir. Wolf is a wonderful young man. I know that you are very proud of him. You have taught him well," the Medicine Woman said.

Bear smiled and graciously accepted her sincere compliment, but when their eyes locked on each other, her smile wilted.

"Where is Wolf?" she pointedly asked.

Bear quietly replied, "We don't know. We thought he was still here and have come to bring him home, but Chief Red Eagle said that he left about five days ago. He never arrived back home and we did not see him anywhere along the way." At that point Bear stopped speaking and stared at the Medicine Woman hoping she would have some answers to share with him.

The Medicine Woman sighed as her eyes turned to stare at the ground. Using her big toe, she began to rub a rock which was lying on the bare ground in front of her. After a rather uncomfortable silence, she looked up and said, "I was afraid of that. He had gotten stronger and was eager to go home, but every time he would awaken from his sleep, he would relate the strangest stories. I believed that it was being caused by the fever, but there was something different about these dreams. They were so vivid that he would describe them as if he were traveling to another world. I had prayed for him to make it home."

The others began to back away as Bear engaged her in conversation to extract as many details as possible. She took Bear by the hand and led him into her hut, closing the buckskin flap behind him to signal that this was a private conversation.

Chief Red Eagle and Chief Long Feather recognized that as their cue to retire to other quarters. The long shadows of late afternoon were beginning to lengthen as the sun descended toward the horizon. Chief Red Eagle called the two attendants to him and said something. They turned quickly and hurried away. He then turned to Chief Long Feather and said, "Please return to the council house with me. There will be something arriving momentarily for us to eat."

In the flurry of all of the activity, Chief Long Feather had forgotten about the gifts he and Bear had brought. "That would be wonderful. We can certainly take care of other important matters there while Bear is conferring with your medicine woman," Chief Long Feather answered.

The boys were not sure what they were supposed to do, so they just continued to follow some distance behind the two chiefs as they walked and talked. It certainly seemed that it was destined to be a very beneficial alliance between the two villages. When they had been there previously, they had slept in a hut which was unoccupied. The thoughts of eating and then getting to bed were certainly foremost on their minds despite the pervading sadness of not finding Wolf as they had hoped.

As they reentered the council house, several women were coming out. The smell of fresh flat bread greeted them warmly once they were inside. Sitting on a bench near the fire, the chiefs found a pot of stew and several loaves of bread. Chief Red Eagle invited the boys to join them near the fire. Everyone sat down, and with a minimum of formality they began to eat.

Chief Long Feather finished eating and opened his knapsack, retrieving several small items from it. As he handed them to Chief Red Eagle, he expressed his personal appreciation for the hospitality and generosity that had been shown to him and his companions. Chief Red Eagle graciously accepted the gifts and, after genuinely looking them over carefully, he placed them on the bench beside the remnants of food.

After everyone had eaten their fill, Chief Red Eagle turned to the boys and said, "If you boys are ready for sleep, the empty hut is still available. You know where it is. Help yourselves. Chief Long Feather and I still have some business to attend to."

The boys looked at each other and quickly rose to their feet. They thanked him for the food and quickly slipped out into the night. It was now dark and they had to stop and get their bearings so they could find the vacant hut. When they arrived at the door, Arrow cautiously lifted the cover and called out, "Is there anyone in here?"

When there was no reply, they entered and groped around in the dark until they found their respective beds. It was not long until all three were fast asleep. It had been a stressful day.

Chapter 4

Light was filtering through the doorway as Deer awoke. Morning had come and it was time to get up. At first, he could not figure out where he was, but as the cobwebs cleared from his mind, he remembered. Arrow and Rock were beginning to rouse. Both had rather confused looks on their faces and Arrow could not help but snicker. In a few minutes, they were all up. Each collected his few belongings and then stepped outside. They needed to determine what the plan was for the day. If they were going to head for home, they knew that it would be best if they got started soon. Furthermore, if Wolf was out there – somewhere, they felt like they really needed to start searching even though they each felt that it would be futile. Once outside, they looked all around hoping to see Chief Long Feather or Bear, but neither one could be seen.

"What do you think we should do?" Arrow asked.

"I think we should either sit right here and wait for Chief Long Feather or Bear to show up or we can go back to the council house and see if they are there waiting on us," Deer responded.

"Let's go the council house," Rock interjected.

With three nods indicating a consensus, they started across the bare courtyard to the council house. Since the hut where they spent the night was actually behind the council house, they could not see the door of the council house from where they were standing. As they approached the front door, they could hear voices coming from inside. One of the attendants from the day before was sitting just outside.

"Is Chief Long Feather and Bear inside?" Deer asked.

"Yes. They are waiting for you. I believe they intend to begin the journey home as soon as possible," the young man said.

Deer led the other two inside where they found Chief Red Eagle, Chief Long Feather, Bear, and the Medicine Woman sitting around the council fire praying. The boys did not interrupt the prayer. They just stood reverently near the door with their heads bowed until the adults had finished.

At the conclusion, Chief Long Feather said, "Boys, let's head for home."

Each of those seated by the fire stood and began to walk toward the doorway. The three boys stepped aside as they passed, then followed them back out into the morning sunlight. Their eyes had just gotten adjusted to the dim light inside. Now back out in the bright light, they squinted and rubbed their eyes trying get adjusted once again.

Chief Red Eagle led the group to the edge of the town where there was a brief exchange of words and farewell embraces. It was clear that a new friendship existed between the two villages even if neither one ever visited the other again. Just knowing that your nearest neighbor is not your enemy is a great comfort.

The Medicine Woman pulled Deer aside. She had a special word just for him. "Search for your friend. He needs you to attend to him. In exchange, he will be with you forever." When she finished speaking, she turned with no further ado and walked back to her home.

With the general flurry of activity, no one really noticed that she had singled Deer out, but her words burned into his mind as he replayed them over and over, pondering what they meant. When he came to his senses, Chief Long Feather and Bear had already started up the trail that led toward home. Rock and Arrow had started that way, too, but stopped to be sure Deer was coming. Deer shook his head slightly and turned to catch the group. In a few moments, the main clearing where the town existed was once again obscured by the lush new vegetation which was springing up from the forest floor.

Bear followed close behind Chief Long Feather as the group made their way back up the ridge. There was very little conversation. The journey seemed especially slow since they were following the oldest member of the party up the side of a mountain. Chief Long Feather did quite well for his age and overall physical condition, but it was clear that the borrowed walking stick was providing a much needed helping hand on the rough terrain.

After a few brief rest breaks on the ascent, they finally reached the saddle of the mountain and looked down the other side toward home. "This is the last place that anyone saw Wolf alive," Deer thought to himself. His next thought was, "I must find him. He needs me," reinforcing the Medicine Woman's words that were echoing in his head.

Bear had been conspicuously silent all morning. His own mind was replaying the stories that the Medicine Woman had shared with him last night. The insights she had were so much greater than his own, and even she was mystified by the illness and the subsequent wild stories that Wolf had shared with her.

As the troupe started down the ridge, a sense of purpose seemed to unify them under a single objective: find Wolf. While Chief Long Feather stuck to the dim

23

trail, Bear and the boys strayed well off the trail looking for any sign of the missing boy. The reality, however, was that with the progressively warmer days during the past six days since Wolf was last seen, it would be their sense of smell that was most likely going to lead them to his current location. All of them were acutely aware of this fact. None of them mentioned it.

Chief Long Feather was moving downhill when he caught sight of the clearing with the abandoned farm just a short distance ahead. He looked around and could not see or hear Bear or the boys, so he whistled in Bear's direction. Bear responded with an agreed-upon response-whistle. The boys, hearing both signals, began to converge from the margins of the search area. They met at the clearing.

"It is time to rest and eat our midday meal," Chief Long Feather announced. "It will give us time to discuss our strategy for searching on the remainder of our journey home."

They continued across the clearing, past the old hut, and down toward the creek which had led them to this place the previous morning. "With all of the things which have happened since yesterday, it seems like ages since we passed this place," Deer commented. Everyone nodded in agreement as the procession reached the creek.

"This looks like a good spot," Chief Long Feather stated as he stopped and sat down on the ground.

The other four sat down nearby and began to pull out an assortment of food from their packs. The women from Chief Red Eagle's town had provided each of them with a supply of food which would be more than ample to last until they made it back home. Arrow and Rock were making short work of a loaf of flat bread, while Deer was digging deep into a bag of pecan halves. None of the boys had had time to eat that morning and they were all quite hungry. Chief Long Feather and Bear had eaten some dried deer meat and some parched corn before the boys arrived that morning, but they were ready for a small snack just the same.

After the feeding frenzy subsided, Bear said, "I believe that we should pair up and walk parallel to the trail especially from here down to the Big River. Chief Long Feather will walk the trail, Rock and Arrow will take the right side, and Deer and I will take the left side. Each pair should stay just within calling range of the trail." He continued on with details of the different calls to be used for staying in contact and which special call to be used if something is found. It sounded very logical and they agreed that it was the plan they would use. Bear felt sure that Wolf had made it off the mountain, but he never reached the first village on the Big River. He had to be here – somewhere.

Unfortunately, it was still many miles to search and it was the most perilous section of their journey.

With lunch completed, the five searchers took their assigned positions and proceeded to make their way north. Initially, they were almost within sight of each other because of the narrow nature of the valley coupled with its steep side walls. However, they soon were able to spread out more and the plan took shape as proposed. Despite their diligence, no sign of Wolf was found.

As they neared the Big River, the shadows of the late afternoon were once again beginning to stretch well beyond the trees that were casting them. Chief Long Feather gave the call to reconvene and the flank members once again converged at the main trail.

"It is time to make camp for the night. With the extensive shadows, it would be difficult to see anything if it were there," Chief Long Feather declared.

He was right. They truly wanted to keep searching, but it was necessary to get some rest so they could resume the effort afresh in the morning. The boys gathered wood for the fire, while Bear cleared some leaves and underbrush from the campsite, then gathered some rocks for the fire ring. Soon, there was a nice fire crackling and they ate a final bite of food for the day. With an adequate pile of leaves raked together to meet their individual preferences, each person settled in for a final night under the stars before they would return home. Within a few minutes, the only sound that could be heard was from the crickets that seemed to be singing to the rhythm of the dancing flames in the center of a ring of men, bound together by the mission they were on.

Morning light was breaking over the horizon when they began to stir. There was no need to get going immediately. They needed to have sufficient light so they could resume the search. Bear added some wood to the embers remaining from last night's fire. Within a few minutes the flames were dancing again and they each pulled up closer to it. It was getting warmer during the day, but the early mornings were still just a little cool.

Before long, the sun's rays were filling the forest and the fog which had been hanging in the valley began to lift. The fire was doused with water from the nearby creek and the search parties spread out once again in a final effort to find Wolf.

They had been making steady progress north when Chief Long Feather signaled for them to converge. When everyone arrived, they realized that they had indeed arrived at the place where the northward trail met the trail that lead back home. They had returned to the Big River Valley.

With the minor adjustment of direction from north to west, the searchers spread back out and continued their effort, whistling periodically to maintain contact with Chief Long Feather back on the trail. About midday, they arrived at the eastern-most village of their own tribe. They entered the village, briefly sharing the story of their journey over the mountain, the people they met there, their helpfulness and friendliness, and the apparent fate of Wolf. Before long, the five men were back on the trail. From this point on, they all remained on the trail. Additional searching was not necessary because if Wolf had made it this far, the people from the local village would have seen him go by or discovered his body.

For the remainder of the trip, most of their conversation was muted and minimal. They were officially in mourning.

Just before dark, they walked back into their home town. Messengers from the neighboring village had run ahead and informed everyone of the bad news. The atmosphere of the town certainly reflected that news, too. Weeping could be heard coming from several huts.

Before they dispersed Bear said, "Thank you, Chief Long Feather, for your leadership and efforts to find my son. You are indeed a great leader for our people."

Chief Long Feather stepped forward and gave Bear a long embrace, then he turned and walked to his own home.

Bear turned to Deer, Arrow, and Rock and said, "When we left here four days ago, you were boys. Today, you have returned home as young men. Hardships will come and when they do, you will face them as men as you have these past two days. Your parents can be as proud of you as I am. Return to your homes. You have earned your rest."

Each of the three quietly thanked Bear for the kind words and promised to continue to be men that make him proud. They each turned and shuffled toward their respective homes.

Once alone, Bear turned and headed for the council house. He wanted to spend some time with the ancestors knowing that Wolf was with them now.

Chapter 5

The next few days around the village seemed very strange. Gray clouds seemed to have filled the sky and the wind was blowing hard all day and night. The town was in mourning and it certainly appeared that the earth was joining them in that effort. However, on the fourth day, the sun broke bright and clear. It promised to be a beautiful day.

Deer dropped by Arrow's home to see if he would like to go spear-fishing down at the river.

"That would be great! I think Rock is caught up on his chores as well. Let's get him to go, too," Arrow added.

"That sounds great. You go get Rock and I will go get my spears," Deer replied.

Arrow headed one direction and Deer headed the other. In a few moments, they returned. Deer had several spears while Arrow and Rock had gathered some cord, a stone knife, and a split-cane basket in case they actually caught anything.

The young men made their way down through the woods to the river. Despite the occasional rains that had fallen this Spring, the river was still fairly low, which was certainly advantageous for spear fishing. You could wade out in the shoals and the water would never be over waist deep.

With the bright sunshine, the air temperature was very pleasant. However, the water was still chilly. Regardless, they did not want to get their buckskin pants wet, so they slipped them off and laid them and their shirts on a log on the bank. Before long the three naked boys were stalking through the clear water in search of anything that moved, especially those big gar fish that like to linger on the shoals in the Spring to spawn. Deer's mother made the best gar cakes and he was really in the mood for eating some.

The boys were so intent on fishing that they did not notice the three teenage girls who had overheard their plans and followed them down to the river. With their clothes left unattended on the bank, the girls seized upon the opportunity to make an impression. They each were particularly sweet on a different one of the three boys, but the boys had just not been responding to their advances as intently as desired. They waited until all three boys were facing away and one of the girls slipped from her hiding place and gathered up the shirts and pants before retreating back into hiding. The boys never saw a thing.

Once securely out of sight, each girl slipped out of her own buckskin dress and into the pants and shirt of their specific choice for a future husband. Then, with cat-like stealth, the clothes-snatching girl slipped back down to the log and left the three dresses in their place before she returned to the cover of the riverside vegetation. They had initial thoughts of just taking their clothes but decided that was too mean, so they left their own dresses behind. Besides being a clever calling card for the caper, it would give the boys something to cover themselves with so they could get back home.

After a few hours of wading and jabbing at things in the water, the boys had managed to spear a few sucker fish, but nothing else. The cold water had turned their legs numb and they decided to get out on the bank and warm up. As they approached the log where they left their clothes, the sound of girls snickering nearby shifted their attention from fishing to their total nudity. While they were certainly comfortable with their own bodies, it was a completely different matter for some girls to see them naked. They made a dash for their clothes only to discover the sheer magnitude of the prank which had been played on them.

Their first thought was to chase the girls down and get their clothes back, but they also knew that the girls would have taken the proper precautions to maintain a safe distance that would prevent themselves from being caught. Secondly, the thought of being stark naked and chasing a girl through the forest was downright embarrassing, almost as much as standing there naked holding a dress. They recognized the beadwork on each dress and knew exactly who each dress belonged to. Before they could really figure out what to do, the ring-leader of the heist, named Snowflake, called out and said, "Deer, if you will bring my dress to my home, I will give you your clothes back."

Deer yelled back, "How do you propose I do that – just walk into town naked and deliver it to you?"

"Well, I don't think that would be a terribly good idea. Use your imagination, great adventurer," she challenged playfully.

Deer turned and sat down on the log. He held the dress up and said, "There is no way I would wear a dress into town. There has got to be another option."

None of the three girls were half as big as any of the three boys and there was no way they would have put one of the dresses on anyway.

Rock had been standing with his mouth open in total disbelief of what had just occurred. Arrow was more inclined to chase them down even if it meant running through the village naked.

Deer looked at what they had and said, "Rock, give me your dress and some cord. Arrow, give me your dress, too." After a second, both naked boys handed over the dresses and simply stood there dumbfounded. Deer continued, "I am going to tie these three dresses together and make a tunic. I will walk back home and get my other clothes and then get some clothes from your homes and bring them back to you before we go get our stolen clothes back."

That plan certainly appealed to Rock and Arrow even though it meant they had to sit naked on the river bank until Deer returned. It was all right for little boys to run around in public naked, but for men to do that was just – well, weird. Bear had said that they were young men now and that they should act like men. In their minds, this was certainly going to be a setback on their road to responsible adulthood.

Deer tied the three dresses together where one dress hung flat in front and one down his back like a poncho. He wrapped the third one around his waist underneath the other two. Finally, using a piece of cord as a belt, he tied the configuration together.

"I'll be right back," Deer said as he turned to leave.

"We'll be right here," Rock responded with disgust.

Deer made his way toward town as directly as possible without passing through any places where he suspected that people would be gathered. That meant it would take a few extra minutes, but certainly well worth it. Arriving home essentially unnoticed was a considerable relief.

After putting on his other shirt and pants, Deer walked to Rock's home, got him some clothes, then on to Arrow's house to get his. Deer was glad that no one was in any of the three huts. He had pondered just what kind of story he could tell that would justify the need for the clothes without compromising their collective dignity.

With clothes in hand, Deer hurried back across town and made his way down to the river. Upon his arrival he found Rock and Arrow still sitting silently watching the water flow by. Deer's approach brought two sighs of relief followed by a flurry of rapid dressing.

Deer expected that they had probably spent their time plotting revenge, but when Arrow finally spoke, the question caught him completely by surprise.

"When are we going to go find Wolf?" Arrow asked in a very matter-of-fact way. Now dressed, he had picked up the basket of fish and turned to go home.

However, the lack of response from Deer caused him to stop, turn slightly, and look back.

Deer's eyes were fixed on his feet. It was as if he were frozen.

"I'm serious. You know he is still out there – somewhere. I know we can find him," Arrow said in a voice that showed that he had been thinking about this for some time.

"Let's go in the morning," Rock interjected. "We could go today, but it would be dark before we could get to the area where we would need to start searching. Besides, we have to retrieve our clothes first!"

The quest was so captivating that they had momentarily forgotten about their clothes.

"All right, we will go in the morning, but we will tell our parents that we are just going exploring and that we will be back in a few days. There is no need to worry them and I would prefer that this be our own effort without any grownups interfering with our mission," Deer declared. Three unanimous nods confirmed their intentions.

"Now, let's go get our clothes," Rock reminded them.

With a definite idea of what they needed to accomplish today, they set out for Deer's house to get the dresses.

"Should we retaliate on the girls?" Arrow asked.

"Eventually we will, but not today," Deer answered. "We have to come up with a good plan so they know we have pranked them back but without completely embarrassing them. After all, they kept their prank private. We should do the same."

"I have an idea," Arrow stated. "Let's rub some poison ivy leaves on the inside of each of the dresses right where their bottoms touch their dress. If they are sensitive to poison ivy, it will be really annoying to them. Their back ends will be itching badly and they won't be able to scratch because girls just don't do that. They are always so delicate and proper." He had obviously had plenty of time to think about this while sitting naked on the river bank.

"What if we TELL them that is what we did, but not really do it, because that would be really mean. These girls are just flirting. I say we flirt back without causing any harm, that way they will know that we have noticed their efforts and want to play along. After all, they are really cute even if they are mischievous, which is rather intriguing as well." Deer speculated to himself more than to Rock or Arrow.

As the trio reached Deer's house, they saw Snowflake standing in the doorway of her home just a few huts away. When Deer pointed at her, she ducked inside to appear to hide. However, she positioned herself so she could watch for Deer's approach.

The boys stepped inside and each got the dress of his respective admirer. With a brief review to set the details of the "poison ivy story" in their minds, they each set out to confront their particular prankster.

Deer folded the dress in thirds and walked straight to Snowflake's door. As he neared, she stepped out to meet him.

"I believe that we need to exchange clothes," Deer stated while extending his arm to offer the dress to Snowflake. "That was a well executed prank. My congratulations to you."

"Well, thank you, Deer. That is very nice of you to admit that we pulled one over on you guys," she replied as she revealed the neatly folded shirt and pants that she was holding behind her back.

With a wide grin on both of their faces, they returned each other's garments.

With his own clothes securely in hand, Deer said, "By the way, we might have rubbed some poison ivy leaves on the inside of your dress. I hope the skin on your backside is not sensitive to it. We only did it to one of the dresses, but I don't remember which one. Happy scratching!"

"You better not have put anything in my dress. My mother will get both of us!" Snowflake exclaimed in a panicked but stifled yell.

Deer could not keep a straight face. "We did not do anything. We just made up that story to get you back. Your dress is fine."

"Whew! You scared me," she muttered. "That would have been a real problem because I am very sensitive to poison ivy. I can just imagine the rash that I would have had to sit on."

"Truce?" Deer asked as he stuck out his hand to shake like boys are taught to do.

"Truce," Snowflake replied. She stepped forward as if to shake his hand, but stepped past his outstretched hand and gave Deer a big hug.

Deer was momentarily caught off guard, but immediately decided that the hug was much nicer than the handshake. In fact, he lingered with the hug long enough that Snowflake pulled her arms from around his waist and stepped back slightly.

Deer was speechless, but the broad smile across his face definitely told her that he was not going to ignore her anymore.

"I'm going home. I have to get some supplies together for another adventure that we are going on tomorrow. The guys and I are going back out to look for Wolf, but you have to keep it a secret. We don't want our parents to know," Deer explained. "I know we can find him, if we give it just one more shot."

Snowflake looked deeply into Deer's eyes and she could see the determination that he felt. "Your secret is safe with me," pausing for effect, "if you come back to me."

Deer smiled once again and simply said, "Agreed." He turned and then strolled back across the short distance to his own home. Once there, he picked up the basket with the few sucker-fish and carried it into the smokehouse. Arrow or Rock had already removed the entrails while they were waiting for him to return with their replacement clothes. Deer removed the fish from the basket and placed them on the smoke-rack to dry. Once back home, he made a concerted effort to gather the needed supplies for their quest.

Chapter 6

"Deer! Help me!"

Deer sat bolt upright in bed. "Who's there?" he whispered quietly. Darkness fully surrounded him. The night had not ended and he could hear the steady, rhythmical breathing of the rest of his family sleeping nearby. There was no reply to his question.

"I must have been dreaming," he breathed aloud as he laid back down. He may have been dreaming when he heard the voice, but he was fully awake now. Eventually, his heart stopped racing and he drifted back to sleep and began to dream.

In the distance, he could see a long path winding through the forest. As he glided along he recognized various trees and rock formations that existed on the way to the Medicine Woman's village beyond the mountain. Her words were echoing in his mind, "Search for your friend. He needs you." Effortlessly, he seemed to float along the path until he spotted a particularly gnarled thorn tree a short distance off the path. Hanging from a cluster of thorns on the trunk of the tree, Deer saw a scrap of red cloth that seemed to point up the hillside. Deer floated up the hill side until the slope became a massive limestone bluff towering high into the sky, but at the base of the bluff was a small cave opening. As he moved toward the opening, the form of a body could be seen lying between a flat rock and the wall of the cave just a short distance inside. As he stretched his hand toward the body, he suddenly awoke. He was sweating profusely and his heart was racing once again.

While the meaning of the dream was clear enough, Deer had no idea how to share it with Rock and Arrow, so he decided to keep it to himself for the time being. He knew that they were depending on him to take the role of leader on this journey. He did not want them to think he had gone crazy. Additional sleep was highly unlikely, so he got up and slipped out into the night to wait for Rock and Arrow.

Morning broke clear and beautiful and the trio was up and gone before most of the people in their town began to stir. The boys had each slept poorly for one reason or another and were glad when the first rays of sunlight lit the distant horizon. They had each told their parents that they wanted to go exploring down the Big River and they would be home in a few days. It was not an outright lie, but it did evade the whole truth slightly. While none of their parents were fooled by the story, they played along and gave their permission to their respective sons, but followed it with a stern, cautionary lecture.

Talk was minimal as they set out. The sense of solemn purpose pervaded each of their minds. This was almost the same scenario that they had embarked on several months before except that previously, Wolf had been with them to lead the way into the unknown. The apprehension they each felt manifested itself in varying degrees of butterflies in their stomachs. They knew about how far they were going before they planned to start searching because they had been through that area three times recently.

"Hey, Rock. How did Meadow react to the story about the poison ivy in her dress?" Arrow asked.

"She just shrugged her shoulders and said that poison ivy did not affect her," Rock replied.

"That is exactly what Sunflower said," Arrow added. "What did Snowflake say, Deer?"

"She said that she was very sensitive to it and I thought she was going to cry, so I told her the truth. She was so cute and we all know that they were just flirting. I got a really good hug out of the deal. Did your girl give you a hug or anything?" Deer asked.

Rock grinned sheepishly and nodded. "Girls are SO soft."

Arrow looked back and forth between Deer and Rock in disbelief. He had not gotten even a handshake and he felt cheated. "That's not fair," he started. "I said the same thing you guys did and you two got lovey-dovey hugs and all I got was my own clothes thrown at me! That's just about how life seems to go for me…" His words trailed off as he kicked at a small stick in frustration.

Deer knew that he needed to change the subject so he said, "Guys, I know where Wolf is."

The matter-of-fact way that he said it caused Arrow and Rock to stop dead in their tracks.

"How do you know where he is?" Rock blurted out.

"If you knew, why did you not take us to him when we were searching before with Running Bear and Chief Long Feather?" Arrow added.

Deer stopped and turned to face his friends and said, "It is so bizarre that it is hard to explain. Do you remember when we were leaving the village where we left Wolf?"

34

They nodded that they did.

Deer continued, "In the flurry of activity just before we left, the Medicine Woman pulled me aside and told me to 'search for my friend because he needs me to attend to him.' I had no idea what that meant and it has been on my mind ever since. I just could not figure out what she meant. Last night I had a dream and her words just kept echoing in my head as I moved through the woods. At one point, I spotted a really ugly thorn tree and there was a piece of red cloth on a cluster of thorns that pointed up a hillside. I went up the slope and found a small cave. Wolf was lying there in the cave. He looked dead. I think the Medicine Woman was saying that we are to bury Wolf where we find him."

The silence between the three boys hung like smoke on a calm day. Neither Arrow nor Rock was prepared for such a revelation. They just stood motionless and stared at Deer as they processed this new information.

"I did not ask for this task. The Medicine Woman dumped it on me. However, Wolf is my friend and I am going to help my friend." Deer turned quickly and started walking once again. He could feel the tears welling up in his eyes and he did not want the others to notice.

Rock and Arrow looked at each other and then started walking quickly to close ranks with Deer.

"Man, what an incredible story. Why did you not tell us before?" Rock asked.

"I wanted to. I just did not know how to bring it up without sounding crazy, or even worse, better than you guys. I am not better and I am not crazy. I just got a special job handed to me and I am going to do it," Deer replied.

"We know you aren't crazy," Arrow interjected. "Besides, you were Wolf's best friend. It is obvious why the Medicine Woman chose you."

"So, Deer, where is this ugly thorn tree?" Rock asked point-blank. He was obviously convinced of the supernatural intervention at work in this matter and wanted Deer to know that he had his support.

"I am not sure, but I know I will recognize it when I see it. The best I can figure, it is a couple of hours past the east village, but before we turned up that creek that takes us back up and over the mountain," Deer explained.

"Sounds close enough to me. I believe that will be easy enough to find," Arrow added.

Much of the remainder of the walk to the east was occupied with small talk about girls, fishing, trees, and the weather, but not much was said about Wolf.

Without Chief Long Feather, the boys were able to walk much faster and reached the east village just before lunchtime. They had already agreed to say nothing to anyone in the east village about their true mission or about the dream. In fact, they decided that they would just pass through and stop somewhere on the far side to eat their lunch.

"We will just wave as we pass through," Deer recommended. "If anyone stops us and wants to visit, that will be fine. However, we just don't want to lose any daylight. If I remember the details of my dream correctly we will have just enough time to find the tree, climb the hill, and bury Wolf before it gets dark."

As the trio neared the east village, they saw very little activity. It appeared that most of the people were away from home, probably foraging for food or preparing their garden for planting. The boys tried to look as inconspicuous as possible. They could not afford to lose the time and they certainly did not want anyone tagging along.

After successfully clearing east village with just a few simple waves and an occasional "hello," they agreed it was time to stop for just a few minutes and eat some food.

"Let's stop at the next little stream crossing and rest for a few minutes," Rock suggested.

"I agree," Arrow chimed in.

Deer's nod made the decision unanimous.

No sooner than the plan was agreed upon, a small feeder stream could be seen a short distance ahead. As they approached it, they pulled their packs off and began to rummage for the food they had packed. After each boy had satisfied his thirst with a long, cool drink of clear stream water, they sat down to talk.

"Do you recognize anything from your dream yet?" Arrow asked.

"It all looks familiar because we walked through here just a few days ago, but I don't recognize anything from the dream," Deer confessed. He had been so sure that he would just walk right to the thorn tree and everything would fall right into place.

"Are you pretty sure this is even the right trail?" Rock tentatively inquired. He did not want to suggest that this was a wild goose chase, but he was beginning to doubt the degree of good sense that they had employed to chase this strange dream.

"I can't say for sure, but I am almost positive this is the right trail that was in my dream. As for the rest of the dream, I have no idea what is real and what is just a wishful creation of my restless mind," Deer replied. He knew how bizarre it must be to Rock and Arrow for him to seem so convinced that this dream would reveal the location of their missing friend. However, in his heart he knew it was not an ordinary dream. This was a premonition with a higher purpose, but he just could not explain it to them. He could not explain it to himself. He just knew it was true.

Following the brief rest, the trio got back to their feet and resumed their journey. They had not traveled very far when Deer stopped dead still in the middle of the narrowing trail. Rock almost ran into him before he could get stopped.

"What's wrong?" Rock whispered directly into Deer's ear.

Without moving a muscle, Deer breathed back, "This is it. This is where the dream began."

Rock looked over at Arrow as if asking what should they do, but before Arrow could reply, Deer bolted down the trail in a steady run.

Without a word, Arrow and Rock were also running through the forest. Deer was well ahead of them and they were steadily falling behind until Deer was no longer visible in front of them. Regardless, they kept running. They intuitively knew that he would stop eventually and they would catch him then.

Sure enough, several minutes later, Rock and Arrow rounded a bend in the trail and Deer was standing in the middle of it pointing out into the underbrush.

As they coasted to a stop beside him, Deer said, "There it is – the thorn tree! Go look and tell me that there is a piece of red cloth stuck on a thorn on the back side."

Without a word, Arrow pushed through the tangled vines and walked the short distance to the thorn tree. As he circled to the far side, Rock and Deer heard an audible gasp from Arrow. In a few seconds, Arrow stepped back around the tree and held up the small, red strip of cloth that had been impaled on the cluster of thorns growing out of the tree trunk.

Rock looked at Deer. His eyes were almost as wide as his mouth but he was speechless with amazement. Deer's eyes were filling with tears. He knew that the dream was true and that he would soon be burying his best friend.

Without a word, Deer pushed through the tangled underbrush to get to Arrow. Arrow handed the cloth to Deer as he passed him, but Deer's focus was on the rising hillside. With a determination like they had never seen in Deer before, he charged straight up the side of the hill. Rock and Arrow had trouble keeping up, but they figured that there was a cave straight ahead and they would catch Deer there.

The higher Rock and Arrow climbed, the steeper and more boulder-strewn the slope became. Deer was well ahead of them when the towering bluff appeared above them. Sure enough, when they reached the base of the bluff, Deer was standing motionless in front of a small cave opening at the base of the bluff. Rock and Arrow, gasping for breath, approached Deer.

"Is he there?" Arrow obligingly asked although he could tell by the faint smell of initial decay that the answer would be yes.

At the sound of their approach, Deer dropped his pack and pulled an extra blanket out and began to unfold it. Inside the blanket there was a wooden scoop and a pouch filled with cedar boughs and tobacco. Deer had prepared for this moment before he had left home. The other two boys had not realized the depth of his resolve until this moment.

Moving into the cave, Deer knelt down near Wolf's body and began to dig. The powdery, loose soil had many small rocks in it, but it was still quite easy to dig since it was completely dry. Before long, a hole was dug that was large enough to hold a body. However, it would take almost another hour before the hole was deep enough to get the body in as well as get it covered with an adequate amount of dirt and rocks to secure it.

Wolf had been dead for over a week, but the cool air flowing from the cave had minimized the decay. Deer draped the blanket over Wolf and then with Rock's help carefully rolled the stiff corpse into the blanket. Once contained in the blanket, they gently dragged the bundle the short distance over to the hole and placed Wolf in it. Deer took the pouch of cedar and tobacco and opened it. Using his fingers to pinch small amounts of the contents from the bag, he knelt back down beside the hole and sprinkled the items on top of the blanket roll that contained Wolf's body. As he sprinkled, he recited prayers that he had heard the elders say at funerals. It took several pinches to empty the bag. Deer then rummaged around in his pack once again and retrieved a bear claw and the small arrow point from the last turkey that Wolf had killed before he got sick. Deer placed the claw and the point inside the empty bag along with the piece of red cloth, said one last goodbye, and tucked the bag inside a fold of the blanket beside Wolf's body. Finally, Deer seized the scoop once again and began to fill the hole, which he then capped with several medium-sized flat rocks. While Deer refilled the hole, Arrow took some red paint that Deer supplied and drew Wolf's symbol on the cave wall above the grave.

Except for the prayers that Deer had said, there were no other words spoken. However, with the impromptu funeral complete, Deer stepped out of the mouth of the cave where Rock and Arrow were now standing and said, "Thank you for your help. I could not have done this without you."

Arrow and Rock simply said in unison, "You are welcome."

"Let's get down to the creek, get cleaned up, and set up camp before it gets dark," Deer said in a rather matter-of-fact way.

Deer was exactly right. However, following such an emotional event, it sounded humorous and Arrow began to snicker quietly.

"I know that sounds rather callous, but we accomplished what we came to do and now it is time to get away from this place and back to our normal lives," Deer explained as he slung his pack over his shoulder and started down the slope.

Rock looked at Arrow, shrugged his shoulders and headed down the hill, too.

Arrow took one quick glance into the cave and soon followed Deer and Rock to the stream far below.

At the stream, Deer scrubbed his hands and arms thoroughly before returning to the place where Arrow and Rock had built a fire. They sat down by the fire as the long shadows of evening merged together and soon faded to black as the night surrounded the three young men just sitting by the fire sharing story after story about their dear friend Wolf.

Chapter 7

Despite the fatigue that racked his body, Deer could not turn his mind off and go to sleep. Rock and Arrow had tossed and turned for a while, but now lay motionless in the dim flickering light of the fire that they were camping beside. They had decided to start toward home in the morning so that they could deliver the sad news of Wolf's demise to his father.

Haunting questions raced through his mind. How did the Medicine Woman know? How could he dream about a place he had never seen and then know that he would find Wolf there? How did the little red cloth get on the thorn tree? If Wolf put the cloth on the tree, how did he then climb that steep hill in his condition? The questions just bubbled to the surface like a spring. Unfortunately, the corresponding answers were not so forthcoming.

The rhythmic crackling of the fire continued to slowly dissipate until there was virtually no sound. The glow of the remaining embers pulsed slowly as if the fire was trying to mimic the breathing of the two lumps cuddled nearby in their blankets. Deer closed his eyes and focused on the sound of the water tumbling down the streambed nearby. Soon, the fading light of the fire dimly lit three motionless figures.

Deer looked down at his hands. He was holding his bow and an arrow was resting on the string, ready to launch. He glanced to the right and a doe deer was strolling down a trail that would pass directly in front of him. Wolf leaned in behind him and said, "Wait until she clears that last tree before you shoot." Deer waited. The deer needed to take three more steps. One. Two. Three. Deer drew the bow, took careful aim and released. The arrow buried deep into the doe's chest. She jumped and started running away but within a few steps, staggered, and fell lifeless to the ground.

"Good shot, Deer," Wolf whispered over Deer's shoulder. "I knew you could do it, with the proper coaching."

Deer rose to his feet and walked to where the dead deer laid.

Wolf patted him on the back in congratulations. "Deer, the Medicine Woman told you that if you helped me, I would be with you forever. I need you to help me do one more thing. I need you to take my spirit back home. I don't want to stay here around this cave by myself. I need to be with our ancestors. However, it sure would be nice if we could go on one last adventure. If you, Rock, and Arrow are willing, I will be your guide."

Deer looked at Wolf and smiled . . .

"Wake up, Deer. It is time to get started home. We aren't going to get there if you don't wake up," berated Rock.

Deer's eyes flung open wide as in a panic. Sunlight was already abundantly illuminating the camp. Jumping to his feet, He began to flit all around looking behind trees, in a large bush, and even in a small cavity under a fallen log.

"What are you looking for?" Arrow asked with a very perplexed expression on his face.

"I saw Wolf! Well, I did not actually see him. I dreamed I saw him and he talked to me like I am talking to you – only somewhat more calmly, I suppose," Deer added, still glancing around to be sure it really had been a dream.

"Man, oh man! I don't think you are feeling too good. I was afraid that you would catch something as much as you touched that dead body," Rock mused.

"I feel fine. In fact, here is what Wolf told me. He needs me to take his spirit back home. He does not want to stay here. He said that he also wanted us to take one last adventure and that he would be our guide."

Bewilderment and shock was readily apparent on Rock and Arrow's faces.

"I know it sounds crazy, but these dreams and these unexplainable events – like finding Wolf exactly where I knew we would – have got to mean something important," Deer added. "Wolf helped me kill a doe in my dream. I know he will help us. The Medicine Woman said he would." With that, Deer simply sat down.

Rock and Arrow looked at each other, then at Deer. Rock finally asked, "How do we get word back home that we found Wolf and that we are going to be gone longer than we told them?

Arrow piped up, "Let's go back to the east village and tell them about Wolf. We can tell them that we are going on down the river for a few more days. They will send someone back to inform Running Bear. We can even pick up a few extra provisions while we are there."

"That is a good plan. We might as well get started," Deer agreed as he began to gather his blanket and reload his pack.

Arrow went to the creek and got water in the wooden scoop and began dousing the remaining live embers of last night's fire. He had to make several trips to complete the task.

As they made their way back to the east village, it was decided that they would not mention anything about Wolf's spirit accompanying them on this adventure. They thought that it would just require too much explanation. To be honest, they really did not understand what they would be trying to explain anyway.

Upon entering the village, Deer took the lead and sought out one of the elders.

"Sir, my name is Deer. May I speak to you?" Deer quietly said to the withered old man that he saw sitting in the shade of a nearby hut.

"Certainly, young man. You and your friends should have a seat," he said as he gestured toward the ground. "What can I help you with?"

"Sir, we're from the village of Chief Long Feather and we have made several journeys through this area recently. The past three have been in search of our friend Wolf." Deer paused to see just how much explanation was required.

"I have seen you boys passing by. Let me guess. You found your friend and want some help." The old man glanced amongst the three boys, but fixed his final gaze on Deer.

"Yes and no. We did find Wolf, but we buried him where we found him because he had been dead for many days. There was no other choice," Deer began. "What we need help with is that we are going to go on a memorial adventure before we return home. We told our parents that we would be home today or tomorrow but we really want to take this one last trip. The help we need is to get word back to our village that we found and buried Wolf and that we will be home in a week or two."

A broad smile crept across the old man's face. "It just so happens that we have a group of traders that will be going through your village tomorrow on their way out west to gather buffalo hides. I will tell them to deliver the messages on your behalf. Is there anything else you need in the way of supplies? I don't see any weapons. How were you planning to feed yourselves?

"Yes, sir, we had wondered that same thing. If you could spare a bow and a few arrows, I believe that we will be able to survive just fine. We plan to make the spears that we need. I have a really good feeling about this trip," Deer added.

The old man nodded knowingly. He did not have to ask any more questions. He had had a very similar experience when he was a young man. His

42

"memorial adventure" had remained the most important single outing that he had ever undertaken. He slowly struggled to his feet and said, "Follow me."

Deer followed the old man around the corner of his house and waited outside the door as the elder slipped inside. In just a moment, he reappeared and handed an old but highly polished hickory-wood bow to Deer.

"I am too old to hunt anymore," the old man began. "I believe that you can certainly make good use of it. Here are five arrows that used to fly well out of it. My grandson shot it when he was younger but he has made his own bow and arrows now. There is no one around that needs it. It is yours."

Deer was almost speechless but the broad smile on his face generated an equally broad smile across the old man's face.

"Thank you very much. This is the nicest thing that I could have ever dreamed of." Deer cut his eyes up from the bow to see if the wise old man picked up on the slip of the tongue. The sparkle that filled his old eyes did not tell, but the wink that immediately followed told Deer that he had met someone who understood what was happening to him.

"You boys will need to get moving if you plan to go beyond where you have already been. New adventures don't happen in your own yard."

Deer thanked him again and rejoined Rock and Arrow. "Let's go!"

"My goodness – that is a nice bow," Arrow exclaimed as they turned east and headed back out of the village.

"It sure is. The most incredible thing is that it is identical to the one that I dreamed about last night," Deer added to see how Arrow and Rock would react.

"Reeaalllly?" Arrow asked in amazement.

"Yep. Exactly. I know this will be a good adventure," Deer concluded.

Rock and Arrow pondered the realization that Deer's dreams were not normal. They were powerful and extremely accurate. There was certainly a higher power at work in the matter and they would simply trust that Deer was in control of this newly acquired gift.

As they arrived at the crossroad where the trail continued east down the Big River or south to the village of Chief Red Eagle and the Medicine Woman, they had to decide which way to go.

"We could continue down the river," Deer started, "or we could head south and let the good people of Chief Red Eagle's village know about Wolf. Which way do you think we should go?"

"South," Arrow and Rock responded in unison.

Without hesitation, the trio turned south. They knew they could not reach Chief Red Eagle's village before dark, so they decided to go as far as the abandoned farmstead that marked the trail leading up the mountain. Clouds were building in the west and it looked like it could blow up a storm before nightfall anyway.

"Do you think it is going to rain hard?" Arrow pondered aloud as he gazed up toward the treetops that were beginning to sway more noticeably.

"I don't know, but I am fairly sure that it will rain some," Rock answered.

"Let's make sure we make it to that old farm. I believe that old hut will give us some protection from the rain. I really don't want to sleep in a wet blanket if I don't have to," Deer chimed in. The other two nodded vigorously in agreement.

The poor condition of the chosen trail did not go unnoticed by the travelers, but it only slightly hindered the pace. They were committed to getting to the old farm as quickly as possible. They knew that they would need to gather some firewood, patch up any minor leaks in the roof, and get the rats and debris cleaned out before dark. There was no time to waste. The distant rumble of thunder echoing through the forested valley announced the coming storm.

"Deer, now that we are headed back into the mountains, do you think that maybe we ought to find shelter under one of the bluffs instead of trying to make it to the old farm?" Rock suggested.

The idea had not occurred to him, but it certainly sounded like a good one if they could actually find an acceptable shelter up in the bluff line. Deer said, "That is a good idea. Let's get off this trail and head directly uphill to see what we can find. If we don't find anything, we can always come back to this trail and proceed to the old farm."

Once they left the trail, forward progress was significantly slower, but they each felt that their chances of staying dry while tucked back in a crevasse in a bluff was better than staying dry even if they got to the old farm before the rain started. The rumble of the approaching storm clearly indicated the time for remaining dry was short.

Within a few minutes the towering rock face of the bluff line could be seen up slope from them. This was a continuation of the same bluff where they had found Wolf the day before. Knowing that there was one cave, there were surely others.

"This hill just does not get any easier to climb," Arrow mumbled as he grasped a sapling to halt his slide back down the hill when he came upon some loose rocks and slick leaves.

Deer reached the base of the bluff first and started picking his way through the large detached boulders and underbrush as he made his way south. Since they were intending to go south to Chief Red Eagle's village anyway, they might as well continue that direction as they searched for shelter for the night.

Rock and Arrow soon reached the base of the bluff as well and caught up with Deer. "I think a rock shelter will provide better protection than that old hut would offer," Rock offered again. "I hope we find one …"

His words were cut short by the sharp crack of a lightning bolt and the simultaneous "BOOOOOM" that accompanied it. All three boys instinctively dropped to the ground.

"That was too close for comfort!" Arrow exclaimed.

"Double time, guys! We need shelter – NOW!" Deer commanded.

The three boys stopped picking their way through the boulders and briars and just started tearing through the foliage in a trot. Before long they came to a small pocket in the bluff face that was not big enough to hold all three boys but might be able to hold their packs and gear.

"This is too small, but it may indicate that there is something not too far ahead," Deer shouted over his shoulder to Rock and Arrow, who were close behind. The first rain drops were beginning to pepper the dry leaves around them, but along the bluff they remained somewhat protected.

"I see our shelter," Deer shouted back as he continued to increase his lead over the others. "It looks perfect."

Deer ducked inside and dropped his pack, bow, and quiver still containing the five arrows. Rock and Arrow soon dashed into the shelter and dropped their belongings as well.

Rock and Arrow then dashed back out of the shelter to gather firewood while Deer started gathering leaves to make each of them a bed. Large piles of leaves were already accumulated inside the shelter where a favorable wind had deposited them, but several more armloads would make the beds that much better.

Dark clouds were passing overhead as the wind continued to increase. The pitter-patter of raindrops was now steady but the most unnerving component of the storm was the lightning. A veritable non-stop explosion of thunder pounded all around them. Even in the late afternoon light, the flashes of lightning were exceptionally bright, hurting their eyes to look at it.

Arrow and Rock returned as quickly as possible with as much firewood as they could carry. It was certain that soon they would be challenged to find any more dry wood. But with a small supply of firewood now gathered, Arrow turned his attention to building a fire as soon as he pulled his fire-starting materials from his pack.

Deer had cleared an area of leaves just inside the drip line of the shelter and had arranged a ring of large rocks to form a fire pit. In the process of doing that, Deer exposed a large spear point that had apparently been lost in the shelter by some other visitor of the distant past.

"Hey, look at this," Deer exclaimed, holding the projectile up for Rock to see.

"Did you just find that?" Rock asked.

"Yep. It was just laying here under the leaves. I don't think I have ever seen one shaped like this before," Deer concluded as he handed the ancient point to Rock.

"That is a beauty," Rock commented as he turned the point over and over admiring the craftsmanship of the person who had made it. "Do you see this fluted channel running from the base up to the middle of the body? That is extremely hard to do. The man who taught me how to flint knap explained how to do this technique, but he said that he did not have the skill to actually flute a point successfully. This is a real treasure."

"Since you appreciate the talent and effort that obviously went into making it, just keep it. I don't need it. Maybe you can show it to your teacher when we get home," Deer said. "For now, let's just get this fire going."

Deer began to arrange the smallest twigs in a small, neat pile. Rock began to shred some bark-fiber that he had collected from a red cedar just outside the

46

shelter. The cedar bark was tucked under the pile of twigs. Arrow knelt down and placed the fire-board near the future campfire and using his fire-bow and spindle, he quickly was generating smoke, then a few glowing embers. Gently placing a few strands of cedar bark on the embers, he began to blow. Almost immediately, a tiny flame appeared which he transferred carefully to the cedar bark and twig pile. As the flame spread, small limbs were added to the pile and eventually larger limbs until a roaring fire was guarding the boys from the raging storm just beyond the drip-line.

With a definite sense of accomplishment, they reclined into the large pile of nice, dry leaves and relaxed as the afternoon passed into dusk. The lightning and thunder only lasted for a short time, but the rain fell in varying degrees of downpours all night long. Each of the boys was especially grateful for a dry bed and a safe, comfortable shelter from the storm. Before long, the casual chatter ended and the rhythmical rain serenaded them off to a long, pleasant night's rest.

Chapter 8

The last drips of rain fell sporadically to the ground as morning broke. Since they were within a half-day walk of Chief Red Eagle's village, they knew there was no rush to leave the wonderful shelter which had protected them so well all night. Besides, this was an adventure and there was no reason that the adventure must start AFTER they visited with the distant Medicine Woman.

"What are you thinking about?" Deer asked Rock, who was leaned back in a leisurely pose with arms crossed behind his head, his eyes closed, and a broad grin on his face.

Rock did not even open his eyes. He knew Deer was talking to him and he said, "I was thinking about those girls we saw at Chief Red Eagle's village. Since we are not in a big hurry, I was thinking about stopping and getting to know one – or two – or three of them." The ear-to-ear grin only got broader.

Arrow leaned forward. "I had not even thought about the fact that we are kind of famous and I bet the stories that the adults told each other about our last visit would really impress the girls." Arrow rolled onto his knees and probably would have stood up, but the ceiling of the shelter was too low. "This is an adventure. What better adventure than meeting some girls!"

Deer almost laughed out loud but restrained himself to a casual snicker. "I suppose that we can take our time at the village. I plan to spend a little time with the Medicine Woman if she will talk to me. I have got to get some more information on these dreams."

"Did you have another one last night?" Rock asked.

"Not that I recall. I just have a feeling that I will though and I want to know if she has any more insights on the matter," Deer answered. Changing the subject, he continued, "I would like to take a look around that abandoned farm that we had planned to spend the night in last night. I wonder why it is abandoned."

The subject change brought the three boys back to thinking about the original mission of exploring the world and away from the topic of girls. Deer had had a dream last night, but it involved Snowflake, and he was not the least bit ready to be teased about having a girlfriend. However, he was keenly aware that he was thinking about her more and more since the clothing-theft incident.

The light breeze wafting through the valley below had shaken almost all of the remaining rain from the trees. It was time to resume their odyssey. After drowning the embers of the fire, they gathered their personal belongings and left the shelter.

Rather than dropping straight back down the hillside and finding the trail, they decided to continue exploring the bluff line. They had seen the trail. They wanted to see something new. For quite some time, they carefully made their way along the bluff and around the huge boulders that had detached from it so long ago that huge trees now grew in the space that existed between the boulder and the bluff. Several other shelters were discovered. Some were bigger. Some were smaller. Each boy still felt very fortunate to have found the one they did when the storm passed through yesterday.

"We better drop back down to the trail and see if we can find the old farm before we get turned around and lose our landmark for finding Chief Red Eagle's village," Arrow suggested.

"I agree," Rock chimed in and the trio turned downhill with the expectations of finding the trail. However, when they reached the creek at the base of the hill, not only was the trail not found, but the stream was flowing east instead of north.

"Something is not right," Deer stated as he stopped and began to assess their location. "Based on the shadows, the water in this stream is flowing the wrong direction if it is the stream we were following yesterday. We better head back downstream and figure out where we are."

Although not panicked, they were duly concerned that they had gotten so disoriented in such a short time and distance. However, before they had walked very far, they realized that the bluff had apparently bent slowly around a corner and that the stream they were following was a tributary to the stream they wanted to find. Sure enough, they soon found the trail they were searching for just before the two streams merged. The rain from last night had greatly increased the volume of water in both streams and crossing even the small tributary involved getting wet up to their knees.

Without any further detours, they continued up the valley, following the dim trail until they came to the clearing where the abandoned farm was located. Even though it had only been a few days since they passed this place with Running Bear and Chief Long Feather, a major change was readily apparent. While only a couple of trees remained in the clearing, one large oak tree stood directly over the little hut. From the evidence, it was obvious that one of those tremendous lightning bolts from the night before had struck the ancient oak, splintering a large slab of wood from one side of the trunk and stripping several enormous limbs completely off. The largest limb had fallen directly on the little hut, completely demolishing the humble dwelling.

49

The three boys ran across the clearing to where the wreckage of the hut now laid. Without a word, they simply stood and stared at the scene in utter disbelief. The realization that they could easily have been killed the night before sent cold chills through each of them. One by one, they sat down and silently pondered the situation. It was a very sobering time of observation and reflection.

"We should get going," Deer stated. "I don't want to think about how this could have ended. It makes me sick at my stomach."

"I agree," Rock seconded and rose to his feet. Arrow was apparently in shock.

Rock was the first one to reach the trail heading up the mountain from the clearing followed closely by Deer. As they entered the forest edge, they looked back and verified that Arrow was indeed up and moving in their direction. No conversation interrupted the sounds of the birds singing happily or the breeze rustling through the trees. A close brush with death has a way of darkening even the best of times. The positive benefit, however, was that they barely noticed the steep, difficult climb until they were nearly to the top.

"I need to rest," Rock wheezed as he sat down on the next available boulder. Arrow had caught up with them and he and Deer sat down, too.

"This is a really steep mountain," Deer commented. It was not normal for him to be the one that minded the strenuous effort. Even though he knew that the other two were probably hurting worse, he wanted to say something to try to make them feel better. The smiles that reappeared on all of their faces were reassuring to everyone. Despite the clear realization that their lives were fragile, they also realized that, for whatever reason, they had been spared. For that they were grateful.

Following the short rest, the final ascent to the top began again. It was nearing midday when they arrived at the big bluff where Chief Long Feather had rested and taken the walking stick. They kept on moving, knowing it was relatively flat and then downhill into Chief Red Eagle's village below.

The spring rain had washed the air especially clean and the view from the top of the ridge was amazing. It seemed as though they could see forever.

"I did not know the world extended so far," Rock announced as he stepped up on a large boulder and peered back down the mountainside.

"I suspect that there are many things we don't know," Arrow added.

Deer nodded in affirmation, but opted to not insert his own musings. Instead, he turned away and walked with determination through the saddle and began the winding descent toward Chief Red Eagle's village. Rock and Arrow followed close behind.

As the slope of the mountain began to decrease, they once again encountered the fringe residences of the village. This being their fourth trip through the village in such a short period of time, most of the residents recognized the boys and waved as they strolled by. Rock and Arrow were definitely on alert, hoping that some of the local girls would venture out into the open and engage them in conversation. They had already agreed that regardless of what Rock and Arrow did, Deer would proceed to the main village area and make the necessary contacts with the elders as well as the Medicine Woman.

As before, most of the people they saw along the way were women and small children until they reached the one hut where that very old man was once again sitting. As the boys approached, he stood and shuffled over to the trail.

"Greetings, sir," Deer began.

"Hello, boys," he replied. "It is so good to see you passing through once again. To what do we owe this pleasant surprise?"

Deer launched into a somewhat abbreviated but still lengthy recitation of their previous return trip to their own home with Running Bear and Chief Long Feather. He followed that with their own search for Wolf and that they had found him. Finally, he concluded with their decision to come here and share the news of Wolf's fate.

Rock was wondering if the doddering old man would be able to stand up as long as this story was obviously going to take. However, instead of tipping over, he seemed to actually straighten up and stand more erect as Deer's monologue rolled on.

Arrow reached out and nudged Rock. He had spotted two especially cute girls who appeared to be just their age and as planned, they excused themselves from the historical recap. Rock and Arrow had barely made eye contact and started easing in that direction when one of the girls smiled warmly and motioned for them to come on over. The two boys lost their inhibitions and with wide smiles on their own faces made a beeline to join the two lovely young ladies.

"That is quite a series of adventures, son," the old man finally commented. "I appreciate you letting me know. I will spread the word in this part of town. I suppose you will find Chief Red Eagle at the council house. You will want to tell him, too."

"Yes, sir, I was hoping to share the news with him," Deer concluded.

As the old man shuffled back to the spot where he obviously spent most of his time, Deer stepped back onto the path alone. He had spotted Arrow and Rock chatting with the two local girls. Before reaching the village, they had agreed to eventually meet at the hut where they always slept unless it was not available and then they would meet at the council house. Deer had agreed to go ahead of them and spread the news as well as verify their accommodations for the night.

Walking on down to the main village alone was a strange feeling. Even though he had been there before, he had always had one of his close friends with him to bolster his courage. Being alone and away from home was new. He did not like it at all. The people he passed were still quite friendly, but somehow he just felt out of place. The closer to the main part of town that Deer got, the slower he walked. Although he was not afraid, his nerves were certainly on edge.

"Deer." The soft, woman's voice emanated from directly behind him.

Deer wheeled around and recognized the rapidly approaching person as the Medicine Woman. He had not seen her but she had obviously seen him and was quickly closing the distance between them. "What are you doing here?" she inquired in a friendly yet inquisitive tone of voice.

"I am so glad to see you. I have been having these amazing dreams and I really need you to explain some things to me," Deer blurted out. As they walked on into town, Deer regained his composure and shared the long story including that he had found Wolf's body after having a dream that told him where to look.

The Medicine Woman smiled knowingly and simply said, "Let's go see Chief Red Eagle. He is in the council house. He and I will be able to shed some light on your dreams and your questions."

Time passed quickly as the two novice adventurers regaled the girls with the many details of their various treks through the wilderness back and forth between their two towns as well as beyond. The two girls had been perfect hostesses, listening intently as the boys embellished the otherwise dull truth and spun it into a montage of mysterious events and supernatural intrigue.

As the sun began to reach the horizon, Rock and Arrow bid the young maidens farewell as they walked them to their respective homes. Then with a dignified and courteous bow the boys turned to leave.

"I do hope you will come visit again – soon," said the taller girl. The expression on her face clearly relayed her sincerity. Her eyes were locked directly on Arrow.

Arrow smiled and replied, "I will do everything possible to pass this way again – soon."

Just before reaching the main trail to the lower part of town, Arrow looked over his shoulder. The beautiful girl was still standing in the doorway. He knew that there was a definite connection with her. He did not really understand how it had happened so fast, but the butterflies in his stomach were flapping harder than he thought possible.

"That went well," Arrow quipped.

Rock leered at him. "We were just going to talk to these girls and see if they are like the girls back home or not. You weren't supposed to fall in love with one of them. How do you plan on getting back here any time soon to conduct a proper courtship? What are your parents going to say?"

Arrow had not thought about how his parents would react. He knew that his father was already thinking about finding his son a wife from their own village. He could only hope that nothing would be arranged before he could get home and talk to his father. Finally, Arrow said, "I don't know, but I do know that none of the girls back home make me feel like this girl did."

As they entered the center of town, they noticed that the streets were deserted. They made their way to the council house and stopped at the door to listen, but there was no sound coming from inside. Apparently, there was no one inside. Without looking in, they proceeded on to the hut that had unofficially become their home away from home. Arrow poked his head inside the hut long enough to determine that it was indeed unoccupied. "Looks like home for the night," he announced.

They stepped inside and began to settle in when Rock asked, "I wonder where Deer is?"

There was no sign that he had been there. The two boys looked at each other and then in unison said, "He is at the Medicine Woman's house." Arrow added, "We will join up with him in the morning."

Rock nodded to indicate his agreement, pulled a handful of nuts from his pack and popped them in his mouth. Arrow soon secured a few morsels of his own. Before long they settled into their familiar locations and drifted off to sleep.

As the first light of morning filtered through the doorway of the hut where Rock and Arrow had slept, the two boys began to rouse around. Deer had not shown up all night, but as they gathered their blankets, he arrived at the door.

"Good morning!" Deer exclaimed.

Arrow had his back to the door and he jumped at the sudden announcement before spinning around to face the door.

"There you are," Arrow responded. "We were wondering what happened to you."

"I spent the night at the council house with Chief Red Eagle and the Medicine Woman. They explained many things and I have a much better understanding of what is happening with the dreams and visions," Deer explained. He briefly shared a few of the things he had learned, but the chorus of their growling stomachs changed the priority away from dreams.

"We can talk about this stuff after breakfast. I understand that an elder's wife baked some bread. Chief Red Eagle sent me to get you," Deer reported.

"That sounds good to me," Rock said as he stepped past Deer and out into the fresh morning air. Deer and Arrow dropped right in step with him.

Once inside the council house, they sat down around the council fire. The fresh bread was already waiting. Rock and Arrow substituted a handful of nuts for supper and even though they were quite hungry, they minded their manners and ate in moderation. It would have been rude to eat ravenously despite their hunger.

A few of the local men had joined them this morning. Chief Red Eagle related what Deer had shared with him regarding Wolf. While open displays of emotion are usually rare, several of the men were clearly saddened by the news. Talk around the room was subdued, but soon lightened as conversation gravitated away from Wolf. The boys were certainly glad that the focus of attention was shifting elsewhere.

After some time, Deer quietly announced that it was time for them to move on. Chief Red Eagle nodded approvingly and leaned close to Deer, giving him a fatherly hug. Without further ado, the boys grabbed their belongings and slipped out of the council house. The next decision they had to make was where they were headed. Deer had a cave on his mind. One located well to the south – one that had changed all of their lives. The vision-quest from the night before made that destination a priority. It had been promised that more answers were waiting there.

Chapter 9

The trail leading south was well used and easy to follow. Chief Red Eagle had given Deer a tail-feather of an eagle that had had the tip dyed red. Chief Red Eagle had said, "This will ensure your safety and good treatment from all of the people and towns of the region to the south because this feather is my stamp of approval for your passage." Deer wore the feather proudly and prominently on a braided lanyard around his neck. The Medicine Woman had braided the delicate lanyard from her own hair and had given it to him when she blessed the upcoming journey. It had truly been an incredible evening in the council house.

Rock and Arrow had asked Deer several times during the first couple of hours of their trek away from the village to share some details of the previous evening. Deer would simply smile. Finally he said, "It was so amazing that it is impossible to really describe. The sights and perceptions would not make any sense if merely described. You have heard the young warriors from home talk about their vision-quests and what a surreal experience it is. Now I understand it better. However, it is something that you must experience for yourself to fully comprehend it." Then he added, "I'll tell you more details later. I am still sorting it all out myself."

"That sounds incredible. I wish we had gone into the council house when we came into the village instead of going to the hut and going to bed," Rock lamented.

"I have a question," Arrow interjected into the conversation. "Did you have any dreams or vision last night about where we are headed?"

"That is a question that I can easily answer. Yes. Sometime during the night, I apparently was asleep because I got a clear message about our objective in this journey. We are going back to that tiny little cave where Rock and Wolf went exploring before we started for home on our first adventure. Wolf's spirit desires to revisit the cave. I must get a token from the cave to take back to our council house. Otherwise, Wolf's spirit can't find closure." Deer had stopped walking and turned to face his friends. The mission was crystal clear to him, but he could tell from the expression on their faces that this was just about the most preposterous story that he could have told.

"Are you kidding?" Rock finally blurted out. "I'm not going back in that cave! That is the craziest thing you have said since we left home!"

Rock's reaction was so extreme that Deer burst into laughter. When he started laughing, Rock and Arrow quickly joined in. Deer turned and started walking again. He did not have the heart to tell them that he was not kidding.

Regardless, their expressions and reactions were wonderful and released much of the tension that had surrounded their conversations most of the morning.

The trail that the trio was following paralleled a very nice stream. They had traveled this route with Wolf several weeks before, but had not really noticed that it was a truly beautiful waterway with numerous waterfalls. On that trip, they were struggling to get their friend home or at least to find someone that could help him.

"I propose that we stop at the next waterfall and see what there is to discover. There aren't any waterfalls on the Big River and I think that they are absolutely amazing," Arrow suggested.

"That sounds like a great idea. The water is flowing strong and I believe that I would even like to go for a swim," Rock added.

Before long, the distinctive sound of crashing water could be heard coming from just downstream of their current position. While it was clearly the sound of a large waterfall, it also seemed somewhat muted as if they were hearing an echo rather than the real thing.

"That sounds like a waterfall, but somehow it sounds odd," Deer quipped.

"Last one there is a rotten turkey egg," Arrow shouted as he dashed past Deer.

Rock was close behind Arrow with Deer bringing up the rear. The boys did not have far to go on the main trail until a secondary trail veered off in the direction of the roaring water. Arrow scampered down the trail first and came to a sliding stop right where the trail ended – at the edge of a *precipice* that was as high as the tops of the trees growing up from the base of the cliff.

"WHOA!" Arrow screamed because he knew Rock was only a few steps behind him.

Sure enough, Rock burst onto the rock glade and almost crashed into Arrow before he could get stopped. Arrow had immediately anticipated Rock's reaction and was prepared to catch him, if necessary, to keep him from knocking both of them over the cliff.

Deer, hearing the screaming, had already begun to decelerate and entered the rock glade at barely more than a jog. "I started to mention that it was probably not a good idea to go sprinting toward a waterfall because there had to be a cliff there somewhere. Looks like you already figured that out."

Arrow, still wide-eyed and slightly more pale than normal, said, "No more running DOWNHILL toward waterfalls!"

With all three safely reigned in, they carefully eased up to the edge and peered over. It was a spectacular sight. The stream that was coursing through the mountains was plunging over the cliff right beside their current vantage point into a large, clear pool directly below them. There were some very large rocks visible in the plunge basin, but for the most part it seemed like a very good place to swim – if they could find a way down.

From their position on the right flank of the falls, they could see a trail on the other side. The only problem was that they had to cross the stream above the falls to reach it. It was fairly obvious from their precarious perch that the bluff leading downstream provided no access to the pool from their side.

"I think that we are going to need to cross the creek if we intend to swim in that pool," Rock noted, pointing over the edge.

"I believe that you are probably right based on what we can see," Deer started. "The question I suppose now is whether we really want to go to that much trouble just to go swimming."

"This little trail led down here and there is a trail on that side," Arrow pointed out. "If we can find a decent crossing, I am still interested in going down to the pool for a refreshing swim under the waterfall. That is something I have never done before and may never get a chance to do again."

"Let's give it a try," Deer relented.

As they stepped back from the cliff, they turned and headed over to the stream's edge. The solid rock slab that the water was flowing across proved to be both a blessing and a curse. While the water itself was only about knee-deep, it was flowing fairly rapidly. Furthermore, the solid rock bottom provided smooth but very unsure footing for them because of the slimy, green algae that was growing on it.

After moving a sufficient distance back from the edge of the waterfall, the stream did not seem to be flowing quite as strongly. That was partially due to the slightly greater depth of the water, but also due to the bottom having a few large cobbles which gave the solid bedrock a less slippery appearance.

"I'll go first," Arrow announced. It was not really in his nature to be a fearless leader, but his adrenaline was still flowing pretty well. Without further words, Arrow stepped off into the water and waded carefully yet confidently across.

Once to the other side, he turned and reported, "The bottom is quite slick, but if you keep your balance, it is not too bad."

Deer waded in next. Gripping his bow and small quiver full of arrows tightly, he eased more gingerly across the stream than Arrow had. However, without any perceptible missteps, he emerged from the water successfully.

Rock was certainly not the most adventurous nor sure-footed person, but the relative ease with which the other two had crossed gave him an unjustified sense of security. Rock simply plowed off into the stream like it was not there. Taking long strides and high steps, he generated tremendous splashes that looked like a plodding buffalo. Just then, Rock stepped on a loose cobble and it rolled out from under his foot, causing him to lose his balance. Unfortunately, his momentum further compounded the problem and down he went with one big splash.

Under normal conditions, this would have proven to be no more than a clumsy and embarrassing event. However, when his entire body dropped into the current, the force of the water immediately began to sweep him along. The further downstream he flowed, the faster he went and the slicker the bedrock stream bottom became. Panic swept over him like a grass fire because he instantly knew that he was headed for the falls and there wasn't anything that he could do to stop it from happening.

Deer and Arrow were dumbstruck. It happened so fast that they were not fully aware of what was about to happen. By the time they realized what would happen in the next few seconds, it was too late to do anything.

Despite flailing wildly, in an instant Rock vanished over the edge. The roar of the cascading water never changed.

Simultaneously, Deer and Arrow sprinted for the trailhead that led to the pool below. They had no idea whether their friend was alive or dead. The flood of emotions that swept over them in that instant ran the full range from shock to terror to anguish and back again. However, they knew that nothing could be done from above the falls. They had to get to that pool as quickly as possible. Rock had fallen from a height almost as high as the surrounding oak trees into a pool of unknown depth with no shortage of big rocks.

The trail proved to be less passable in reality than what it had appeared from the other side of the falls. Nonetheless, they scrambled down the apparent deer path as fast as their legs would carry them.

Partway down the trail, Deer stopped and looked over toward the pool. Although fearful of what he might see, he had to know if he could catch a glimpse of Rock. Just as he stopped, Rock bobbed to the surface, still flailing his arms wildly and screeching like a mountain lion.

"He's alive!" Deer exclaimed.

Arrow never slowed down, but he did hear the wonderful news and let out a decidedly joyful whoop of relief and happiness.

Rock had managed to swim over to the rocky shallows and was sitting in the edge of the water when Arrow and Deer arrived.

"Are you hurt?" Arrow asked.

"I don't think so. Nothing is throbbing and I don't seem to be bleeding," Rock replied.

Deer ran up at that moment. "I am so glad you aren't dead! Your parents would have killed us! What were you thinking? We told you the rocks were slick!"

"I thought that since you guys had no trouble getting across, it wasn't nearly as treacherous as it really was. I have to tell you, I clearly saw my life flash before my eyes and it was way too short. It was an incredible feeling, though. You are flying through the air and everything starts moving in slow motion. You see every individual drop of water that is floating down with you. Then you slam into the water and everything goes back to happening too fast. However, after I hit the water and realized that I was not only not dead but not even hurt, it occurred to me that that was the MOST exciting thing I have ever done, but I don't ever want to do it again." Rock chattered on and on, repeating himself and waving his arms wildly as he described every minute detail of the experience.

Arrow and Deer, once again, stood speechless.

After Rock had settled down, Arrow looked at Deer and asked, "Aren't we going to go swimming?"

Without another word Deer and Arrow slipped out of their clothes, carefully stashing them in a safe place this time before splashing out into the surprisingly deep pool. They did not want to have their garments snatched again. Despite Rock's clothes already being wet, he decided to slip them off as well because it was much easier to swim without them.

The cold water reminded them of wading and fishing in the Big River recently, except this water was perfectly clear. Deer and Arrow swam out into the pool near the edge of where the falling torrent was entering the pool. The roar was deafening.

Deer then swam below the surface of the plunging water to see what it looked like. Arrow and Rock followed. The bubbles completely obscured their vision, and the churning current made it difficult to even tell which way was up. However, they each soon popped to the surface and determined that it was not a good idea to swim directly into the impact area. Arrow started around the right end of the impact area while Deer and Rock swam around the left end.

While there were no massive boulders directly under the falls, there were many around the perimeter of the plunge area. As the three boys reunited behind the falls, they crawled up on the base of the bluff to talk.

"That was amazing," Arrow exclaimed.

"Absolutely!" Deer agreed.

It was Rock's turn to comment and all he could say was, "I sure am glad those big rocks weren't under the waterfall."

Deer and Arrow nodded vigorously in agreement.

Once behind the veil of falling water, the boys found themselves sitting on the lip of a rather expansive *bluffshelter*. The shelter was not really visible from in front of the falls nor was it accessible today without getting wet. When they turned their full attention to investigating the shelter as opposed to visually scouring the details of the waterfall, they realized that they were not the first people to spend quality time in this shelter. The walls were adorned with a wide variety of painted scenes. Arrow was the first to exit the water and walk up into the shelter. Deer and Rock soon followed. None of the boys spoke a word. Even though they had seen similar kinds of imagery before, the quantity in this place was incredible. This was clearly a special place.

The smooth limestone along the back wall was literally covered with painted figures of deer, buffalo, and other animals. There were scenes showing people with weapons. The images depicted hunting or fighting while others seemed to illustrate things from the spirit world. Geometric shapes and numerous parallel lines were apparently important, but their meaning was certainly unclear.

The boys slowly eased through the gallery of imagery. Suddenly, Rock stumbled over a small woven basket. It was sitting beside a large slab of rock that had apparently fallen from the ceiling of the shelter long, long ago. Inside the basket was an odd assortment of items including a roll of twine, a highly polished clay pot, many very well made arrow points, a bundle of dried corn on the cob, a carved wooden smoking pipe, a limb from a cedar tree, and several other small items.

"What do you think this is?" Rock asked.

"I don't know for sure, but if I were guessing, I would say that it is an offering of some sort. These paintings are highly symbolic and I think we have stumbled onto a very sacred place to Chief Red Eagle and his people," Deer theorized. "Look at that line of stacked rocks. That is not natural. It must mean something very special."

"I think you are right. We need to get out of here," Arrow added.

With that, the boys walked back over to the water's edge and waded in. Swimming back around the waterfall, they found themselves back out in the sunlight. Within a few strokes they had crossed the pool and were reunited with their clothes, which they were quite pleased to see. The water was cold.

"Glad there weren't any pesky girls around to steal our clothes again. That would have been a real problem this far from any replacements," Rock quipped.

All three boys laughed loudly. While this second close call with death was not out of their minds completely, their youthful sense of invincibility had certainly limited the impact of the lesson that should have been learned from the experience.

Within a short time as they proceeded downstream, they found a footpath that lead back up and out of the narrow canyon. They followed this trail which led them back to the main pathway they had followed before the waterfall detour. Much of the remainder of their journey downstream passed uneventfully. Just before dusk, they selected a campsite for the night and made the necessary preparation to get some rest because tomorrow they would leave the comfortable trail, turn east, climb up and over the ridge, then descend into the stream valley below.

Chapter 10

Sunrise had passed and the birds were singing sweetly when the three boys finally got up and broke camp.

"Guys, I must go to Wolf's cave. I won't ask you to go in because this is something that I must do," Deer announced almost apologetically.

Based on what Deer had said after leaving Chief Red Eagle's village, Rock and Arrow already knew that was to be the ultimate destination of this odyssey and that Deer had not been kidding yesterday. Both nodded affirmatively as they set out.

Chief Red Eagle had told Deer that Eagle Village Creek would turn toward the setting sun about one day's journey to the south. Deer was also told that he would see a large pine tree in the middle of the path near that major curve that had a large X carved into it. That marked tree is where they would need to turn east, cross the creek, and follow a path up the mountain. It was reported to be the easiest place to cross the eastern ridge and gain access to the next valley. Although Chief Red Eagle had never traveled to the adjacent valley himself, the cross-country merchants had told him that the stream beyond the eastern ridge flowed north and eventually merged with Big River. From there, they figured that they could find their way back home.

Leaving the well used trail that led south was somewhat unsettling but necessary. By using the landmarks that Chief Red Eagle had supplied, Deer would be able to identify and follow the dim path that would lead to the top of the ridge and into the adjacent valley.

"Here is the X that marks the trail which we need to follow," Deer announced as they approached the large, gnarled pine.

"What trail?" Arrow asked, glancing all around and seeing nothing but dense vegetation.

"Chief Red Eagle said that the trail we want is just across the creek but he did not say exactly how to get across the creek," Deer said, pointing in the direction of the creek. Without another word, he turned off the well established trail and headed into the thick, lush vegetation.

Arrow and Rock glanced at each other and fanned out on both sides of Deer in hopes of finding something that even resembled a trail. All three boys reached the creek bank simultaneously, but were separated by about an average arrow shot.

63

"Do you see a good place to cross?" Arrow asked from his position farthest upstream.

"Not really. It actually looks a little deep," Deer replied.

Rock added his observation, "I suspect we can cross down here, but it looks like we will get wet when we do." Then as an apparent afterthought, Rock added, "It would not be as rough as the last place I crossed."

All three boys laughed heartily. It was an excellent tension breaker. The mood had gotten too serious and, after all, they were on an adventure.

Without looking further for a better place to cross, Deer stepped off into the creek. Despite flowing rather swiftly, it proved to be less than waist deep and the bottom was covered with small cobbles. Without incident, he waded right across and emerged on the other bank. He noticed what appeared to be a game trail leading away from the stream's edge, across the *floodplain* and eventually to the base of the eastern ridge. Rock and Arrow quickly converged on the place where Deer had crossed and followed his lead.

At the sound of Rock and Arrow splashing across the creek, Deer glanced over his shoulder and steadily strode toward the base of the ridge. Arrow and Rock only managed to match Deer's pace, but as the trio started up the slope, Deer slowed down and was soon rejoined by his friends. The lower slopes of the ridge were not steep or difficult to ascend, but the occasional rock outcrop reminded them that there was bound to be tougher going in the near future.

"Did you see that rotten log back there? It looked like a bear had rolled it over to search for grubs," Rock mentioned quietly as if hoping that the bear would not hear him.

"I bet these woods are full of bears. I intend to make enough noise tromping up this trail to the summit to let them know that we are coming," Deer replied. "My father says that that is the best way to not surprise a bear. The last thing we need is to startle a bear because I know I can't outrun one."

Arrow glanced back at Rock and added, "Deer, we don't have to outrun the bear. We just have to outrun Rock."

"Very funny," Rock sneered.

With a grin on his face, Arrow paused momentarily to let Rock catch him. Rock knew that Arrow was joking and he took no real offense to the good-natured ribbing. That was just the kind of friendship that they shared. They could poke fun at each other one minute and passionately defend each other's honor or very life in the next.

The easy part of the climb was soon behind them and the arduous task of scaling the steep slope was at hand. The trail was easy enough to follow because it ran in a fairly straight line and at a steady upward angle. Having enough traffic from occasional merchants as well as deer and bear, apparently, its visibility was reasonably well maintained.

Pressing upward became increasingly more strenuous and the steady pace of the lower slopes was reduced to more of a slow, scrambling climb. The loose rocks and deep leaves only served to inhibit progress, making it seem like they were moving three steps forward while sliding two steps back. If it were not for the occasional trees that provided a stable handhold, they wondered if they would have been able to scale the mountainside at all. They paused frequently to catch their breath, although they claimed it was to admire the spectacular scenery.

"Look ... at ... the ... horizon. I think ... I can ... see ... all of ... the way ... to the ... edge of ... the earth." Rock finally wheezed out.

Arrow and Deer simply nodded agreeably. They were unable to speak at that moment.

After several minutes, Deer looked at Arrow and said, "We crossed this ridge with Wolf and I don't remember it being this steep."

After a reflective moment, Rock replied, "Downhill never seems as steep as uphill, I suppose."

Deer nodded and then stated, "I guess you're right. I do know one thing though. I don't want to climb many more mountains before we get home. Chief Red Eagle indicated that the valley we are headed to will lead us back to Big River. After we visit Wolf's cave, we can follow the creek and once we get back to the Big River, we can find our way back home without climbing any more mountains."

Arrow was silent throughout the discussion. As much as he wasn't looking forward to climbing any more mountains, he had been thinking about the cute young lady he met at Chief Red Eagle's village. If they followed Deer's plan, they would bypass her and he may never have the chance to see her again. The deep, contemplative expression was easily noticeable. He did not try to hide it, but he was not ready to talk about it either. Not returning home with Deer and Rock was not an option.

Deer once again rose to his feet, picked up his bow, and resumed scrambling upward. He had noticed Arrow's expression, but decided that it was not the proper time to get into a lengthy discussion. Pulling themselves past ancient oak, hickory, and occasional pine trees would require that they remain focused and, above all, moving.

By the time that they finally reached the saddle of the ridge, the sun was slightly past midday. Sprawling out on the ground under an old majestic oak tree to rest, Rock declared that he was going to take a long break. No objections were voiced by either of his companions and all three were soon stretched out in the shade watching the newly *unfurled* leaves rustle gently in the cool breeze. While lying there and nibbling on a few stashed morsels that they were carrying, the cares of life seemed to melt away.

"I hate to say it, but that climb was almost worth it just to lay here and relax," Rock declared softly, not wanting to disrupt the magic of the moment.

Deer simply smiled. Arrow looked at his dear friend and whispered, "But only with friends like you guys."

Once the trio was rested and fed they gathered their meager belongings and walked to the far side of the saddle, looking down into the eastern valley. The poorly defined trail that they had followed up the mountain was just as poorly defined going down the other side, but they had already noted that going down did not seem nearly as steep. Their progress downhill was almost *euphoric* as they intentionally allowed themselves to slide from tree to tree almost as if racing to see who could get to the bottom first.

"That was fun!" Rock declared as he reached the bottom.

"It sure was. Let's go back up and do it again," Arrow mockingly challenged.

"No way!" Deer and Rock replied in almost perfect unison and then they both broke into an extended period of laughter at the mere idea of climbing a mountain just to slide back down. None of them could imagine doing such a silly thing just for fun. However, it WAS fun!

When the *frivolity* subsided, the realization came that they were still on a serious mission. Each of them looked around to see if anything looked familiar because no one was entirely sure whether they needed to go upstream or downstream from their current location to find Wolf's cave.

"I propose that we make our way over to the stream and see if anything looks familiar. If it does, we should head upstream. If is does not, then we go downstream because the cave was at the farthest point that we traveled up the creek," Deer offered.

"That sounds like a solid idea," Rock responded. Without further discussion, they all headed for the creek.

The underbrush was certainly more lush along the creek bank because there was abundant water and the valley floors were more insulated from the cold winds that embattle the ridges throughout the winter. In their carefree descent of the ridge, they had lost the trail. At this point, however, it did not really matter except that they had to fight their way through the vines and briars to actually reach the creek.

Arrow was the first to arrive at the creek, where he quickly knelt and got a refreshing drink of crystal-clear water. Deer and Rock were not far behind and they also took advantage of the stream's delicious taste.

"I don't know if this water just tastes better than other water, but it sure is good," Arrow remarked before going down for a final mouthful.

"I don't know either, but I sure needed it," Rock added.

With their bellies filled, they began to study the creek and the scenery of the area when Deer asked, "Does anything look familiar?"

"Not really," Rock answered. "However, we have seen so much in the past few weeks, I am not sure if I would recognize it anyway."

"It looks vaguely familiar but I would like to look upstream regardless," Arrow announced.

"I agree," Deer chimed in and the boys turned upstream. Before they had traveled very far, they crossed the trail that they were supposed to have followed down the mountain into the valley. A short lateral venture up and down the trail revealed that everything looked new to them. Returning to the creek bank, they continued upstream until mid-afternoon before they spotted an especially large and oddly shaped boulder sitting in the edge of the creek.

"Look." Arrow said pointing at the boulder. "I know I have seen that boulder before. We HAVE been through here before."

Deer maneuvered closer to the creek so he could get a better view. Immediately upon seeing it, he shouted, "You're right! We have been through here before." The confirmation of a prominent landmark that they had seen on their first adventure was exciting. Aside from being on the right creek, they were headed in the right direction.

"I remember that rock," Deer stated confidently. "We are about a half day's walk from the little valley where Wolf's cave is located." Looking up toward the western ridge, he continued, "Unfortunately, there is not enough daylight left to walk that far today."

"I think we should walk a little farther and find a good place to camp for the night," Arrow proposed. "That way, we can leave our packs at the camp, walk on to the cave, get whatever it is that Deer needs to get, then walk back to the same camp. We will save the effort of hauling our stuff unnecessarily and our camp will already be there waiting for us to return."

"That sounds like an excellent idea, Arrow," Rock offered. Deer agreed as well, and they all started working their way toward their anticipated overnight camping area. Conversation became fluid because the anxiety of seemingly being lost was gone. They knew where they were and they knew how to get home. Everything else was relegated to enjoying the trip.

Before long, a nice, high spot overlooking the creek came into view. "This looks like a good spot. We can set up camp and then go down to the creek for a swim," Deer suggested.

"Perfect spot and a perfect idea," Arrow commented.

The camp was quickly cleared of undergrowth, a ring of stones was set up, firewood was gathered, and leaf-bedding was collected. Before long, a modest fire was burning and they made their way down to the creek. Climbing the mountain and subsequently sliding down it had resulted in the collection of an inordinate amount of sweat and dirt. A swim was just what they needed to help them to sleep comfortably under the stars.

Splashing around and skipping rocks not only washed their dirt away but also much of their natural caution. They knew that they were totally alone and did not give a thought to any dangers that may be present. No bears or mountain lions had been encountered. No people lived in this area. For all intents and purposes, they felt safer here than any place they could think of.

With the late afternoon sun dipping behind the ridge, Arrow recommended that they head for camp. With one last rock successfully skipped all the way across the creek, they filed out of the water and scurried back to camp. In addition to being wet, the temperature was dropping as fast as the sun. The heat from the campfire felt wonderful and Arrow was glad that he had thought to build it before they went swimming.

Once dry, they slipped their clothes on and settled in next to the fire to eat a final meal for the day. The dried nuts, cracked corn, deer jerky, and flat bread that Chief Red Eagle had given them was good, but it wasn't their mother's home cooking.

"I was wondering," Rock pondered. "Since we are coming back to this camp tomorrow, do you think that we could set up a trap and catch a squirrel to eat for supper tomorrow night? I really would like to have some fresh meat at least once in a while. I would even volunteer to clean it and cook it if we could catch one."

"I was thinking about that," Deer replied. "I have been carrying this bow and arrows for several days and I have not even tried to shoot anything. We have seen many squirrels and several rabbits. I am sure that I can get one or two. As we walk to the cave tomorrow, we will proceed more quietly than we have been and I believe that I can get a shot."

Rock smiled and nodded. "I know you can if we put a little effort into it." Conversation flowed amongst the three as they discussed different strategies for getting a squirrel versus ones used to hunt rabbits.

Arrow decided he was ready for bed and reached into his pack to get his blanket. Grabbing the blanket by one corner, he pulled it free of the pack, allowing it to unfold. As it unfolded, something dropped to the ground with a thud. Startled by the unexpected object dropping at his feet, Arrow jumped back and dropped the blanket. Deer and Rock whipped their heads around just in time to see the blanket hit the ground. However, the blanket did not reach the ground before they saw the large black snake that it covered. Apparently, the snake had crawled into Arrow's pack while the boys were swimming only to be dislodged when Arrow removed the blanket.

Uncertain just what kind of snake it was, the boys moved back momentarily to formulate a plan. The poor light cast by the fire was not adequate to determine whether the snake was dangerous or not, so Arrow eased in and lifted the blanket carefully until the snake was fully visible.

"It's just a rat snake," Rock blurted out. "It won't hurt you."

"I know that. It startled me, though, and that will make me hurt myself," Arrow snapped.

"We could kill it and then we would have fresh meat," Deer offered.

"I have eaten snake and it's not too bad, but I think I will hold out for squirrel if it is all the same to you guys," Rock responded.

With that, Arrow reached down and grabbed the snake by the tail and tossed it out into the darkness beyond camp where it hit the ground with another resounding thud.

"I don't mind snakes, but I don't like it when they surprise me," Arrow muttered. As sleepy as he was a few minutes before, now he had trouble going to sleep.

Before long, all three boys were stretched out and the sound of the crickets ebbed and flowed with the breathing of the young explorers.

Chapter 11

The first good light of morning had the three boys up and moving. The best chance to get a squirrel was early in the morning. While the creek bottom was certainly rich with nut- and acorn-bearing trees of all sorts, they felt that the lower slopes of the ridge would be just as productive but with fewer briars. The new growth of leaves would limit visibility well up into the canopy. Using a bow and arrow was not the most effective weapon for shooting small game anywhere, especially in the tree tops.

Arrow and Rock fanned out on either side of Deer as they moved up the valley. Moving much slower than they had in days past, they were able to slip through the forest with great stealth. The occasional squirrel would be spotted high in the trees ahead or it would go scampering wildly across the forest floor as they approached. Dozens had been seen, but none offered any hope of a shot.

"There is no shortage of squirrels in this area, but I think we should make our way on up to Wolf's cave. We need to take care of the business there and just plan on returning to camp in time to hunt more this afternoon. You guys can stay in camp and I will slip out alone. I think there is just too much commotion with all three of us walking through the woods even though we are not making much noise," Deer proposed.

"That sounds fine," Rock agreed.

"We can just hang out at camp this afternoon and wait for you to bring in supper," Arrow jokingly chided.

All of the boys laughed as they picked up the pace and abandoned the official effort of the morning hunt. However, after being highly focused on watching for squirrels, not one passed unnoticed. There was indeed an abundant quantity of squirrels in this valley. As they walked, the conversation turned to squirrels and odd squirrel behavior.

Deer was the first to share a story with the others. "I was walking through the woods one day with my father and he spotted a squirrel up in an acorn tree. Every time he tried to maneuver for a shot, the squirrel would simply run around to the back side of the tree. Dad must have made three or four laps around that tree before he determined exactly where it was. Holding his bow in one hand, Dad bent over and picked up a large chunk from a dead tree limb that was lying on the ground. Then he walked straight away from the tree about ten paces before turning around and facing the tree. Staring up into the tree, he spotted the tip of the squirrel's tail, but the rest of the rodent was hidden by the tree. Dad tossed the chunk out into the woods about ten paces

71

on the far side of the tree. When the chunk hit and went crashing through the dry leaves on the ground, the squirrel quickly dashed around to our side of the tree. Dad took careful aim and drilled the squirrel perfectly."

Arrow waded in next. "I have seen my father do that same thing. That is an excellent strategy, especially for red squirrels. Gray squirrels are more *skittish*, and they usually head for the very top of the highest tree. If they can get into an adjacent tree, they will huddle up in a clump of leaves at the very top. It is almost impossible to see it unless it moves.

One story led to another and soon Rock topped them all when he told about a squirrel that his dad had killed last winter. "Dad was slipping along one morning," he began, "when he heard something odd. Dad said that the snow was only about ankle deep, but that the surface had refrozen overnight making it crusty. He could tell that the animal was walking toward him. He could also tell that it was following the dry creek channel very near to his current position so he just stood perfectly still, hidden by the cedar tree that was nearby. The sound of the approaching animal got louder as it got closer. It was a mother bobcat with two small kittens. They were easily within range, but dad said that the kittens were so cute that he decided to just watch them because they were so playful. Apparently, the mother bobcat sensed that something wasn't right because she gave a low growl and the two kittens made a dash up the hillside and into a tiny hole in the bluff."

Arrow and Deer had not heard this story before. They stopped walking and turned to face Rock.

He continued, "Dad said that his attention was on the kittens, and before he realized it, the mother bobcat was nowhere to be seen. When she got out of sight, the two kittens resumed their wrestling and nipping each other at the mouth of the little cave. As he stood there, he heard a squirrel crossing some frozen limbs above him on the hillside behind him. When he stepped into the clear, the squirrel apparently spooked and jumped out of the tree just a few steps from him. As the squirrel ran directly up the hillside, Dad took quick aim and let an arrow fly. It hit the running rodent right through the back legs which stopped it, but also made it very mad. Needing to finish the job, dad *nocked* another arrow and shot it again. With the dead squirrel in hand, he started back down the hillside when he spotted the two kittens lying in the mouth of the cave watching the whole show. Without giving it another thought, Dad cut the squirrel's tail off to prove his story and tossed the squirrel up to the bobcat kittens. Dad said that he had certainly been entertained by the whole show and that he felt like it was his way of giving something in return."

"That is an amazing story," Arrow blurted out.

"Rock, are you making that up?" Deer quizzed.

"Honest. It is the absolute truth. I can't believe I had not told you guys before. I guess it just slipped my mind," Rock responded as he shrugged his shoulders.

"I suppose if we hunt long enough, really cool and interesting things will happen to us also," Deer commented. He then turned and resumed walking toward the cave.

Arrow and Rock took up the trail immediately behind him and the remainder of the walk to Wolf's cave hollow passed fairly quickly and without incident including encountering any squirrels that were interested in being shot and eaten by the three novice hunters.

When they arrived at the mouth of the hollow, they barely slowed down except for Deer pointing at the location of the camp site where they had stayed during their previous and ill-fated trek into this area. They quickly covered the short distance up the hollow and soon arrived at the base of the bluff that led up to Wolf's cave.

Deer looked at the others and said, "I know you don't want to go inside, but I must. I know what I have to get and I don't think it will take long."

"I've been thinking," Rock started. "I went in with Wolf on the first visit and I did not get sick, so it must not be the fact of going inside that makes you sick. I think it was that pile of bat droppings that Wolf fell in that made him sick. Since I know where he went, I think it is a good idea for me to go in with you. I can at least stay by the opening in the big room that leads to the outside and help you find that important feature."

"That would be fantastic, Rock," Deer said with a sigh of relief. "I have to tell you – I was pretty nervous about going in there alone. I did not know where to find what I was looking for and there is no telling whether there might be something dangerous in there or not."

"By the way, Deer, what are you going in there to get?" Rock asked.

"The Medicine Woman told me to get a bat from inside the cave and take it back home," Deer answered.

Rock stopped. He wondered if he had volunteered too quickly. Then he asked a second question. "Did she tell you how you were supposed to catch a bat and get it back home?"

With a sly grin Deer bent over and picked up a short section of dead limb about half as big around as his arm but about as long. "She did not say that it had to be alive when we collect it. She just said that we had to get one and take it to the council house back home."

Rock nodded his head slowly as he formed a mental image of the scene that was about to take place inside this cave. He remembered seeing some bats in the cave but he was not exactly sure how Deer thought he was going to hit one with that stick.

Meanwhile, Deer emptied the arrows from their quiver and pulled a small pouch from the bottom of it. It was like the pouch in which he had transported the cedar and tobacco that he used during Wolf's burial. With the pouch removed from the bottom of the quiver, he placed the arrows back in their proper place then laid the bow and quiver full of arrows at the base of a tree.

Arrow had already begun to build a fire because Deer and Rock were going to need light once they got back into the cave. Rock joined Arrow and began to feed the fire while Arrow worked on a temporary torch that they could use until they got inside. Once inside, they could retrieve one of the good torches Rock left behind when he and Wolf exited the cave about fifteen days before.

"I think this will last long enough for you to get inside and find one of the good torches left inside. You can then light one of the good torches with this one," Arrow instructed.

With the temporary torch in hand and lit, Deer scrambled up to the mouth of the cave and quickly went inside. Rock was close behind him. Deer soon located the torch that Wolf had dropped just where the natural light ended. He managed to get it lit, then left the temporary torch propped against the wall for Rock.

Deer scurried along the narrow passage and soon emerged into the large room. Rock soon appeared and stood up beside him. The sound of squeaking bats told them that they would have no problem finding the object of their quest. Whether they could collect one remained to be seen.

As agreed, Rock stayed by the exit hole as Deer started easing along the wall. He did not go far before he spotted a single bat hanging from the bottom of a rock ledge right above his head. He had imagined that he would find himself flailing wildly in the near pitch dark as the chaotic creatures darted past his head. Whacking one that was sitting still, while less sporting, would surely be more effective. He raised the stick and with one swift swat, the mission was

74

accomplished. After using the stick to rake the unfortunate bat into the pouch, Deer turned back toward the exit. Rock led the way with Deer close behind. When daylight was plentiful, they each extinguished their lights. Upon reaching the wide-open spaces, they dropped their torch just outside the mouth of the cave and descended to the place where Arrow was waiting.

"That did not take long," Arrow noted.

"No, I got lucky and found one that I could collect easily," Deer responded. "Let's get away from this place."

"No argument with that," Rock quickly agreed. "To be honest, I am ready to head for home. I think I have had just about enough wilderness-exploring for a while."

With no further discussion on the matter, they retraced their route back down the hollow and just before dark, arrived back at the camp where they had left their belongings.

As evening fell, the three young men sat around the fire and reminisced about the events since Wolf's incident and how dramatically their lives had been changed. Visiting the cave had stirred up feelings that, generally speaking, had been laid to rest or at least thoroughly suppressed. With the collection of the bat, stories about Wolf dominated the conversation. Rock recounted the story once again about his first trip into the cave with Wolf and, initially anyway, how funny it was to see Wolf covered in stinky bat guano. "Wolf was the best hunter, woodsman, and adventurer of all the young men in our tribe. Seeing him that way was so uncharacteristic," he concluded.

Fatigue finally overcame conversation and the boys settled in for another night under the stars. The crackling fire and the babbling brook soon serenaded them to sleep and into their separate dreamlands.

Deer looked down at his hands. He was holding his bow and an arrow was resting on the string, ready for launch. He glanced to the right and a doe was strolling down a trail that would pass directly in front of him. Wolf leaned in behind him and said, "Wait until she clears that last tree before you shoot." Deer waited. The deer needed to take three more steps. One. Two. Three. Deer drew the bow, took careful aim and released. The arrow buried deep into the deer's chest. She jumped and started running away but within a few steps, staggered, and fell lifeless to the ground.

The sky was full of stars on the moonless night when Deer opened his eyes. He had not dreamed about Wolf during the past few nights and he had wondered why. Rock and Arrow were still quite oblivious to his struggles.

Deer sat up and using a future piece of firewood, he stirred the remaining coals. Adding a handful of small twigs and medium-sized sticks first, Deer then added a couple of large chunks. Within a few moments, new flames were licking at the fresh fuel and as they grew, the light that emanated from it began to push the shadows well beyond the edge of camp.

Lying back down in the badly compressed bed of leaves, Deer pulled his blanket up to his chin and stared up into the expansive night sky. Occasionally, a bat would dip and dive through the fire light and snatch a bug out of the air before disappearing back into the darkness. Deer wondered where the bat lived and if bats missed their friends as badly as he missed Wolf. Thoughts ran wild as he pondered his own short past and then about what the future held for himself and his buddies sleeping nearby. Before too long, sleep crept back into its rightful place and Deer was soon resting comfortably once again.

A chorus of birds joyously announced the new day. Before long the three boys were stirring, gathering their belongings and preparing to start the long journey home.

"I had another dream last night," Deer started. "Actually I had the same dream that I had before – the one where Wolf helped me kill that doe."

"What do you think it means?" Arrow asked.

"I don't know. It might not mean anything, but it was so vivid," Deer mused, then continued, "I think that just in case it is a vision of something that is about to happen, I should probably take the lead this morning."

Rock looked at Arrow and then said, "That sounds fine to us. In fact, I would love to see this dream you keep having come true. I would really like to eat a fresh deer steak!" With that Rock laughed heartily not because he did not think Deer was capable of killing a deer, but because the idea of having a dream come true seemed so unlikely.

Deer laughed, too, but in his heart he knew that today the dream would come true. He did not understand it and he could not explain how he knew. He just knew.

Since no people permanently lived in this valley, there were no established trails to follow. Therefore, they picked their way downstream along game trails and through natural clearings, all of which slowed homeward progress tremendously.

Just before midday, Deer stopped and raised his hand to stop Rock and Arrow who were following a short distance behind.

"I heard something walking in the leaves," Deer whispered back toward his friends. He followed that with the simple yet direct command to "Stay." With that, he turned his full attention to locating the source of the sound. As he scanned the underbrush just ahead, he pulled an arrow from the quiver and *nocked* it on the bowstring.

At that moment, he heard Wolf's voice in his head say, "Wait until she clears that last tree before you shoot."

A broad grin covered Deer's face as the young doe stepped out of the brush completely oblivious to Deer's presence. He knew that this was providential and that the deer would soon be his.

One step. Two steps. Three steps. Nothing to deflect the arrow. Draw. Aim. Release!

The arrow found its mark perfectly and disappeared right behind her front leg. She jumped straight up and hit the ground in a full run, crashing through the brush and making a tremendous amount of noise. However, that only lasted as long as that last breath she had taken because the arrow had done its job in an instant. The doe only ran a short distant before crumpling to the ground in a lifeless heap.

The forest was silent once again, but only for a moment. As soon as the reality of the situation dawned on them, a raucous explosion of whooping and yelling broke out from all three of them as they celebrated their unparalleled personal accomplishment.

Rock and Arrow ran up to join Deer beside the carcass. Now it was Deer's turn to be pumped up on adrenaline and talking non-stop. "Guys, it was just like the dream. I heard Wolf talk to me. He said to wait until she cleared the last tree. Well, I don't think there was an audible voice to be heard, but I heard it in my mind just like the dream was playing out while I am awake! I can't believe it. This is the most amazing thing that has ever happened to me . . ."

Deer jabbered on and on. Rock and Arrow just stood there in stunned silence. How could a dream come true in such minute detail? Neither one knew, but the evidence was lying at their feet as well as flowing from the mouth of their good friend who had always seemed so rational and stable until the past few weeks. They were not sure what to make of it.

Deer finally hushed long enough for Rock to say, "I said I would clean it if you killed it. Let's drag her over to the creek and see how much meat we can collect. She isn't all that big, but it is going to be more than enough meat to carry all the way back home – minus what we will be eating for lunch!"

Without discussion, Rock grabbed the deer by the front legs while Arrow grabbed the back legs. Deer cleared a path back down to the creek bank. Once there, Rock dug into his pack and pulled out his stone knives and a piece of antler for resharpening the edges. Nothing dulls a stone blade like deer hair.

Rock quickly cut all four legs off and dropped them into the shallow creek to cool. He then turned his attention to the *back-strap*, the tender meat along the backbone. While he had left the hide on the legs to help insulate those portions during transport, he had removed the hide from the two lean strips of prime fare. Arrow was busy building a fire and Deer was gathering wood. In just a few minutes, the smell of *tenderloins* cooking over an open fire had each of their mouths watering with anticipation.

"I hate to leave so much of the carcass behind because there is some really tasty meat on the ribs, but I just don't think we can carry everything home. I think we can carry the legs for sure and I figure we will eat most of the *back-strap* for lunch and supper today," Rock postulated. "By leaving the hide on the legs, it will stay cool longer, and every so often we can drop them back into the creek to re-chill them. Since we don't have any salt to cure them, we will have to be careful that they don't spoil before we get them home – assuming that we don't eat them before we get there."

Deer laughed at the thought of the three of them gorging themselves on the meat to the point that they would be unable to even waddle home at all. "That sounds like a good plan. I figure that we will certainly eat some of it as we go. After all, WE earned it!"

They chattered continuously until the fresh meat finished cooking. At that point, conversation pretty much ceased and the only sound that was heard was chewing, smacking, and groans of deep satisfaction from the incredible meal that they were feasting on.

"I was thinking," Arrow started as he swallowed another bite. "We will need to move on down the creek before we make camp for the night. With the smell of blood in the area and a fresh carcass nearby, we will probably have bears or cougars coming to visit us tonight."

"I had not thought about that," Rock replied. "I agree. We need to camp well away from this place and based on the position of the sun, we better get moving so that we have time to get there and get settled before dark. I'll

78

retrieve the legs from the creek while you guys figure out how to transport the rest of the cooked meat so we can have it for supper in a little while."

"I'll use some of the hide from the torso of the doe and make a temporary pouch out of it by perforating the edges and lacing them up with some cord," Arrow offered.

"That will work!" Deer exclaimed. "It will provide a good bag and will minimize the amount of dirt and flies that would get on it otherwise." He smiled as he took note of just how resourceful they had become as a result of the many days they had successfully survived thus far while out in the wilderness.

Soon Rock had the four leg quarters strung together and draped over a makeshift meat pole. Arrow then added the hide-bag full of cooked *tenderloins* to the pole. With Deer taking the lead to clear the path, Rock and Arrow grabbed opposite ends of the pole with the meat hanging safely between them.

Progress was slow but steady as the threesome picked their way toward home. Just before dark, they reached a favorable camp site. Returning the leg quarters to the cool water for overnight storage, the boys opened the bag and pulled out several pieces of meat. Although it had cooled, it was still delicious. The additional cargo had forced them to work much harder than they had been and the fresh meat was an extremely important component to sustaining their strength for the remainder of the journey home.

Fatigue was so great that they did not even bother to build a fire before wrapping up in their blankets for the night. Sleep came quickly and the dark of the night surrounded them without even being noticed.

The following morning, everything was gathered, packed, and hoisted onto their collective backs for another day of marching through the wilderness. While the route they chose eliminated the difficulty of traversing several ridges, it still proved to be an arduous trek and was no shorter in the number of days that it took them to get home. However, they finally reached their home village after almost six full days of walking from the time they left Wolf's cave. Beleaguered and exhausted, they were grateful to be home and even delivered both hindquarters to the smokehouse for final cleaning and curing before parting company for their respective homes. Deer was instructed to come to the council house tomorrow.

Chapter 12

Deer slept so hard that he barely felt like he had slept at all. Being back in his own bed, however, was a wonderful improvement to the weeks of sleeping in a pile of leaves and waking up covered with dew. The smell of fresh flat bread filled the air inside his home because his mother had risen early to prepare him a special "welcome-home" breakfast. It was indeed good to be home.

A definite change had occurred in Deer during this last trip. His parents saw it immediately. Deer had passed from youth to adulthood. He had closed one chapter of his life as he stumbled headlong into the next one. It was bound to be an interesting transition back into a normal day-to-day life.

"Snowflake dropped by a few days ago to see if you were back yet. Obviously, I told her that you were not," Deer's mother said softly as she tended the baking bread. She did not need to say anything else.

Deer had been just lying in his bed soaking up the sounds and smells of home with his arms crossed behind his head and his eyes tightly closed. However, with the mention of Snowflake he opened his eyes and a crooked little grin crept across his face. A moment later, he sat up. There was a burning question that had been riding in the back of his mind ever since the clothes-theft incident.

"Mom, do you like Snowflake?" Deer asked, not sure how to wade into the subject that he really wanted to talk about.

"Snowflake is a high-spirited girl. She has plenty of energy and initiative," she replied. His mother kept her back to Deer because she could not help but smile and she did not want to embarrass her son.

"I've been thinking about her lately and I want to get to know her better. I know we have lived close to each other all of our lives, but I don't really KNOW her. I'd like to know what she likes to do for fun, what her favorite food is, and – who she intends to spend her life with," Deer concluded abruptly as he intently watched his mother's reaction.

Without so much as a flinch, she gently responded with, "I suppose you can go ask her those things right after breakfast. I believe that she will be glad to know that you are home," then for effect she added with a smile, "safely."

Deer returned her knowing smile with a sheepish one of his own. With no further discussion, she handed Deer a loaf of hot, fresh bread and a bowl of honey. Conversation was indeed halted as he turned his full attention on the simple yet fabulous meal prepared just for him.

As he ate, he realized that his most urgent destination had to be the council house. Between bites he juggled what he knew he had to do and what his heart was urging him to do. All of the days and nights beyond the village had passed reasonably conflict free. Now that he was home, a tug of war was in full swing even though he knew that he had a sacred duty to fulfill in honor of Wolf.

With the last bite of bread swallowed and several sticky fingers licked clean, he stood up and returned the honey bowl to its place. As his tongue vigorously rubbed his teeth clean, he mumbled to himself, "There is plenty of time to get to the council house. I want to at least tell Snowflake that I am back." With that decision made, he stepped out into the light of a beautiful, new day.

The short walk to Snowflake's home was completed quickly. However, upon arriving he discovered that no one was home.

"Where is she?" he mumbled to himself as he tried to imagine what daily activity might have her away from home this early. He had really wanted to show her the feather that Chief Red Eagle had given him. It was a little tattered from the trip, but it was clearly something that should impress her. At that moment, it occurred to him that he had been gone for two weeks, had seen many amazing things, but had not brought her back a single object to show that he was thinking about her. In retrospect, he was glad she wasn't home.

Deer walked back home and retrieved the little pouch that contained the dead bat before making his way across town to the council house. One of the elders was sitting on a log just outside the doorway. He looked up and smiled as Deer approached.

"Welcome back, Deer! We have been awaiting your return," he said as he stood to greet him. "Chief Long Feather and Running Bear are inside. I'll announce that you are here."

Deer only had to wait for a few seconds before the elder stuck his head back through the deerskin flap covering the doorway and motioned for Deer to enter.

Slipping through the deerskin door was almost surreal. The bright, cheerful day had certainly not managed to sneak inside. The darkness was not only real in a physical sense; it was quite tangible in a spiritual sense as well. Deer was not expecting that. As his eyes adjusted he grew increasingly nervous about what was about to happen – whatever that was. The only light filtering into the structure was coming through the hole in the roof that existed primarily to let the smoke from the fire escape.

Chief Long Feather spoke in a low, quiet tone as he instructed Deer to "take a seat."

Bear was sitting motionless directly across from Chief Long Feather staring at the ring of stones that marked the sacred fire circle. An ample amount of wood was piled inside the circle, but there was no fire. The few times that he had been in Chief Red Eagle's council house, there had always been a small fire burning. The only thing that he could figure is that this was part of some ceremony that was to be performed or already had been. The lack of the fire served to make the darkness that much more oppressive.

As Deer took his place, Bear look up at Deer with eyes that were filled with questions. Deer managed a weak smile but Bear's expression never changed. Feeling extremely uncomfortable, Deer lowered his eyes and simply stared at the would-be fire hoping that something would happen soon to cut the tension.

With a long sigh, Chief Long Feather broke the silence as he said, "Deer, many days have passed since I led the unsuccessful search to find Wolf – a journey in which you participated. When you and your two friends left town on this latest excursion, you told your families that you were just going exploring. However, from the reports that came in from the traveling merchants just a few days after you left, it appears that you walked straight to Wolf's body. I have to tell you, we are very confused by all of this and just need you to tell us the whole story – from the beginning. We are simply baffled by the series of events that have transpired. We need to know what is going on."

Now it was Deer's turn to give a long sigh because it was going to be a long story. There was so much that he now understood that had only become clear after much time had passed. "Sir, I would truly love to tell the entire story. It is eating me up to hold it in. However, I will warn you – it is a long story and parts of it are unbelievable even to me. Regardless, I swear that everything I am about to tell you is the complete and honest truth." Deer looked first at Chief Long Feather and then to Bear. Both nodded supportively, so Deer launched into the tale.

Deer started with the first adventure and how they had wandered so far from home that they did not know where they were. He told about Wolf exploring the cave and what had happened there and the return trip home via Chief Red Eagle's village. Deer shared many details that initially seemed unimportant and had not been shared before, but in hindsight the smallest details turned out to be the biggest aspect of each segment of the story. Much of this portion of the story had already been related to the two men before the group traveled to meet Chief Red Eagle.

When the story reached the part in which they returned home after the visit to Chief Red Eagle's village, Deer slowed down and really shared as much as he could remember. The two men sat mesmerized as Deer described the various dreams, the red cloth, and burying Wolf. Then he shared how the vision quest at Chief Red Eagle's had lined out exactly what needed to be done to bring Wolf's spirit back home and how the bat guano had caused Wolf's delusions and ultimately his death. When Deer got to the part of the story in which he killed the bat and put it in a sack, Deer presented the sack to Bear and said, "The Medicine Woman said that I must bring the bat to you and that you would know what to do with it."

Bear's eyes were wide and his mouth was open. The words that the Medicine Woman had shared with him on his visit to her home came flooding back as he related her instructions, "Receive the offending individual gladly, and his smoke will release Wolf from bondage." Until Deer handed him the bat, he had no idea what her instruction meant. Now it was perfectly clear.

Deer continued the story by telling how he had dreamed twice about killing the deer before it actually came true. He explained how Wolf had guided him in the dream. Chief Long Feather and Bear hung on every word. The long faces that he had initially been confronted with upon entering the council house were now transformed by contented smiles. The last thing Deer shared was that he stopped by the east village and gave one of the deer legs to the old man that had given him the bow. Deer felt that that was the least he could do in exchange for the beautiful bow that he had given Deer.

Bear sat up straight, clearly brimming with pride at the effort and dedication that Deer and the other boys had demonstrated. "There is only one thing left to do. We must rekindle the council fire and burn this dead bat. Wolf is home. His place among the ancestors is almost complete."

With no further discussion, Bear handed the fire-bow to Chief Long Feather who rolled onto his knees and as he recited prayers, the smoke began to rise. Within moments the tiny embers captured in the cedar bark led to flames. As dry wood was added to the fledgling flame, the fire began to grow. As the flames increased, the smoke actually dissipated until good light filled the house.

After several minutes, the fire became fully engaged, so Bear stood up. With one hand raised to the ceiling, he began to pray. When he finished, he tossed the dead bat – bag and all – onto the fire. Without a word, the three men stared into the fire as the bag ignited. In a matter of minutes, it was finished and all traces of the bat were consumed.

Deer looked up at Bear as if waiting for a signal that said he needed to do something else or that he was free to go.

Bear turned to Deer and softly said, "Come here."

Deer stood quickly and moved around the fire circle to join Bear.

As Deer approached, Bear turned to face him and with tears in his weary eyes he simply said, "Thank you. You have accomplished a tremendous feat. I am more grateful than words can fully express. I may have lost my son, but in my heart I am as proud of you as I ever was of him." With those final words, Bear reached out and hugged Deer tightly.

Chief Long Feather rose to his feet and announced, "Deer has certainly proven his right to manhood, and with his special connection to the spirit world, he has proven himself worthy of full access to the council house as well."

Deer finally stepped back from Bear's embrace and said, "Thank you both for giving me the chance to explain what happened, for believing me, and for accepting me. I give you my word that I will conduct myself with honor and dignity. I will not let you down."

After a few minutes more, Deer excused himself and slipped outside the council house. The mid-afternoon sun peaked through the fluffy clouds that were floating by. He was not sure how long he had been in the council house but most of the day had already passed.

"I need to go find Snowflake some flowers," Deer muttered to himself and headed out of town toward the large meadow.

Birds were singing happily as he walked. Their songs were so cheery that he began to whistle as if he could talk back to them.

The meadow was not far from town. It was the town's old garden but when the new garden space on the other end of town was cleared several years ago, the old garden was abandoned. In the spring and summer, wildflowers covered the whole area and he could certainly find Snowflake a handful of flowers there.

Chapter 13

Deer made his way back into town with a handful of pretty yellow flowers. It had been another very eventful day. In retrospect, there had certainly been many of those since Wolf first discovered that cave. He daydreamed as he walked but mostly his thoughts were on Snowflake.

"I really hope she is back," Deer thought to himself.

As he approached her home, he could tell from the sound of the various voices that her family was home. They should be, since it was supper time. He stood outside for a moment before he mustered the courage to actually approach the doorway. He had done many courageous things recently, but the thought of knocking on her door had unleashed all of the butterflies that his stomach would hold.

Holding the flowers behind his back, Deer shyly inquired, "Hello? Is Snowflake home?"

Much to his relief, the first head to emerge through the doorway covering was Snowflake's.

"There you are!" she blurted out as she popped outside.

All of the suave and clever things that Deer had rehearsed and wanted to say vanished when he opened his mouth to speak. In a weak attempt to recover, he simply whipped the flowers from behind his back and thrust them her direction.

"For me?" Snowflake asked as she reached out to take the bouquet and give it a big sniff. "How thoughtful!" The twinkle in her eyes told him that she was indeed pleased with the meager gift.

"Are you busy or can we go for a walk?" Deer asked. The butterflies were certainly settling down.

"I was just about to eat supper, but that can wait. Where do you want to walk to?" she inquired.

"Let's walk down to the river. It will not get dark for a while. I think we have plenty of time," Deer suggested.

As they started away from the house, Snowflake's mother stuck her head out the door to be sure who Snowflake was leaving with. When she saw that it was Deer, she simply smiled and resumed her meal preparations. Snowflake had been talking non-stop about him since Chief Long Feather's expedition to find Wolf had returned. She recognized what was going on and she thought that Snowflake had certainly chosen well.

Deer and Snowflake strolled through town. A few people stopped them briefly to welcome him back and congratulate him on solving the mystery of Wolf's fate. News of the events at the council house was beginning to spread.

As they reached the edge of town and started down into the river bottoms, Deer reached over and took Snowflake's hand. The entire time he and his buddies were gone on this last trip, Deer imagined what it would feel like to hold her hand. That hug she gave him before they left had sparked his imagination and curiosity had finally overcome his shyness. To his delight, she gladly accepted his hand and they proceeded down to the water's edge holding each other, letting the warmth of their grasp fuel the lively conversation.

"Have you seen Meadow lately? Has Rock gone to visit her?" Deer asked.

"I think Rock went to tell Meadow that he was home before he even went to his own house. Meadow told me that she really likes Rock," Snowflake reported.

"From what Rock said while we were gone, he really likes Meadow, too," Deer confirmed. "Arrow was not really that interested in Sunflower, though. He met a girl at Chief Red Eagle's village that he flipped for and I think that she felt the same way. What did Sunflower say about Arrow?"

"Sunflower was never very interested in Arrow. Basically, she picked him because he was the only guy that one of us girls had not already taken a serious interest in. I don't think she will care if he decides to go after that other girl," she added.

Deer let the obvious hint – that Snowflake wanted him – pass without comment.

Upon reaching the river, they sat down on the bank and talked some more. Occasionally tossing a stick or a stone into the current helped facilitate the growing ease that they were feeling with each other. Deer regaled her with some of the stories from the various adventures. He watched her eyes as he spoke, searching for clues to her willingness to hear more. To his delight each story was received with enthusiasm, so he would tell another. Deer knew that there was not enough time to tell her everything, but then again, he needed to save something for their next walk. He abruptly stopped talking and asked, "What's important to you?"

The question seemed to come out of nowhere and Snowflake just sat there for a moment formulating a response.

Deer, fearing that he had said something wrong, began to stutter and sputter as he tried to back-peddle to safe conversational terrain. "You don't have to answer that if you don't want to …"

"I don't mind," Snowflake began. "I was thinking. I think the most important thing is family. My mother has always impressed upon me that if I will take care of my husband, he will take care of me." She cut her eyes over to Deer and turned the tables on Deer by asking, "What do you think is important – especially in a wife?"

"Wow. That's a hard question," Deer replied as he tried to buy some time. "I don't guess I have really thought about the details, but generally I think that she should be someone like you."

Snowflake tucked her chin against her chest to hide the smile that filled her face. She had not kept her feelings hidden from anyone up to this point and there was no use in acting shy now. Everyone in town knew that she really liked Deer. Although Deer may have been the last to know, he had gotten the message and came to realize that he liked this spunky girl as well.

"We better get started home," Deer said as he rose to his feet.

Snowflake stood up quickly and turned to face him. The smile on her face made her big brown eyes twinkle just that much more.

Deer took her by the hand and as they began their walk back home, he said, "We will talk tomorrow and many, many days to come."

PART 2

Chapter 14

The school bus came to a squealing stop as the brakes announced the final pickup for Sam and Jim for the week. In the mountainous portion of north Arkansas, a school bus ride started early and often felt like the roller-coaster at the amusement park in Branson, except without seatbelts or lap bars.

"Did you see the photograph on the bulletin board at the Marble store? That buck must have had twenty points!" Sam said. "That must be the luckiest guy in the county to get that deer."

Jim looked up from the lunar phase chart that he had been studying intently. "Haven't been over to Marble in a while. When did he kill it?"

"Thanksgiving Day. The story goes that he agreed to go to his mother-in-law's for lunch if he could slip off afterwards and do a little hunting. His wife was not too happy, but she decided it was better than having him sulk around the house all day. I'd say he has two things to be thankful for," Sam added with the kind of independence that an unmarried young man would display.

Jim chimed in his two-cents worth for good measure, "Poor hen-pecked fellow. I'll hunt whenever I want to. Ain't no woman gonna tell me I gotta go out to eat on the best huntin' day of the year."

Most people thought that Jim Flagstone and Sam Jefferson were brothers. They were always together. They liked and disliked the same things. They were both seventeen going on twenty-five. Jim and Sam even lived close together and got on and off the school bus at the same crossroads near the community of Alabam. This was their senior year and the Christmas break was just one week away. The two boys were planning a camping and hunting trip to take advantage of the "doe days" that were scheduled for December 27th, 28th, and 29th at Taylor Wildlife Management Area. People joked that Sam and Jim lived so far out in the sticks that they probably had to come toward town to hunt. The truth was both boys regularly saw ample game around their homes. The trip was more about camping than hunting. Hunting was just a good excuse.

"You may think differently someday, Jim Flagstone," Sarah Jackson whispered sweetly in Jim's ear as she leaned forward from the seat behind. Sarah had a major crush on Jim even though she was only a sophomore. Jim and Sam were two of the first riders on the bus and Sarah was only a mile up the road at the previous stop. She typically would move so that she could get the seat nearest to Jim.

Sam rolled his eyes and turned to look out the window. Gray clouds filled the early morning sky. The weatherman from the television station in Fayetteville said that it could snow in the afternoon.

Jim looked over his shoulder and grinned at the cute face that was perched there. "Sarah, you know what I mean. A guy that doesn't do anything but work and whatever his wife wants is going to be miserable. A miserable guy would not be any fun to live with."

Sarah's imagination was in overdrive and her face said so, but she managed to keep any comments to herself. However, the playful wink said volumes as she settled back in her seat to brace for the next hairpin turn in the road.

Jim was certainly flattered by the attention, but his personal experience with girls was extremely limited. His mother had died in a car wreck when he was five. His father, the local pastor at the Alabam Community Church, had never remarried and spent all of his daylight hours as a handyman or, seasonally, doing lawn care. The little church could not afford to pay Pastor Flagstone a regular salary, so the reverend had sustained a meager existence for his son and himself on the money made doing odd jobs as far away as Huntsville.

Sam's father had inherited a twenty acre farm on the top of a hard scrabble mountain overlooking the Kings River Valley. It was a gorgeous view, but the opportunity to make a living was limited. About fifteen years ago, Mr. Jefferson had given up on the cattle business and built five large chicken houses. The chickens were delivered when they were just beginning to lay eggs and for the next six months, the Jeffersons were busy from morning to night. The money is good, but more significantly, they were too busy to enjoy it.

Sam's sister Martha had helped in the chicken houses until she moved to Fayetteville with two of her high school buddies about two years ago. Martha wanted to go to college and find a job that did not make her long black hair smell awful. The family understood, but her decision left them in a slight bind with the work that had to be completed every single day. Soon thereafter, Mr. Jefferson struck a deal with Sam and Jim. Every afternoon after school, the boys would spend several hours working in the chicken houses. Despite the smell and the loss of their afternoons spent playing basketball or pursuing whatever game animal happened to be in season, they both enjoyed the freedom that money brought. Jim also knew that the money would take some of the financial strain off his dad as well.

As the bus pulled up to the stop sign at the highway, the doors opened and several younger kids boarded. They were followed closely by Dustin Rogers and Bill Perkins. They lived by the highway just a few miles out of Huntsville. Bill and Dustin grabbed the empty seat in front of Jim and Sam, as usual.

Dustin had just turned seventeen and Bill was a few months younger. All four seniors had grown up riding the same school bus for eleven and a half years and were looking forward to graduation in May.

"I bet it snows a foot before morning," Bill declared.

"I wouldn't be surprised. It has already dropped six inches in Oklahoma City. Everything they get usually comes right through here," Sam added.

Jim had returned to scanning the lunar chart in search of the perfect day for asking Mr. Jefferson for a day off to go duck hunting down by the river.

Sam glanced over at Jim. "I don't know why you mess with that chart. If it snows, Dad will let us off to go hunting. Even if it is a weekday – school would be cancelled."

"Yeah, I know. I just like to see if I can tell any difference from one day and time to another," Jim explained.

"Did anyone catch that hockey game on ESPN last night?" Dustin asked. The other three boys shook their heads 'no.' "It was a good game! The Flyers really whipped the dog out of the Oilers!"

"I thought the Oilers were a football team," Sam teased.

"You guys! Hockey is so much better than football and it takes skill and grace to boot!" Dustin countered. Jim laughed and slapped Dustin on the back. Dustin was a fanatical hockey fan, but the other three had never caught the bug.

The bus began to slow down as it made the sweeping turn into the schoolyard, crossed the parking lot, and came to a squealing stop. Bill mumbled to himself as he exited the bus, "I wish they would let me fix those brakes. That screeching can't be a good sound."

School dragged by with the anticipation of the coming snow, but when the kids reconvened at the bus for the return trip to their homes, not one snowflake could be found. Mr. Weaver, the bus driver, was probably the only one who was truly glad. Sam and Jim, followed closely by Sarah, got on the bus and found their normal seats. Bill and Dustin waited at the front of the bus. Bill's twin sisters, Mary and Terri, came strolling up from the elementary school. They were in the third grade and no one could tell them apart. It was Bill's job, at least for another semester, to be sure that the girls got on and off the bus safely. With both girls secured, Bill followed them onto the bus.

Dustin's brother Tim was always the last to arrive. Tim was the teacher's pet and he seemed to always find some way to hang back and do some little task for her before he had to catch the bus. Dustin figured that Tim was sweet on his sixth-grade teacher. He had seen her and she was definitely the youngest and prettiest teacher in the whole school system. Dustin thought to himself, "at least he has good taste." Tim came scampering across the yard just as the bus roared to life, ready for one more trip into the boondocks. The last two riders found their seats and the bus headed for the highway.

"Jim, are you ready for semester tests?" Sam asked.

"I'm ready for them to be over. I don't figure I will do good enough or bad enough, for that matter, to make any difference. I kind of like being in the middle of the pack. You don't get messed with from either end," Jim said.

Sam and Bill both nodded in agreement.

Dustin was the best student of the foursome. He was capable of being on the honor roll, but he did not like being in the spotlight, so he did just enough to make a solid "B." He did not comment on the question, but the other three knew the truth anyway.

It did not take long before the bus turned off of the highway onto the rough gravel road. It squealed to a stop and Bill and Dustin herded their respective siblings off the bus. Bill stopped momentarily and hollered back to Jim, "See you Sunday." Jim smiled and waved goodbye to his two friends. The door closed and the bus pulled away.

Sam knew Jim's dad was a preacher and that Jim was always at church on Sunday. Mr. Jefferson's career of working chickens required an everyday commitment, which pretty much eliminated more than the rare visit to the local church. The Jefferson family had never had anything against "church folks." They just did not see the appeal. Sam and Jim were best friends, but they did not try to influence each other on the issue of religion because they certainly had different opinions on the matter.

As the bus rumbled along the rugged mountain road, Sam and Jim talked about the camping trip. Sam's dad had said that the boys could have the three days off – without pay – and they could borrow the old farm truck to drive themselves and their gear to the state-owned Wildlife Management Area northwest of their homes. They had saved enough money to buy an Army surplus tent that would sleep four. Blankets were plentiful. The list went on and on until the bus pulled to a stop and Mr. Weaver opened the door for them to get out.

Sam and Jim grabbed their book bags and headed for the door.

Sarah tossed a coy parting in Jim's direction, "See you Sunday, Jim."

Jim stopped, turned, and smiled back at her. "Sounds good. See you then."

As the bus pulled away, Jim could not help looking up at the bus window where Sarah was. He was not disappointed. She was waving and smiling from ear to ear.

"She's plum goofy over you, Jim," Sam commented.

"Yeah, but I figure she'll forget about me shortly after May. I might as well enjoy the attention while I got it. Who knows what the future holds, but I don't expect to be collecting eggs all of my life," Jim replied.

"Well, you're probably right. I don't have a clue what I want to do after school, but the thought of gathering eggs for the rest of my life does not really excite me, either. It is too restricting. There are deer to be hunted and fish to be caught," Sam added.

The two boys laughed and turned toward the Jefferson farm. There were eggs to be gathered as well as nastier tasks to be handled. Homework was minimal and they figured there was all weekend to get to it.

Chapter 15

Pastor Flagstone grabbed the wooden mallet and began to strike the bell in front of the Alabam Community Church. After twelve resounding rings that echoed through the crisp mountain air, Pastor Flagstone reentered the small wood-frame structure to see how Jim was progressing with the fire in the pot-belly stove. The temperature was perfect for sitting in a deer stand or a duck blind but the church was in need of some heat. Jim had acquired enough wood from their personal supply at home to last for a couple of hours. He had loaded it in the old pickup last night.

Satisfied that Jim would soon have the cold driven from the sanctuary, Pastor Flagstone patted Jim's back and headed for the little room behind the piano to pray and go over his notes one more time. Jim knew his father's routine. He was glad that his dad would give him something to do so he could help. Building a fire was certainly not new, but it was important.

Smoke was rolling out of the flue and the room was beginning to warm nicely when the sound of crunching gravel wafted by Jim's ears. He did not really have anything else to do, so he was simply sitting in a folding chair near the fire, enjoying the warmth and the aroma of the old stove. As long as he could remember, this was the focal point of his life – the church. Even without knowing his biological mother, he had many adopted moms that he loved as if they were his real mother.

The door swung open and Dustin hurried in ahead of his parents and little brother. "Hey, Jim, want to go sledding after church?" Dustin chided. The weatherman had heightened everyone's expectation of snow and, when it was finished, there was only a light dusting. The clear skies and moderate breeze would quickly erase even that.

"Okay. I'll get a broom and dustpan and see if I can find enough to ride a sled on," Jim countered with a laugh. Jim tried to hide his disappointments with humor.

Dustin laughed, too. "Those weathermen missed it again. I can't figure out how someone can be wrong more often than right and still keep their job! It doesn't work that way at school. If you are right less than two thirds of the time, you will probably flunk," he continued.

The door opened again and Mr. and Mrs. Rogers, followed closely by Tim, slipped into the cozy facility. Mrs. Rogers came and stood by the stove to soak up some extra warmth before she made her way down to the second pew on the left side, where the Rogers family always sat.

A virtual parade of vehicles soon began to arrive and the little building quickly became a church. Pastor Flagstone had emerged from the makeshift study and began to shake hands, hug necks, and get the latest updates on about a half-dozen different members' "ailment-of-the-week." He always showed the proper amount of concern, because he truly was concerned. He wholeheartedly believed 1 Corinthians 12:26 that says, "Where one member suffers, all the members suffer," and that it was his duty to pray for those needs.

Mrs. Perkins arrived shortly after the Rogers. Bill made his way down to the second row on the right where Jim and Dustin were now sitting. She was more comfortable about half way back and Bill's twin sisters always sat with her. Mr. Perkins was on the road again. He is a long-haul trucker and since the twins arrived, he has had to work as much as possible to keep his family sheltered and fed. But when he is home on Sunday, he is present.

Several other families came in, made a general "thank you" for the nice fire, and mingled briefly before taking their seat. One of those was Sarah Jackson and her grandparents. Sarah always came with them because her parents worked nights at the chicken processing plant and they did not come. She used to sit with her grandparents, but for the last few months she has chosen to sit on the third row on the right side. Grandma Jackson certainly approved of Sarah's choice. She says, "Jim is a very good boy."

The Pastor looked at his watch and noticed that it was eleven o'clock and time to get started. Mr. Rogers grabbed his songbook and Mrs. Rogers headed for the piano. Tim stayed put, knowing better than to act up.

"Since we are just over one week away from Christmas, I have decided that Christmas songs are certainly in order. Please rise, take your hymnal, and turn to page 143," Mr. Rogers announced. Mrs. Rogers pecked out the introduction to the first song. Then, like an old Victrola that needed a few more cranks, the music began, and the congregation started singing. By the time everyone reached the last verse, the group had finally harmonized and was beginning to actually sound like they knew the song.

Four or five songs later, Mr. and Mrs. Rogers returned to their seat beside Tim, and Pastor Flagstone stepped up to the pulpit. "It is so good to see everyone," he said. "I am so pleased that you have chosen to be here on this blustery winter day. There are so many places you could have been, but you chose to be in the Lord's house. I trust that you will receive a blessing today."

"Despite this being the Christmas season, I felt impressed of the Lord to bring you a sermon on another topic," Pastor Flagstone continued. About that moment, a small slip of paper dropped over Jim's shoulder onto his lap. Passing notes in school was bad enough, but to pass notes in church was taboo.

Jim inconspicuously opened the small slip of paper. It read, "Dear Jim, I don't know how to tell you this, but the seat of your pants is ripped. It's not too bad, but if you go to the altar to pray, it could be bad. Thought you should know. SARAH."

Jim was mortified! He thought that he heard something when he squatted down to start the fire. Now he was trapped in front of the whole church, sitting between two good friends who would certainly run to school and tell everyone. His mind was racing with thoughts of how to avoid this embarrassing situation, when it occurred to him that Sarah had apparently been checking out his rear-end during the song service. Jim's mind rewound to Sam's declaration regarding Sarah, "She's plum goofy over you, Jim."

As quickly as total chaos had racked Jim's mind, he solved the problem. He would simply wait until the altar invitation and slip his coat back on before he stood up. That would not draw attention from Bill and Dustin and that would also cover his backside. He decided right there that Sarah was right about one thing – no trip to the altar to pray today.

Jim completely missed the sermon. His mind was reeling. The coat took care of the ripped pants. Bill and Dustin gave no indication that they noticed, but somehow he needed to talk to Sarah – privately. When the last prayer was finished, people began to visit and make their way to the parking lot. Bill and Dustin worked their way through the small crowd and reunited with their families. Jim motioned to Sarah to meet him in the corner, which she happily did.

"I have to thank you for that heads-up." Jim sincerely confided. "That could have been awful – not that having you see it was bad enough."

Sarah smiled from ear to ear and eased up as close to Jim as she dared and said, "It was my pleasure – and our secret." With a flirty wink and a crooked grin, she wheeled around and headed for the door.

Jim just stood there, replaying her words, not to mention that look. He was in shock again. Not so much for what she said and did, but for how he felt about it. He was really starting to look forward to seeing her face and hearing her voice. This was new territory. He needed to find a quiet place to get alone and do some thinking. He wondered if Mr. Jefferson would need any help at the chicken house this afternoon…

Martha walked through the door of her parents' farmhouse just in time for Sunday lunch. It was only nine days before Christmas, but she had finished her semester tests at the University the week before and was feeling a little homesick. She had worked all day Saturday at the public library and then met her roommates for an end-of-the-semester celebration. None of the three girls could afford to celebrate much, but they had decided to treat themselves to a night of dancing and socializing at one of the establishments on Dickson Street. After staying out too late, they all slept in Sunday morning.

The wonderful smell of fried fish had greeted her when she stepped onto the porch. She had forgotten how much she missed her mother's cooking. It had been almost a month since she had come home, even for a brief visit. Mrs. Jefferson hopped up, walked around the table, and gave her a big hug. Martha laid her coat in the recliner just outside the kitchen door, made her way into the dining room, grabbed a plate and fork, and approached the table. Everyone had already started eating, but no one had gotten very far.

The antique pedestal table was decorated with a beautiful poinsettia. Her mother had gotten out the Christmas place mats and red paper napkins. The fireplace in the living room was crackling with light and warmth. But the large spruce tree, fully decorated and strung with hundreds of tiny twinkle-lights, made the whole scene look like a Norman Rockwell painting.

After giving her father a kiss on the cheek, Martha sat down and began to fill her plate. Her former place at the table was still available and it felt so good to be home. Conversation bounced around the table at a furious pace. There were so many topics to discuss: school, work, roommates, Fayetteville, and the future, just for starters. Everyone wanted to know everything.

"Fayetteville is SO BIG! There are people everywhere. Everyone is in a hurry and time just flies by," Martha said. "But it is so cool! Most of the stores are open until midnight and you can buy anything you can imagine – if you can afford it. Money sure doesn't go as far as it needs to. The part-time job at the city library is a breeze, though. You just sit at the desk and check out books. Most of the people use the University library, which is huge, so many times there is nothing going on. It gives me a chance to read or do my homework. It's much easier than gathering eggs." Martha shot a grin and a wink at her father, who merely chuckled in response.

"School is getting better. I have finally figured out what I want to do with my life." Martha let the words soak in for effect. "I want to be a history and science teacher." She grabbed another piece of fish and waited for the feedback.

"Well, that sounds like a better idea than what I figured you went to college for – a husband – not that that is a bad plan, either. An educated man can certainly get a better-paying job and provide my baby girl with the things I couldn't," Mr. Jefferson declared.

"Oh Daddy! I don't even have a boyfriend. There is plenty of time for that," Martha said. "Besides how could there ever be another man as wonderful as you – no matter how much money he makes. Money doesn't make people happy anyway."

Sam had been sitting and listening but had kept his mouth busy with the delicious lunch. He had certainly missed having his sister around the house to pick on and tease. However, she was not a girl anymore. She was a woman and he was so proud of the strides that she had made to rise above her humble roots and make her own way in this rough-and-tumble world. All of a sudden, he realized that he was getting teary-eyed. He grabbed his tea glass and quickly exited the dining room and headed for the kitchen to get some more ice. When he was out of sight, he wiped his eyes on his sleeve and called back, "Anybody need anything while I'm up?"

"No, thanks," came three replies. When Sam returned to the table, Martha was describing the Introduction to Archeology class that she had just completed.

"… Dr. Smith told us all about the Indians that once lived right here in Arkansas – how they made tools, what they ate, what they believed – all kinds of stuff. It was so interesting. There were days that the class would actually go into the lab and look at real artifacts and Dr. Smith would explain all about them. He is the best teacher that I have ever had because he is so passionate about the subject. I told him that I had never thought about being an archeologist, but that I think I'd love to go on a dig someday. He told me that he would call me the next time he needed a crew member."

"Well, dear, that sounds very exciting," Mrs. Jefferson remarked. "How long has Dr. Smith been in archeology?" She was fishing to find out how old this guy was and if he was really interested in archeology or in getting a spunky twenty-year-old co-ed out in the woods.

"I don't really know. He has been teaching at the University for almost thirty years. I am guessing that he is about sixty. Do you remember the newspaper articles about that cave that the University archeologists were digging in last year? Dr. Smith was leading that team," answered Martha.

"Oh, him! Yes, I do remember that story. He is quite well known. Going on a dig would be a valuable experience for a future science and history teacher," Martha's mother added, discarding her initial concern.

Sam simply sat there, amazed at the conversation and realization that there was a whole world outside of Madison County that was ready to be explored and experienced. The potential was mind-boggling. He was going to visit the school's guidance counselor as soon as he got the chance.

Lunch was winding down and everyone had eaten their fill. Martha and her mother both got up and began to clear the dishes and the leftovers. Mr. Jefferson and Sam retired to the living room, where they settled in to watch whatever football game was on the television. Living way out of town is great if you love being outside, but if you want to watch TV, you are limited to the two or three stations that you can pick up with an antenna. Mr. Jefferson made it known that he would never pay for cable TV even if he could get it, but he finally did give in and upgrade the "rabbit ears" to an outside antenna. In particular, he wanted a clearer picture when the evening weather forecast was broadcast. In his opinion, there was "no time to waste sitting around watching that stupid box – there was work to do or sleep to get."

In a few minutes, Mr. Jefferson was snoring louder than the announcer was talking, so Sam got up, slipped on his coat, and walked outside. The light snow had not affected the roads and a bluebird sky made it look considerably warmer than it actually was. Sam pulled his collar up around his neck, jammed his hands deep into his pockets, and headed out toward the barn. He needed time to think. The past hour had been like a whirlwind that had sparked a whole new set of possibilities and perspectives. "This life is very complex but very simple all at the same time. What am I going to do? I never considered that I am racing toward a fork in the road of life. Which way is the right path? Wow, this is serious…"

Sam opened the door of chicken house number three and started back in where he left off just before lunch. He was glad he was alone – as alone as you can be with 10,000 clucking chickens. He needed to think and the barn was always good for that.

99

Chapter 16

The telephone rang in Dr. Smith's cluttered office, which had previously served as a storage closet. It was the third ring before he dug down through the pile of maps, charts, and notebook paper and grabbed the receiver. "Archeology Department, this is Jerry," Dr. Smith said in his usually cordial and energetic style.

"Dr. Smith, my name is Billy Bob Jackson. I live over in Madison County and I was walking across my pasture this morning and I think I found something that you might like to see," came the slow Southern drawl from the other end.

Jerry sat up straight and began to search for a notepad to write on. "Well, Mr. Jackson, let me find something to write on and then you can tell me all about it." Jerry had gotten many calls from people all over northwest Arkansas since the regional newspaper ran a feature article on him and some of the discoveries that he had made along the White River. Most of the calls did not amount to anything spectacular. He was virtually married to his career, so working nights and weekends had become a lifestyle. With that kind of dedication, he was bound to be successful.

"All right, I'm set. What ya got?" Jerry asked.

"Well, like I said, I was walking down through the pasture this morning, checking on my cows. I got forty heifers and most of them are getting close to dropping their calf, so I take a walk every morning to keep tabs on their progress. Can't afford to lose one if it comes early. Cold weather is tough on a newborn calf. It's too bad the price of calves is down; those things are almost costing me more than they're worth."

Jerry leaned back and laid his pen on the tablet.

Mr. Jackson continued, "Anyway, I was walking down through the valley where the field road drops off the flat into the part of the valley that floods every spring. I guess that's why they call it a *floodplain*. Well, I was strolling along and noticed a stone spear point. There's lots of flint rock along Kings River, but I have never found any arrowheads on my farm before. I've owned this piece of ground about twenty years. Bought it from old Mr. Taylor's wife when he passed away, God rest his cranky old soul. Anyway, I started looking more closely and found a couple of broken points. I was just wondering if you would be interested in coming out and looking at the spot and telling me something about all that stuff."

Jerry rubbed his eyes and tried to think of a diplomatic way to tell Mr. Jackson no. Then he thought about how little is known about the Kings River Valley, especially the upper reach of it. This might be an opportunity to make friends with a primary landowner. In that area of the state, people are reclusive and suspicious of the government and university professors. Stories abound about how somebody knew somebody who knew somebody who lost their whole farm because of a single rare bug that was discovered during some encounter with "the government." Details are always missing, but the end result is always the same. However, having an ally could open many doors later.

"Where is your farm, Mr. Jackson?"

"Just north of Highway 68, near Marble. It's hard to describe. If you would meet me at the store at Marble – there's only one, you know – you can't miss it – I'll show you the way."

"Hmm. This is the last day that I am going to be in the office before the Christmas break. How about January second? Would 10:00 in the morning be all right?"

"That would be great! It will give me time to check my cows beforehand. We can look at the Indian rocks and the place where I found them. Then, Momma can fix us some lunch. That's the least we can do, if you have to drive all the way out here." Billy Bob had started calling his wife "Momma" when his two boys were small because that is what they called her. forty-eight years later, he still called Peggy "Momma." She thought it was sweet.

The plans for Wednesday were already sounding like a better arrangement than he had initially feared. If nothing else, he had hopes for enjoying some stunning scenery. Who knows, maybe Mr. Jackson would let him come back someday and do some fishing. "10:00, Wednesday. I'll see you there." As they hung up, Jerry's mind began to go through the checklist of equipment and records that he might need. It was about a one-hour drive to Marble. He certainly did not want to forget anything critical.

Jerry rolled his chair up to the overstuffed bookcase near his only window and pulled the notebooks that contained all of the archeological site records for Madison County. Then he rummaged around in a cardboard box in the corner and pulled out a county highway map that had the site numbers referenced on it. Marble is in the upper reach of the Kings River and very few sites have been recorded in that area. Blank spaces on the map are always perplexing, Jerry thought. Does it mean there are no sites or that no one has ever bothered to look? Jerry muttered to himself, "Next week there should be a few more dots added to this old map. Unfortunately, that means filling out more of those site forms. I hate paperwork." Like most archeologists, Jerry loved fieldwork, but hated being tied to a desk while he completed the laborious but necessary documentation.

As he looked at the map, he realized that he really had no idea where Mr. Jackson's farm was. To complicate matters, he did not even have his phone number so he could call back and ask. He laid the notebook and map in his chair, wrote the appointment on his calendar, and headed out of his office, down the hall, and into the lab. Becky looked up from the pile of stone tools that she was numbering to see who was coming in.

"You look deep in thought," she quipped, returning to the tedious task she had chosen for the day.

"Yeah, I just got a call from a farmer over on the Kings River. He found some artifacts and I am headed over there in a couple of weeks," Jerry explained as he passed by. Without slowing down, he rounded the corner and slipped out the back door into the parking lot.

Behind the building sat his trusty companion: an old blue Dodge pickup truck. The University had asked him last year if he was ready to trade it in on a newer one, but Jerry just could not stand to part with "Ole Blue." Besides, the places he went in search of pristine archeological sites, he did not want to answer for the dents and missing parts that surely would occur. Jerry raised the lid on the camper shell with one hand while simultaneously opening the tailgate with the other. It seemed that more often than not the camper door would slip out of his hand and bang him on the head before he could get it propped up with the old shovel handle. He never thought about getting the props fixed until he was juggling the doors.

Becky glanced out the window to watch the absent-minded professor wrestle with the two doors. The entertainment value was only part of her reason. The primary reason was that if he gets whacked in the head, he will be mad when he comes back in and she will know to keep her distance.

With the back of the truck opened without incident, Jerry climbed into the back of the truck. There were two large wooden footlockers filled with forms, hand tools, and artifact bags sitting end to end across the front of the bed. Various sizes and shapes of tools and sifting screens lay in a tangled pile – evidence of the last hasty field trip. Jerry squatted down in the back of the truck to contemplate all of the gear on hand and tried to think of what might be added. After a few minutes, the only thing that he seemed to lack was a couple of plastic buckets. He could not imagine what he might need them for on this trip, but he figured that they could make a handy seat and they could ride in the truck as easily as not.

When he came through the lab door, he stopped and scanned the room for empty five-gallon buckets. Not seeing any, he looked across the room to where Becky still sat. "Where are the buckets?"

Without looking up, Becky replied, "In the old storage trailer out back."

Jerry turned and headed back out the door. Becky laid her pen down and headed to the key cabinet, retrieved the key for the trailer door, and started toward the back door of the lab. As Jerry yanked the lab door back open, Becky was standing there grinning with the key in her outstretched hand. Jerry's aggravated expression was instantly replaced with a sheepish acknowledgement of her ever-present help as he took the key and headed back outside.

After getting three buckets from the trailer and locking the door, he placed the buckets into Ole Blue and returned to the lab. A quick glance at Becky instantly reminded him to put the trailer key in its proper spot. Without a word, Becky returned to her numbering and Jerry headed back to his office.

Jerry picked up the two notebooks and map from his chair and sat down. There were three sites recorded along the river, but none of them seemed to amount to anything more than a surface scatter of artifacts dating to about 3,000 years ago. He felt certain that there should be more recent artifacts in the valley, but the pasture grass eliminated all visibility. He figured that what Mr. Jackson would show him would be more of these Archaic period artifacts. "Oh, well, you can't assemble a puzzle without the little pieces, too," Jerry declared to no one as he stuck the notebooks, map, and his camera into the backpack that he reserved for fieldwork. "Now, back to what I was working on before the phone rang."

Chapter 17

Jim triple-checked the lists of supplies and equipment that they figured they might need. Sam reported to Jim that Dustin and Bill were both ready and waiting. "Man, we've got everything, including a kitchen sink. It's time to go. Besides, we are going to be less than thirty minutes from home. If we forgot something critical, we can always just come get it."

Jim nodded affirmatively and the two boys piled into the old farm truck. The motor roared to life as if it too was eager to be part of the first-ever "Four Friends Annual After Christmas Campout and Deer Hunt." The boys had barely managed to contain their excitement regarding the anticipated event.

"Just imagine, four good friends on our own in the great outdoors without supervision!" Sam exclaimed as they cleared the driveway and headed toward Bill's house.

Jim was also excited about being on his own, but there was a certain anxiety there as well. In seventeen years, he had never spent the night away from home. He had pretty much raised himself because his father was either out working or ministering to a church member, but they were always both home at bed time. The next thought that raced through his mind was that he would not see Sarah until next Sunday. She was there last Sunday and mercifully things were back to normal as far as church went, but Jim found himself thinking about Sarah more than the sermon. He told himself that a week apart was going to allow for some perspective in this growing relationship. At the moment, he was not convinced.

"What's bugging you, buddy?" Sam asked. "You have a strange expression on your face."

Jim had not confided his feelings about Sarah to anyone. He believed that this was a passing phase and that things would get back to normal soon. He just did not want to deal with the teasing or the questions. "Nothing. Just thinking about where I want to hunt this afternoon," Jim answered in half-truth.

Sam had been watching Jim for quite some time and probably knew him better than anyone else. Sam knew that Jim was one of those rare jewels that most guys would never have for a friend – the kind that would be willing to die for you. However, Sam also knew that Sarah saw that high quality, too. Choosing to not press the most likely true issue, Sam said, "Yeah, I was thinking about that, too. I bet that the deer are slipping out into fields to eat right before dark. The acorns have either been eaten or they have gone sour. This time of year your best bet is either a green field or a honeysuckle thicket."

Jim was eager to focus on hunting and he chimed right in. The two boys discussed the value of cover scents, different camouflage patterns, and watching the wind yet again. Both boys struggled to concentrate on reading a schoolbook, but a hunting magazine was devoured from cover to cover at least twice. They were still talking ninety miles an hour when they pulled into Bill's yard.

"It's about time! I was about to go stir crazy with anticipation," Bill said as he jumped off the end of the porch landing beside the old farm truck. He grabbed his gear that he had already piled by the driveway and tossed it into the truck.

Mrs. Perkins stuck her head out of the front doorway to see the boys off. "Have a good time. Get a big one!" she hollered as the boys piled into the front of the truck. Three eager waves and three big smiles reassured her that they would have a good time even if they came home empty-handed. They waved again as the truck left the yard and pulled onto the highway for the short drive to Dustin's house.

As they turned in, Dustin could be seen through the picture window of the Rogers' home hugging his mother goodbye. Dustin gave Tim a high-five as he turned and dashed out the door. His gear was piled on the porch. Bill had hopped out and started toward the porch. Dustin grabbed most of it and Bill got the rest. In about one minute, the four boys were back on the highway headed for "Taylor's Woods."

Several years ago the Arkansas Department of Natural Resources bought a large tract of rugged country and had opened it up for public hunting and fishing. It was once owned by an old miser named Mr. Taylor. He had inherited several thousand acres and then managed to parlay that into a larger holding through the money that he made on cattle. Every time an adjacent farm would go up for sale, Mr. Taylor would buy it. Unfortunately for the locals, he would only let a very select few people onto the property to hunt and fish. When the ADNR got the land, it was teeming with deer, turkey, black bear, and many other animals that were generally scarce in other parts of the Ozarks. The mountainsides were covered with mature oak, hickory, and pine trees, and many of those old pastures were converted to wildlife food plots. Most people believe that it is the most beautiful land in Madison County and possibly all of northwest Arkansas.

Over the years, the four boys had each spent a considerable amount of time hunting Taylor Wildlife Management Area, but this was the first time that the four boys were going to be there together without any adult supervision. Despite the distance from home and the lack of direct supervision, each boy knew that any misbehavior would be met with harsh consequences – namely, never getting to go again.

The old truck rumbled down the highway away from town with its four tightly compressed passengers. The sign marking the turn-off had been riddled with bullets by some irresponsible person, making the writing illegible, but the truck seemed to instinctively know the way. Before they knew it, they had arrived at The Woods.

They drove quite a ways into the area before arriving at their predetermined campsite. To their surprise, there were no other people camping there. As soon as the truck stopped, the boys piled out of the cramped cab and began to unload the truck. In just over an hour, everything was set up and a fire was going.

As they sat and discussed strategy, it was clear that Jim and Sam had their minds set on hunting one of the old fields. Bill and Dustin were headed downstream to stake out some honeysuckle thickets. The way they figured it, that covered the best possibilities on the first evening and they could adjust their strategies tomorrow, if needed. After all, they only had three days, and half of the first one was gone.

The other decision that the group had agreed on was that they were not going to do any cooking. They had packed several pounds of bologna, cheese, mayonnaise, and bread for lunch and supper. A bowl of cereal or a sweet roll would suffice for breakfast.

The brisk air temperature was invigorating until they stripped down to their underwear to start layering up with their warmer hunting clothes. It did not take long to get a pair of long-handle underwear back on and break that rapid heat loss from the wind chill. The cold north wind was blowing about 10 miles per hour, but after getting properly dressed, it was not a problem. The boys each successfully passed the hunter safety course offered during shop class at school, so their guns remained in their cases until it was time to actually go hunting.

After they ate a sandwich for lunch, they settled down close to the small fire. They did not need a large fire with all of those clothes on and they wanted to conserve the firewood for that evening. Bill spoke up, "Besides hunting, what else do we want to do for fun while we have the chance?"

Jim tossed in the idea, "How about doing some cave exploring? We used to crawl around in caves all the time when we were younger."

"Hey, that would be neat. We have not been spelunking in a while." Bill said.

106

The wheels started turning and Dustin asked, "Do we have the gear for cavin' with us?"

"Oh, yeah, that was one of the hold-ups this morning. It took me a while to find dad's old carbide headlamp." Sam added. "I even grabbed some walkie-talkies that we can use either cave exploring or while we are hunting. I guess they work underground."

Discussion had swirled around spelunking for almost an hour, when Jim stood up and said, "I'm heading to my deer stand." The other boys followed his lead and started gathering the specific items that they wanted to take to their stand as well. Jim grabbed a shovel and covered the pile of embers and coals with dry dirt. He hoped that would contain the current fire while preserving the coals for the evening fire.

Jim and Sam picked up their guns and started walking south from camp. Bill and Dustin headed north. Each boy settled into his chosen spot and waited.

Jim selected a good-sized bench just above the Kings River *floodplain*. The bench once held a long, narrow pasture and ADNR had planted it in clover. The plentiful tracks and droppings assured him that he would definitely see a deer here before the three days passed.

Sam made his way further upstream and came to an actual pasture that was still being farmed for hay. There was a series of *scrapes* along the edge of the field, so he decided to sit down along an old fencerow at the end of the field so that he could watch the *scrapes*.

Bill and Dustin decided to stay together. An old field north of camp that had been abandoned, probably before Mr. Taylor died, was now a massive thicket of sweetgum trees and honeysuckle. They decided to set up near the corner of the old field. Bill would watch one way and Dustin would watch the other. They figured they could cover the old field more thoroughly.

A couple of uneventful hours passed for each of the boys and the sun was beginning to set when Jim spotted the first deer stepping into the food plot. The big doe was followed closely by two fawns. She casually fed along while the two yearlings wandered, fed, and frolicked. Jim did not even raise his gun; he just sat in his ground blind approximately fifty yards from the trio and watched them. Just before dark, Jim could see a couple of other brown forms enter the field and begin to feed.

Sam had decided that he was so far from camp that he was not going to shoot a doe on this first hunt. He really had his heart set on the nice buck that he was sure had made the *scrapes* that he had been staring at for several hours. Daylight faded to black, but no deer appeared.

Bill and Dustin were leaned against different sides of the same large oak, but neither one could get comfortable. The ground was cold and the roots were hard. Bill's legs kept going to sleep and that would make him fidget and squirm. Just before dark the two boys decided that it was imperative that they get still. This was the absolute best time for hunting.

"WHEW! WHEW!" blew the deer that had slipped up behind them without being noticed. The deer had not necessarily seen them, but had come in downwind and caught their scent.

Dustin and Bill both jumped a foot! The deer reversed direction and vanished back into the forest. The two boys looked sheepishly at each other. They had been discovered and knew that there was no good reason to sit there for the last ten minutes of fading daylight.

"Ready to go?" Bill asked.

"Yep." Dustin replied with a deep sigh. He really felt they would have had a better hunt than what had transpired.

Four flashlights converged on camp at about the same time. Jim grabbed the shovel and uncovered the coals and began to stoke up the fire again. After they put their guns away, Bill lit the Coleman lantern, Dustin retrieved the supper materials, and Sam helped Jim with the firewood.

Each boy took a turn telling his particular story about the afternoon's hunt. Then they discussed the strategies for tomorrow morning's hunt and any adjustments that they wanted to make. The glow of the fire and the warmth of the company made the evening absolutely wonderful, despite a second meal of bologna sandwiches, chips, and fruit. However, everyone was having such a good time. No one complained.

Everyone turned in early to get some sleep. The old army tent was excellent. All four boys crowded in and settled down for a peaceful night's rest.

Chapter 18

"RIIIIIIIIIIIIIIIIIIIIIIIIIIIIIIIIIIIIING," blared the wind-up alarm clock. It was 5:00 – time to get up and head for their deer blinds. Four groggy lumps began to stir. The strange surroundings of the tent as well as the utter darkness caused general confusion, until the cobwebs began to clear from their minds.

"Wow, it's cold in this tent." Bill remarked.

"Yeah, and if you touch the sides, you'll get wet, too," Sam added, having just stretched his arms and encountering the condensation collected on the inside of the canvas.

Jim slipped on his heavy coat and stepped out of the tent. They had left the Coleman lantern just outside the door. He bent down and lit it. Then he handed it back through the door of the tent where Sam took it and hung it on the ridgepole in the middle of the tent.

One by one they emerged from the old tent with new enthusiasm for the upcoming day. The fire was out and they opted to not start another one. Sam dropped the tailgate on the truck and placed the lantern on it to provide light for the camp. Dustin rummaged around in the food box and found a package of sweet rolls. Jim had gotten the milk out of the cooler and poured a couple of plastic glasses full. Conversation was limited as they ate and drank a hurried breakfast.

With the overnight hunger pangs subdued, they disposed of the cups and plates in a trash bag and began to gather up their gear for the hunt. The general consensus was that everyone was going to give his previous stand another try. It was agreed that they would reconvene at camp about 10:00 for lunch.

Each hunter was settled in as the first rays of the sun began to peek over the horizon. Being on the west side of the river valley, those early rays were a welcome sight. The water jug at camp did not have any ice in it, but the air temperature felt cold enough to have frozen the water.

As the first light illuminated the food plot where Jim was hiding, he could see a couple of deer already in the field. He did not know if he or the deer had arrived at the field first, but he was certainly glad to see them. They were well over a hundred yards away and he did not even pick up his shotgun. The sunshine felt good on his face and he decided to wait and see what was going to happen before he changed his location or strategy.

Sam had returned to the line of *scrapes* and nestled back into the thick brush of the fencerow to wait. "The sun is certainly taking its time coming up this morning," he thought to himself. He had gotten sweaty walking to his stand and now he was getting chilled. After leaning his dad's 12-gauge against the fence post nearby, he dug down into his backpack and found a hand warmer that he had brought in case of an emergency and this was quickly looking like just such a case.

By the time he finished fumbling in the backpack, found the hand warmer, got it lit, and reloaded the backpack, the sun was beginning to chase the shadows from the field. Sam had intentionally avoided the *scrapes* because he did not want to leave any human scent around them. The curiosity to know whether the *scrapes* had been worked overnight was driving him crazy. Maybe he could slip out there and take a quick look. He knew better, so he stayed put.

Just as good light revealed the features of the field, a single doe came bounding out of the woods into the middle of the field about 100 yards away. She stopped and looked back as if to see if something else was coming. Sam knew that she was running from the buck that he had his heart set on. He picked up the gun and wiggled around to get set, in case there was an opportunity for a shot. The big doe wagged her tail, turned and bounded on across the field toward the river. In just a minute, he heard her splashing through the water, followed by the sound of hooves crunching up the gravel bar on the other side.

"I don't know what pushed her, but she certainly didn't wait on it," Sam mused. He maintained his intensity and focus for another fifteen minutes, but nothing else appeared in the field. Sam sat patiently until the predetermined time, gathered his stuff, and vacated his hiding place. Before he left the field, he eased over close to the *scrapes*. They had not been worked. "That's a good sign – I think. He has not been here yet. Maybe this afternoon."

Meanwhile, elsewhere that same morning, Dustin and Bill had decided to separate a short distance. Bill set up by the same tree where they had hunted yesterday. He decided it was still a good idea to face the thicket. That deer last night had to be the exception to the rule. Dustin moved down to the other corner of the thicket. With this plan they could cover three sides of the overgrown field. As the sun came up, they realized that they could see each other quite well and that made both of them feel more confident.

As the anticipation of "first-light" changed into the anticipation of seeing something in the clear light of day, both boys began to worry that the morning was going to be a waste of perfectly good sleep. The morning was quickly passing and less than an hour remained before they were to return to camp. Dustin and Bill had not looked in each other's direction for quite some time, when a glimpse of movement between them caught both of their attention at the same time.

There, broadside and halfway between the two boys, stood a fabulous eight-point buck. Dustin and Bill were each frozen with indecision. The buck looked both ways and realized that he was in a quite dangerous situation. In a flash, he darted back into the thicket and vanished. Neither boy could risk a shot because of the danger of shooting toward his friend. Prior to their hunter education class, they might not have recognized the danger. They were grateful for having learned something in school that was actually of practical use. The rest of the morning passed with both boys keeping a vigilant eye in each other's direction. There seemed to be a pattern of bad luck following them.

The cold temperature eased as the sun climbed higher in the sky. At 10:00 the four hunters reassembled at the camp and rummaged through the ice chest and the other boxes for the elements of lunch. As they settled in to eat another meal of cold sandwiches, they shared the events, such as they were, of the morning's hunt. Conversation quickly turned to the day's next activity – spelunking some caves in "Taylor's Woods."

Jim and Sam knew about two caves down by the river. The caves were readily accessible, so the foursome decided to go have a look. Sam grabbed the Coleman lantern and a lighter while each of the others secured two flashlights each. When they arrived at the mouth, it was obvious that there had been many visitors before them, based on the graffiti on the walls and the amount of litter on the ground. It was really quite disappointing. A cave is such a unique environment – equivalent to the bottom of the ocean or outer space. Caves should be treated with the utmost care, but, alas, that was not the case for this unfortunate opening in the earth.

"I can remember coming to this cave when I was a boy," Sam reflected. "It was in pretty good shape then. Maybe the dirt-bags that did all this did not go into the cave." It certainly was wishful thinking, because the chances of all the damage being confined to the mouth were remote.

Sam lit the lantern and led the way into the tunnel. The others followed. There was little need for the flashlights because the lantern lit the way very well. In fact, it lit the way so well that it removed some of the mystique of exploring the dark recesses of the underworld. The main shaft rose slightly as they lost sight of the outside world, then narrowed down to no more than a hallway about four feet high. After about fifty feet the hallway opened into a single room that measured forty feet in diameter with a ceiling just over fifteen feet above the floor. Sam set the lantern in the middle of the room and they fanned out to explore. Jim made his way to the large rubble pile directly across from the hallway. He surmised that the passage continued beyond this pile, but he was not interested in moving it to find out for sure.

Dustin was looking at the rock walls with much interest. "These walls are limestone, which is pretty soft. Water once flowed through here and eroded this cave into its current formation. Limestone formed on the bottom of the ocean and is actually the solidified remains of shells and bones of sea creatures. That is why there are so many fossils in these rocks," Dustin said as he pointed to a particularly complete shell impression.

There were no fancy *stalactites* or *stalagmites*. There were no formations of any kind. There were no bats or cave crickets. In fact, there was very little trash and graffiti. Except for the thrill of seeing someplace that is so absolutely different from the outside world, it was really pretty boring.

Sam grabbed the lantern and the four boys duck-walked back through the hallway and eventually back to the outside. The most noticeable thing was that the air temperature was about twenty degrees warmer inside the cave than outside the cave. Sam extinguished the light.

"Do we want to go look at the other cave?" Jim asked.

"Sure," was the simple reply in unison from Bill and Dustin. Then Dustin added, "We don't have a deer to butcher. What else is there to do?"

It seemed like a relevant question, so they continued on down the bluff. The Kings River long ago had undercut the bluff. As such, the base of the bluff was set back about twenty feet from the top, forming a drip line at the edge of an area that was perfectly dry. Jim was walking along the drip line when he saw something glossy. He bent down to pick it up only to discover that it was a perfect Indian arrowhead.

"Hey, look what I found!" Jim exclaimed.

"Wow, that's a good one." Sam remarked. "My sister, Martha, was talking about arrowheads and archeology just the other day. She had a class at the University where she learned about the Indians that once lived in these parts."

The boys passed the point around and looked at it carefully. After a brief search of the immediate area, nothing else was found and the journey to the next cave continued. They had not gone too far, when the bluff seemed to dip away from the general line that it had followed up to this point. When they arrived, Dustin and Bill simply stood speechless. The cave opening was probably 200 feet across and fifty feet high. It looked like an amphitheater. The boys approached the looming opening with the kind of awe that one might experience from looking at a huge cathedral.

112

Sam lit the lantern again and led the young explorers inside. "This cave was once used as a kind of summer dance hall. The cool air rushing out of the cave was better than modern air-conditioning – it was free. The band would set up on that high rock over there and the people would show up and square dance on most Friday afternoons from June through August. Dad tells me that my grandparents met here and started dating because of this old cave."

The boys were truly impressed with the cave and its history.

"It seems impossible that this used to be a dance hall. There is nothing left to indicate it." Bill commented.

They made their way deeper into the cave and it started to constrict down to a narrow passage. They continued for about 100 feet before the passage became too small to pass without crawling on their bellies. The rushing air hitting their faces certainly attested to the fact that the cave continued, but this time of year was no time to be getting wet and muddy slithering around in a cave. They decided to save this leg of the adventure for warmer weather.

They made their way back to the bluff line and then back to camp. It had been an interesting day but it was time to turn their attention to the afternoon hunt. Each boy was certain that this coming hunt was going to be "the one" in which they bagged that trophy deer. After a few moments in camp, they decided that they could sit in their stand as easily as sitting in camp, so they struck out for their respective blinds.

Jim settled into his hiding place once again. He had seen several deer on both of the previous hunts and fully expected that to continue. He was not terribly eager to shoot a deer because his father did not own a deep freeze and he would have to give most of the meat away. "Why go to so much work just to give it away?" He decided that it would have to be a perfect shot at the perfect deer before he would kill it. He was thoroughly enjoying just watching the magnificent creatures. As he got comfortable and warm in the afternoon sunshine, he found himself nodding off. He figured that was all right, because it was still a couple of hours before the deer should arrive.

Jim awoke with the sudden realization that there was a young doe standing about ten yards from him. It was looking straight into his eyes. Jim regained his composure and did not move a muscle. The deer, uncertain what was sitting in the tall weeds, decided to put some distance between herself and "it." The deer turned and bounded across the field into the edge of the woods. Two other does that were feeding at the other end of the field looked up and watched her bound away. They did not seem too concerned and soon returned to feeding. Jim was fully awake now. He had never had a deer that close before. He saw her nose twitch. He could have counted the individual hairs of her eyelashes. But those big brown eyes, full of curiosity, reminded him of another pair of big brown eyes that he had not seen since last Sunday.

Sam decided to move to the other end of the field that he had been watching. He did not want to give up on the *scrapes*, but he wanted to watch them from a different perspective. As he settled in, he realized that the wind was not going to be as good, but he rationalized that it would not matter just this one afternoon. He was actually closer to the path where the doe had crossed this morning, but his heart was still set on a buck.

The afternoon seemed to fly by as he watched the birds and squirrels go about their business. "The world is an amazing show, if people would just take the time to stop and watch," Sam thought to himself. He became so involved in watching two gray squirrels chasing each other up and down the trees that he almost forgot why he was hiding in a brush pile.

When Sam glanced back into the field, there was a doe walking down the edge of the field next to the river. About fifty yards behind her was a *spike buck*. He was maintaining his distance but was clearly intent on not letting her get out of his sight. Sam looked at his gun and then back at the young buck. If they stayed on track, they would probably walk past him at less than forty yards. Sam relaxed his grip and opted to simply let them both grow up. It had been a great day and he just did not want to disrupt the flow and wonder of nature. He simply chose to melt into the background and be an observer. Sure enough, the two deer passed him at twenty-five yards. Sam decided that was more exciting than actually killing one of them.

Bill and Dustin returned to the thicket that they had been watching. They decided to position themselves at opposite corners so they would not run the risk of shooting toward each other and so they could cover all four sides. Bill stayed at the original tree and Dustin made his way around the overgrown field.

Dustin looked around and found a couple of trails accessing the thicket that appeared well used. He found a fallen tree and settled in behind the trunk. As he sat and contemplated the geology around him and how much he had enjoyed going into the caves, he became aware that he was not alone. He slowly scanned the woods and as he turned to look over the log, he spotted the lone doe standing at the edge of the thicket. She was scanning the forest for danger before leaving the dense cover behind. Satisfied that she was safe, she started down the trail. Dustin let her get into the clear, then aimed, and squeezed the trigger.

Fire exploded from the end of the barrel, but Dustin knew it was a good shot. The doe hit the ground before the echo of the shot stopped. Dustin's heart was pounding so hard he thought it would jump out of his chest. He had killed his first deer and he had done it all by himself! Dustin laid the gun down, stood up and began whooping and hollering like he had won the lottery.

He grabbed his pack and his gun and crossed the forty yards of forest to claim his much-sought-after trophy. When he reached the carcass, he decided to mimic the guys on television. He eased up behind the deer and poked it with his gun. She was dead. The whooping and dancing started all over again.

Dustin looked up just in time to see Bill running through the woods toward him. When he got to Dustin he said breathlessly, "Thank the Lord you're okay. All that yelling, I thought you'd shot yourself!"

The two boys exchanged a vigorous "high-five" and then dragged the deer away from their hunting spot to *field dress* her. They certainly did not want a large pile of entrails stinking up their spot and they did not really want any scavengers visiting their spot either. The old doe was a handful but they managed to drag her several hundred yards out into the forest before finishing the messier part of the process.

Jim and Sam got back to camp first. Jim started working on the evening fire. Sam lit the lantern because it was totally dark. "Wonder where Bill and Dustin are? They should be back by now." Sam commented.

"If they aren't back in thirty minutes, we will head out to find them," Jim responded.

In about twenty minutes, Sam spotted their flashlight coming through the woods. "Here they come," Sam reported.

Jim and Sam walked to the edge of the lantern light and watched as Bill and Dustin came dragging the deer into camp. Excited conversation exploded as they listened to the various experiences that had transpired that evening. It had truly been a special day. Jim looked at Dustin and said, "We need to thank God for such a wonderful day. This is truly a gift and we need to let Him know how much we appreciate it."

Each boy bowed his head and, one by one, they each offered a simple prayer of thanks for this day that they would remember and cherish forever. Even though Sam was not used to praying, he gave it his best shot and shared from his heart.

Afterwards, Dustin said, "I know we said that we were not going to cook, but what do y'all think about cooking some fresh *back-strap* instead of ANOTHER bologna sandwich."

They all heartily agreed and set to the task. Soon the deer was hanging from a tree limb where they would leave it overnight. A strip of *tenderloin* was removed and placed on a spit over the open fire. The stars never looked brighter nor the smiles bigger than what could be seen that magical night.

Chapter 19

"RIIIIIIIIIIIIIIIIIIIIIIIIIIIIIIIIIIIIIING," blared the alarm clock for a second and final morning. It was 5:00 again and the adrenaline rush from last night had subsided, leaving each of them drained. Sam finally mustered enough strength to climb out of bed and get moving. Jim and Bill soon followed, but Dustin declared that he was sleeping in.

The three gathered outside to admire Dustin's deer and get some sugar into their systems. Soon the conversation began to flow.

"Do you think we should take Dustin and his deer home at lunch?" Bill asked.

"Probably. It is not as cold as it was last night and it might get too warm for it to just hang there all day," Sam said.

"I vote that we break camp after the morning hunt and head for home," Jim proposed. Bill and Sam agreed. Bill stuck his head back into the tent and told Dustin the plan. Dustin said that he would start gathering the equipment when he got up.

With the understanding that this was the last hunt, there was a sense of urgency. While there was time left, there was no rush to get a deer. This was the bottom of the ninth inning and they were behind one to nothing. Even though they were almost as excited about Dustin's success as he was, there was still that spark of competition that seemed to drive them to excel in physical contests. It wasn't personal; it was nature.

Jim had left his backpack in his blind last night. It seemed silly to carry it out then carry it back. He moved the pack and settled into the spot. He had spent so much time there that he had it wallowed out and it had become quite comfortable. All that was left to do was to wait.

Bill decided to move down to the corner where Dustin had sat the first morning. The wind was more favorable there than anywhere else. He found a good vantage point and waited. He could see every place that a deer had been seen in the previous two days from this location and with his dad's .30-.30 rifle, he could cover them all, too. Bill felt very good about his "last stand."

Sam returned to the far end of the field and settled back into the spot that he hunted the previous evening. As the sun began to push the darkness back into the forest, Sam heard the familiar sound of running deer. It did not sound like they were trying to escape. It sounded more like they were chasing each other back and forth just out of the field. Sam strained to see them, but it was still too dark.

Just then, a doe burst out of the woods and made an arc out into the field. She stopped, turned back toward the darkness, and waited. Sam could see the steam from her nostrils as she stood trying to catch her breath. The sound of soft shuffling could be heard approaching the field. "It's got to be a buck," Sam thought. Just then, a young buck with several points protruding from his two small main beams stepped into view. It was not the monster that he had hoped for, but he was a "shooter" just the same.

The doe turned and bounded toward Sam's end of the field and passed his position about thirty yards away. He knew the buck would take the same general path, so he eased around and got set. The buck watched the doe disappear back into the woods and he started that way, too.

As the buck closed the distance, buck fever began to set in. Sam closed his eyes and tried to suppress the surging adrenaline, but it was no use. He was shaking so hard that he looked like he was sitting on a paint shaker. The buck was within range and still getting closer. Sam decided to let him get as close as possible because as much as he was shaking, he was afraid he would miss him. What he had not counted on was the fact that the closer he got, the more he shook. When Sam just could not stand it any longer, he slipped the safety off, aimed as carefully as he could manage, and squeezed the trigger.

In an instant, time almost stopped. The shotgun fired and the rifled slug seemed to drift down the barrel and float toward the deer. The recoil was unnoticed because of the convulsions that he was already suffering. The buck's foot seemed frozen in mid-air with his attention focused on the doe ahead of him. When the slug finally reached its mark, the deer simply stopped and fell over – all in slow motion.

Sam just sat there. He was ecstatic and stunned all at the same time. As time returned to its normal pace, he noticed movement over by the *scrapes*. A large-racked buck was bounding across the field headed for the cover of the forest. It was the big buck that Sam felt sure was there – somewhere. He did not even lift his gun. He was emotionally drained and just laid there for several minutes until he could regain his composure.

Jim heard the shot and knew that Sam was focused on getting a buck. He looked out across the empty field in front of him and grabbed his stuff. He wanted to be with his friend. By the time he reached Sam's field, Sam was up from his hiding place and was walking toward the deer. Jim laid his gear down at the end of the field and started toward him.

"Did you get him?" Jim shouted.

"Yes, I did," came the reply.

"Fantastic!" Jim exclaimed as he came running across the field.

Sam had knelt over the buck and thanked God for the gift before Jim arrived. He then turned his attention to the antlers with its modest arrangement of eight tines as Jim got to him.

"Way to go, Sam. He's a nice one," Jim remarked.

Sam was still quivering, but, mercifully, the hard shakes had stopped. "This is my first buck all on my own. I can't wait until Dad sees him! He is not the 'big one,' but he is a dandy to me."

Jim and Sam each grabbed an antler and began the chore of dragging the deer back to camp. They did not go very far until they decided to *field dress* it. That would reduce the weight considerably.

Dustin had finally gotten up and gone outside to look at his deer and start breaking camp. "I sure hope the guys have a good morning," he thought. He sat down on the tailgate and unwrapped a sweet roll. He was eager to get his deer home, but on the other hand, he was not ready for the "hunt" to end. It was certainly a dilemma. Dustin had unloaded the truck and had begun to put the table and chairs and other such items that belonged to Sam in the truck first.

Sam spotted Dustin as they approached camp. "Hey, Dustin, come give us a hand."

Dustin wheeled around and looked Sam's direction. Then he realized that Jim and Sam were dragging a buck.

Dustin jumped out of the back of the truck and ran up to the two boys. They were both smiling so big, he wasn't sure who had killed it. "Who got him?"

Jim pointed at Sam as Sam admitted that the buck was his. Dustin took both boys' guns and dropped in beside them as they covered the short distance back into camp.

Sam looked behind the truck seat and found a second rope. He tossed an end over the same limb that the doe was hanging from, tied one end to the deer's rack, and they hoisted the buck up beside the doe. Sam related the story to Dustin, while Jim ducked into the tent to get his camera. He wanted some pictures of this historic moment.

Dustin took his place beside the doe and Sam slipped in beside the buck. Jim snapped the picture and said, "You two guys look like the happiest fellows on the planet."

"I don't know about Sam, but I could not be any happier than I am right now." Dustin replied. Sam simply nodded his head 'yes' and the ear-to-ear grin confirmed it.

With two deer to add to the load of gear to take home, they decided that they should get the tent loaded next. After sorting all of the bedside personal items into separate piles, the cots and blankets and pillows were removed from the tent. The poles were pulled and the tent collapsed to the ground. In less than ten minutes, their shelter for the past forty-eight hours was stowed in the back of the truck. The cots went in next.

It was almost 10:00 and the three boys were anxiously awaiting good news from Bill. They continued to pile stuff into the back of the truck, intentionally leaving a large space by the tailgate for the two, and hopefully three, deer. There were only a few items left to load when Bill came strolling into camp.

He glanced up at Dustin's deer but did not immediately realize that there were two hanging there. As the image penetrated his weary brain, he stopped and looked directly at the two deer. "Holy mackerel, those things are multiplying! Who killed the buck?"

Sam sheepishly stepped forward and joined Bill beside the deer as Sam shared the story one more time. Bill confided that he did not see anything.

"Me either," Jim added.

With the deer being the last two major additions to the back of the truck, Dustin untied the ropes and lowered the deer to the ground. Deciding that Dustin would be the first one dropped off, they would load the buck first and then put the doe on top.

One final sweep of the campsite collected the last of the trash. Sam got into the truck and started the engine. The other three squeezed in from the passenger side and they started the bumpy ride out of "Taylor's Woods."

When the truckload of hunters pulled into the Rogers' yard, Mrs. Rogers stepped out onto the porch. She about halfway expected the boys to be home around lunchtime despite their "guarantee" that they would hunt until dark. The four boys piled out of the truck and started lifting Dustin's gear out of the back. But when they lifted the big doe out of the back, Mrs. Rogers' eyes got big and she came down into the yard for a closer look.

"Dustin, did you kill this deer?" she asked.

"Yes, ma'am. Yesterday afternoon with one shot. I'll tell you about it later," Dustin beamed.

"Y'all carry it around back so I can get some pictures before we start processing the meat," Mrs. Rogers said.

Tim emerged from the house as each boy grabbed one of the deer's legs and headed around the house into the backyard. There was a good tree with a perfect limb where they could hang the deer back up and start butchering it.

Mrs. Rogers came out the back door with her camera. "I want a picture of all five of you – six, counting the deer."

The boys laid the deer out and knelt down behind it. After five or six shots, she finally released them to finish hoisting the carcass into the tree. Bill offered to stay and help, but Dustin declined. Mrs. Rogers used to work in the butcher shop at the grocery store and she was fully willing and able to take on the task.

The three boys piled back in the truck and eased on down the road to Bill's house. He hopped out and grabbed his gear. "See ya Sunday," Bill said as he headed toward the porch.

"Sounds good," Sam replied. Jim shot a surprised look at Sam, but did not say anything. Sam saw the look, grinned, and asked, "I guess it would be okay if I went to church with you guys, wouldn't it?"

"Absolutely!" Jim's instant reply shot back. "I can't think of anything that would make me happier, Sam. Dad and I would be glad to pick you up if you need a ride."

"I'll let you know, Jim," Sam said. Then he turned the truck around and headed for home.

Chapter 20

Dr. Smith returned to northwest Arkansas after a brief vacation over the Christmas holiday. School was not scheduled to resume until next Monday, so the campus was almost deserted. Dr. Smith typically enjoyed the few times when the students were not around because it was quiet and he could think without being interrupted. Yesterday he was almost able to get his desk cleaned off. He had not managed that feat since he moved into his new office. It might be smaller, but he did not have to share and he could close the door if he chose to avoid interruptions.

The clock read 8:30 a.m. as he left the office and headed through the lab to the parking lot. "Ole Blue" was right where he had left it two weeks ago, so he did not bother to recheck the back end other than to be sure that the camper shell door was still locked. He opened the cab and tossed his "day pack" into the passenger seat before sliding in and starting the engine.

The weather was cool but nice for early January. He let the truck warm up for a few minutes before pulling away from the building. He had not heard from Mr. Jackson and he hoped that he would be at the Marble store to meet him as planned. But if not, he figured that he could ask around and get directions to the Jackson farm.

The drive to Marble was pleasant. He did not travel that area very often and he had forgotten just how much more rugged it was. He turned into the parking lot, such as it was, of the Marble store about 9:45 a.m. He made it a habit to be most places fifteen minutes early so that if something goes wrong, you have a cushion of time to work with to avoid being late. Dr. Smith parked Ole Blue and decided to wait inside. He wanted a cold drink anyway.

Dr. Smith opened the door and headed toward the beverage cooler.

"Good morning, sir," said the cheerful storeowner.

"Good morning to you," Dr. Smith replied without changing course. When he made his selection, he walked over to the counter.

"I don't believe I know you," the owner remarked as if searching his mental database for the person's name.

"No, sir, probably not. I'm Dr. Jerry Smith. I'm an archeologist from the University in Fayetteville. I've made arrangements to meet a local farmer by the name of Billy Jackson. Do you happen to know him and where his farm is?

"Oh, of course, I know Billy Bob. He stops by here regularly to get odds and ends or just *chew the fat*," the owner elaborated. "His farm is north of here, but it's a booger to get to if you aren't familiar with this area."

"We're supposed to meet at 10:00. I'll just wait on him." Jerry turned and walked over to a bench near the door and sat down to wait. A large collection of photographs covered the bulletin board. Each one was a portrait of a dead animal or fish along with a person sporting a really big grin. Jerry used to hunt when he was younger, but work had squeezed that activity out of his life. He still managed to go fishing, but not as often as he knew he should. One photo caught his attention. The deer lying in the back of the truck was huge and the rack on its head was taller than the side of the truck bed. It was dated Thanksgiving day. Most of the pictures were from October and November, but another one caught his eye that was dated December 29. The deer was average, but the boy holding the head had a smile that said "I just won the lottery!" Jerry couldn't help but smile.

The door swung open and an older gentleman in bib overalls strolled through the door and stopped. "Are you Dr. Smith?"

"Yes, sir, I am. You must be Mr. Jackson," Jerry replied.

Billy Bob turned to leave. "Can't stay and visit this morning, Buddy. Got an appointment with the good doctor. I'm here to show him those Indian rocks that I found in my field."

"See ya later then," Buddy responded.

Billy Bob and Dr. Smith returned to the parking lot. "Follow me back to the house," Billy said as he got into his truck.

Jerry got into Blue and hurried out onto the highway to catch up with Mr. Jackson. From the time Billy turned off the highway, Jerry was basically lost. He made mental notes of the numerous turns because he knew he had to find his own way out. Jerry was relieved when the lead truck turned onto what appeared to be a long driveway, although no house could be seen. Two miles later they pulled into the yard of a traditional white-frame farmhouse, complete with an old red barn, a chicken coop, and what he decided must be the outhouse. It was unclear whether it was still an active outhouse or not. He certainly hoped there would be no need to find out.

Mr. Jackson stopped the truck and started walking toward the house, pausing to allow Jerry to catch him before both men climbed the steps to the big front porch. Mr. Jackson opened the door and led the way into the living room. The smell of fried chicken permeated the house.

"Momma, we're back," Billy called into the kitchen.

Billy walked over and sat down in his recliner and pulled the old cigar box out from under a stack of magazines on the coffee table. He handed the box to Jerry who took a seat on the couch. The kitchen door swung open and Peggy and a pretty, young teenage girl entered the room.

Dr. Smith sat the box down and stood to greet Mrs. Jackson. "Hello, Mrs. Jackson. I'm Jerry Smith."

As they shook hands, Mrs. Jackson said, "I'm Peggy. It is so nice to meet you. I feel like I already know you from what I have read in the newspaper."

Jerry shrugged and tried to downplay the notoriety. "I guess that may be true, but it has been mostly old-fashion work with the occasional opportunity to meet really nice people like y'all." Jerry looked at the young girl and asked, "What's your name, young lady?"

"My name is Sarah Jackson. I'm their granddaughter," gesturing toward Billy and Peggy.

"Let's have a seat and see what you have found," Jerry said as he sat back down on the couch and opened the cigar box.

There was quite a nice collection of stone tools in the box. "Did all of these come from the one location?" Jerry asked.

"Yes, all of it was picked up by Sarah and me during the past couple of weeks. I walked down through there this morning and noticed that there is still quite a bit that we have left behind," Billy said.

"That's good. I would like to see it on the ground after a while before you collect it, too." Jerry interjected. "What I see is nice, but not unexpected. These large projectile points are the kinds of points that we find all over the Ozark Mountains and beyond. They relate to the time period that archeologists call the "archaic." Based on the various dating techniques that we use, we believe that these artifacts are between 3,000 and 5,000 years old." Jerry paused and looked at each one of the Jacksons to see if they were following his abbreviated lecture.

"How do you age them?" Peggy asked.

"We can't actually perform any test on the stone tools to tell us how old they are. We have to find them in association with other things, like fire hearths or charred wood. Through years of research, we have learned that the style or shape of the point would remain similar for a while, then change into a different style. When we date charcoal, for instance, using *carbon-14*, we learn that people during a specific time preferred a certain style of point. Then, when we find that particular style of point, we make the supposition that the point relates to the same time period as all of the others like it that came from a datable context. That is why finding sites that have features other than just stone tools is so very important. We need a better sample of datable material right where the Indians left it."

"That is absolutely fascinating," Billy remarked. "Sarah, let's take Dr. Smith for a walk."

Billy, Sarah, and Jerry rose from their seats and walked out the front door. Jerry stopped at his truck and grabbed his pack, then quickly caught up with the Jacksons. Jerry rummaged around in his pack and pulled out the map and finally figured out where he was. With his current position in the universe settled in his mind, Jerry began to scan the landscape for the telltale signs of the numerous sites that he knew must be present. As they walked down the point toward the *floodplain*, Jerry slowed to check a bare spot where an armadillo had been digging. Sure enough, there were flakes in the dirt.

Billy stopped and looked back, "Those stupid armadillos are a pain in the rump. They dig holes in the fields and if a cow steps in the hole, she could break a leg. Wish they were fit to eat."

Jerry rejoined Billy and Sarah and they continued down to the edge of the first terrace. The cows had worn several trails in that area and there were many artifacts visible on the exposed surface. "How long since this ground was cultivated, Mr. Jackson?"

"I've had it twenty years – never plowed it. Mr. Taylor had it fifty. I don't think he had plowed it since the 1930s when they used to grow some cotton in here. It did not do very well, so everyone went back to raising cattle," Billy explained.

Sarah did not say much. She was listening and absorbing more information than she could have ever imagined. She kept pointing to artifacts and Dr. Smith would graciously explain what it was, what kind of raw material it was, how it was made, how old it was, and why it was important.

When Dr. Smith had drawn a sketch map and taken some notes, they started back up the hill to the house. Dr. Smith's personal interest rested in *bluffshelters* and caves. He explained, "The Indians would live in those places and, because of the dry conditions, items that normally decay would be preserved. These

125

areas were also poor agriculturally, so they have remained virtually undisturbed for thousands of years. Unfortunately, people have started digging carelessly in these caves and shelters looking for these rare artifacts. In the process, they are totally destroying these extremely important resources."

Billy thought about that for a moment, then said, "There are lots of bluffs on this farm and I don't think anybody has ever messed with any of them. You're welcome to go take a look and see if there are any sites there. In fact, you have my permission to look and record everything on the whole place. I know that there is a hollow just to the north that has some overhangs and caves. Help yourself, but let's go eat lunch first."

The four of them sat down to a wonderful spread of fried chicken, as well as corn, green beans, and potatoes from last year's garden. Dessert was apple pie with a scoop of ice cream. Billy explained that the apples came from the tree in the yard last fall but that the ice cream came from the store because it was too much trouble to make ice cream when you could buy it.

When lunch was finished, Jerry said, "Billy, do you mind if I go for a walk to get a feel for the place? I would like to evaluate the potential for archeological investigation."

"Help yourself, but I think I am going to stay here. My arthritic knees are acting up today. Must be a cold front coming," Billy added.

Sarah piped up, "I would like to go with you, if that is all right."

"Oh, of course it is all right. I would love to have the company - especially someone who knows their way around," Jerry said. He was more serious than they realized by the joking way he said it.

Sarah and Dr. Smith went out and got into Ole Blue and drove back down to pasture where they had been looking before lunch. Jerry got a shovel out of the back and dug a couple of shallow holes to see what the soil looked like. He placed the shovel back in the truck and they started walking and looking.

They chatted casually about school, career, and other things of interest, including fishing. Sarah was a good student and Jerry was quickly impressed with how quickly she grasped new concepts. They were walking along one particular hollow that had a significant bluff along one side but no shelters, when Dr. Smith noticed a small dark opening. He and Sarah carefully climbed the broken bluff face and discovered a small opening with a significant airflow rushing out of it.

"I believe this is a good little cave. I doubt that there is anything of archeological interest, but it would be fun to explore nonetheless," Dr. Smith shared rather matter-of-factly. They did not have a flashlight, so neither one even considered crawling inside.

"That is a tiny little opening. A fat person would get stuck quickly," Sarah joked, but in the back of her mind she thought, "I'll tell Jim and Sam. I bet they will check it out."

Jerry was very encouraged by the overall condition of all of the archeological sites both in the fields as well as the bluffs. Vandalism was almost non-existent. Jerry and Sarah spent most of the afternoon walking and looking. By the time they returned to the truck, the sun was beginning to set. They drove back to the house and went in and shared what they had seen. Dr. Smith promised to come back in the early Spring and do some additional investigation when he had some college students to help him.

Dr. Smith declined the offer to stay for supper even though lunch had been fabulous. He made his way back out to his truck and headed out. He wanted to find his way to the highway before dark. By the time Jerry got back to the University, it was dark and he realized how tired he was. "I'm getting too old to work this hard. This is a young man's profession," he thought to himself as he backed Ole Blue into its parking space and killed the engine. Jerry grabbed his pack and headed for home.

Chapter 21

Jim and Sam stood, talking in hushed tones in the morning twilight, while listening to the world around them begin to awaken and start another beautiful day in the Ozark Mountains. The hills, as far as they could see, were covered with a sea of leafless hardwoods dotted by the occasional pine tree, all standing strong and still, seemingly waiting for the sun to break the horizon. Winter's grip had begun to loosen and hints of spring could be found in such signs as the bright yellow blooms of the jonquils that had recently risen above the brown grass that would soon become a lawn. A few warm days at the end of February had apparently tricked these early bloomers into emerging. Jim and Sam both knew that at least one more stretch of cold weather could be expected because the opening of turkey season was always miserable and that was still three weeks away.

It was the last week of school before "spring break" and both boys knew that mid-term tests were coming. School had certainly seemed like it was winding down in the past few weeks. Maybe it was the boys who were winding down. Either way, they were not terribly concerned. The squealing brakes of Mr. Weaver's bus could be heard in the distance stopping to pick up Sarah. The two boys were looking down the road in the direction of the approaching bus, when two mature does slipped across the gravel road less than 100 yards from them.

"Hey! Look at that! We have been standing here just talking and those two deer just walked across the road like they own the place," Jim commented.

"They know that hunting season is closed and that we are no threat," Sam added.

Just then the bus rounded the corner and squealed to a stop at the crossroads. Jim and Sam climbed in and took their seat. Sarah was already leaning up to slip Jim a peck on the cheek even though it was against school rules. That just made it more exciting. Sam had resigned himself to the apparent reality that Sarah had become a major, if not permanent, part of Jim's life.

"We missed you at church yesterday, Sam," Sarah said as she looked toward him.

"Yeah, I got busy helping Dad clean out one of the chicken houses and could not make it. Once you get that mess stirred up, you just gotta finish it before you lose your nerve," Sam explained.

"Sure sorry I missed out on that," Jim said, rather unconvincingly.

"Are you guys coming to Grandpa's farm this weekend?" Sarah asked.

"We're still planning on it, if the weather is decent. If it turns off cold and rainy, we'll postpone," Jim answered.

"I have already told Grandpa that we are going cave exploring. He said that it was fine and that he wished he were younger because he would like to join us. Grandpa said that he used to do some cave exploring when he was younger, but his knees will not let him get down and crawl around in the rocks anymore," Sarah elaborated. She was possibly more excited about the adventure than Jim or Sam because she had never done anything like that before. After the time that she spent with Dr. Smith, she had gotten very interested in the history of the area and had read several books on the subject. She could only imagine what kinds of spectacular artifacts and geological features might be awaiting them.

"I was reading last night about some of the first archeological investigations that were done in the Ozarks. The museum at the university hired some guys back in the 1930s to explore the caves and dry bluffs along the White River. They found mummies, woven bags full of acorns, twine, sandals, clothes, and all kinds of stuff that normally rots away. Reportedly, they were between 600 and 1,000 years old!" Sarah shared. "Most of those sites are now under Beaver Lake or have been *dug out*. I just know that we will find some really cool artifacts on Grandpa's farm because Mr. Taylor did not allow strangers on his land and neither does Grandpa."

The bus continued to swerve, wind, and bounce toward the highway, making periodic stops to collect passengers. When they finally reached the highway, Bill and Dustin herded their younger siblings onto the bus and flopped into their own seats. The bus pulled away and soon arrived at school.

Saturday morning broke with the most perfect weather that anyone could remember for mid-March. Sam hurried into the kitchen to prepare a sack lunch. Mrs. Jefferson was already in her sewing room working on a new dress for Martha. She enjoyed sewing and it was a nice change from the routine of cooking, cleaning house, and working with the chickens. As Sam threw together a bologna sandwich, he thought to himself "Bologna sandwiches always taste better outside on some sort of adventure." With a bag of chips and an apple added to the lunch sack, he headed for the door. He had promised his dad that he and Jim would be back in the middle of the afternoon to help in the chicken houses. He certainly wanted to get moving before he lost any more time.

"Have a good time, dear, but don't take any stupid chances – like crawling around in a hole in the ground isn't stupid enough," Mrs. Jefferson said as Sam dashed by the door.

"We'll be careful," he answered as he bounded out the front door.

Sam and Jim had gained permission to use the farm truck for the trip and they had loaded their gear in it the night before. Sam hopped in and headed down to Jim's house with an unbridled enthusiasm that he rarely exhibited. Jim was scurrying around making sure that he wasn't forgetting anything when Sam pulled up and honked the horn.

"Let's go. We're burning daylight!" Sam yelled toward the house.

Jim dashed out the door and jogged toward the truck. He tossed his backpack, which was full of odds and ends that they might like to have in an emergency, into the back of the truck as he climbed in. "Gee, you're pumped up this morning," Jim commented.

"No time to waste – if these caves have never been explored, there is no telling what might be waiting for us to discover," Sam replied as he backed the truck onto the road and started toward Bill's house.

Dustin had spent the night with Bill because both boys had gone to the basketball game at school on Friday night. As the truck pulled into Bill's driveway, both boys dashed out the door and jumped in the truck. In half a minute, they were back on the highway toward Marble.

Even under the cramped conditions, it did not take too long to get to the gravel road off the highway. However, the crooked graveled county road was a different matter. The winter weather had taken a toll on the rural road and the county had not gotten the grader out of winter storage to begin repair to the ruts and mud holes that now reduced travel speed to a seeming crawl. By the time they reached Grandpa Jackson's driveway, Bill and Dustin had both decided that they were willing to ride in the back of the truck on the return trip. Sam and Jim agreed that it would not be too cold and that they could get back in the cab when the truck reached the highway.

"It is unbelievable how rough these back roads get by the end of the winter," Sam remarked.

"All that freezing and thawing is tough on any road, but with all those chicken trucks, feed trucks, school buses, and propane trucks, it's no wonder they get almost impassible," Bill added.

The driveway was in much better shape and the farm truck finally got out of second gear as it glided along the forest trail slowly descending down into the Kings River Valley. Jim and Sam had been there once before, when they had driven Sarah there so she could try on some newly altered clothes that Grandma Jackson had been working on. Bill and Dustin had never seen the place before.

"Wow! What a cool farm! This is great!" Bill exclaimed as the living example of a Norman Rockwell print came into view. "What a spectacular view!"

The truck had barely come to a stop when Sarah appeared on the front porch. She was dressed in a red flannel shirt and an old pair of Grandpa Jackson's double-knee overalls. She had to wear a belt around her waist, because they were several sizes too large for her small frame. Grandma Jackson had folded the pant legs up a couple of turns and tacked them so they would fit, more or less.

The boys piled out of the truck as Grandpa Jackson stepped out on the porch beside Sarah. "Looks like a fantastic day for caving," Grandpa remarked. "The fields are fairly dry. You can drive on down to the river bottoms. That will save you a few steps especially coming back up the hill."

"Thanks, Mr. Jackson," said Sam.

When the truck had stopped at the house, Bill and Dustin had climbed into the back. Jim held the passenger door of the truck open for Sarah. She climbed in and then Sam and Jim took their respective places by the doors. The truck started again and eased on down the hill toward the river as Mr. Jackson waved to Bill and Dustin and then returned to his easy chair in the living room.

As soon as the truck was away from the house, Sarah eased to the right and got right against Jim's leg. Jim lifted his left arm over her head and rested it on the back of the seat. Jim had previously been very careful about how much interest he returned to Sarah's increasingly obvious advances when he was around his friends. However, the walls were coming down and he was beginning to see a future for this situation. She was so close that Jim could smell her hair, and it was certainly nicer than chickens or his sweaty buddies. All at once he wondered what HE smelled like. He had never really contemplated that question before. At one point, a covey of quail flushed from the side of the field road directly beside Sam's door. When Sarah's face jerked to the left to see the birds, her shoulder-length auburn ponytail slapped Jim on the chin, but he certainly did not mind.

Sam guided the truck to the bottom of the hill along the two-track field trail. As the trail turned toward the creek, Sam yelled back to Dustin and Bill, "Hold on, this could be bumpy." Everyone braced. Three seconds later the truck lunged

131

into the water, bouncing over the large rocks in the bottom of the stream. The clear water was deceptive. It appeared to be about six inches deep but was actually closer to sixteen. Then the truck climbed out of the water as quickly as it had entered.

"Hope Dad wanted the truck washed," Sam quipped, trying to downplay the rougher than expected crossing. "Besides, we did not want to get our feet wet before we even got started."

Sam steered the dripping vehicle off the trail, stopped, and killed the engine. Sam hopped out of the truck and looked in the back where Dustin and Bill were now laying. Before crossing the creek, they had been sitting confidently on the side of the bed against the cab. By the time the truck stopped, they were both laying in the bed of the truck tangled in the ropes, bailing twine, and other farm equipment that seemed to always be in the back of the truck.

Bill and Dustin quickly extracted themselves from the pile of junk in the bed of the truck. "My goodness, that was interesting," Bill said, as he sat back down on the side of the truck bed.

Dustin did not say anything. He just sat up and rubbed his elbow. Jim and Sarah slipped out of the passenger side, and the teens began to drag the spelunking gear out from amongst the jumble of debris. Jim turned to Sarah and asked, "Where do you suggest that we start exploring? You have walked around this farm more than we have."

Sarah looked up with a somewhat stunned expression. She had not really thought about the fact that the boys had no clue where they wanted to go. She stepped up between Jim and Bill and said, "When Dr. Smith and I were hiking down the bluff by the river, we did not notice any big cave openings. However, there were several small openings that he said could develop into substantial caves once we get through the openings. They won't be for the claustrophobic. Then again, we did not go all of the way down the bluff, either."

Being the most adventurous of the four, Sam grabbed his lantern and flashlight and said, "Lead the way, Miss Sarah Jackson! I'm going explorin'!"

The other three boys nodded in agreement and soon all five of them were hiking straight across the field to the river. The boys were wearing boots, but Sarah was wearing tennis shoes. They turned downstream until they found a shallow riffle, where they could cross easily because the bluffs were on the opposite side of the river. When they reached the water, Jim handed his backpack to Dustin and bent down so Sarah could hop on his back. She shuffled quickly up behind Jim, planted a hand firmly on his strong shoulders, and hopped astride his back. Jim staggered slightly but quickly regained his balance, grabbed her legs, and headed out across the icy stream.

Sarah was fairly petite, but the loose gravel and the swift water still made the short crossing dicey. Jim was glad to get to the dry land on the other side. The other boys followed close behind. They could see the enormous bluff through the forest and directly above their current position.

When Sarah's feet hit the ground again, she tapped Jim on the back and sweetly whispered, "Thank you, Jim." Then she scampered out ahead of the boys to lead the way up to the dry bluff.

Even though it was not very far, the steep slope left all of them slightly winded. Sarah spoke first, "Dr. Smith and I searched upstream. We only found two small openings that I am not sure Dustin could squeeze into, but Grandpa told me that he used to see a bunch of bats coming out of the bluff downstream. I suggest that we go downstream and look for that cave first. If we don't have any luck, we will come back and check on those little ones upstream."

With a unanimous vote, the five explorers started walking downstream. Sam led the way, followed closely by Bill and Dustin. Jim and Sarah lagged behind because Sarah insisted on looking for Indian artifacts along the drip line of the bluff. The three lead explorers soon progressed out of sight around an outcropping of rocks. It was the opportunity that Jim and Sarah had been waiting for. They both simultaneously realized that they were alone, albeit for only a moment. Sarah looked up from scanning the ground to find Jim standing on a large rock watching her.

"What are you looking at?" Sarah coyly asked.

"The cutest girl I know," Jim responded and then continued before she could say anything. "Are there really any caves downstream or were you just getting rid of the guys so we could have a minute alone?"

Sarah climbed up on the rock beside Jim as she formulated her reply. "Yes – to both." Then, she leaned in close to give Jim a peck on the cheek, but at the last instant, Jim turned his head toward her and planted a kiss right on her lips.

As quick as a flash, they realized that this was their first intimate moment. Neither would be the same nor did they regret it. "In fact," Jim thought, 'with a little practice, this could be habit-forming.'

"Are you guys coming or what?" came the distant voice of Sam as he realized that the two sweethearts had lagged behind.

133

"We were looking for artifacts. We'll be right there." Jim called back. Sarah and Jim stepped down from the rock and hurried to rejoin the others.

Chapter 22

When Jim and Sarah caught up to Sam, Bill, and Dustin, they were standing in front of a rather deep inset in the bluff. The back wall was not clearly visible in the distant shadows. Sam was kneeling down to light his lantern. "About time you two got here. Did you discover anything exciting?" The smirk on his face told Jim that the double meaning in the question was not accidental.

"We didn't find any artifacts," Jim said, dodging the question. He then stepped around Sam and started back into the shadows. "This looks like a good place to start."

"We thought so. When this lantern gets going, we'll see just how good it is," Sam said.

"I have the rope in my backpack," Bill chimed in.

"I have four extra flashlights plus the one I plan on using," Dustin added.

The lantern flared to life and the novice explorers converged on the back of the *niche*. Sam took the lead followed by Bill and then Dustin. Jim and Sarah took the rear. The *bluffshelter* was generally dry and flat, but large slabs of rock that once were on the ceiling of the shelter now lay on the floor. It was a clear reminder that spelunking came with a definite set of unique hazards.

Sarah was diligently searching for evidence of any Indian artifacts that might be exposed on the surface. "This place looks exactly like what Dr. Smith described as the setting and size of the shelters where he has made his most amazing discoveries. I just know that he would be interested in digging here."

"You'll have to give him a call and let him know about this place," Jim replied as he followed the other three boys into the retreating darkness. "But for now, if you are goin' cavin' with us, you better come on."

The mouth of the cave, which Dr. Smith would call a shelter, was about fifty feet across and fifteen feet tall. However, by the time they had gotten deep enough into the cave to actually need their lights, the cave more closely resembled the hall at the school building. It had become a fairly uniform shaft about eight feet high by twelve feet wide while gaining slightly in elevation. The group proceeded at a steady pace, not paying particular attention to the details of the rock walls they were passing, eager to see if there were any classic cave features like *stalactites* or *stalagmites*.

As the teens strolled deeper into the mountain, the shaft followed a more *sinuous* path, whereby Sarah and Jim could not see Sam because he was continually around the next corner. That left Jim and Sarah more dependent on their flashlights than the others.

"This is so exciting," Sarah whispered to Jim. "I can't believe how awesome this is."

Jim simply smiled, reached over, and gently grasped her hand as they lagged a few more steps behind the others.

"Cool!" Sam exclaimed. "You guys have got to see this!"

The group quickly converged on Sam's position. They found themselves standing at an opening, looking into a very large room. They all entered the room and formed a fan at the opening, but no one said a word. The awe of the moment was soaking in as each one of them quickly scanned the new sights, and then, slowly began to take in the details of their subterranean discovery.

The ceiling of the room was at least thirty feet high and the wall directly across from where they entered the room must be over 100 feet away. The ends of the room to the left and right lay beyond the reach of the light.

"Listen," Sam breathed as five pairs of eyes turned toward the ceiling. The squeaking of bats was growing as they objected to the intrusion of light into their home. Some of the bats dislodged from their perches and began to dart nervously around the room, which in turn elevated the nervousness of the explorers.

"I am going to kill the lantern. It is too bright for the bats. If I don't, they are all going to be diving at our heads," Sam announced as he extinguished the bright light and sat it in the opening that marked the exit.

Everyone's eyes were accustomed to the brightness and when it went out, they were all rendered temporarily blind. No one moved and they kept their flashlights trained on or near the floor to further avoid disturbing the bats. Slowly, their vision returned and a new plan was quickly formed to continue the exploration.

Bill and Dustin agreed to go to the right and see if there were any more passages to be explored or if the room ended somewhere that direction. Sam, Jim, and Sarah headed to the left.

Sam led the way and within 200 feet they came to a large column in the middle of the room where an ancient stalactite and stalagmite appeared to have met and then proceeded to grow in circumference. Jim and Sarah headed around the left side while Sam went to the right. They soon discovered that the column was not in the middle of the room. It was located at a split and was actually a flow stone formation attached to the wall. Sam continued for some distance when he came to an apparent avalanche. He scaled the rock pile and found that the passage had taken a vertical turn and was continuing almost directly above the passage that he figured that Jim and Sarah were exploring.

As Sam had disappeared to the right Sarah cocked her head to one side and said, "It looks like a frozen brown waterfall. I think I'll name it 'the waterfall' unless we actually find a real waterfall in here somewhere." Jim only nodded approvingly and continued his slight descent behind the left side of the "waterfall." Their passage went down a short distance and then took an abrupt left turn before narrowing significantly.

Jim turned to Sarah, "I am going to crawl into this tight passage. You stay here at the opening in case I get stuck and need help."

"Okay, but you be careful," Sarah cautioned.

Jim slithered into the hole and after about forty feet decided it was too narrow to go any further. He lay silently, listening for any sense of what may lie beyond, but all he could hear was his heartbeat and breathing echoing off the extremely confined space. Crawling out of the passage was easier said than done, but he eventually backed out to find Sarah sitting on a boulder shining the flashlight around the room, checking out the walls.

"Well?" Sarah asked.

"It got too tight. I couldn't see or hear anything beyond that point," Jim answered.

They shared a brief look at a couple of interesting features that Sarah had spotted and then returned to the "waterfall." Sam's light could be seen approaching from the other fork of the passage. Jim and Sarah did not wait on him but began to retrace their steps back to the lantern. Sam followed close behind. Bill and Dustin's lights could be seen approaching from the right. Sam picked up the lantern and started into the exit passage before he stopped to light it. Jim and Sarah waited until Bill appeared then followed Sam.

When Bill and Dustin rejoined the others, they reported that the large room just kept going. "As far as we could see, the room looked very much like what we all first encountered," Bill said. "We didn't see anything special." Dustin nodded in agreement.

After Sam relit the lantern, they decided to continue the discussion back outside in the sunshine. Once again, Sam led the way, followed by Bill and Dustin with

Jim and Sarah close behind. The return trek to the outside world did not seem nearly as far as the trip into the cave. Clearly, it was just another distortion that occurs when you anticipate a big adventure versus when it concludes. Regardless, the five *intrepid* explorers were absolutely thrilled with the total experience.

"That was the coolest thing I have ever done!" Dustin declared.

Bill, Jim, and Sarah affirmed that sentiment with a resounding, "AMEN!"

It was only 10:00, but each of them picked a spot in the mouth of the shelter and started digging into their individual backpacks. Collectively, they brought out a smorgasbord of sandwiches, chips, cookies, crackers, fruit, and candy that had been earmarked for lunch, but the excitement of the moment justified a celebration feast. They laughed, talked and related their individual experiences with attention to detail as if the four members of the audience had not just been there, too.

Sarah watched and listened to Jim intently. She hung on every word because as he shared what he saw and did, she wanted to know how he would present her to his friends.

"When we got down to that tight spot, I crawled right in there. Sarah could have certainly gone farther than I did, but I wasn't about to put her into a situation where she might get trapped or hurt. I just couldn't let her be in serious danger," Jim said.

Sarah just sat and smiled. She knew that Jim did truly care about her and that eventually his shyness would subside and he would openly express his feelings regardless of who was present. She had learned in Sunday school that patience is a virtue and she knew that it was true.

As the meal and the conversation began to wind down, Sam asked, "Where shall we go now? Jim and I don't have to be back to collect eggs for several hours."

Sarah sat up straight and said, almost apologetically, "There is a little cave up the hollow from where the truck is parked that we can go check out. It is a very tiny opening – maybe 18 by 24 inches. There was a good airflow coming out of it when Dr. Smith and I found it, but we didn't go inside."

"That sounds intriguing. I vote for checking it out," Sam declared, raising his right hand. A quick glance around the group discovered four other hands shooting into the air. "Looks unanimous! Let's check it out!"

They gathered their trash and their gear and headed for the truck. The four waders and one passenger quickly crossed the river once again and soon returned to the truck. Everyone but Sam piled into the back of the truck and found a good handhold. Sam cranked up the truck and soon forded the stream again before shutting the engine off. Sarah's little cave was across the creek and there did not seem to be a good reason to wade the little creek twice if it wasn't necessary. With trash and leftover food consolidated into a single sack and left in the truck, the young people set up for the short hike up the hollow.

When they arrived at the location, it was not readily apparent that the little *niche* in the bluff actually was a cave. They stood there and looked at each other and then at the bluff for several seconds before Sarah spoke up and said, "I know it doesn't look like much, but there is a bunch of air rushing out of that little hole. It must be coming from somewhere."

Sam turned without saying a word, and started up the bluff. He had left the lantern in the truck because it was almost out of gas and he did not want to carry it if it was not worth the effort. Bill and Dustin were close on his heels. All of the backpacks had been left in the truck, too, but each person was armed with two flashlights.

When Sam got to the opening and stuck his head in front of the hole, he was truly surprised. He shined his light into the darkness but could not see an end to the cave. He stopped and looked down to Jim and Sarah and said, "Are you two coming?"

"We're right behind you." Jim replied.

Satisfied with the answer, Sam turned, wiggled into the opening, and crawled into the darkness before he reached into his back pocket and grabbed his small flashlight. When he cleared the opening, Bill slipped in next, followed by Dustin. When only Dustin's feet were left protruding from the bluff face, Jim grabbed Sarah's hand and they started up the jumbled path together.

As Jim bent down to look into the hole, Sarah slipped past him and said, "I don't want to go last. You follow me." Then, with the agility of a mink, she dropped to her belly and wiggled into the hole.

Jim could not help but grin. Sarah was great. She was rough and tough like his lifelong buddies, but she had the qualities of a woman, too. The thought passed quickly through his mind, "I believe God has chosen a real jewel for this country boy. She likes to go spelunking, fishing, and hiking. We are going to have a great time together, and an occasional kiss would certainly be an additional perk." Jim snapped out of his daydream and scurried into the hole, intent on catching Sarah so he could tease her by messing with her feet.

To Jim's surprise, Sarah had wriggled well into the passage and was out of reach. He also noticed that the opening that he had just entered was actually the tightest point he was passing. Soon he was on his hands and knees crawling as fast as he could on the sharp rocks to catch the others. He could hear excited voices coming from somewhere ahead. The tunnel-like passage did not last too long before it opened into a substantial room. When Jim entered the room, the other four were huddled just to his right, looking at something on the floor lying against the wall.

"What is it?" Jim asked.

"It would appear to be four bundles of dry river cane," Dustin answered, since he was the one that spotted them. "I don't know much about Indian artifacts, but they look really old. See the twine that binds them? It appears to be made from woven grass."

Sarah piped up, "If it is old, I bet Dr. Smith would like to see it! We should look around and see if we can find anything else, but we should leave it where we find it in case it is really important."

The boys and Sarah fanned out, momentarily forgetting that the goal of the mission was to explore the cave. When nothing else was found, they reconvened at the opening in the wall that led to the outside world.

"Let's split up like we did before. Bill, you and Dustin go right. We'll go left," Sam suggested.

They all agreed and started moving in opposite directions. The cave was eerily quiet, unlike the previous cave. Bill and Dustin soon encountered a substantial drop-off. They shined their lights over the edge and a series of ledges could be seen, but the actual bottom could not. Without ropes, neither boy was interested in trying to climb down the apparent sinkhole.

"I think we should save this descent for another day," Dustin advised.

"I think you're right," Bill agreed. "Let's go after the others."

They turned to go and realized that they had not gone far from the exit, but that they could not see any of the other three teens. Dustin chose to lead the way. He soon discovered that the room bent hard to the left shortly past the exit, which is how the other three had gotten away so quickly. As they rounded the corner, they spotted several flashlights in the distance. Although they were hurrying to catch up, they noticed a small opening in the wall.

140

"I'll duck in here and see if this goes anywhere. You stay here and watch to see if they make any detours," Dustin said as he bent down and stepped through the opening.

About the time he tried to stand up, he noticed that the floor was sloping down into another apparent sinkhole. He eased up to the edge when a rock shifted under his weight. As his foot dropped over the small *precipice*, he found himself sliding down a muddy slope. Fortunately, he only slid about six feet before hitting bottom. It happened so quickly, he did not even have time to call for help. Then he noticed that the mud smelled like manure. A quick check confirmed his initial assessment. His next look was toward the ceiling for the most obvious source, but no bats were present although they clearly had been. Dustin regained his composure, scaled the guano-covered slope, and returned through the opening.

"Gee, what happened in there?" Bill asked upon seeing Dustin reappear, covered with bat guano.

"I fell. Wouldn't you know it would be in a bat's bathroom!" Dustin replied in a state of disgust. "I've got to get out of here and try to get cleaned up. I've got it in my ears as well as other more critical places. You go on and tell the others that I am headed for daylight. I'll meet y'all at the truck. I hope I have some soap in my lunch sack."

Dustin headed for the exit and Bill hurried to catch up with Sam, Jim, and Sarah. They had not gone too far even though the room was continuing beyond them.

"Here comes someone," Sarah remarked to Jim and Sam when she noticed a light coming their direction.

Bill rejoined the others and said, "We were blocked by a large sinkhole, so we decided to follow you guys. Dustin spotted a small passage off the main room right back there and decided to check it out. He fell in a huge pile of bat guano and has headed for the truck."

"Yuck," Jim exclaimed. "Well, it looks like this cave is as extensive as the first one. We can come back later and check it out more thoroughly. Sounds like we need rope anyway."

The four agreed to not finish exploring the cave today, so they turned and headed for the exit. When they got to the torches, Sarah selected one to show to Dr. Smith, but left the other three. Soon all four young people were back outside and headed toward the truck. Upon their arrival, they found a guano-covered Dustin sitting on the tailgate eager to go home.

141

After a brief stop at Grandpa Jackson's house to let Sarah out, Sam pointed the truck toward home. Dustin volunteered to stay in the back of the truck for the entire trip, so the other three settled into the front seat as they got underway.

Chapter 23

The phone in the archeology office was ringing when Dr. Smith got his door unlocked on Monday morning. He dropped the armload of papers on his cluttered desk and grabbed the receiver.

"Archeology Department, Dr. Smith speaking," he said.

"Dr. Smith, this is Sarah Jackson. You and I took a hike on my Grandpa Jackson's farm a couple of months ago. His farm is on the Kings River." She paused to see if he would remember the experience.

"My goodness, Sarah. How are you?" Dr. Smith exclaimed, remembering the wonderful outing that they had shared. "To what do I owe this pleasure?"

"I don't know if it is anything important, but some friends of mine and I were out exploring some caves on Grandpa's farm on Saturday. We went into one of those tiny little caves and found four really old-looking torches way back in one of the caves," Sarah reported.

"Really! Describe one to me," Jerry said as he sat down and found a notepad to write on.

"We left three of them where we found them, but I brought one out so you could see it if you'd like to. They were all basically identical, being made of sections of cane about 18 inches long and lashed together with some cord that looks like woven grass. We did not find anything but the torches." Sarah said.

"I believe you have correctly identified the specimen. When would be a good time to come out and document this discovery?" Dr. Smith asked.

"I am on spring break all week. I can be at Grandpa's almost any day." Sarah responded.

"Wednesday worked well before. I'll be out to the Jackson farm about 9:30 a.m." Jerry said. "Tell your Grandmother not to fix lunch."

"I'll be there and I'll tell her, but I don't know if she will listen." Sarah concluded as she hung up the phone. As soon as she hung up, she called Jim's house, but after three rings the answering machine picked up. "Jim, this is Sarah. I just got off the phone with Dr. Smith. He is coming out on Wednesday at 9:00. I sure was hoping that you could be there, too. Please give me a call."

"It's 8:00 in the morning. I bet he is already working over at Sam's. He'll call later," Sarah mumbled to herself as she headed to the laundry room to get started with her chores.

About thirty minutes had passed when Sarah's phone rang.

"Hello. Jackson residence," Sarah announced politely.

"Sarah, this is Jim. What's this about some doctor making a house call to check you out," he said, pretending to be confused by Sarah's message.

"No, silly. Dr. Smith is that archeologist that came out and looked at the caves back at the first of the year. I called him and he wants to see that torch that we found in that keyhole cave," Sarah explained.

"I was teasing you. I knew what you were talking about. You're so cute when you get serious," Jim quipped. "What am I saying? You're cute all the time."

Sarah just giggled.

"How are you getting to your Grandpa's farm?" Jim asked.

"I will be spending the night there Tuesday night," she explained.

"I'll talk to Sam and see if we can borrow the farm truck for a little while," Jim thought out loud, then added, "It is really good to talk to you this morning. Even though we sat together at church yesterday, we don't get to talk. We will have to do this more often, but right now, I am late for work."

Jim and Sarah exchanged "goodbyes" and hung up. Jim grabbed his baseball cap and jacket then dashed out the door. His feet were going to work but his mind was racing down toward Sarah's.

Wednesday morning Sarah looked out the window when she heard the approaching truck. She had struggled with just what she would wear. She wanted to look nice, but she also wanted to crawl back into the little cave with Jim and Dr. Smith. She settled on a pair of jeans that were lightly faded but still fit well and a flannel shirt. The old "Jefferson farm truck" coasted to a stop beside Grandpa's truck. Jim and Sam exited the vehicle dressed in their cave-crawling clothes and made their way to the porch. Sarah opened the door and invited them in.

"Where's the doc?" Sam asked.

"Not here yet," Sarah replied. "Should be here in a few minutes. Come on in and take a seat. I am so glad you guys could come. I just did not feel right crawling in that little cave without y'all."

Sam and Jim both smiled, but Jim was certainly pleased to hear that Sarah wanted to include them in the experience as well as the security. Jim was more than happy to protect his investment.

The sound of crunching gravel announced the arrival of Dr. Smith. The three teens met him at the door.

"Grandpa is out checking his cows, but he said for you to come right in and make yourself comfortable," Sarah greeted Dr. Smith. "This is Jim Flagstone and Sam Jefferson. We are three of the five who discovered the torches."

Everyone shook Dr. Smith's hand and they all returned to the living room and selected a seat. Sarah unwrapped the torch and handed it to Dr. Smith.

"Wow! That is a beauty!" Dr. Smith exclaimed as he examined the torch closely. "This is almost certainly a torch that was made by Indians. It is interesting that it is not burned. Apparently, it was not used but possibly stored in the cave for a future use. Were the others burned?"

Sam spoke up, "No, sir. All four of them were identical, as far as we could tell."

Dr. Smith wrinkled his nose and muttered, "That is strange. If they were as far back in the dark as you indicated on the phone, I would have expected one of them to be burned, at least a little. We'll have to check to see if there might be some other evidence of what these torches mean. If we can find some charcoal, we will be able to get a *carbon-14* date. That would be fantastic."

"I brought my lantern. Let's go look," Sam said as he stood, signaling his desire in the matter.

As if on cue, the others rose to their feet. Dr. Smith looked at Sam and said, "I like your enthusiasm. I'm not getting any younger. Let's go look in a cave!"

Sam volunteered to use his truck, but Dr. Smith said that he would like to take his own as well in case he needed any particular equipment out of it. Sam agreed that that was a good plan, but still chose to take his own truck in case he could not stay as long as the others.

Sam, Jim, and Sarah got into the Jefferson farm truck and led the way down to the creek. Dr. Smith followed closely behind. Grandpa Jackson stepped out of the barn and waved to everyone as they drove by. When they stopped at the creek, the teens piled out and began to gather their gear. Dr. Smith grabbed his camera, notebook, and small metric tape measure along with a couple of flashlights.

The entourage made their way up the hollow discussing the plan of action as they went. "I would like to see the remaining torches in their original position when we get there. There may be some significance to their arrangement," Dr. Smith explained.

Sam scurried up the bluff to the mouth of the keyhole cave and proceeded to light the lantern. Dr. Smith followed close behind. Jim and Sarah brought up the rear. With the lantern lit, Sam dropped to his belly and began wiggling into the shaft. Dr. Smith got down, with a few grunts and groans, and headed in second. Jim motioned for Sarah to follow Dr. Smith but what he really wanted was a second kiss.

Sarah dropped down to enter the hole, but then stood back up as if reading Jim's mind. With lips puckered and eyes closed, she turned her head toward Jim. In an instant, Jim gently held the sides of her face in his hands and pressed his lips to hers. It only lasted a few seconds and would not win any contests for style, but the impact was more profound than their first kiss. This one seemed mutually premeditated and sealed the growing bond that had formed between them. When Sarah eased back slightly from Jim, there was a peace that settled on both of their faces. No words were said. None were needed.

With a twinkle in her eye, Sarah dropped to the ground and disappeared into the cave. Jim was reeling from a deluge of thoughts and emotions. He took a deep breath, glanced to the heavens in thanks, and dropped to the ground to enter the cave.

When they assembled inside, Dr. Smith was kneeling over the torches. "This is how they were lying when you found them – stacked up between this rock and the wall?"

"Yes, sir," Sam replied. "We have not touched those three other than to lift the top two to determine that there really was three, well, four, counting the one we collected."

With the bright light of the lantern, they spread out to search for other artifacts or possibly artwork that might be present on the wall. Dr. Smith explained, "In France, there are several caves where the ancient hunters would go to perform 'rite-of-passage' ceremonies. The walls of those caves were decorated with successful hunting scenes and stories of other significant events. It would be unlikely to find a similar pattern, but we can't rule it out."

A thorough inspection of the walls discovered nothing. Their attention then turned to the floor of the cave. "We should look for anything that doesn't seem to belong, like sticks, grass, charred plant material, or chipped stone tools. Someone was in this cave hundreds, if not thousands, of years ago. They must have had a reason," Dr. Smith continued to lecture.

They found nothing to the right of the opening, except the ragged sinkhole that seemed to block their investigation in that direction. They returned to the exit shaft and proceeded left. As the cave bent to the left, Dr. Smith kneeled down on the floor once again. "Here is something," he said while pointing to a rock slab. "It appears to be some charred plant fiber." He pulled a small magnifying glass from his pocket and trained the beam of his flashlight directly on the object. "Yes, burned cane, I believe. Someone was apparently in here and used one of the torches for light. I bet if we look closely, we will find more."

As they proceeded, they indeed did find several more pieces of charcoal. Dr. Smith suggested a working theory. "I believe that at least one person entered this cave and used a cane torch to look around in this cave. I can't see any reason why, but that may be the real answer. Someone came in here possibly looking for something, possibly did not find it, and apparently did not come back. I can't figure out why they left those perfectly good torches behind, though. They must have intended to come back and just did not."

Sam, Jim, and Sarah were soaking up every word the professor said. Furthermore, they were extremely eager to help the professor in any way possible. This was a true mystery and they were on the case. Conversation ricocheted through the cave much like the actual echo of their voices as thoughts and ideas were bantered about. Finally, Dr. Smith declared that he should document the torches in his notes and take some photographs before they exited the cave. He indicated that he expected that task to take about an hour, if "you kids want to go exploring for a while." Then he added, "Keep your eyes open. There could be other hidden treasures deeper in the cave – like the skeleton of the owner of the torches, if he didn't find his way out."

That possibility had not even crossed their minds. But with the mere suggestion, they were doubly inspired to search every nook and cranny in search of the "explorer's bones." Jim, Sam, and Sarah decided to leave the lantern with the professor so the photographs would be better and they continued in the direction of their previous exploration from four days before.

They looked and looked, but found nothing archeological. The cave amounted to a single shaft with occasional cracks and tiny holes too small for even Sarah to enter. After about thirty minutes they agreed to return to the professor.

He was just about finished and, after carefully packing the three remaining torches in his backpack and collecting several pieces of charred material from inside the cave, they crawled outside.

When they reached the flat ground near the creek, directly below the mouth of the keyhole cave, they sat down to discuss what they saw. Jim was still in an exploring mode and found it difficult to sit still, so he began to pace and wander. Each bare spot of ground was scanned thoroughly for whatever there might be to discover. While Dr. Smith, Sam, and Sarah discussed the findings inside, Jim worked his way to a gravel bar in the creek. Standing at the edge of the water looking at the bed of brown rocks, a shimmer of white caught his eye. He bent down and pulled a complete miniature triangular arrowhead from the gravel bar.

"Cool!" Jim exclaimed.

The other three stopped their discussion and looked in Jim's direction. He was returning quickly to their location.

"Look what I just found in the creek," Jim announced as he handed the point to Dr. Smith.

Dr. Smith took the tiny point that was less than an inch long and held it up where everyone could see it. "This is a Fresno point. It is an actual point that would have been used on an arrow, as opposed to a spear or a dart. It is a common point style of the late prehistoric time period – 1200 A.D to 1700 A.D. I will make a note in the records that it was found in the gravel bar in front of the cave. By the way, does this cave have a name?"

Sarah spoke up and said, "I have been calling it Keyhole Cave because of the tight little opening, but I don't guess it has a name."

Jim chimed in, "Keyhole Cave sounds good to me."

Sam nodded his approval.

"I guess that is settled then. It is now Keyhole Cave," Dr. Smith announced as he handed the point back to Jim. "You can keep that. The museum has plenty, and it will make a nice keepsake."

Jim simply beamed with the idea of having a piece of history to hold in his hand. With much of the day spent, they agreed that they had accomplished what they set out to do and with no additional fanfare, made their way back to the trucks. Dr. Smith thanked the young people for their help as he slipped into his truck and started back up the hill. Sam, Jim, and Sarah got into their truck and followed close behind.

Dr. Smith stopped briefly to retrieve the fourth torch before he continued back to the University. Sam and Jim offered to take Sarah home. She graciously accepted, trotted into the kitchen to tell her grandmother, and then to get her things. When she returned to the truck she slid into her designated spot in the middle. Jim then climbed in and deliberately threw his arm onto the back of the seat. Before they reached the highway, his hand was resting comfortably on Sarah's shoulder where it stayed for the remainder of the trip.

Chapter 24

"I wish that Bill and Dustin could have gotten loose last Wednesday to hear what Dr. Smith told us in the cave," Sam said as he flopped down on the seat of the school bus. Spring break had seemed extremely short and getting back in the swing of school was the farthest thing from his or Jim's mind.

"I was telling Bill all about it at church yesterday, but Dustin was not there. Bill said that Dustin was sick. His folks were there but they didn't say too much about it other than to request prayer for him to get well," Jim responded.

Sarah leaned forward and asked, "Did Bill say what Dustin's symptoms were?"

"Not really. All he said was that Dustin was extremely tired and was running a low fever. It sounds like the flu to me," Jim said as he shifted around in his seat to get a better look at Sarah. School rules prohibited them from acting upon the feelings that they were experiencing, so they had decided to keep a low profile even on the bus.

Sam had accepted the fact and figured that there wasn't any reason to get into Jim and Sarah's way. He knew that he would quickly become the "odd man out" and he truly wanted to be friends with both of them, if at all possible. Truthfully, he was envious that they had such a strong connection. He certainly wished the best for them, but he wanted someone special to waltz into his life, too.

As the bus reached the highway, Bill guided his sisters onto the bus followed closely by Tim, Dustin's little brother, but Dustin was absent. Bill dropped into the seat in front of Jim. As Tim passed by, Jim asked, "How's Dustin?"

Tim slipped into the empty seat across from Jim as the bus began to roll again and said, "He is still running fever and this morning he was talking crazy. He said that he dreamed all night long about hockey. He said that he has never had such a real dream. It was almost like he was actually at a hockey game. Mom is taking him to the doctor this morning."

Bill sat quietly, just listening to the morning's report. When Tim finished, he turned to Jim and Sam and posed the question, "Do you think Dustin caught something when he fell into that bat guano? He looked like he rolled in it. He could have inadvertently gotten some in his mouth or nose. I have a really bad feeling that this is not your average illness."

"Don't go burying him over a head cold, Bill," Sam retorted. "Dustin has a bug. He'll get some antibiotics, and then he will have to suffer through the remainder of school just like the rest of us."

The wise crack was meant to lighten the mood and it did. Everyone chuckled and agreed that Sam was right, although, there certainly seemed to be an unspoken, ominous feeling hanging over the situation. No one talked about it anymore, but it rode heavily on their minds as the bus swung into the schoolyard.

Meanwhile, Mrs. Rogers had taken Dustin to town.

"Hello, Dustin," said Dr. Jones, the family's physician. "What seems to be the problem today? Too much spring break?"

"I wish," Dustin replied. "I don't really know what's wrong. I am totally exhausted and all I have wanted to do for the past three or four days is sleep. Mom says that my temperature has been running just less than 100 degrees. I have no appetite. I just feel generally rotten."

"Sounds like the flu, but I would like to get a blood test and a saliva culture to be sure. You sit tight and I will have a nurse in here in a minute." Dr. Jones pulled his stethoscope out of his lab coat pocket and listened to Dustin's breathing and heart beat.

The frown on his face did not look good, but at least the stethoscope was not ice cold when it touched his bare chest and back. The doctor made some notes on the chart and exited the room. Dustin's mother had stayed in the waiting room. He was a high school senior and did not want his mother to go with him. But the frown on the doctor's face made him reconsider that choice. He was wishing that she had been there to see the doctor frown. He felt quite alone and that just made him feel all that much worse.

The door opened and a jolly-faced nurse stepped into the room wearing rubber gloves and a mask pulled down on her chin. "Hello, Dustin. Dr. Jones asked me to get some samples," as she walked right up and grabbed his arm. In no time she was finished and scurried toward the door. "You can slip your shirt back on and return to the waiting room. We'll call you when the tests are complete."

Dustin slipped his T-shirt back on and shuffled toward the door. He stopped and reached for the doorknob but the darkness was quickly shrinking his vision to a single point of light, which lingered for a moment then faded to black.

Dustin awoke with a start. "What is that awful smell? Where am I? What happened?" As his mind and eyes began to focus, he could see Dr. Jones, the nurse, and, most reassuringly, his mother. All three were smiling.

"Welcome back! We heard a thump on the door and came in to find you passed out on the floor. I know you said you were tired but I guess my nurse drained your last speck of energy right out of you!" said Dr. Jones, trying to lighten up the situation. "You and Mrs. Rogers can just stay right here in the room while we get back to those tests."

Mrs. Rogers and the medical staff helped Dustin up out of the floor and into the chair in the corner. The nurse slipped out and quickly returned with a couple of sugar cookies. Handing them to Dustin, she and the doctor left the room again.

"What happened, son?" Mrs. Rogers asked quietly.

"The doctor came in and asked me some questions, then sent the nurse in to take blood and saliva samples. When I got up to go to the waiting room, I guess I fainted," Dustin recounted.

"You go ahead and eat those cookies and just sit there until they come back and tell us what's going on," she declared.

The next hour passed slowly, but when the doctor returned, he had a perplexed look on his face. "Dustin, let's go take a chest x-ray. I heard a strange rattle in your chest that does not sound like pneumonia. I would like to see if there is anything that would show up on film. The good news is that the blood and saliva tests came back normal, but something certainly seems to be wrong. Otherwise, you would be sitting in school!" he jokingly concluded.

Dustin stood up and followed Dr. Jones down the hall to the radiology department. The x-rays showed nothing abnormal. Dr. Jones was clearly confounded by the case but instinctively knew that there must be infection, bacteria, or a virus to blame. As a precaution, he prescribed a round of strong antibiotics and sent Dustin home to rest until additional tests could be performed on the blood samples. Those results could take several days.

Mrs. Rogers pulled the car into the driveway and parked. After a stop at the grocery store and the drugstore, Dustin had nodded off and did not rouse until his mother started trying to get him out of the car.

"I can make it, Mom," he mumbled as he pulled himself out of the car through sheer determination.

She helped him into the house and straight to bed. The door hardly closed behind her before he drifted off to sleep again. Mrs. Rogers walked down the hall to the telephone, where she dialed her husband. The details of the morning took several minutes, but his recommendation was the same as hers – call

Pastor Flagstone. Immediately after she got off the phone with her husband, she dialed the Flagstone residence. The reverend was not home, which was not unexpected, so she left a brief message asking him to call her "as soon as possible."

Dustin looked around. He was standing at the mouth of a cave. There was no recollection of how he got there, or for that matter, where he was. He was drawn inside and the mere thought of going seemed to cause it to happen. The corridor had no discernible light source, yet it seemed luminescent. He could feel himself gliding into the passage and could tell that the cave walls were quickly evolving into a concrete block-lined hallway and that the dirt and rock floor had become a poured concrete floor.

"I'm having that dream again," Dustin told himself. "I wonder what this means?"

The hallway ended at a large opening. Dustin looked at himself and he was now wearing a hockey uniform, complete with gloves, helmet, skates, and a stick.

"COOL! Last time I was watching. I am going to get a chance to play!" he perceived.

Dustin skated onto the ice and up to the puck that was sliding toward him. He looked in the direction of the incoming puck to see another boy standing at the far end of the rink also wearing a hockey uniform with a large number eight on it.

"Welcome to the 'Dream Rink' #44. I'm #8. You're new. What's your story?" he asked.

"Yes, I'm new. I don't know why I'm here and why did you call me #44?" Dustin replied.

"We don't use our names here, just our jersey number. It makes it easier when guys get 'promoted to the next league,' if you know what I mean," #8 explained.

"You sound like there are others," Dustin began. "Where are they?"

"They come and go depending on when they are sleeping. The majority of the team is here every night. That is when we practice or choose up sides and play a practice game."

"Where are we?" Dustin continued to pump for information.

"I'm not really sure, but this is what we have pieced together. Each of us is very ill in reality, but when we sleep, we assemble here. Nobody has figured out where we are, but it is a very nice change from being sick, so we don't complain. We don't know how we got lucky enough to get this 'escape' but we figured that it was just one of God's little perks. Like I said, we don't ask too many questions. We are afraid that we will lose the privilege. Now, if you're through talking, it's time to get in a little extra practice, so hit the puck."

Dustin raised his stick and slapped the puck toward the goal beside #8. It was the first time that he had ever been on the ice playing the game that he loved to watch. It was exhilarating. He started skating toward #8, but #8 stopped the puck short of the goal and raced past him. Dustin reversed direction and started skating after his impromptu teammate.

The two boys skated and skated. They each made numerous goals in a hockey version of "one on one." Then as quickly as it began, Dustin stopped and announced that he had to go. Number 8 waved goodbye and the hockey rink faded away as he slowly opened his eyes to see Pastor Flagstone, Jim and both of his parents standing around his bed.

"Hey, Jim. Hi, Pastor Flagstone. How are y'all doing," mumbled a groggy Dustin.

"We are doing just fine, Dustin. How are you feeling?" Pastor Flagstone asked.

"To be honest, I don't feel bad. I just feel drained," Dustin answered. "I'm sorry I missed church yesterday. I wanted to go, but I just could not muster the energy and Mom said there was no use in going if all I was going to do was sleep."

Pastor Flagstone chuckled and nodded his head in agreement then added, "Of course, that does not stop some folks from coming. There are a couple of folks who have never missed a Sunday and still have never heard me preach."

Everyone laughed because they all knew to whom he was referring. Then Pastor Flagstone stepped closer to the bed and picked up Dustin's hand as a silence fell across the room. Then the preacher began to speak. "Dustin, the doctors don't know what's wrong, but we know the Great Physician and He has this situation firmly in control.

Each person present around the bed knelt down as Pastor Flagstone began to pray. "Dear Lord, we call upon You at this time to ask for Your intervention in healing Dustin. The doctors don't know what the problem is, but we know that

You do. Dustin is a child of Yours and we believe that, as our Heavenly Father, You will take care of your children because You want the best for us. Lord, we put our trust and faith in You, standing on your Holy Word, that You are God and that You will restore Dustin to us soon."

As everyone left the room, Jim lagged behind. He wanted to speak to Dustin in private. "I wanted to let you know that Dr. Smith did an investigation in Keyhole Cave, where you found the torches. We found some charcoal down by the little passage where you had your mishap. He is supposed to have all of that stuff analyzed and let us know how old it is. Then while we were sitting outside the cave discussing everything, I found this arrow point. Dr. Smith said it could be over 800 years old, but probably closer to 400 years old. Either way, it was exciting to find."

Dustin looked closely at the little point, admiring the symmetry and obvious craftsmanship. "That is a beauty, Jim. What are you going to do with it?"

"I think I am going to have it mounted on a necklace and give it to Sarah for her birthday," Jim replied. He could see that Dustin was drifting off, so he wished him well and slipped out of the room.

When the room was quiet, Dustin closed his eyes and faded back to sleep. As he did, he felt the cold breeze on his face and became aware of the guys skating past him. A smile crossed his face as he entered the rink and joined the group.

Chapter 25

Three boys were skating around and passing the puck between themselves as they sped toward the distant goal. Dustin glided out toward the blue line and waited for them to return to center ice.

"Hey, #44! Glad you're back. Let's play some two on two," #8 suggested.

The other two boys agreed with the suggestion and formed one team. Dustin and #8 took the opposing side. They skated for what seemed like hours, laughing and talking as they played. Dustin could not remember having a better time than he was currently experiencing.

The longer they skated, the more players and fans began to appear. Soon, there were enough people to fill two full teams, when the announcer declared, "Ladies and gentlemen, welcome to tonight's game. It looks like we have many excellent participants on the ice. Set the clock and let the contest begin!"

No one actually chose sides. Everyone just seemed to know who was on which team. Even though the scoreboard kept the statistics, the outcome was inconsequential. Both sides had so much fun and when the game was over, every player was still a friend. Soon the crowd and players alike began to disperse and Dustin knew it was time for him to leave as well.

As his mind slipped into neutral for a brief instant, Dustin became aware of his mother sitting on the side of his bed and reading from her Bible. He reached up and touched her elbow, which made her jump slightly.

"Oh! You startled me. I was sitting here reading and praying. How do you feel this morning, dear?" Mrs. Rogers asked.

"Surprisingly good for having played hockey all night," Dustin replied.

She looked over the top of her reading glasses with such an incredulous look that Dustin started giggling. His mother smiled. It was the best sign she had seen in several days.

"I guess it was a dream. It is the most awesome thing," he started, and then proceeded to tell her all about the dream.

"No wonder you're tired," she responded. "Are you hungry? You haven't had anything to eat in a couple of days."

"Kind of," he answered. "I would like to have something to drink, for sure. Can I have some macaroni and cheese?"

"I don't have any prepared, but it won't take but a minute to whip some up. Can you get up and come to the kitchen? Your father has already gone to work and Tim caught the school bus about an hour ago. It will be good for you to get up and stir around a little bit," her words trailing off as she passed through the bedroom doorway bound for the kitchen.

Dustin swung his legs over the side of the bed and sat up. The room spun momentarily, but soon stabilized. He pulled his robe off the back of the chair beside the bed, slipped it on, and made his way into the kitchen.

As he entered the kitchen, Mrs. Rogers glanced over her shoulder to reassure herself that Dustin was all right. He eased up to the table and sat down in a chair. "I'll have your macaroni ready in a couple of minutes --." She did not get to finish her sentence because the phone rang.

"Hello?" she said.

The voice on the other end spoke for quite some time before she broke in and said, "He seems better. He is sitting here at the table asking for something to eat and drink."

More muffled speech could be heard coming from the other end of the phone. Finally, Mrs. Rogers sighed and said, "We'll meet you there about 10:00."

"Who was that and what was that all about?" Dustin asked with genuine curiosity.

"That was Dr. Jones. He said that your blood test came back and there are some abnormalities that they can't identify. He wants you to go to the hospital in Fayetteville for some more thorough tests," she relayed. What she did not tell Dustin was that they had observed an extremely aggressive and fast-growing virus that he could not identify.

She finished the macaroni and poured Dustin a glass of iced tea. While he ate, she went and packed an overnight bag for both of them for the trip to the hospital. While she was away from Dustin, she telephoned Mr. Rogers. She instructed him to stay at work until school was out and then bring Tim to Fayetteville. Next she called Pastor Flagstone's house and left a brief message.

Dustin had finished most of the macaroni by the time she returned. "I have packed some clothes, but I encourage you to take something to read or a hand-held game to play. Dr. Jones indicated that it would be an overnight stay."

That information was unnerving. He looked into her eyes searching for definite reassurance. Without saying a word, he smiled and shuffled off toward his room to get dressed. Her rock-solid faith was intact and visible. Dustin knew that no matter what happened, the godly faith of his mother, as well as the whole family, would stand through any trial.

Dustin soon emerged from his room. He was dressed and ready to go. Mrs. Rogers followed him out the door, locking it behind her. The macaroni and cheese tasted fine, but the butterflies were keeping it from settling on his stomach. He kept that to himself.

She started the car and soon they were moving west toward Fayetteville. Dustin peered intently out the window. He had lived in this area since birth, but somehow, everything looked so bright and new. He convinced himself that it was just the first big push of spring. He was not really scared, but the feeling of having no control over what would happen somewhat reminded him of riding the school bus. He tried to relax and watch out the window for deer or turkey. Both were commonly seen in this area and today he really wanted to see them. He desired to know that the world was still right-side up and that everything would be fine.

The winding highway to Fayetteville essentially ran through the White River Valley occasionally passing within sight of the water. The riffles cascading over the dull brown cobbles of the gravel bar brought back memories of swimming in the streams around the area. "Those Ozark Mountain streams have the best skipping stones in the world," he thought to himself.

Houses got more frequent, traffic got heavier, and nature was less evident as they approached the city limits of Fayetteville. After a few turns, the car pulled into the parking lot of the hospital. Although he was not sleepy, he struggled to muster the energy to get out of the car. Dustin could not decide if it was the illness or his aversion to the upcoming ordeal. Mrs. Rogers got out of the car and walked around to the passenger side and opened the door. "Dear, you have to get out of the car. They can't make you well unless you go inside."

Dustin looked up at the fatigued smile that rested on her face. He wrinkled his nose slightly and said, "I know, but I think my feet are stuck to the floor. Not really. I'm just, well, you know, scared." There, he'd said it. It was the truth and he was so relieved to get it off his chest.

"Of course you're scared," Mrs. Rogers continued, "You'd have to be out of your head to not be scared. I'm scared, too. But you know as well as I do that God is in control and He has a master plan. Our family has never faced anything critical before and I believe that He is testing our faith to see if we are ready for the next level that He has planned for us. I would gladly take your place, but that is not how the cards were dealt. It is okay to be scared, but you must never back down from the faith in God that we have instilled in you. Have faith and He will see us through."

Dustin stood up and gave his mother a big hug. "I love you, Mom. Let's go see what miracle God wants us to be a part of." With their arms around each other, they walked slowly across the lot and into the front door of the hospital.

Dr. Jones was waiting when they entered. He had already secured a wheelchair for Dustin. Dustin sat down and looked over his shoulder and said, "Hey, Doc. If you'll get yourself a chair, I'll race you to the elevators."

The doctor laughed out loud and said, "I'll take a rain check on that. I got thrown out of the last hospital that caught me racing wheelchairs. It was worth it, though. That cute little nurse that I was racing later became my wife! You might want to challenge one of these young nurses to a race later. Who knows what you might win," he added with a wink.

Mrs. Roger started coughing and sputtering at the thought of Dustin chasing girls around the hospital in a wheelchair. His being sick was disturbing enough. "Thanks, Dr. Jones. I almost choked on this piece of hard candy I was working on."

Dr. Jones laughed again and headed Dustin down the hall. "I have already registered Dustin with the hospital and we'll get him settled in his room before we start the advanced tests." They eventually turned into room 44. It contained an official hospital bed and a couch. "I figured that someone would spend the night, so I got a room with adequate accommodations for both of you."

As he stopped the chair by the bed he instructed Dustin to get undressed and put on this hospital gown. "Don't forget to wear a robe if you walk out in the hall. There isn't a back in that thing. You don't want the girls fighting over you."

Dustin certainly appreciated the doctor's humor and he wished that he felt well enough to play along with him. However, he had been up several hours and really needed to lie down. While Dustin followed the doctor's orders, his mother stepped into the hall with Dr. Jones. They discussed the proposed procedures and then attended to the required paperwork for the hospital. When Mrs. Rogers returned to the room, Dustin was asleep.

The cold air of the hockey rink cleared the cobwebs from Dustin's true reality. He felt like he had been away from the rink for so long. As he stepped onto the ice, he realized that he was alone. This was the first time that he had not seen #8 upon his own entry to the arena. Dustin decided to simply practice his skating and puck handling. He was eager to try some fancy moves, but really preferred to not have anyone watching in case they did not look as cool as he hoped.

Dustin slapped the puck ahead of him and then accelerated to catch up with it. As he passed the puck, he spun around and started skating backwards. Using his stick, he reached out and hooked the puck once again. As he skated right beside the net, he flicked the puck in, then he cut the skates sideways and stopped just before hitting the end wall.

Dustin continued to experiment with different moves as well as doing them faster than the time before. His talent and skill were increasing rapidly. He pushed the physical envelope as far as the sharp angles and abrupt direction changes. Nothing seemed impossible and he felt as though he could perform anything that his mind could imagine.

In the middle of a drive toward the net, complete with spins, jumps, and reversals, Dustin noticed that he was no longer alone. People had begun to gather in the stands as well as a few players that were beginning to venture onto the ice. Most of the players wore recognizable numbers, but a few new numbers had joined the game.

"Nice moves, #44," said #30 as he skated closeby, obviously intending to join the action. "How long have you been playing hockey?"

"I'm not really sure. About a week, I think," Dustin replied as he passed the puck to #30.

"Wow! You're good for only a week's worth of playing," #30 remarked with surprise. "You're a natural. You will get promoted to the Big League soon."

"What's the Big League?" Dustin asked.

"We are not quite sure, but whenever a player demonstrates enormous skill, the announcer will declare, usually at the end of an especially good performance, that the really good player has been selected for promotion to the 'Big League,' whatever that is." Number 30 shrugged his shoulders as he finished his explanation, stole the puck from Dustin, and shouted over his shoulder, "Bet you can't take the puck away from me before I can score, Superstar!"

The race was on but when Dustin skated past #30 backwards, #30 knew that he was no match for the exceptional skill that he faced. Dustin refused to gloat, but for the first time in his life, he clearly excelled at a sport even if it was in an alternate reality. They continued to spar as others continued to choose up sides and join the fray.

When the impromptu warm-up session seemed to wind down, a booming voice announced, "Tonight's contest will be especially significant, because Big League scouts are in attendance to evaluate some of the players for promotion!" The crowd cheered loudly and the game began.

Dustin was fabulous. He skated like he was born on a pair of skates. Steals, passes, and checks performed with the intensity of a bull but with the grace and finesse of a figure skater. Dustin performed so far above the skills of the others that none of the other players, including #8, were left with any false sense of their own preparedness for the Big League.

When the final buzzer sounded, Dustin had proven his ability to all present. As the players all congratulated him on an outstanding performance, the booming voice of the announcer rang out. "Ladies and gentlemen, it is with great pleasure that I report to you that the scouts have consulted and agreed that a new member of the Big League has been selected for promotion."

A spotlight that Dustin had never seen before shone down from above center ice and illuminated the far end of the arena. A section of the arena wall slid back and a dark curtain just beyond began to part, exposing a glowing hallway.

The announcer then continued with even greater enthusiasm, "#44, you have proven yourself worthy of promotion to the BIG LEAGUE!" The crowd stood and cheered as Dustin waved to them. He was being promoted. He had no clear idea exactly what lay ahead. However, the warmth and love that seemed to be emanating from the bright light at the end of the tunnel was clearly drawing him to find out. As Dustin entered the hallway, the curtain closed behind him, the arena wall returned to its position, and the other players and fans resumed their normal activity.

Dustin had slept through several of the hospital procedures that afternoon without waking up, but about midnight, he drew his last breath and slipped into eternity.

Chapter 26

Pastor Flagstone pulled into his driveway. He looked at his wristwatch. It was 4:30 a.m. He turned the headlights off and just sat there in the quiet pre-dawn morning. He had spent the evening at the hospital in Fayetteville with the Rogers family, all of whom were present when Dustin passed away.

The grief and sorrow that he felt could not be released there, and now a flood of tears came pouring out. He slumped over the steering wheel and sobbed uncontrollably. He had not felt so utterly helpless and bewildered by such an unexpected death since his darling wife was taken from him fourteen years ago. But in some way this was so much harder. Dustin was just on the brink of actually starting his life. "God, I don't understand. Tell me why." Pastor Flagstone was still sitting in the truck when the sun rose.

He had wept until exhaustion produced sleep, but the rays of a spectacular sunrise peeking over the eastern ridge roused him awake. He stepped out of the pickup and faced the rising sun. In that early morning light, words of the Bible poured through his mind like a tidal wave and he dropped to his knees and began to praise the almighty, omniscient God that he knew was in complete control. In an instant, he was washed with a peace that surpassed all possible human understanding.

"The Psalmist David was right when he wrote in chapter eight, 'O Lord, our Lord, how excellent is thy name in all the earth! Who hast set thy glory above the heavens.' You are in control just like with Job and even though our hearts are heavy with loss, I will trust You, because as it is written in Matthew 10, You know when a sparrow falls to the ground." Pastor Flagstone eventually rose from his knees and took a good look around him. He could hear a turkey gobbling in the distance. Other birds were singing. Two squirrels were playing "chase" in a nearby tree. The Holy Spirit had taken his broken heart, raised him from the ashes of this circumstance, and comforted him in a profound way. The reverend made his way to the house. He had one more unpleasant task ahead. He had to tell Jim.

Jim was awake when his father came in, but he was nowhere near ready for school. He had been up much of the night praying for Dustin and his family. When he heard his dad's truck pull up to the house but his dad did not come in, he knew that was not a good sign, but he also knew that his father needed time alone. In the Old Testament, Jacob wrestled with an angel all night to get an answer from God. He knew that scene was being rerun in the front yard.

"Jim, I am so sorry to have to tell you, but Dustin passed away last night."

Even though he thought he was ready, the words hit him like a punch in the stomach. Being a seventeen-year-old young man is supposed to mean that you are tough, and tough guys don't cry – at least where anyone can see. He turned his back to hide the welling tears and said, "Somehow, I already knew."

Pastor Flagstone recognized the body language and only patted Jim on the shoulder briefly before turning and walking down the hall to his bedroom.

Jim was numb. He was sad but the loss was so surreal that it seemed more like a bad dream. His next thought was about Bill and Sam. Someone needed to tell them. Jim walked part of the way down the hall and said, "Dad, I need to borrow the truck. I have to tell Bill and Sam before they get to school."

"Drive carefully. I am in no shape to work this morning and you are in no shape to go to school. Do you want me to go or is this something you would prefer to do yourself?" Mr. Flagstone asked.

"This is something I have to do myself," Jim said as he turned to leave the house.

Jim looked at his watch. It was still an hour before he and Sam would normally convene at the bus stop. He climbed in the truck and reached for the ignition, when he thought, "How am I going to tell them?" He bowed his head and prayed, "Father God, I have read in Your Word that when Your children stand in need that You will give them the words to speak. I have no idea what to say to Sam and Bill, but I need the right words to say because Sam is not a Christian. Please guide my words. Amen."

He started the truck and headed for Bill's house. It did not take nearly as long without all those bus stops and he turned into Bill's yard in about fifteen minutes. Bill was standing at the window, when Jim turned in. By the time Jim was out of the truck, Bill was standing there.

"This looks serious, Jim," Bill said with a grimace.

"There is no easy way to say it. Dustin passed away last night," Jim blurted out. In his mind, he thought back to his prayer for the right words to say. Somehow, he did not feel that blurting it out was all that inspired, but it does cut right to the chase.

Bill just stood there, momentarily speechless, his piercing eyes begging for a different news-flash. When Jim did not flinch, Bill simply dropped his head and stared at the ground.

"Dad was there, but he did not give me any details. Apparently, he went to sleep and just did not wake up," Jim added.

Bill lifted his tear filled eyes and in a choked voice said, "Thanks for coming and telling me in person. I think I am going to go for a walk now. I need to be alone."

Jim fully understood, so he got back into the truck to go tell Sam. In his mind Bill was, in some ways, the easy stop. The fifteen minute drive to Sam's house was torturous as he bounced through an emotional roller-coaster that was mostly spins and drops without very many "high points." As he pulled into the yard, Sam saw Jim through the window and knew something was amiss. He stepped outside to find out.

"Sam, let's go for a walk," Jim said as he stepped out of the truck.

Sam trotted over to join his friend who was heading away from the house. "What's wrong, Jim? You look awful. Spit it out."

Jim stopped just before reaching the gravel road and turned to face Sam. "Dustin died last night." Once again, his mind rewound that prayer for the "right words to say in a time of need." He was not known to be terribly diplomatic, but this was abrupt even for himself. "I have the bedside manner of a train-wreck," he thought to himself.

Sam's mouth fell open and his eyes widened in shock. "NO WAY!" he exclaimed. "What happened?"

"I don't really know. Dad came in early this morning after being at the hospital all night. He didn't share any details other than he just went to sleep and did not wake up," Jim related.

Sam was stunned. He bent down and picked up a hand full of rocks and walked on out into the road. He spotted a beer can laying about forty yards away and proceeded to throw the rocks at the can without saying a word. He just threw those rocks as hard as he could and when he ran out of rocks he would simply bend over and reload.

Jim just stood and waited. Everyone vents their emotions in their own way, but the one common denominator is that they all need time and space to express themselves before any words of comfort can be effective.

After four or five minutes of steady throwing, Sam just sat down in the middle of the road. Jim started to leave him alone, but he figured Mr. Weaver would run over him like he did the old hound dog several years ago that was sleeping in the road. Jim got close enough to hear that Sam was crying. To the best of his recollection, he could not remember ever seeing Sam cry. Mr. Jefferson was a man's man and Sam was a chip off the old block.

Jim walked up beside Sam, knelt down, and placed his arm around Sam's shoulder. Sam turned and gave Jim a genuine hug that said "Thank you, friend."

The sound of squealing brakes in the distance meant that the bus would be arriving for them in about a minute, but neither boy had any interest in catching it. They stood up and decided to wait by the mailbox where they would flag the bus down and tell Mr. Weaver – and Sarah. Jim had forgotten all about Sarah. She did not know. Jim had to tell her.

The bus sat at the bus stop for a moment, waiting for someone to appear, but when neither Jim nor Sam did, Mr. Weaver continued on his route. Within a few seconds the bus rounded the curve and began to slow down as it approached the two boys standing in the road. When it stopped, Jim climbed on and signaled for Sarah to come to the front. Upon her arrival, she knew the news was bad.

Jim looked at Mr. Weaver and said, "Dad was at the hospital in Fayetteville last night. Dustin passed away." He had said that phrase so many times this morning that some of the shock had worn off for him. However, it affected the hearers of the news with similar consequences as his first hearing.

Mr. Weaver was clearly stunned and kept saying, "No ... no ... no."

Sarah just exploded in uncontrollable sobbing. Jim reached out and grabbed her, pulling her in close. For a couple of minutes, the idling bus just sat in the road as the occupants coped with the news.

Sarah pulled her tear-streaked face out of Jim's chest and whispered, "Can you take me home? I don't want to go to school today."

"Sure. I have dad's truck here at Sam's. I would be glad to run you home," Jim assured her.

Mr. Weaver thought that would be fine and agreed to pass the bad news to the school, so that the officials would not think the kids were simply playing hooky.

Jim thanked Mr. Weaver and helped Sarah off of the bus.

As the bus eased away, Jim found himself standing in the middle of an old country road in the back woods of Arkansas with his best friend and his girlfriend, all grieving the loss of their buddy, Dustin. At that moment, reality began to settle in on each of them, that life was precious but temporary, because like the Bible says in James 4:14, "For what is your life? It is even a vapor that appears for a little time and then vanishes away."

Jim, Sarah, and Sam walked back to Sam's house where Mrs. Jefferson was standing on the front porch waiting. The threesome approached the porch and Jim, feeling like the spokesman for the group, said to Mrs. Jefferson, "Our good friend Dustin died last night. We aren't feeling like going to school. I think we need to go talk to my dad. He was there. We want to know more."

Mrs. Jefferson nodded in agreement and said to Sam, "I'll let your father know what has happened and that you will be with Jim. It will be fine with him. He'll understand."

They thanked her and proceeded to get into the Flagstone truck. "Let's run over to Sarah's house first and tell her parents what is going on before we go talk to Dad," Jim suggested.

Sarah and Sam agreed.

After turning the truck around, Jim pulled out onto the road to Sarah's house. Conversation was absent. Everyone was still reflecting on this terrible turn of events.

Jim pulled into Sarah's driveway, parked, and let her out. She was gone for several minutes then reappeared at the door with her mother. Sarah gave her mother a kiss and returned to the truck. Jim stepped out and let her in. As they backed out of the driveway, Jim and Sarah waved to Mrs. Jackson, but Sam just kept staring at the floor. He was simply devastated.

Driving into his own yard, Jim wondered if his father would be asleep after such a horrible night. He decided to slip in and check before inviting the others in. When he opened the door, he could hear snoring from the back room. Jim quietly crept in and left a note on the kitchen table that said that Sam and Sarah, as well as himself, were going to Bill's house and they would all be back later to talk to him. He did not know if he would get a chance to read it, but it was there just in case.

Upon returning to the truck, Jim proposed that they go see Bill. Sam and Sarah agreed. They really wanted to be together. There was a need to console each other that was incomplete without Bill.

As the Flagstone truck pulled into Bill's driveway for the second time, Mrs. Perkins stepped out on the front porch. The three youths joined her there.

"How's Bill?" Jim asked.

"He's doing okay, I guess. That was not the news that we wanted to get," she confided.

"Us either," Jim continued. "Where is Bill?"

"He is out in the storage building. I have not checked on him, but it sounds like he is building something. I thought I would give him some time alone, but I think he would be glad to have your company," she said as she pointed toward the backyard.

The threesome descended from the porch and proceeded to the workshop in the backyard. Jim eased up to the slightly open door and stuck his head in and asked, "Bill, can we come in?"

"Sure, Jim. Come on in," Bill responded with a decidedly more upbeat tone. "I decided to build a bird house. I needed something to do while I was thinking and this seemed better than anything else I could come up with."

The four each pulled up a chair inside the little building and they began to share. Jim and Bill did most of the talking. Sarah made occasional input. Sam sat quietly most of the time and listened. The other three had a unique perspective that he did not fully understand, but he was quickly coming to realize that this life is not all there is. In fact, the sermons that he had heard Pastor Flagstone preach recently were making more sense, too. The more they talked, the better he began to feel.

Chapter 27

Jim rolled into the Flagstone yard at about 2:00 in the afternoon. The time that the four of them had shared in Bill's workshop had been very therapeutic for everyone. They had laughed and cried for a couple of hours. It was hard to believe that they had so many stories to tell from Dustin's short lifetime.

After he dropped Sam off at home, Jim drove Sarah to her home. They had sat in the cab of the truck and just talked. Life had thrown them a decidedly serious curve and it was certainly a wake-up call to not take any gift that the Lord gives for granted.

As he walked toward the house, he wondered if his dad was still asleep. When he walked through the door, Jim heard his father's voice from the back bedroom. "Jim, is that you?"

"Yes, sir. I am sorry I was gone so long," Jim apologized. "We were talking and the time just got away from us. We did have a wonderful time, though," he added as he headed down the hall.

"Oh, that's fine. I was snoozing. I can't go without sleep like I could when I was younger. I woke up about thirty minutes ago when the phone rang. I found your note and figured you would be home soon. How did everyone take the news?" Pastor Flagstone asked.

"After the initial shock, everyone handled it better than I expected. Sam is having the hardest time. He isn't saved and just doesn't have that peace that comes from knowing that 'to be absent from the body is to be with the Lord.' Bill, Sarah, and I tried to explain it, but he just could not make it add up. We did not think that it was the right time to push too hard, but the ground is definitely plowed. I am praying that Sam will get saved as a result of Dustin's death."

Pastor Flagstone had stopped getting dressed to devote full attention to what Jim was saying. He was truly pleased to hear that the youth under his teaching had learned the lesson that he had taught from the pulpit. The information about Sam pricked his heart and solidified his intentions to preach a salvation message at Dustin's funeral.

As Jim turned to leave the room, Pastor Flagstone said, "By the way, the phone call that woke me up was from Mrs. Rogers. They are home and would like for me to come to their house this afternoon to talk. I could not believe how upbeat she was on the phone. Would you like to go with me? You might have a chance to talk to Tim while I talk to Dustin's parents. If you don't want to go, that's fine. I understand."

168

"I think I would like to go with you," Jim replied. "I need to fix myself a sandwich before we go. By the way, Mrs. Perkins said that she would call the ladies from church about bringing food to the Rogers house. She said she would be glad to handle that detail."

Pastor Flagstone smiled to himself. "There isn't another family on earth like the church family. A tragedy welds us together like nothing else."

Jim rummaged through the refrigerator and found some lunchmeat and cheese. The bread was stale, but at least it wasn't molded. He sat down at the kitchen table and began to eat. Although his heart was not in it, his stomach was grateful.

The Flagstone truck pulled into the Rogers driveway about 4:00 in the afternoon. There was a car present that they recognized as a church member. Jim and his father stepped out of the truck and proceeded to the house.

Mr. Rogers opened the front door when Jim knocked. He was obviously tired. You could see it in his eyes, but you could also see a peace in his eyes that made Jim smile. Mr. Rogers graciously hugged Pastor Flagstone for his spiritual support and guidance. Then he hugged Jim because, despite the obvious relationship that Jim and Dustin had, he was truly glad to see him. Mr. Rogers also fully understood that life is temporary and the real significance of life lies in eternal decisions you make during your life.

The Flagstones came in and found their seats. A steady stream of people from the church and the school dropped by. Most brought food or some other item, but all of them came to console and express their genuine grief. There were many tears and many hugs, but each time Mr. and Mrs. Rogers would fall back to the fact that Dustin knew Jesus as his personal savior and that there would be a happy reunion someday in the future.

Soft music was playing in the background. In fact, it was playing so softly that it was barely noticeable. Jim recognized the genre as instrumental versions of common hymns although he could not remember the names of most of them. Dustin's little brother was energetically playing video games in the adjacent room and seemed to be quite content, so Jim chose to leave well enough alone. Jim really preferred to stay with the adults anyway.

The Rogers had lived in the area for many years but they were not native to the area. Mr. Rogers and his wife had moved to Huntsville because of a job transfer when Dustin was a baby. From what Jim knew, they really did not have any close family. Dustin had indicated that his grandparents were all dead and that he was not close to what few cousins he knew about. Biological family ties just weren't important to their family. They had always relied on their church family, and Pastor Flagstone was a key ingredient of that family even though he was only a few years older than Mr. Rogers.

Soon the kitchen table was loaded with food and the refrigerator was full, too. Mrs. Perkins and the twins had done an outstanding job of rallying the cooks, but it was obvious that there was too much. Mrs. Rogers was absolutely overwhelmed by the support that the community had demonstrated, but she told Pastor Flagstone that "he was either taking some food home with him or he was going to have to stay the night."

The reverend laughed and agreed to take some food "for long-term storage" to his refrigerator.

Jim had not said much. He was truly uncertain what to say so he had just sat and listened. This was really his first experience of sitting with a grieving family, but as far as he could tell, this had to be one of the best that had ever been.

Pastor Flagstone finally raised the issue of the funeral when he asked, "Did you make any arrangements for the funeral?"

It was an extremely awkward question and although he had been wondering the same thing, Jim would not dare ask. He was glad that his father had.

"We have talked to the funeral home and have taken care of the casket, flowers, and gravesite. However, we can't set a date or time for the service because Dustin's death was ruled mysterious and the coroner's office is performing an autopsy," Mrs. Rogers explained. "I really hate the idea of an autopsy, but I feel like it is important to know why Dustin died."

That answer was fully satisfactory to all that were present. The question of what killed Dustin was riding on everyone's mind. There was a definite fear that there was some deadly virus about to attack the community, but what was the source? That was indeed an important question that needed to be answered and only an autopsy was likely to help.

Exhaustion was clearly taking a toll on Pastor Flagstone, so he stood up and said, "I think it is time to go home, but let me tell you – tonight will be the hardest night of your life. When the guests are all gone and the reality of the situation sets in, you will be emotionally challenged. If you need me, do not hesitate to call. God has placed me here to be a minister to the hurting. You guys clearly qualify."

Mr. and Mrs. Rogers hugged and held Pastor Flagstone. They knew he was right and they appreciated his loving compassion more than they could ever say or express. In a moment, Jim and his father made their way to the truck, each carrying a couple of plates of food. Pastor Flagstone made his way to the passenger side and climbed in, signaling that it was Jim's job to drive them home. Although they had not intended to make off with a substantial quantity of food, it was certainly a welcome addition to the generally barren refrigerator in their own home.

Mrs. Rogers had been told that it would take a couple of days for the coroner to perform the autopsy. She was hoping that they would release Dustin's body on Friday. When Friday morning arrived, the anxiety spiked to an all-time high before the phone rang about 10:00.

"Mrs. Rogers?" came the tentative voice on the other end.

"Yes?" she cautiously replied.

"This is Dr. Jones' nurse. Dr. Jones asked me to call you and let you know that the coroner's report was faxed to our office this morning and that Dr. Jones would like to go over that report with you and your husband. He said that was standard procedure for the family doctor to explain the findings to the family. Would there be a good time for you to come in?"

"I will be there in about thirty minutes," Mrs. Rogers responded.

"That will be fine. Dr. Jones said that he figured that you would be here almost as quick as I called. I can't imagine being in your place. Please know that we are praying for all of you," the nurse concluded.

"I really appreciate that. We will see you in a few minutes," Mrs. Rogers said.

After she hung up, she immediately called her husband. He had gone to his office for a few minutes to visit with co-workers more than to work. He felt like he needed to keep them informed. He said that he could be at Dr. Jones' office in thirty minutes.

Mrs. Rogers arrived first but opted to remain in her car until her husband arrived. She was certainly a strong woman emotionally, but she wanted his support to face what was coming.

171

Mr. Rogers pulled into the lot a few minutes later and they walked into the reception area together. Dr. Jones had spotted her sitting in her car and was nervously waiting. This was absolutely the hardest thing that he had to do as a family doctor.

"Come right in," Dr. Jones said, leading them to his personal office. "The coroner faxed his report to me and I thought it was better to show you what it said than just try to describe it over the phone."

They all turned into his office and Dr. Jones closed the door behind them as the couple took a seat together on the couch. Dr. Jones grabbed a chair and pulled it over in front of them.

"First, let me say how incredibly sorry I am for your loss." Dr. Jones began. "I have been beating myself up ever since you brought Dustin in on Monday. I must admit that this report made me feel better regarding why I did not recognize the problem. If you look here on page two, it states as a cause of death 'previously unknown virus that apparently entered through a cut on the back of the neck. The virus apparently settled on the base of the brain causing rapid deterioration of the basic bodily function of breathing and consciousness.' In other words, he went into a deep sleep and stopped breathing. The mystery is where the virus came from. Do you happen to know where Dustin got that cut on his neck?"

Mr. Rogers looked at his wife who seemed poised on the brink of an answer but following a pregnant pause she said, "I don't know for sure. He went spelunking with some other kids over on the Kings River and fell into a pile of bat guano, but I don't know if that is where he received the cut or not. That was last Saturday."

Mr. Rogers looked at Dr. Jones and asked, "Does the report say when they will release Dustin's body?"

"Yes, it does. The body will be released as soon as you tell them where to deliver it. You can call them from here and Dustin should be at the funeral home by this afternoon," Dr. Jones replied.

Dr. Jones turned around, lifted the telephone receiver, dialed the coroner's office, and handed the phone to Mr. Rogers. In a few minutes, he hung up the phone and said, "They promise that Dustin will be here by 3:00."

The Rogerses rose from their seats and thanked Dr. Jones for his help and started for the door. Dr. Jones opened the door and followed them to the parking lot. He stood there watching them drive away before returning to his other patients.

Time seemed to pass very slowly waiting for 3:00 to arrive. At about 2:30 p.m., the Rogers family got into the car and drove to the funeral home. True to their promise, the coroner's vehicle arrived just after 3:00. Dustin was unceremoniously encased in a large black bag and was quickly transported into the back of the funeral home so that final preparation could be made to the body. The family was not allowed to see Dustin, but the funeral home director reassured them that he was in good condition and that they could certainly have an open-casket service if they desired.

Mrs. Rogers was quite relieved by that information. She could only imagine what the coroner might do while searching for the cause of death. With their minds put at rest, they sat down and finalized the arrangements for the funeral service for Sunday afternoon. Sunday was Dustin's favorite day. It seemed fitting that his funeral should be held then.

Chapter 28

Pastor Flagstone had spent the majority of the day Friday landscaping yards in Huntsville, but had wrapped it up earlier than normal. He arrived at home to find the light on his answering machine blinking. Still covered with dirt and sweat, he pressed the play button.

"Pastor, this is Mrs. Rogers. I know you are out working, but if you could give me a call or come by, we would like to discuss the funeral arrangements. Dustin's body was delivered to the funeral home this afternoon and we would like to have the funeral Sunday afternoon. Thanks."

The grungy preacher stood there staring at the machine debating whether to call her or get cleaned up and go over there. He wanted to go, but he was quite tired. He decided to go take a shower and eat some supper before he called her back.

After his shower, Pastor Flagstone had gotten dressed and had warmed up some leftovers in the microwave for his supper. He thought it was strange that Jim was not home yet, but he knew that he had to get going so that he would not be gone all night. He called Mrs. Rogers and set a time for his arrival. Since Jim was not home, he left a brief note on the kitchen table.

Jim and Sam were just about finished with their chores at the Jefferson chicken houses for the day. They had worked together all afternoon. It was not the most efficient way, but for them the conversation was more important than the eggs. Sam was full of questions about what Christians believed about life and death. Jim had explained his understanding of eternity.

"Sam, everything we believe about God comes from the Bible. It tells us how to live. It tells us how to treat others. It even gives us some idea about what happens when you die. The Bible says that during life we are given the opportunity to find out who Jesus is, what he did, and what that means to each of us," Jim said, trying to find the proper explanation of what it meant to be saved and why it was important.

"Jim, I've been to church and hung around with Christians enough to know that Jesus is God's Son and that He was crucified by a bunch of church people about 2,000 years ago. I know that His death was supposed to 'wash away my sins.' That is what that song said. However, I am a good person. I work hard. I treat people right. What do I need to be 'saved' for? I'm as good, or better than, everyone else," Sam concluded.

That was the opening that Jim was desperately searching for. Jim reached into his back pocket and pulled out the little New Testament that he carried and opened it to the back cover. He and Sam sat down on two plastic buckets and began to look at what was written there.

Jim started by showing Sam that God loved him. He read John 3:16, "For God so loved the world that He gave His only begotten son that whosoever believes on Him should not perish but have everlasting life." Jim looked up at Sam and said, "You said just a minute ago that you believed that Jesus was God's Son."

Sam nodded and said, "Sure, I have heard that verse all my life and I believe that it is true."

Jim continued, "Did you know that Romans 3:10 says, 'There is none righteous, no, not one?' Verse 23 goes on to say, 'For all have sinned and fall short of the glory of God.' That means that being good is not good enough to get to heaven. We must be righteous and that is so much better than 'good' that there is no comparison. In fact, righteousness is so high, we cannot attain it in our own ability. We need a savior and that is where Jesus comes in."

Jim was rolling. The words that he longed to say for so many years were finally pouring out. He felt a boldness and an empowerment that he had not experienced before.

"If everyone has sinned then Romans 6:23 says that 'the wages of sin is death' – which means eternal separation from God – 'but the GIFT of God is eternal life in Jesus.' Then in Romans 10:13 it says that, 'whoever calls on the name of the Lord shall be saved,' and John 1:12 says that 'as many as received Him, to them He gave the right to become children of God, even to those who believe in His name.'"

Jim looked into Sam's eyes and he knew that Sam finally understood that he was a sinner and that he had to be saved if he wanted to go to heaven when he died. Jim point blank asked, "Do you believe that Jesus died and that He paid the price for your sins?

Sam simply said, "Yes."

Jim asked another question, "Do you believe that if Jesus gave his life for you, you should devote your life to him?"

Sam replied without hesitation, "Absolutely! Buddy, if you saved my life from some mortal danger here on this earth, I would feel indebted to you forever. If Jesus paid the price for all my sins, the least I could do is live for Him!"

"The only thing left to do then is pray. I'll be glad to help you," Jim added.

Sam bowed his head and following Jim's lead quietly prayed, "God, I believe that Jesus is your son and that he died to pay for my sins. Thank you for that. I just want you to know that I am sorry and that I want Jesus to live in my heart forever. Amen."

After they prayed, Jim shared some more Bible verses with Sam that reinforced the verses that they had already looked at. Jim and Sam spent quite a while discussing other Biblical principles, until Jim realized that it was dark outside and he was late getting home.

"What do you think about going to Taylor's Woods. We could do some listening for turkeys and maybe some fishing in the morning?" Jim asked, changing the subject abruptly.

"Sounds perfect! I'll be ready about 6:00. I'm sure Dad will let us borrow the farm truck and I'll pick you up," Sam responded.

With a parting "high-five," both boys slipped out into the cool night air, headed for their respective homes.

All of the way home, Jim was virtually walking on air with the joy he felt over Sam's decision. It had been his prayer, but he had not expected God to work so quickly. Then again, God is God and He works on His own timetable and agenda whether we understand it or not. Jim was still ecstatic when he got to the yard, but was somewhat disappointed when his father's truck was not home. Now he could not share the good news with him. Jim made his way into the house and found a note on the table. He determined that he would stay up until his father returned from the Rogers' house, even though he needed to get some rest before his trip to Taylor's Woods the following morning.

Mr. Rogers met the pastor at the door and eagerly invited him in. "Have you had supper?" He asked.

"Oh, yes. I am still eating on those plates full of food that you sent home with us a couple of days ago," Pastor Flagstone replied as he made his way into the living room.

Mrs. Rogers was already seated there. Mr. Rogers came in and sat down beside her. Pastor Flagstone sat down in the old wooden rocking chair across the room.

Mrs. Rogers started the conversation by saying, "The funeral home said that they would be ready for the service on Sunday if we wanted to do it then. What do you think?"

"I have been doing a considerable amount of thinking about this funeral. First, I would like to run some things by you," the reverend began. "I think that Sunday would be a wonderful day to hold the service. In fact, I was wondering what you thought about having the actual funeral service at 11:00 a.m. in place of our standard service. Here is my thinking. If we have a standard worship service at 11:00, with a funeral planned for 2:00 p.m., everyone will have their mind on what happened and the upcoming funeral. If we would have the service at eleven, we could go right ahead and get to business. Numerous people have indicated that they were planning to attend our church service this Sunday anyway. Secondly, I would truly love to make this service a celebration of Dustin's faith and use that as a springboard into a salvation message. There will be a number of non-Christians in the service and I believe that God has laid it on my heart to use this untimely death as an example of always being ready to meet your Creator," Pastor Flagstone concluded and then waited for a response.

"I could not agree more," Mrs. Rogers said. "We have talked about what benefit could come from this and the only thing that we could think of was that Dustin's death could serve as a wake-up call. If someone gets saved because of this, it will help lessen the pain."

Mr. Rogers chimed in, "We were also discussing how awkward a standard worship service would be with a funeral service afterwards. I believe that having the service at 11:00 is perfect."

The three adults discussed various other details and then retired to the kitchen to eat some cake. Following that, Pastor Flagstone had a prayer with the family asking for God's comfort on them and that He would see fit to prick the heart of the lost through this situation that they would be saved. A hearty chorus of "amen" closed the prayer and Pastor Flagstone excused himself, making his way home.

Jim was standing at the door when his father came in. In fact, it somewhat startled him. Jim did not normally meet him at the door.

"Hey, son. What's up?" Pastor Flagstone said.

"Sam and I were working at the chicken houses this afternoon and Sam started asking me questions. One thing led to another and Sam got saved! He finally understood. It was like a light came on. We talked for a long time. That is why I was late getting home," Jim blurted out, still very much excited by this decision.

"Praise the Lord!" exclaimed Pastor Flagstone as he reached out and hugged his exuberant son.

"I am convinced that he came around and saw the light because of Dustin's death," Jim offered.

They sat up for a while talking about Jim's conversation with Sam and the funeral arrangements on Sunday. Finally, both agreed that it was past time for going to bed, so they called it a night.

Jim's alarm clock went off at 5:45 a.m. The annoying racket eventually cleared the cobwebs enough that he rolled onto the edge of the bed and sat up. However, he wondered if it would be worth it. The adrenaline rush from last night's events had carried with it a physical energy drain that was correspondingly low. Jim was there.

He made himself get up and get dressed. He had gathered his fishing gear last night as well as a cooler for any fish they might catch. He was certainly glad because he would have surely forgotten something critical if he had waited until this morning to get it all together.

By the time he reached the living room, he saw the headlights from Sam's truck turning into the driveway. Jim slipped on his camouflage jacket, grabbed his possessions, and slipped out into the chilly morning air. After placing his things in the back of the pickup, Jim slipped into the cab.

Sam looked over at Jim and said, "I did not want to get up this morning. I feel absolutely wrung out."

Jim nodded and replied, "I know what you mean. I did not know that I could be this exhausted after just waking up."

Sam turned the truck toward Taylor's Woods and the remainder of the fairly short trip passed with very little conversation until they arrived at the location of their deer camp. Sam stopped the truck and got out. Jim joined him. They stood for almost a minute and stared at the ring of stones that had encircled their campfire. Neither boy said anything, but both of them were reflecting on that trip and contemplating future hunts without Dustin. It simply would never be the same.

Sam looked at Jim and mumbled, "Let's go fishing."

Neither one of them foresaw how difficult that stop would be. Without further delay, they resumed their journey on down to the river and found a place to park.

"I think I am going to work my way downstream to the next riffle and try to catch some *Brownies*," said Jim.

"Sounds like a good plan. I'll go with you," Sam declared.

The two boys slipped on their knee-high rubber boots and started walking, occasionally easing over to the water and making a few casts where the vegetation was sparse. Much like the deer hunt, this trip was more about fishing and being out in nature than actually catching something. Consequently, they had a wonderful time together walking and talking.

Chapter 29

Sunday morning arrived with overcast skies and a fifty-percent chance of rain. Pastor Flagstone slept fitfully, when at all. When daylight began to illuminate his bedroom, he decided to go ahead and get up. He had spent most of Saturday preparing for the service, but now that the time was nearly at hand, he felt so unprepared and inadequate to present the message that was burning on his heart. Kneeling at the foot of his bed, he began to pray for strength, wisdom, and courage. It would undoubtedly be the most difficult funeral that he had ever officiated.

Eventually, the sound of footsteps in the hall told him that Jim was up, so the reverend concluded his prayer time, slipped on his bathrobe, and walked to the kitchen. Jim was sitting at the table eating a large bowl of cereal. The reverend took a bowl from the dish-drainer and sat down, too.

"Good morning, son," he said, quietly. "How did you sleep?"

"I can't be sure that I ever got to sleep, except that the night passed fairly quickly. I am sure that is the least restful night I have ever had," Jim replied. His voice clearly exhibited the fatigue that he was feeling. "That's two nights in a row."

Mr. Flagstone poured himself a bowl of sugar-coated cereal, a meal he only partook of when he needed a morning energy boost. "I can sympathize. I got no rest out of my sleep either. Good thing we have this turbo-charged cereal to get us going," he said with a wry smile.

Jim looked up from his dwindling bowl to see that his father was clearly trying to lighten the mood. Jim returned the smile and dug back into his bowl to chase down the last few morsels. Finally, he drank the remaining sugar-laced milk from the bowl.

"Dad, is there anything that I can do to help at the service today?" Jim asked.

"I don't think so, unless you would like to say a few words about Dustin." Mr. Flagstone stopped eating and waited for a response.

"I have been thinking about that. I would love to, but I know that I could not hold it together. I think I will just keep quiet. I will probably just be there to comfort Sarah," Jim said without thinking how it sounded.

A fleeting image of a young man looking for every opportunity to nurture his relationship with his girlfriend zipped through his mind. Mr. Flagstone chuckled quietly. He knew that was not what Jim intended, but he was also aware that Jim and Sarah were becoming inseparable.

Jim ignored his father's snicker, figuring that it was best that he not know what he was laughing at. Jim rinsed his empty bowl with water and placed it in the sink. When his father indicated that he did not want a refill, Jim put the milk back in the refrigerator and the cereal box back in the pantry before returning to his room to get dressed for church.

Pastor Flagstone quietly finished his cereal and placed his rinsed bowl in the sink beside Jim's. He tightened the belt on his robe and made his way to his own room to get dressed as well.

Jim drove the truck to church while Pastor Flagstone made one last scan of his notes. They had arrived somewhat earlier than normal in expectation of others arriving early as well. However, there were no other cars on the gravel lot. Jim got out and walked up to the front door. The drab gray skies were certainly reflective of his mood. He unlocked the door and proceeded to turn on all of the lights. The door opened again and Pastor Flagstone slipped inside, made his way to his office and closed the door behind him.

After opening the church building, Jim made his way outside once again. The cemetery was located right beside the church, so Jim walked over into it. There was no fancy fence or mausoleums. It was simply a well-manicured section of lawn with about forty headstones of different sizes and shapes.

A large pile of fresh earth rested beside a large rectangular hole. A piece of green carpet covered the dirt, simulating grass. A small canopy covered the grave and ten ordinary folding chairs that were set up there. Jim looked into the hole but it was so dark under the canopy that he could not discern anything specific.

The sound of crunching gravel disturbed his concentration. He turned to see a long, black hearse backing up toward the front door. Jim made one more glance into the hole as if expecting to see something amazing, then turned and started toward the hearse.

The funeral director and his assistant were sliding Dustin's casket onto a gurney. The church had installed a wheelchair ramp on one of the two front doors several years ago. The old wood-frame church was built long before anyone thought about making public facilities handicap accessible. Today, the ramp was certainly earning its keep. He and his father had built the ramp out of scrap lumber and some plywood. The weight of the casket was sure to be an acid test of their craftsmanship.

Despite the creaks and groans from the bowing wood, the load was successfully delivered inside the sanctuary. Jim breathed a sigh of relief, as did the funeral director. Dustin was wheeled down to the front of the church and positioned exactly where the communion table normally sat. A second vehicle arrived. The driver began to unload many baskets and floral arrangements. The church immediately brightened and took on the wonderful smell of spring. He had never noticed how dull the sanctuary was before, but the flowers had truly transformed the somber room into an atmosphere of celebration.

With the commotion in the sanctuary, Pastor Flagstone decided it was time to leave the solitude of his office. He was relieved to see that the casket had been delivered along with so many beautiful flowers. The reverend and the funeral director sat down on the front row and began to go over the basic program of the service. With no major changes, they both agreed that the order of service looked feasible as well as focused on its mission.

While the director and the preacher discussed the service, the driver of the hearse had slipped out and moved the car away from the door. It had been decided that the casket would be carried from the church to the grave without using the car.

It was barely after 10:00 and people were beginning to arrive. Pastor Flagstone made his way to the vestibule and stood by the front door, greeting people as they came in. Jim made his way down to his usual pew and settled in.

Sarah and her parents and grandparents all arrived about 10:30. She made her way towards Jim and eased in beside him. The remainder of the adult-aged Jacksons settled several rows behind her. Jim placed his arm on the back of the pew and gave her a comforting hug. The Perkins family arrived next and sat in front of the Jacksons, but Bill came down and sat beside Sarah.

A general din of hushed conversation filled the sanctuary as the room began to fill. Most of those who were present were members, but many new faces dotted the crowd. Jim had heard someone say that Dustin's parents were out in the lobby visiting with everyone who entered. A reserved sign on the front row was undoubtedly holding them a place.

Jim, Sarah, and Bill were leaned forward talking, when someone slipped in and sat down beside Jim. Jim turned and looked directly into Sam's face. As glad as he was to see Sam, it was an even bigger thrill to see both of his parents. Sam had said that he was going to bring them to the funeral, but Jim wondered.

The Jeffersons sat down right behind Sam and Jim because it was just about the last seats left without sitting on the front row with Dustin's family. Jim greeted the Jeffersons warmly. It was not an act. He was truly thrilled to see them there.

In a moment, Pastor Flagstone made his way to the pulpit and said, "Would you please stand."

As the congregation stood, the funeral director escorted Mrs. Rogers to her seat followed by Mr. Rogers and Tim. After they sat down, Pastor Flagstone directed everyone else to sit down, too.

Pastor Flagstone then opened a hymnal and said, "I have asked the music teacher from the school to play the piano for us today and she has graciously agreed. As most if not all of you know, we have decided to combine our Sunday morning worship service with a 'home-going celebration' for Dustin. Although our hearts are certainly heavy with the loss of this fine young man, there is also a sense of joy knowing that he was a child of the King. Someday we will be reunited with him for eternity in heaven. So, having said all that, I would like to start this service by singing a few hymns. Take your hymnal and turned to page thirty-five. Let's sing 'When the Roll is Called up Yonder.'"

The majority of the congregation seemed somewhat confused by the merger of what traditionally would have been two services. However, they gladly accepted the concept of the service being a celebration.

After three stanzas of "When the Roll is Called Up Yonder" were finished, Pastor Flagstone announced the next song. "Turn to page thirty-three and let's sing 'When We All Get to Heaven.'" As usual, the singing got better the longer everyone sang. "Now turn to page 107, 'Blessed Assurance' and that will be followed by 'It Is Well With My Soul' on page 108."

At the conclusion of the last song, the reverend closed the song book and said, "Some of you know the origin of this last song, but I am going to share it with you again. The author sent his wife and daughters on a ship from Europe to America. He was delayed and decided to take a later ship. While enroute, the ship with his family on it sank and they all drowned. He got the news while on his way across the ocean. In his utter sorrow and despair, he sat down and wrote the words of this song. They include 'when sorrow like sea billows roll – whatever my lot, Thou hast taught me to say, it is well, it is well with my soul.'

"How could he write such profound words in the face of such devastating loss? Because he knew that he and his whole family were Christians and that they would be reunited some day. Today, we are here to celebrate the short life of Dustin Rogers. He was among us for seventeen years, but God saw fit to take him home. We grieve the loss, but the comfort of God has reassured those of us who have a personal relationship with Him that it is only for a short time."

Pastor Flagstone spent about twenty minutes telling everyone that it is "appointed once for every man to die – then the judgment." He also said that if anyone has not accepted Jesus' sinless sacrifice of His own life on the cross, then that person has condemned himself to eternal separation from God in a place that the Bible calls the "Lake of Fire."

The preacher kept pointing out that Dustin had accepted Jesus as his Savior. Then he would repeat the point that "Jesus is the way, the truth and the life and no man comes unto the Father except through Him." As he concluded, he made a fervent plea that anyone who wanted to could be saved today.

Jim glanced over his shoulder to get a look at the Jeffersons. They were visibly moved by the aggressive message and repeated plea to be saved, but when the brief invitation time was given they did not move. However, three teens from the school came forward and accepted Christ as their personal savior.

As the service was concluded, the formal viewing time was allowed after the casket was opened. As Jim, Sarah, Bill, and Sam stood there looking at the body of their friend, Bill placed a hockey puck inside the casket. Sam placed an empty shotgun shell and piece of tanned deer hide from Dustin's first deer. They each said goodbye in their own way, but the bond that they had was unshakable.

As the congregation filed out, they reassembled in the cemetery. After the family passed by and said farewell, the director closed and locked the lid. Jim, Sam, and Bill along with three other fellows from school had agreed to be pall bearers. With everyone else outside, the director wheeled the casket to the side door nearest the cemetery. The six boys lifted it off the gurney and made their way down the steps, across the yard, and to the grave.

Pastor Flagstone said a prayer for the family and those who were grieving the loss. He asked God to comfort and heal the hurt. As he concluded, a hole in the clouds opened up directly above them and the warm rays of a spring sun began to shine down on those assembled there. It was as if God Himself had sent a sign down to that sad place and said "fear not for I am with you, and I have all things in the palm of my hand."

The graveside service passed quickly and the crowd mingled for a while but soon made their way to their cars and returned home. The funeral director and his assistant lowered the casket into the ground, gathered up the chairs and canopy, then called for the backhoe to come fill in the hole. By 1:00 in the afternoon, the grave was filled and the flowers had been arranged over the fresh soil.

The service was over, but the ripples were still spreading across the community.

Chapter 30

Monday morning broke bright and clear. The events of the previous several days seemed like a very bad dream. By all evidence, it would be an absolutely gorgeous day. Jim hurried down to the bus stop and found Sam standing there waiting. The telltale sound of the approaching bus could not be heard yet.

"I was wondering if I was going to have to come down there and drag you out of bed this morning," Sam said as he jokingly jabbed at his best friend.

Jim laughed and said in reply, "I finally got a good night's sleep. I have not slept worth a flip for a while. You probably think that it's related to the stress and strain of everything that has been going on. I've decided that it's not. The problem is that the nights were too short. I am hoping to take a nap during study hall to make up the difference."

"You're pitiful!" Sam exclaimed shaking his head in exaggerated mock disbelief.

Jim just laughed. It felt good to laugh. Several dark days had come and gone, but Jim just felt like this was the start of a definite upturn. About that time, a turkey gobbled in the distance and the conversation instantly swung to the pending turkey season that would open the following week. However, in a few minutes, the sound of the squealing bus could be heard approaching their position.

"Sam, how many more bus rides do we have before graduation?" Jim asked out of the blue, not expecting an answer.

"Approximately sixty-seven, not counting this morning," Sam immediately replied as if he had been prompted that the question was coming.

"Approximately? sixty-seven sounds like you know exactly how many more trips we have," Jim said.

"Well, there are thirty-four more days of school and two trips per day would be sixty-eight. However, the school usually gives the seniors a couple of days off before everyone else escapes. I also had no way of knowing just how bad of a case of turkey fever I might contract next week. So with all of those variables, I figure sixty-seven is the most that we will have to endure," Sam explained as the bus squealed to a stop. "The real question should be whether those brakes will hold together for sixty-seven more trips!" Sam added with a chuckle.

The last crack hit Jim funny. He was laughing so hard that he had trouble getting on the bus. When he passed Mr. Weaver, he took note of a big smile on the portly driver's face. He had also heard Sam's final crack and he too found it humorous. Mr. Weaver was glad to see the fellows back to their normal upbeat selves.

Jim started down the aisle and the sight of Sarah's smiling face simply topped off his morning. "This will indeed be an excellent day," Jim thought to himself.

Sam grabbed a seat across the aisle from Sarah while Jim slipped in beside her. When they were seated, the bus began to roll toward its next stop. Sarah inquired as to what Jim and Sam were laughing about when they boarded the bus.

Sam went through the rationale regarding the bus rides and Jim added the crack about the brakes. Sarah smiled widely but did not find it nearly as funny as they did. She realized that she only had sixty-seven more bus rides sitting beside Jim.

Jim sensed what was going through her mind and leaned over and whispered in her ear, "Maybe you won't have to ride the bus at all next year."

Sarah whipped her head around to look squarely into Jim eyes. There was a mischievous twinkle that she had rarely seen, but she knew that there was something profound hidden in his words. Her mind raced. "What could he be hinting at?" She vowed to get him alone and find out what he had on his mind, because the suspense was killing her.

The bus bounced and swerved through the mountains making the usual noise and the same regular stops. When it pulled up to the highway, there stood Bill and the twins. They piled onto the bus and quickly found a seat. Bill slipped in beside Sam. No one was surprised that Tim was not present.

"Good morning, Bill," Jim said in a tone that was so bubbly that it surprised Bill.

"My goodness, you're chipper this morning," Bill said in a voice that sounded half asleep.

"Yes, I suppose I am," Jim declared. "I have made a decision that life is meant to be enjoyed and my first thing to enjoy is that I have one less bus ride than I did an hour ago!"

Sam looked at Bill and shrugged his shoulders as if to say "I don't know what has gotten into him."

Jim just laughed and gave Sarah a light slap on her knee. She was speechless. She was seeing a side of Jim that she did not know existed. She thought he was quiet and reserved, but this morning he was apt to say or do anything. She was not unhappy with his demeanor, just surprised.

The bus wheeled into the school yard and eased to a stop. When the door opened, almost everyone stood and began to file off. Sarah and Jim remained seated because she wanted Jim to lag behind so they could talk.

Sam looked back to see if Jim was coming and realized that he would be along later.

"I'll see you guys at class," Jim said as Sam and Bill went down the steps onto the gravel lot. When most of the bus was empty, Jim and Sarah stood and made their way to the front also.

Once out of the bus and somewhat separated from the other students, Sarah stepped around in front of Jim and said, "What did you mean about not riding the bus next year?"

Jim grinned from ear to ear and said, "I have been thinking that I don't want our relationship to end when I get out of school. Do you?"

Sarah stopped walking backward, blocking Jim's path and answered him saying, "Absolutely not. I want us to be – be – oh, you know – boyfriend and girlfriend even if you aren't in school."

"That is what I want, too. The way I figure it, I am going to have to get a job, but when I do, I will have a car. If it works out right, I was hoping to drive you to school on my way to work. It will just depend on what kind of job I can get and the hours. But that is what I would love to do. Otherwise, I will only get to see you on Sunday and on a few evenings. I don't think that would be satisfactory for either of us," Jim concluded.

The gears were really turning as Sarah spun around and resumed her journey to class. Jim walked beside her all the way to her class before continuing on to his own. Despite his exceptionally good mood, he still wasn't looking forward to class.

When the final bell rang, Jim made his way to the place where he and Sarah had designated to rendezvous for the walk to the bus. Another long day at school had finally come to an end. Sarah was, as usual, the first to arrive. They did not talk too much as they walked; they just enjoyed each other's company. Sam was walking just ahead of them, so they stepped up the pace to catch him.

"We need to go camping this weekend, Sam," Jim said as they caught up with him. "I have been thinking about asking Grandpa Jackson if we could camp out there on Friday night. If he says, 'yes,' then we could do some turkey scouting, fishing, spelunking, and relaxing. What do you think?"

Sam face exploded with a wide-eyed smile. "That would be awesome! When are you going to ask him?"

"I have been thinking about it all day. He said that we were welcome anytime. I thought it would be good to call him this afternoon before we start gathering eggs. Sarah, is there any chance that you could stay at the farm this weekend? I know it would not be possible to actually camp with us, but you could hang out with us until bedtime, then I could run you up to the house for the night."

"That would be the best time, especially if Bill could join us," Sarah added.

"Sounds like we all agree. I will call Mr. Jackson when I get home," Jim said.

The bus ride home found the riders bubbling with hopes and plans for the future. Despite the difficulties of the past week, life had indeed gone on and would continue to do so. The pain gradually lessened and the scars eventually healed, but each of them was changed forever.

PART 3

Chapter 31

"I can't believe how much junk mail I get!" Martha Jefferson muttered under her breath as she pulled a double handful of paper from her mail slot in the office of her apartment building.

"There is no telling how much a normal stamp would cost if the post office was not being under-written by all of that junk mail postage," the manager interjected as Martha turned to leave.

Martha snickered at his comment. She was not actually mad about the mail. In reality, she was lonely and truly wanted to have a relationship with someone – someone who knew her as something other than "occupant."

"I bet you're right," she said over her shoulder. "A stamp would surely cost over a dollar because there is no way they would downsize. Oh well, can't change that mess anyway," she concluded as she hurried out the door.

Downsizing was very much on her mind. The archeology department was being threatened by the university with severe cutbacks or total closure if they did not recruit some new students. Enrollment was down to a mere handful and with the job market waning, new students were not likely to come rushing in.

Martha rounded the corner and started up the outside stairway to reach her second floor apartment. She liked living in the apartment complex because it gave her a sense of being in a tight-knit community without the pressure of actually having to interact with anyone. Most of the tenants were students at the university and since she was the senior professor of archeology, she found it awkward to even try to befriend her neighbors.

As she pulled her door key from her fanny pack, she realized she had left her cell phone at the office. While it was not a problem to be without the phone, she knew the battery would be low if not dead by morning. She made a mental note to put the charger in her pack. Besides, she had a home phone even though it rarely ever rang. As a matter of fact, the cell phone rarely rang either.

Stepping inside, the warmth of the cozy, one-bedroom facility reminded her she had forgotten to turn the thermostat down before she left that morning. "I don't know what has gotten into me lately. I am being terribly disorganized and I don't like that. Who knows when I will forget something important and get myself in real trouble," she muttered to herself.

The late afternoon sun was settling behind the ridge west of town. It had been another long day of teaching, counseling students, and trying to plan a testing project at some sites near Fayetteville. Turning on the light in the room illuminated the many piles of papers, reports, artifact catalogs, and an assortment of other documents. Looking around, she realized her home was looking more like her office every day. The idea that archeology was slowly consuming every waking moment, as well as every available inch of her life, struck her with a definite sense of urgency to find a hobby or a friend.

Tossing the door key and the unsorted pile of mail onto the kitchen cabinet, she opened the refrigerator door to inventory what might be left that had not passed into the realm of a fuzzy, green science project. Lab nights with the local archeological society chapter on the two previous nights had kept her from being home to even attempt to cook. Lunches always amounted to whatever could be grabbed at the student union as she walked between her office and class. More often than not, that fell directly into the category of "junk food" at best.

To her disappointment, the elves had not magically stocked her refrigerator while she was out. Other than a box of leftover Chinese noodles that smelled reasonably edible, there was little else to choose from. She decided to finish off the noodles. While they were warming in the microwave, she took an apple from the counter and without deliberation started biting off mouthfuls as she stared at the slowly rotating turntable that held the grease-stained take-out box.

Losing interest in watching the box do laps inside the microwave, Martha turned her attention to the mail. Most of the pile was indeed garbage that quickly landed in the trash can without even being opened. However, one envelope caught her eye. While she did not recognize the return address, it was hand addressed specifically to her. She slipped it into the hip pocket of her size-ten jeans as she refocused her attention on the apple and the rapidly heating food.

In a moment the oven signaled that the allotted time had expired. She opened the door and could tell she had overheated the noodles. Carefully pulling the box out of the oven, she dumped the contents on a plate. "There was no need to eat out of the box," she thought. "I need to wash a few dishes anyway."

With the apple almost completely consumed, she took the plate and a glass of iced tea and returned to the living room where she settled onto the couch. Martha thought about watching the news but just could not bring herself to hear the same old stories of war, murder, and mayhem. If she wanted to know what the weather forecast was, she would go to the Internet. Rather than picking up the television remote, she grabbed the stereo remote and turned on some relaxing music. As the chaos of the day began to melt away, the small pile of noodles slowly filled her stomach in a warm and satisfying way as well. Before long, Martha drifted off to sleep.

It seemed to have only been a few minutes but when she opened her eyes and fixed her gaze on the clock across the room, it was almost 10:00 p.m. The stereo was still on but the easy listening music that had lulled her to sleep had been replaced by two sports enthusiasts arguing about the best strategy for a successful football team. Martha was not the least bit interested in football or listening to them debate endlessly about it. She finally located the remote, wedged between the cushions of the couch, and turned the racket off.

"That was a good nap. I knew I was tired."

Martha got up and carried the empty plate and apple core into the kitchen. As she dropped the core into the trash she saw the junk mail which reminded her of the letter in her back pocket.

Tearing the end of the envelope carefully, she slipped the letter out. Among other things, it read:

> *Attention graduates of Huntsville High School:*
> *It has been twenty years since graduation and it is time to reunite for a grand celebration of that most important of all milestones. The class reunion will be held on the first Saturday in June of next year at the High School gymnasium. Bring your spouse and children because this will be a family event.*

The letter went on to describe the various events that were planned and numerous other details. For a few minutes, Martha studied the letter and then dropped it in the trash, too.

"High School was not a milestone – it was a prison sentence. I did not enjoy it while I was there and the last thing I want to do is socialize with a bunch of people that I don't care to see." Martha was fully awake now as she fumed momentarily and relived the less-than-pleasant experiences of high school. The idea that she would have any interest in spending time with those long-forgotten acquaintances just further agitated her.

"I have work to do," she said as she began to fill the sink with hot water. Washing the few dishes that were lying in the sink helped calm her down, but mostly it just distracted her because some of the dishes should have been washed three days ago. The food that was stuck on them was now quite stubborn.

With the kitchen cleaned up, Martha returned to the couch where she picked up a recent archeological research journal. Thumbing through it, she settled on an article by an archeologist in Missouri describing the findings from a cave near the state line. As she read, the author described various styles of stone artifacts that had been found and postulated as to the perceived function of each one. Some of the theories were backed up with replication experiments while others seemed to stem from basic intuition.

Martha liked to use a pink highlighter to emblazon key passages. With pen in hand, she marked several key statements and then flagged the top of the page with a small "sticky note" to denote that she had marked something of particular interest or importance. A quick glance at the bookshelf easily revealed which books had been read and which ones had not.

With the article thoroughly dissected, she placed the journal back on the coffee table and headed for the bathroom where she brushed her teeth and washed her face. She glanced into the mirror, briefly thinking about those times when she would comb her long, black hair before retiring. Since her impetuous decision to get her hair cut short in anticipation of the previous summer's hectic dig schedule, it still surprised her when she saw herself in the mirror. The flowing mane that had covered her head since childhood was reduced to a fraction of its former length which barely reached her shirt collar. It was easier to take care of, but it still did not feel right.

With hygiene duties completed, Martha locked the outside door and turned out the living room lights. She had no classes to teach the following day, so she made a mental note of the various things she wanted to accomplish when morning came. Even though the temperature in the apartment was slightly cooler than most people preferred, Martha turned on the ceiling fan. The gray-noise not only drowned out the random racket outside, but the hum of the motor was better than a sleeping pill. Soon, the steady cadence of her breathing confirmed that another night of rest had successfully begun.

Chapter 32

Jim Flagstone and Sam Jefferson were sitting in their patrol car watching a long section of College Avenue. Numerous businesses located along that portion of the street were closed for the night. However, with thousands of college students in town and several bars as well as the movie theater catering to the late night crowd, vehicle traffic on the five-lane thoroughfare was always present. Jim positioned the car where he could be easily seen. It reduced the number of speeders without having to do much.

"We need to go fishing one more time before the weather turns off cold and the fish quit biting," Jim said.

"I don't think Tammy has any plans this weekend," Sam responded. "Where do you want to go?"

"I was thinking about going out to Beaver Lake, but with the temperature dropping so much at night, I am afraid the water temperature may already be falling. I was thinking about going to the Kings River and floating from the Marble Bridge down to our deer camp in the wildlife management area," Jim suggested.

Sam pondered the idea for a few moments, and with a slow, positive nod, agreed with a contemplative, "Yeah, that would be fun and we could get a look at the deer woods, too."

While they sat and discussed the finer details of the plan, a little red sports car came zipping down the street. It was clearly exceeding the speed limit of forty miles per hour by at least twenty more. Sam aimed the radar gun at the car and clocked it at 64 mph.

Jim started the cruiser and Sam hit the blue lights. By the time they got onto the road, the peppy little sports car had already topped the hill and vanished. Jim accelerated rapidly and within a matter of seconds also topped the hill. Fayetteville was not known for being a focal point of major crime. It was a small city that took great pride in its wholesome atmosphere surrounding a multitude of people that were connected in one way or another with the intellectual pursuits of higher education. Crime was almost always centered on college high-jinx and underaged drinking.

As Jim assessed the traffic, he spotted the suspect a short distance ahead and knew he could catch up easily. After 10 years on the job, Jim knew the routine. He would drop in behind the car, they would pull over, he would approach the driver and they would act surprised or heartbroken.

Sam had radioed in to report the chase, but when he returned the microphone to its proper place he said, "I'll bet you a cup of coffee it is a college girl headed back to the sorority house."

"I won't take that bet because I bet you are exactly right," Jim replied.

"Rats! I needed a cup of coffee," Sam responded.

Within a matter of seconds, the police car slipped in behind the red Mazda Miata. The right blinker came on and the car veered into the next available parking lot. Sam called in the license number and verified the registered owner as a Tiffany Weaver, age 21. There were no outstanding tickets or prior violations.

Jim stepped out of his car and cautiously approached the driver's door. Sam took the backup position. As Jim approached the car, the lightly tinted window descended to reveal the broad smile of a wide-eyed college girl. The smell of alcohol was easily detectable.

"Good evening, officer. I suppose you were wondering why I was in such a hurry, weren't you?" the driver said in a shaky but perky little voice.

Jim leaned closer and asked, "Can I see your license please?"

With a decidedly flirty wink, she said, "Aren't they on the back of the car?" She then burst into laughter and added, "I know. That's an old joke, but it is still so funny!" Without further ado, she handed him the requested driver's license.

Jim could not help but smile. This girl appeared to be very drunk. Even though he never thought drunks were funny, he was always amazed at just how badly drunks will embarrass themselves and damage their reputation in the name of fun.

The name on the license matched the information received from the dispatcher. "Ms. Weaver, could you step out of the car for a moment?" Jim requested.

"Well, to be honest, no," Tiffany said almost apologetically.

"May I ask why?" Jim countered.

"It's a little bit embarrassing. I am not wearing any pants," she sheepishly admitted. Jim's sharply raised eyebrows were begging for an explanation, so she continued. "I was at the lake with some friends and one of the guys put a can of beer in the fire. In a few minutes, it exploded and sent a burning piece

196

of wood flying out of the fire. It landed in my lap and the pants I was wearing literally burst into flames. I jerked the pants down but not before the guys started pouring beer on me to put the flames out. When it was all said and done, the pants were too burned to get back on. I was so upset I ran to my car and left the party. I was trying to get home."

Jim was stunned speechless. Even if the story was a lie, it was the best speeding excuse he had ever heard. However, he had to at least try to confirm the tale. Jim leaned forward and shined his flashlight onto Tiffany's legs. She was indeed wearing no pants and the tops of her legs were badly blistered. Jim leaned back and said, "I can see you are telling me the truth but even if you were lying, that is the best excuse I have ever heard. I was just going to write you a warning even if your legs were not blistered. However, I am going to insist that you go to the hospital instead. You probably have second- and third-degree burns. You need medical attention. Please sit right here until I return."

Jim walked back to his patrol car and radioed for an ambulance. He had considered moving her to the police car but thought better of it. Having trained medical technicians to attend to her was certainly a much better plan of action.

The hospital was only a few miles away and the ambulance would be there in a matter of minutes. Tiffany had not realized how badly she was hurt, but when she saw the blisters by the light of Jim's flashlight, she quickly did. Jim and Sam walked back up to her car to find that she had fainted and was slumped over into the passenger seat. Jim could hear the sirens approach so they choose to leave her, but only after Sam reached in and checked her pulse. She was going into shock. Sam walked quickly to the trunk of his patrol car and retrieved a blanket which he then gently draped over her. It was too cool to be mostly naked and soaked in beer even if she had not been badly burned.

Paramedics soon arrived and quickly removed the limp young lady from her little car and placed her on a stretcher. Five minutes later, the ambulance was gone and it was quiet again. A wrecker was summoned and the Miata was taken to the impound yard for safe keeping.

Sam looked at Jim and said, "It is never dull hanging out with you."

Jim just smiled and hung his head as he nodded in full agreement.

Chapter 33

"Dr. Jefferson, may I speak with you privately?" Dr. Hodges asked as he stuck his head around the door frame to peer into her office.

Dr. Hodges was the Chairman of the Department. It really was not a question. It was a command for her to follow him – now.

Martha placed the technical report she was reading back on the pile of journals. She had checked out several from the library to prepare for her next research project. Since she was in her own office at her own desk, she had slipped her shoes off in an effort to get comfortable. Taking just a moment to slip them back on, she took her eyes off the doorway. When she looked up Dr. Hodges was gone.

Quickly stepping into the hall, she saw him moving toward the doorway that led to the artifact storage area. The "stacks" had once been a wing of the old library building. The museum had acquired the space and it was now crammed full of artifacts that had been collected from not only Arkansas but many other states and even a few foreign countries. Most of the artifacts were donated over the years by collectors who were seeking a tax credit or were hoping to clear their conscience because they had looted the object from an ancient grave. Past museum staff had gladly accepted the items but refrained from asking too many questions. That would generate a whole new set of issues. In their defense, most of those artifacts were accumulated during an era when digging up ancient artifacts was not as politically incorrect as it is today.

Martha joined Dr. Hodges just as he unlocked the door and flipped the light switch on. "What's up, Dr. Hodges?" she asked with a rising sense of concern over the apparent secrecy.

He did not respond. Dr. Hodges' hearing was not what it used to be. The wear and tear of time certainly seemed to be more apparent year by year.

As they wound their way deeper into the bowels of the seemingly endless rows of shelves, he eventually stopped at one in particular. Martha was now genuinely curious. 'What was in the non-descript cardboard box?' she thought to herself.

Dr. Hodges pulled the box from the shelf and placed it on the work table nearby. Lifting the lid, he revealed what appeared to be four neatly wrapped handmade torches. Without protective gloves, he declined to lift the objects from the box but turned to face her and asked, "Do you recognize these items?"

Martha leaned over the box and peered at the torches. Ever so gently, she took the ball-point pen from the pocket of her flannel work shirt and prodded at the wrapping to expose one of them a little better. "No, sir, I can't say that I do. They appear to be prehistoric torches and I see from the label on the box, they came from Madison County. Why do you ask? What's the problem?"

"According to the accession log, they were found in a cave near the Kings River by some high school students named Sarah Jackson, Jim Flagstone, and Sam Jefferson. Isn't that your brother's name?"

"Oh, yes," she exclaimed as she remembered the whole event. "I had forgotten all about those. I recall Sam telling me about them, but I never actually got to see them. Those are some very nice specimens."

"I just received a call from an individual that would like to make a financial contribution to the museum if someone would do some research on the archeology of cave use and associated symbolism in the Ozark Mountains. The benefactor asked to remain anonymous and with the size of the contribution, I gladly agreed. I can tell you that he is very well connected to the University and working on his special project would virtually seal your bid to replace me as chairperson in a few years. I know this sounds like an offer you can't refuse, but I just felt it was something that would be especially interesting to you personally as well. Will you take the project?"

Momentarily speechless, Martha just stood there. She had felt that she was certainly well-positioned to get the department chair position someday, but she had no idea Dr. Hodges thought so, too. She came to the realization she was probably standing there with her mouth open, so she blurted out, "I would love to take on the project."

"Great," Dr. Hodges exclaimed. "I will let you do some records checks and see what all there is in the way of material. Get back to me in a few days." With that, he turned and walked directly away, leaving Martha standing there over the open artifact box.

When she heard the door of the stacks close with a resounding thud that echoed through the vast expanse of historical items, she turned her attention back to the ancient torches. She did vaguely remember when Sam and the others found the torches, but she was not quite sure why Dr. Hodges had focused on them. Regardless, she decided it was as good a place as any to start.

Rummaging through the drawers of the supply cabinet, she found two thin cotton gloves. Unfortunately, they were both for a left hand. It seems that no matter how many pairs of gloves are purchased, they rarely stay paired with their respective mate. Digging deeper into a small box containing aluminum foil scraps finally produced one more glove, and as luck would have it, it fit her right hand. The color did not match either of the other two gloves but it would serve the purpose nonetheless.

Returning to the work table, she gently lifted a torch and its protective wrapping from the box placing the bundle on the table. Under the intense fluorescent light surrounding the desktop magnifying-glass/light combination, she carefully began to peel the clear, protective bubble-wrap away from the actual artifact.

The well-fashioned split-cane torch was about two inches in diameter at the base and about 12 inches long. The split river-cane staves were lashed together with cord made from what appeared to be the braided leaves of the cane itself. The cords were still tightly bound around what would have served as the handle. Peering through the magnifying glass in the center of the magnifying desk lamp, Martha could see some sort of white residue that seemed to be sticking the torch end together, but it was not clear what the substance was.

A quick look at the other torches verified that they were exactly alike in size and design but no residue was readily apparent on them. None of the torches had ever been used. Martha took a dental pick and scraped a small sample of the residue off and deposited it in a glass Petri dish. "I need to see what this white substance is," she mumbled to herself.

Rewrapping the torch, she placed it back in the container, closed the lid, and returned the box to its proper location on the shelves. After making a few notes on a piece of scrap paper, which she then stuffed into her pocket along with the pen, Martha made her way toward the exit with her sample in hand. Her mind was racing with the possibilities for research angles. It was not the direction she had been planning but it might actually prove to be more interesting in the long run and clearly a better career choice.

Upon returning to her desk, Martha rolled her desk chair over to the computer in the corner of the room. She had never really liked computers, but it was undeniable that they were excellent tools for searching obscure data. Linking to the archeological database across campus had greatly improved with the installation of new fiber-optic cables. Martha found it easier to stay focused on a specific task when she talked aloud to herself.

"Okay. Let's check to see how many *bluffshelters* and caves are recorded in just the six counties of extreme northwest Arkansas. That should cover the entire White River drainage basin including the major tributaries."

Her fingers pecked around on the keyboard with the appearance of someone with only a rudimentary skill for typing. The typing class she had in high

200

school had proven quite useful, but the lack of practice had never permitted much proficiency.

The database was quite extensive and an enormous amount of data could be searched given enough time and persistence to form the search questions properly. After some time, she was able to print out a list of the known sites which had produced perishable artifacts, including their associated accession numbers. She also produced another list of sites with prehistoric drawings on the wall, commonly called rock art.

While the search reported that there were hundreds of shelters and caves scattered throughout the region, relatively few had ever yielded baskets, clothing, or wooden artifacts. Even fewer had ever had any rock art noted.

"It will not take too long to pull together the collections that are represented by this short list of accession numbers," she commented.

"Excuse me?" Polly asked.

"Oh! I'm sorry. I was talking to myself again," Martha replied. "Dr. Hodges asked me to check on something and, unfortunately, there isn't much to work with. Thank goodness for those collections from all of those digs back in the 1930s or we would not have anything to study from those old caves and shelters."

Polly was still standing in the doorway of the office. After four years as the department secretary, she was accustomed to Martha's idiosyncrasies. However, she had a question of her own and chose to wait until Martha changed gears and focused on her instead of the new research project. If she didn't, Martha would probably never realize that she had been asked a question.

Martha rolled back over to her desk with the printout in her hand. Once squarely settled behind it, she placed the printout on the top of the pile of journals and looked at Polly once again and said sweetly, "Now, what can I help you with?"

"Every year, as you well know," Polly began, "the Archeology Department is invited to the Sociology Department's Thanksgiving potluck luncheon on the Tuesday before Thanksgiving. That's only seven days from today. Dr. Hodges always represents our department and a few others will attend as well. As always, attendance is not required. I just need to know if you are planning to go or not. If you are, what are you going to bring?" With her monologue concluded, Polly ceased her well practiced speech and waited for a reply.

"I really don't like those kinds of gatherings and I really doubt that I will make it this year either. I appreciate the invitation, though. If I change my mind, I'll let you know," Martha concluded.

"That's fine. I already had you down for a 'no' since the list had to be turned in this morning. I know you don't like those things and you have never been to one yet, but one of these days you may HAVE to go and just fake it." With a wink, Polly turned and sashayed back to her office at the end of the hall.

Polly had a point. If she was in line for the Department Chair position, she should start greasing the social skids a little better. That thought had not much more than passed her mind than a second one slipped right in behind it. Dr. Hodges said this new benefactor was well connected with the university and he might be there as well. Martha let out a long sigh and muttered, "I better go. I have no idea what to bring to a function like this. I better go talk to Polly."

Rising from her desk, Martha stepped quickly into the hall and into Polly's office where she asked, "What time is that dinner?"

Polly sat up straight and peeped over the top of the computer monitor. Her wide eyes just barely visible over the top of the monitor immediately reminded Martha of the little cartoon character that is frequently drawn with wide eyes on an egg-shaped head above a horizontal line. Martha could not help but laugh out loud.

Polly quickly leaned around the screen and the broad grin on her face reassured Martha that she had correctly interpreted "the look" and had not offended Polly by laughing at her.

"Are you really thinking about going?" Polly asked with glee.

"I think your insightful comment about HAVING to go some day for political reasons was keenly astute. I believe I should go," Martha paused for emphasis, "whether I really want to or not."

"The meal starts at 12:30 but everyone starts gathering to visit about 11:30," Polly added. "That is when the really important alliances are formed."

"What kind of dish should I prepare?" Martha sheepishly asked, hoping Polly would say it was too late to get on that list.

"Well, the secretary from the Sociology Department said there was already enough food planned for the event, but there is a need for drinks. If you could bring three or four two-liter bottles of soda, that would be wonderful," Polly replied.

The excitement in Polly's voice was so animated Martha could not help but grin. Polly's sweet nature and gentle demeanor was so sincere and unpretentious that Martha wondered if she ever had a bad day or even a bad moment for that matter.

"I would be glad to provide some drinks for this party," Martha said with a well-disguised sigh of relief.

Polly clapped her hands together and softly shouted "All right!" with a genuine joy that was so characteristic of her nature.

Martha smiled broadly and turned back into the hall, quickly returning to her office.

Chapter 34

The late model pickup truck came to a slow stop at the Marble Bridge just after the sun rose. Jim and Sam stepped out into the crisp, fall air and both paused to listen to the water tumbling over some nearby shoals on the Kings River. An ever-so-slight breeze rustled the brilliantly colored leaves that filled the forested hillsides. Blazing yellow hickory, fiery red oaks, and the seemingly misplaced majestic pine formed a mosaic that was literally breathtaking.

"I don't care if we catch any fish or not," Sam whispered. "This is the most beautiful place I have ever seen."

Jim just stood there staring at the magnificent landscape. Living in town for so many years, he had forgotten just how spectacular the view can be along the Kings River. Words would have failed to capture the awe of the moment and unnatural sounds would have only spoiled the magic.

After several minutes, Sam quietly walked to the back of the truck and began unloading the fishing gear. He had to get the fishing equipment out of the canoe so they could get the canoe out of the back of his truck. Jim soon joined Sam. They removed the 17 foot canoe from the truck bed and slid it down to the water's edge. They had already parked Jim's truck downstream at the take-out point. With Sam's truck moved to the parking area and the fishing gear loaded back into the canoe, the two life-long friends shoved off for a day of rest and relaxation.

The current was minimal as the canoe glided through the pool immediately below the bridge. They felt like there was no need to fish this first hole because it was so close to the road and received so much pressure. Surely, any remaining fish were well educated and would require far too much effort to catch. After all, one goal of the trip was to catch fish.

The pool bent gently around the corner of the mountain and the sound of the occasional vehicle crossing the bridge could not be heard at all. Soon, the only sound they could hear was rustling leaves, singing birds, and a frantically chattering squirrel somewhere up the mountainside above them.

"Do you remember this place ever being so radiant in the fall before?" Jim asked quietly. "I suppose as kids we were just oblivious to our surroundings and just how good we had it. This is the most perfect scenery on the most perfect day."

"I couldn't agree more. When we lived here, all we could think about was getting out of this one-horse town and moving to the city. Now, we are amazed at everything we left behind and do whatever it takes to come back just for a brief sanity break." Sam whispered in response, not wanting to disrupt the peaceful voyage.

"Speaking of living here," Jim began. "Have you heard from your parents lately?"

"Dad called about a week ago and said that things were going well. Apparently, they are quite happy living the retirement life in sunny Florida. After they sold the farm, they never looked back. I miss them sometimes, but it is nice to have a place to stay when Tammy and I go to Florida on vacation," Sam explained.

The pair floated leisurely along through several pools, making occasional casts, and even catching a few small fish, which were immediately released back into the crystal clear water. It was the most relaxing activity either one could have ever dreamed of.

"Do you remember those torches we found in that cave when we were kids?" Sam asked.

"I sure do. Those were some amazing items and that university fellow sure got excited about them," Jim replied. "Why?"

"Martha called yesterday. She said that she was going to start working on a new research project concerning caves and some of the really unusual artifacts that had been found in them. She said she had pulled those torches out of the storage area to look at them as part of her study. I had almost forgotten about them myself," Sam concluded.

"I don't know exactly why I remember those torches. I guess I just thought they were so rare that the event just stuck in my mind," Jim explained. "Did she say what she was going to do with the torches?"

"No, she didn't. She just mentioned that she was going to study them. She did say that she hoped to do some additional excavation in some small caves in hopes of finding some additional specimens. Most of the artifacts she intends to study were collected back in the 1930s except for our torches. I guess we really did find something rare," Sam said.

Just then, Jim made a gentle cast behind a boulder that was protruding from the surface of the water. He twitched the small, plastic grasshopper to simulate a real insect that could have fallen into the water. The tiny ripples were still emanating out from the bait when the water exploded immediately under it. A large bass had slipped from his lair in the shadows of the rock and grabbed the lure with a fervor that startled Jim and Sam.

"Whoa!" Jim yelled. "That's a nice one!"

Sam quickly reeled his line in to be sure that Jim did not have any additional obstacles to avoid. Jim was using a spinning reel on a lightweight rod with very thin line. He had to be extremely patient with this fish, which could easily snap the line. Sam kept the boat steady while Jim played the fish. After almost a minute, the fish was rendered too fatigued to resist further, and Jim gently reached into the chilly water and lifted the fish into the canoe.

"That's a very nice fish, Jim. Let me get the camera out of my tackle box and take a picture before you turn him loose," Sam said as began fumbling through the array of loose baits, plastic sacks, and snacks that cluttered the box.

"I would love to have a picture of this beauty. I bet he weighs almost five pounds. This may be the best fish that I have ever caught on this river. I know it is the best I have caught since we moved to Fayetteville."

Jim held the bronze-backed lunker up and turned it around, carefully looking at the splendid color and details of the trophy smallmouth bass.

Sam finally found the camera and lifted it to his face and said, "Smile!"

Jim smiled broadly as the shutter made the characteristic "click." With the picture taken, Jim briefly looked the fish over one last time and eased it back into the water. Releasing his firm grip from its bottom lip, the fish gave one last thrash of the tail and splashed water on Jim and Sam before vanishing into the shadows of the deep pool.

"That was fun!" Jim declared. "Let's get another one."

Sam laughed as he placed the camera back in the tackle box, picked up his fishing pole, and refocused his efforts on catching a nice fish of his own.

Chapter 35

The library at the university was not crowded on most Saturday mornings, but especially not the Saturday before Thanksgiving. Martha usually made Saturday mornings a priority when she needed some peace and quiet as well as some uninterrupted time for doing research.

Having filled her backpack with the books and periodicals related to her previous research topic, she left her apartment. The trip to the library only took a few minutes but the route required her to walk up and down several steep hills. Hauling the load left her asking herself why she kept carrying those books home in the first place.

Making her way to the check-out desk, Martha approached the clerk that always helped her. "Good morning, Dr. Jefferson," Mindy said, greeting Martha with a warm smile. "How may I help you this morning?"

"Hello, Mindy. I suppose you can help me check these books back in. I got them last week and have decided to change directions on my research. I don't need these anymore."

"That's easy enough," Mindy replied. "Set them up here on the counter and we will go through them. What is your new project, if I may ask?"

"Dr. Hodges has asked me to investigate cave usage and associated symbolism in the Ozark Mountains," Martha said. Then, as an afterthought, she asked, "Has there been any other faculty members doing that kind of literature search recently?"

"Well, I'm not really supposed to divulge this information due to patron confidentiality – but I'll look it up for you anyway." Mindy turned her attention to the monitor and pecked around on the keyboard. "It appears that Dr. Anderson in the Sociology Department has checkout out two books on the interpretation of religious symbolism on totem poles on the northwest coast of the United States. I don't see anything else recently."

"That's interesting. I should visit with Dr. Anderson. If I recall correctly, he teaches a course on religious icons and symbols." Martha pulled a small notebook from her jacket pocket and made herself a note.

Mindy happily waded through the many books and cleared Martha's account so the computer would allow her to obtain a new pile of books. With her business concluded, Martha thanked Mindy for her gracious help and made her way to the card catalog. Several computer terminals were present for searching the catalog more quickly, but numerous students, working on term papers, were already camped in front of them. That did not bother her, though. She preferred the old-fashioned system anyway.

After almost an hour, Martha had assembled a lengthy list of references and made her way upstairs to search the shelves. It was like a treasure hunt. "You often start with one target in mind," she mused, "but discover so many others in the process." Martha truly loved the library, but it was second to her love of digging.

Time passed imperceptibly in the vast silence of the book shelves on the third floor. The tendency was to be almost reverent, as if in church, when prowling through the seemingly endless rows.

As the morning wore on, more students began to arrive and the hushed, distant chatter from the lounge area began to draw Martha back to reality – namely, the reality that she was getting hungry. With a dozen books in hand, Martha walked back downstairs where she once again approached Mindy for assistance.

"Did you find everything you were searching for?" Mindy asked.

"More or less. I found most of what was on my list and several others that weren't, but that is usually what happens," Martha answered with a chuckle.

Mindy smiled and began to check out the books to Dr. Jefferson.

It occurred to Martha, as she waited, that she had fostered a fledgling friendship with Mindy. Noticing that it was almost noon, Martha asked, "Have you had lunch yet?"

Mindy stopped and looked up. "No, I haven't, but I was thinking about it."

"So was I," Martha added. "If you don't have other plans, I would be glad to buy your lunch. You are always so pleasant and helpful. I don't know if you are this sweet to everyone, but I just want to take this opportunity to show my appreciation for your wonderful assistance and great attitude."

"I would be honored. That is such a sweet gesture. Let me get these books signed out for you, grab my jacket, and we will go," Mindy responded.

Most of the people working at the library were students. Mindy was somewhat older than the average student but younger than Martha. Based on how much time Mindy spent working at the library, Martha guessed that she was a regular employee. Regardless, Martha wanted to get to know Mindy better. After all, it was the season of Thanksgiving.

Mindy indicated that she only had thirty minutes for lunch and she usually brought something from home. However, today, she had decided to splurge and go to the student union for a change.

"What are you hungry for, Mindy?" Martha asked as they entered the food court.

"I was planning to have a bowl of chili," Mindy answered. "This cool weather has put me in the mood for a hot bowl of chili, Dr. Jefferson."

Martha's initial impression of Mindy was that she was not some sort of health-food extremist. Her answer certainly provided Martha some confirmation and peace of mind because she was craving a greasy hamburger. "First thing, please call me Martha. I don't really get into that formality thing. Secondly, you sound like my kind of person. You eat normal food."

They got their meals and selected a table overlooking the football stadium. Conversation bounced all over the map. They discussed family, hometowns, pets, cars, and briefly, men. It turned out that Mindy was married and had a 10 year old son. Her husband operated a bulldozer and backhoe for a local construction company. Mindy had taken the job at the library because she really liked books and it provided her with some financial assistance when the weather did not allow her husband to work, but mostly for the health insurance.

The thirty minutes passed far too quickly, but Mindy knew she had to return to work. She thanked Martha for a wonderful lunch and for the kindness she had shown her. Promising to do it again soon, they hugged, and then Mindy headed for the door. Martha gathered the two trays and discarded the trash before making her way outside.

It had been a long time since she had felt so warm inside. Thanksgiving time had never been especially meaningful, but today it took on a tangible attribute that would last far beyond the season.

Chapter 36

Martha had no classes on the Tuesday before Thanksgiving, so rather than going to her office she opted to drive to the store and pick up the promised soft drinks for the potluck lunch at the Sociology Department. She needed a few groceries anyway.

Steering her twenty year old Toyota pickup into a parking space midway across the lot, Martha got out and walked to the store. She liked the little truck because it was economical and still reasonably dependable. However, the maroon color was quite hot in the summer, especially since the air conditioner did not work. Martha debated with herself regularly about either fixing the air conditioner or painting the truck. Spending scarce cash on a truck that qualified as an official antique car without the potential resale value always seemed to justify doing neither one. The repair cost would likely exceed the cash value of the vehicle, anyway.

The crowd was fairly light even though it was early in the morning, but there were still more shoppers than normal because of the rapidly approaching holiday. Martha grabbed the first shopping cart that she saw and was pleased when all four wheels rolled smoothly – in the same direction. In about twenty minutes, she had gathered everything on her list, checked out, and returned to her vehicle.

Once home, she put the personal grocery items in their appropriate places then placed the four heavy soda bottles into a backpack. Just before she got to the door, she noticed that the light on her answering machine was blinking. Pausing, she pressed the "play" button.

"Hey, sis! It's Sam. I was just calling to be sure that you knew that you were welcome for Thanksgiving dinner at my house on Thursday night. Tammy said that she hadn't talked to you in a while and we were hoping that you could drop by. We'll be eating our traditional meal of deer roast and corn-on-the-cob, as usual. I called your office and you weren't there, so I guess you're somewhere in between. I'll see you later."

Martha smiled at the thoughtfulness of her younger brother. "That sounds like an offer I can't refuse. It will be good to just relax and do some reminiscing. I would also like to hear the story about those torches and see if there is anything that is not recorded in the files."

With that thought floating around in her mind, she grabbed her belongings and started her hike to the office. Many of the students had already left campus for the holiday break. As she approached her office, she spotted a little book with a bright green cover lying on a bench beside the sidewalk. There was no one around and curiosity got the better of her, so she picked it up.

The words "New Testament" were printed on the front. Standing beside the bench with the book in her hand she looked all around, but the absentee owner was no where in sight. Flipping through the pages, she noticed that there was also no name inside the front cover. There was no way to figure out who it belonged to and return it, so she dropped it into her shirt pocket and proceeded to her office without given it another thought.

Polly was busy making last-minute preparations for the party. When Martha rounded the corner in the hall and approached her office door, Polly said, "Good morning, Dr. Jefferson. Dr. Hodges was looking for you a few minutes ago. He said that he would be right back." Without even waiting for a reply, Polly darted back into the department office whistling as she worked.

Martha just smiled and opened the door into her cluttered little home away from home. Even though there were locks on the office doors, it was not uncommon to find that someone had been in and dropped off a parcel or some other item. Today, sitting in her chair was a large wicker basket. The woven wicker handle arching over it made the basket look like an oversize picnic basket.

Carefully approaching it, she raised the cloth to reveal that the basket was empty. Perplexed, she lifted the basket out of the chair and placed it on ever-growing pile on her desk, placed the backpack full of soda bottles on the floor and sat down.

Just then, Polly poked her head around the corner and said, "I put that basket on your chair. It belongs to the department. I thought you might want to put the soda bottles in it. Archeologists are notoriously utilitarian, but if you wanted to dress up your contribution to the potluck, you are welcome to use it. It is strictly up to you." As quickly as she appeared, she was gone again.

"Thank you," Martha yelled as the frantic secretary dashed back to her office to answer the phone.

Martha looked at the basket and then at the backpack. Polly was probably right. The basket would certainly make a better impression than her tattered field backpack. All of the sudden Martha felt somewhat self-conscious about her own appearance. Jeans and a work shirt had been her official attire since her days as a student. Amongst her peers, it was not unusual or unacceptable. Removing the bottles from the pack, she placed them into the basket and, using the provided cloth, she dressed up the contents as best she could. With a personal flash of creativity, she retrieved two candles, each about the size of a

12 ounce soda can, from the nearby shelf and placed them in the basket as well. Neither candle had ever been lit. They were gifts from former students.

"That will add a little color to this old basket," she thought. "It still needs something, though." Opening her desk drawer, she removed a roll of fluorescent orange flagging tape that she normally used to mark key features on sites. Pulling a long piece from the roll, she began to wrap the apex of the handle of the basket. With that step complete, she finally worked the remaining piece of the orange tape into a large and rather well-formed bow.

"That should be sufficient," Martha whispered softly to herself.

When she looked up, Dr. Hodges was standing in the doorway admiring her handiwork. "You have made that old basket look quite presentable."

"Thank you, sir. Polly said you wanted to talk to me."

"I was just wondering if you had discovered anything new or interesting regarding your new research project," Dr. Hodges said as he stepped out of the hall and into the tiny office.

"I have been doing some reading on religious symbolism of Native Americans and while there is some work on the subject, it is not extensive. I think this is going to be a very interesting project and I would like to involve someone from the Sociology Department to partner with me on it. I think there will be some definite needs for their perspective and even some Cultural Anthropology expertise by looking into some ethnographic studies of indigenous people with stone-age technology," Martha concluded.

They discussed the matter intensely for several minutes before Martha added, "I hope to discuss the matter briefly with Dr. Anderson during lunch today."

"That is a splendid idea. I believe that he is exactly who you could team up with to make this project an amazing success," Dr. Hodges said in conclusion as he turned toward the door once again.

"Dr. Hodges, I have one more question. Can you tell me who this mysterious benefactor is? I promise I won't reveal his identity," Martha assured him.

"Oh, certainly! His name is Ted Wilson. He is a past graduate of the school and has a very successful international trading company. He lives north of town on a large tract of land that he calls a farm. I think the only thing he grows is weeds and wildlife. It is a beautiful place. You will certainly want to go visit with him and be sure that your research is on target for his expectations. I will get his address and phone number." Dr. Hodges stepped back out into the hall and disappeared from view as he strolled toward his own office.

In a few minutes he returned and handed the contact information to Martha and said, "I got an email from him yesterday. He said that he will be back from a business trip today and will be home through the coming weekend. He also said that he had plans to do some hunting and just relax, as well as putter around his farm."

Martha listened as she looked at the slip of paper, then she said, "Does he live alone?" Martha asked the question just to get a feel for this fellow's attitude toward visitors since he will only be home a few days. She did not realize how the question sounded until it was too late to reword it.

Dr. Hodges smiled. "He has never been married. He's committed to his business and, according to him, never saw a need to settle down. He is a natural adventurer and believes in exploring the world and its mysteries. When he asked me about this project, I told him that you would be perfect for the challenge. You are so much like him that I know there will be great energy between the two of you that will be translated into great discoveries for science."

"Interesting," Martha mumbled as her eyes studied the information once again.

Chapter 37

Polly, Martha, and Dr. Hodges as well as a few others from the Archeology Department made their way across campus to the Sociology Building. Since the Sociology Department was quite large, they occupied an entire building. The Archeology Department, while quite popular with the students and faculty for the amazing museum displays, was small and squirreled away in the basement of the Architecture Building. The small staff felt more like family. Most of the large departments felt more like businesses. Consequently, the large departments felt obliged to have social functions to ensure that most of the staff would at least recognize each other.

One of the classrooms had been transformed into a banquet hall. The desks and other educational furniture had been lined up along one wall. Eight large tables had been set up and covered with disposable tablecloths. Six folding chairs were pushed up to each table. A small, wicker cornucopia centerpiece, complete with plastic vegetables, decorated each table. Otherwise, the room was undecorated.

Martha surveyed the room and noticed that other beverages were sitting on a table in the corner. Breaking away from the group she worked with, she made her way toward that table. Just looking at the hodgepodge of bottles and pitchers in disarray on the table, it was clear that the backpack would have been just fine. Removing the bottles from the decorated wicker basket, she placed her contribution on the table amongst the others and then slid the basket under the table.

At the front of the room, many covered dishes were arranged on the longest table. Glancing around, Martha wondered just how many people had agreed to bring food. The second thought that passed through her mind was just how many people were invited to eat all this food. She estimated that there must be enough food to feed a hundred but there were less than three dozen present.

Martha took a plastic glass, placed several ice cubes in it, and then poured herself some tea from one of the pitchers beside the soda bottles. Retreating from the growing crowd, Martha eased over to the window and starting looking out at the trees. The changing colors were vibrant. Moreover, they were a stark contrast to the lush, green grass growing beneath them. The scene was both dynamic and peaceful at the same time.

Without really looking around, Martha sensed that someone was standing behind her. The intrusion into her mental vacation initially agitated her but pasting a smile on her face, she glanced over her shoulder.

"Dr. Jefferson?" the older, gray-haired gentleman asked.

"Yes," she quietly replied.

"I am Terry Anderson. Dr. Hodges said I should introduce myself to you."

"Oh! Dr. Anderson! Yes, I was hoping to talk to you today," Martha stammered along trying to compose a coherent thought. "You caught me admiring the beautiful scenery. My office does not have a window. Well, it does, but it is a small one up near the ceiling and there is a hedge growing in front of it. My office is in the basement."

"I can appreciate that. I have an interior office. The tenured staff gets windows. I am the new guy around here even though I have been teaching for a long time," Terry explained.

Before the conversation could progress any farther, someone rang a bell and announced that it was time to eat. Instructions were made regarding the direction of the serving lines and other such trivia. Martha and Terry joined the crowd of people and made their way toward the end of the line. As they inched forward, Martha began to describe the premise of the research project that she was undertaking and how she had noticed that several of the books she needed were checked out.

Dr. Anderson listened intently and nodded thoughtfully as Martha elaborated on the project. However, before she could complete her sales pitch, they reached the point where they could start selecting from the sumptuous fare. Conversation paused momentarily, but when they selected seats across the table from each other it resumed as if it had never stopped.

"So what do you think? Would you be interested in working on this project with me?" Martha concluded.

"It sounds like exactly the kind of project that I could really get into. I would love to tackle it. I have been looking for a research project that I can sink my teeth into for a while, but nothing has really developed. This sounds awesome. We will certainly need to talk more about what you have discovered in the literature so far and then we can build on that," Terry stated excitedly.

Martha was already sure that he was interested because, although he had a plate full of food, he had barely touched it. She could see the sparkle in his eyes as the mental wheels began to spin wildly with the possibilities. Terry began to talk, so Martha decided to take the opportunity to dig in. It smelled so good. She just had to confirm that it was equally tasty.

Eventually conversation slowed and the crowd began to filter out. Martha rose from her seat and said, "I plan on doing some additional ethnographic literature searches in the main library on Sunday morning. If you would like to join me, I usually arrive around 9:00."

"I will certainly plan on it," Dr. Anderson replied.

Martha deposited her plate in the trash and retrieved the basket from under the table before leaving the room. Strolling down the hall she thought out loud, "That was a nice get-together. I will plan on attending this next year as well."

Returning to her own office, she returned the two candles to the shelf where they had sat previously. After removing the orange tape from the basket handle, she made her way into the main office and placed the basket in Polly's chair for its return to storage.

As Martha sat down at her desk, she decided it was past time to clean off her desk. For the rest of the afternoon, she sorted the various documents and papers into numerous piles. At the conclusion, not only was the top of her desk once again functional, many books and reports had been properly shelved or set aside for return to wherever they came from. It was somewhat embarrassing how long some of them had been on loan. A quick glance out the little window confirmed her suspicion: it was dark and it was time to go home.

With a sense of accomplishment, Martha picked up her backpack and a few other items that needed to be taken home and headed out. As she walked, she briefly contemplated what to fix for supper. She had eaten too much at lunch and her supper menu was definitely going to be light. The closer to home she got, the more convinced she became that an apple would be plenty. It was certainly easy.

As she climbed the stairs to her apartment, she remembered that Dr. Hodges said that Ted Wilson was coming home today. Once she got inside and kicked her shoes off, she quickly flipped through the mail, and then took the phone to the couch.

Taking a few minutes to organize her thoughts, she finally dialed Ted's number. On the fourth ring, the answering machine picked up and said, "Hey! You have reached Ted Wilson – well actually, you got his handy answering machine because I can't get to the phone right now. Please leave me a message and a number where I can call you back. Beeeeeeeeeeeeeeeeeeeeeeep."

The length of the tone assured Martha that Ted was not home yet or he had not checked his messages. Either way, she launched into her speech. "Hello,

Mr. Wilson. I am Dr. Martha Jefferson from the University. I am an associate of Dr. Hodges. He has given me the opportunity to work on a research project that you are helping to fund."

Before she could finish, a voice boomed through the receiver, "Hey, Dr. Jefferson! Sorry I didn't get to the phone before that stupid machine picked up. I was outside looking at the stars and just could not get to it any quicker. I promise, I was not screening my calls," Ted rattled off breathlessly as if he really had been running to get to the phone. "I should remember to just stick the phone in my pocket when I am laying in the grass at night watching for falling stars. Do you ever lie out in the grass at night and just look at the stars? It is so peaceful. I hope to go into space someday. The price tag is too steep for me to even think about it but laying in the yard is cheap. I usually pick a spot that is pretty lush because I don't want to lie down on a big anthill. I'm glad we don't have fire ants here. That would certainly ruin a great night of star-gazing."

Martha was sitting on the couch. Her mouth was open. Her mind was reeling. She had no idea what to say and silence ruled the moment.

"Dr. Jefferson? Are you still there?" Ted asked cautiously.

Regaining her composure, she said with as much diplomacy as she could muster, "Yes. I was just thinking about, uh, stars and ants. Those are two extreme topics to be pondered in the same breath."

Ted burst into laughter. He was laughing so hard that he finally laid the phone down on the counter. After what seemed like several minutes, he was able to speak. "I love your quick wit. I have got to meet you. Have you got any plans for Friday?"

Martha recalled that Dr. Hodges had described Ted as energetic and loads of fun. She also knew that she wanted to meet him to discuss the project so she said, "I am available on Friday. What time would you like to meet?"

"Why don't you come out about 1:00 in the afternoon," Ted began. "I will give you a tour of my farm. I have a place that you will probably want to investigate. It is the place that sparked my imagination to think about Indian religious symbols. I don't know what it is or what it means, but I just know it's important. Afterwards, I would be honored if you would stay and help me eat some barbecued ribs that I was planning to smoke tomorrow."

Martha was doubly intrigued. "1:00 will be great and I would love to join you for some ribs. Could I bring something to go with them?"

"No need," Ted replied. "I already have that taken care of. On my way to the house earlier today, I stopped and bought enough groceries to feed myself through the weekend. I was expecting to be eating leftovers alone for most of that time. This will be a wonderful and unexpected treat. You just bring yourself and if it's not cloudy, we will go outside and count stars after supper."

Now, it was Martha's turn to laugh. "I will come prepared."

As she hung up the phone, she realized that for many years her life had been fully wrapped up in her career, but in the last week she had really moved outside of her shell. Was she turning over a new leaf or was her well-ordered life on a collision course with a greater destiny? She was not sure, but so far, the ride was most intriguing and there was just enough adventurer in her to want to see where the following days might lead.

Chapter 38

Dinner with Sam and Tammy had indeed been a wonderful time. They had not only shared a lovely meal, they spent many hours just talking. Martha could not remember the last time she and Sam had just talked. From time to time, the conversation passed briefly through a work-related story. However, for the most part, they simply recounted tales about growing up on the family farm, antics of old friends, and memories about their beloved parents. They both missed them very much, especially during the holidays. It was almost midnight when Martha returned to her home and got to bed.

Friday morning had broken with clear, blue skies from horizon to horizon. The weatherman had promised that it was destined to be the most beautiful day of the entire fall season. After all of the rain that started falling on Wednesday afternoon and continued into Thanksgiving Day, it was certainly a welcome sight.

Martha rolled over and looked at the clock that boldly announced 9:30 a.m. Lying there reveling in the knowledge that there was no class, she let her eyes slowly close as if she had no other place to be – all day. As her mind began to focus on her plans for the day, she remembered her appointment with Ted Wilson!

Bolting from bed, she jumped into the first pair of jeans she saw, and then frantically rummaged through her tiny closet to find a shirt. Although she owned a reasonable variety of tops, almost all of them fell into the category of "work-shirt" and most showed the evidence of it. As she debated the merits of one over another, she finally sat down on the end of the bed and said, "Get a grip. This is not a date. This is more like a business meeting. Ted is like a client and I just need to make a good impression without looking too dressy or too sloppy. We are going to be wandering around his farm and then eating barbecue." Returning to the closet, she selected a red and black plaid flannel shirt. Slipping her nightshirt off and putting the flannel shirt on, she headed to the bathroom to comb her hair and get ready for the day.

Since she was not expected at Ted's until after lunch, Martha decided that there was time to prepare a late breakfast before driving her own truck over to the university's motor pool and getting her official field truck. All of the archeological field equipment that she could possibly ever need was stowed securely inside the locked camper shell on the back of her company pickup. While she thought about taking her own truck, she really liked the peace of mind of driving the official vehicle. It gave the clear message that this was official business and not a date, as some might postulate.

In college, Martha and her roommates had aggressively pursued guys. The girls had also enjoyed a certain degree of success from their efforts. Both of her friends had dropped out of school after three years, had gotten married, and started families. While part of her once longed for a loving relationship, the drive to succeed as an archeologist won.

Thoughout graduate school and until now, Martha had chosen to completely immerse herself in the science and in her career. While she had enjoyed the occasional dinner and entertainment with a male companion, no one ever sparked any deeper interest to her beyond being just a friend and someone to share an occasional dinner with. At almost forty years old, she had come to the conclusion that archeology was her silent spouse and it was a good relationship. Martha was not interested in turning her nice, neat little world upside down and she wanted to be sure that Ted did not get the wrong impression either.

After preparing and eating a couple of scrambled eggs and a slice of toast, Martha finished off brunch with an orange. She thought about making orange juice, but figured that eating the orange would be just as good in the long run, not to mention far easier.

With a couple of hours before her appointed time of arrival, Martha tried to utilize the time productively. She cleared several piles of books that had been stacked along the wall, sorted them, and placed them onto the proper shelves for easier retrieval. The coffee table, also piled with magazines and other soft-cover manuscripts, was a little more difficult to categorize. However, with a little creativity, she grouped them by subject and placed them in a drawer of the file cabinet with other similar documents.

As the clock neared noon, Martha found a stopping point in her cleaning frenzy, slipped her camouflage field jacket on, picked up her keys and backpack, and walked to her truck. The parking lot was virtually empty. Clearly everyone in the complex had gone somewhere for the holiday. Martha was glad that she had somewhere to go, as well.

The gate at the motor pool was locked because the university was officially closed. Unlocking the gate, Martha pulled her little truck into an available space and transferred her belongings to her work truck. Once she pulled that truck outside the gate, she relocked the compound.

The drive to Ted's farm would only take about thirty minutes. Martha was still a little ahead of schedule, so she decided to take the long route out to Ted's. Driving north, she noticed that many leaves had been blown off of the trees in the recent storm. While the fall colors would be considered passed their peak, many individual trees remained quite radiant.

Her chosen route took her through the countryside. Amazing economic growth in the region had subsequently caused an explosion of construction. Land that until recently had been characterized by large pastures dotted with cattle had now been crisscrossed with new roads. Beside these roads, houses, almost like weeds, had sprung up in the former fields. While the economic boon was great for the local property values and overall well-being of the community, the rampant construction of previously protected environments was erasing the archeological record at a pace that was incomprehensible. The money that was paying her salary and funding her research was the same money that was destroying the resources faster than a team of archeologists could document or preserve. It was a real paradox with disastrous consequences no matter what happened.

Martha turned into Ted's driveway a few minutes after 1:00. Being casually punctual was a point of pride with her. Immediately upon entering the property, she crossed a welded-pipe cattle guard. However, it soon became apparent that there were no cattle on the farm. Dr. Hodges had said that all Ted raised was weeds and wildlife.

The long driveway snaked along the top of the ridge and was bordered by almost a half-mile of weedy, unkempt pasture. There was no livestock of any kind and apparently, he had not even tended the fields so they could produce hay for someone else's animals. At the end of the driveway sat a modest house. While it probably had 2,000 square feet of floor space, it was obvious that it had been built as an ordinary farmhouse almost fifty years before. Two things did make her smile, though. The large front porch reminded her of her own childhood home and an old pickup truck, just like her father's old farm truck, was sitting in the front yard.

Martha pulled up beside the old truck and parked. As she stepped out, the smell of barbecued ribs on the grill greeted her warmly. Making her way up to the front door, she knocked vigorously and waited. There was no response. She knocked again, but still no response. Descending the steps, she made her way around behind the house to see if Ted was in back.

To her surprise, Ted was indeed there. The sight she beheld stopped her in her tracks. Ted was standing in front of the barbecue grill wearing a pair of Bermuda shorts, a flowery Hawaiian shirt, leather boots, and huge set of headphones that were either the remote variety or contained the radio directly in them. Ted was poking at the cooking ribs, dancing a little jig, and singing – badly.

Martha was frozen. She truly did not know whether to proceed and risk embarrassing him or slip away and come back later – much later. However, before she could do either one, Ted made a spin in his dance routine and spotted her just standing there.

"Hey! There you are! I thought it was about time for you to arrive," Ted shouted, not realizing that he was overcompensating for the loud music blaring in his ears. "Let me turn this music down," he said in a slightly more normal tone as he fumbled with the knobs on the unit before simply removing the headset altogether and laying it in a nearby chair.

Martha could not help herself. She was grinning from ear to ear – to think she had been concerned over her own appearance. "I could have worn a clown costume and this guy would not have cared," she thought to herself as she moved toward the obviously eccentric and slightly older man.

Ted jabbed the fork that he had been poking the ribs with into a particularly large slab and walked over to properly shake hands. "I am so glad you could come out today and visit. Dr. Hodges told me that you were the best. I am taking him at his word until I can prove it to myself," Ted boldly proclaimed and then finished with an exaggerated wink to show that he was just playing.

Martha, although still grinning broadly, was struggling for words. She finally blurted out, "You are one of a kind, aren't you? It is so refreshing to meet someone who is honest about his own individuality and bold in his persona. I love both of those things."

Up to that point, Ted's appearance and "show" had distracted her from any further observations of her new surroundings. However, when she looked around, she realized that the view from the rather small backyard was utterly breathtaking. Martha was once again frozen in a slow motion stare that seemed to capture hundreds of square miles of the most spectacular panoramic scenery that she could imagine.

"Quite a view, isn't it?" Ted said rather matter-of-factly. "I did not really like the house but I bought the whole farm just for this view. I have traveled most of the states in the United States and in about twenty foreign countries and I have never seen any view that I enjoy more. You should see the sunrise. This view is nothing compared to that."

The White River occupied a substantial channel far below their vantage point, but it looked like a common stream from this distance and elevation. "How much land to you own right here?" Martha asked.

"I think it is about 2,000 acres," Ted replied. "It is about a half mile to the road and it is about a mile down to the river. I have about two miles of river frontage. The pasture up here is all the cleared ground I have. The remainder is steep mountainside covered with forest. Let me turn these ribs over and I will give you a brief tour."

After shutting the grill down for a long, slow cook, Ted led Martha over to a small barn. Inside there was an old Army Jeep. Ted climbed in and started the engine. It belched and sputtered but soon settled into a steady rhythm that seemed capable of providing cross-country transportation. "Hop in, Doc."

Martha apprehensively settled into the passenger seat then Ted backed the vehicle out. He swung by Martha's truck and suggested that she get her camera, which she did. In a moment, Ted turned the Jeep downhill as he slowly let the vehicle crawl down the slope toward the river valley far below.

The route that Ted chose to travel was nothing more than a set of parallel trails from what Martha could only guess was evidence of previous journeys up and down the mountain. The only solace that she could grasp was that Ted had apparently traversed this path successfully at some time in the past. Otherwise, he would not still be alive to try it again.

Much of the slope was nearing a forty-five-degree angle and it felt like any deviation from a straight down descent would cause the antique Jeep to simply roll over. Without seatbelts, a roll bar, or even a roof, the prospects of unsuccessfully descending the mountain would certainly result in a fatal crash. Martha never took chances with her life. She had invested far too much to throw it away on a stupid thrill ride. To say the least, she was terrified.

Ted, on the other hand, seemed completely at ease. He was chattering about the rocks, the trees, the weather, and a dozen other topics. Martha simply clinched the seat and mashed her imaginary brake pedal through the floorboard.

Far below, the slope began to flatten out slightly so Ted slipped the vehicle out of first gear and into second, still allowing the engine to provide the majority of the speed control. "This old trail was an abandoned logging road when I bought the place," Ted explained. "The locals tell me that back in the 1930s they used mules to skid logs down to the river after they let the logs just slide down the hill on their own. I can't imagine how hard that was. I understand that several men as well as mules got killed in the process. I am glad this old mule is a sure-footed beast. I think it would climb a tree if I could find one big enough."

"Now it's my turn to take your word for it. Please don't prove it to me," Martha said, her voice noticeably shaken.

For the first time, Ted realized that Martha was extremely scared. "I am SO sorry. I did not prepare you for that ride. I drive down here all the time to fish in the river. I did not even think about how you might feel about it. Please accept my most sincere apology."

"I accept. It is good to know that you are quite experienced on this particular part of the tour," Martha answered, beginning to release her death-grip on the seat.

"It is an easy ride on down to the bottom. There is nothing to worry about. The trip down is much more unsettling than the trip back up. Going down, gravity has the tendency to play with you a little," Ted remarked, trying to lighten the mood.

Martha decided to stop playing the tourist and move to a different strategy. "What is down here that you want me to see, anyway?"

"While hiking along the base of the bluff, which is just above the *floodplain* of the river, I found this small cave. I went inside to look around and noticed a strange, faded red symbol painted on the wall of the cave just above the floor. Using the light that I had for cave exploring, I could tell that it had been intentionally painted there, but I could not tell what it represented. I returned several times with various types of lights but nothing would bring the image out enough to identify it. Finally, I just sat and stared at it using an ordinary candle. Then, just as plain as day, I could see a wolf track instead of just a smudge. I don't know why the better lights did not show the image as well, but they didn't. I revisited the cave from time to time and it appeared that there was nothing else painted on any of the other walls and I never found any indication that the cave had ever been used for a shelter or anything. I am just perplexed by that wolf track painted on the wall and I wanted to know more."

"That is quite a story, Mr. Wilson," Martha began. "As crazy as this little ride seemed to be, you now have my undivided interest. I would love to see this cave. In doing research into the symbolism that has been recorded in caves in this region, sadly, there isn't too much. Most of what has been recorded was described by some of the early pioneers of Ozark archeology when they were digging for museum specimens back in the 1930s. I guess those digs were going on during the same era as the logging that you mentioned a few minutes ago. If you really think about it, that was an extraordinary time in history. It is amazing to ponder the accomplishments of all of those rugged men. While many sites have been recorded, virtually no thorough analysis of the so-called 'rock-art' has ever been done."

By the time Martha finished her brief lecture, Ted had pulled the Jeep to a stop and killed the engine. "The cave is up there," Ted said, pointing up the

224

mountain. "Since you don't want to see this 'mule' climb a tree, we will have to walk."

"That is perfectly fine," Martha assured him, smiling broadly. Ted returned the improved mood with a gentle laugh of his own.

Martha stepped down from the Jeep and peered up through the recently *denuded* trees but could not see a discernible bluff, just a steep slope. Ted grabbed a backpack from the back of the Jeep. It contained a few items that he thought might be useful for helping Martha inspect the little cave, including several flashlights and a couple of candles. Before leaving the house, Martha had traded her camouflage jacket for a khaki-colored hunting vest because it provided ample pockets for transporting small things like notebooks, rulers, pencils, and a trowel as well as her camera.

The lowest slope of the mountain was slightly gentler. However, this segment quickly transitioned into a grade that required climbing on all fours and grabbing the available trees and saplings to facilitate sustained forward progress. Not much talking occurred because both were exerting most of their effort just to climb. Fortunately, the climb did not last long and they both arrived somewhat winded but unscathed.

"That is quite a climb for a fellow who's is almost fifty years old," Ted heaved. "I don't suppose that it would be quite so tough if I was not so out of shape." Then, he chuckled and sat down to rest.

Martha, still gasping for air also, nodded in agreement but finally said, "That climb is tough regardless of age or conditioning." Like Ted, she sat down and rested, too. However, she sat facing the bluff while Ted sat facing back down the hillside.

The massive limestone bluff rising above them was clearly the geologic formation they were looking for; however, no cave opening was apparent in either direction from where they now sat. Even without a visible cave, the bluff was absolutely amazing and commanded a definite sense of awe, respect and wonder.

Ted, realizing that Martha was busily studying the bluff, rose to his feet and said, "The cave is this way," as he pointed to the left of their current position.

Martha stood carefully. The ledge that they had been sitting on at the base of the bluff was only about ten feet wide. It was comprised primarily of large boulders and accumulated soil and small rocks that had fallen from the bluff long ago. Despite the extreme vertical nature both above and below them, the ledge was relatively level and provided a reasonably easy place to walk except for the occasional vine or dead limb.

As they proceeded along the base of the bluff, Martha was struck by how the view from the ledge changed dramatically for every 100 feet that they walked. Despite growing up in the mountains of north Arkansas, exploring bluffs and caves was a relatively new experience for her. Her professional expertise was exclusively rooted in the excavation and study of "open sites," a term for sites that are located in fields and forests. The geologic processes inside caves and *bluffshelters* are radically different and far more complex.

Before long, they rounded a slight bend in the bluff and a small opening came into view. The mouth of the cave was no more than fifteen feet wide and six feet high. Rather than being rounded, like many caves, the mouth was more rectangular, thus making the cave seem larger than it really was. Taking a flashlight from his pack, Ted illuminated the area well into the cave to show that the cave did extend well back into the solid rock. Based on the downward sloping ceiling and the relatively flat floor, it appeared that the cave once angled downward but had now been partially filled with rocks and sediment that had washed in over the ages. Approximately sixty feet into the cave, the floor and ceiling almost met. Crawling on their stomachs, they were able to see that the cave did indeed extend further. However, nothing larger than a rat was likely to know just how far unless some serious excavation was undertaken.

Retreating almost back to the mouth, but still well inside the moisture-free zone, Ted stopped and pointed to an irregular smudge on the wall. "There is the wolf track," he declared.

At first sight, Martha was not only unimpressed but generally skeptical that this was even genuine rock art. She started out by staring at the stain and moving the flashlight that Ted gave her slowly taking advantage of many different angles. She gently touched the possible image to see if there was a texture change. Regardless of what she tried, nothing gave her a clear answer.

Without looking back, Martha said, "Ted, you said that a candle makes the best light for seeing this. Did you bring a candle?"

When she looked back, Ted was already holding the candle and the lighter. "One step ahead of you, Doc," he said.

Martha smiled and accepted the candle as Ted lit the wick. Then, moving it over to the stain once again, she was stunned to see the clarity of the edges of the image. The pad of the wolf track was not as defined as the toes. Taking a dental pick from her tool kit, Martha very carefully scratched the edge of the stain to reveal that it was indeed a painted image applied to the solid rock wall.

"Wow!" she exclaimed softly. "That is amazing."

"I thought so," Ted agreed. "I suppose the big question is: What does it mean?"

"That is definitely the big question." Martha stepped back from the image to get a better perspective of not only the wall, but the setting that was around it. She got her tape measure out and began to take some measurements and make some notes. The rock art was far enough back into the cave that natural light was unable to provide adequate illumination for proper photography. However, Martha took a few pictures of the artwork as well as the ground immediately below it. Her instinct told her that if the image was associated with anything, it was probably directly below it.

With that thought, she began to study the arrangement of the natural rocks on the floor of the cave. In most of the cave the angular chunks of rock were turned in all sorts of ways and in no certain arrangement. However, below the wolf track, the rocks were primarily laying flat although still in no particular pattern. The difference was not profound, but quite subtle. Martha wondered if it was real or just her imagination.

Stepping to the mouth of the cave, she took several more pictures looking back into the cave. Photo-interpretation of the rock configurations could be done back at the office. She turned to Ted, who was standing patiently beside her, "This is fascinating and I think there is probably something or someone buried directly below that wolf track. I would love to come back next week and find out."

"I think that would be outstanding. If you come on Monday I would be glad to help you dig," Ted declared.

"Monday would be perfect. Let's go eat some ribs," Martha announced, slapping Ted on the shoulder.

Chapter 39

The ride back up the hill was not as scary as the descent had been. Reaching the top, Ted turned the Jeep back toward the barn, where it was normally stored. Conversation flowed as they gathered their respective possessions and started toward the backyard. The smell of barbecue filled the late afternoon air.

"I don't know about you, but I am hungry," Ted declared.

Martha's stomach had been growling for quite some time, but until now, she had not mentioned it. "I am starving. If those ribs are half as good as they smell, you may not have enough for both of us," Martha responded boldly.

Ted laughed and lifted the lid on the smoker to reveal an overly full cooker. "I am betting they are better than they smell – AND – that there is more than enough."

Martha had stepped up beside him to peer into the grill. "Wow! I think you are correct. That IS more than enough ribs for two. Were you expecting a crowd or just me?"

"Just you. However, it is just as easy to cook a rack full as it is to cook a few, and leftovers are welcomed when you are a bachelor. Cooking is not my strong suit," Ted added.

Now Martha chuckled as she added her two cents' worth, "I hate to cook for one, but when I do, I love leftovers."

Ted stepped into the house momentarily to get a platter for carrying the ribs inside. Martha was not sure what to do to help, so she just stood there and waited for instructions.

When Ted had the platter fully loaded, he turned toward the house again and said, "Let's eat. I have a limited drink selection. Would you prefer water or iced tea?"

"I would like to have a large glass of water, please. I haven't had enough water today and I am thirsty," Martha replied. "Water is the best drink for thirst."

"Water all around!" Ted exclaimed, thrusting a finger into the air as if ordering drinks in a bar. "I like the way you think."

Placing the platter on the dining room table, Ted stepped into the kitchen to fix their drinks, as well as get some plates, forks, and napkins.

Martha spotted the restroom at the end of the hall and said, "I'll be back. I need to wash my hands."

"Make yourself at home. The bathroom is at the end of the hall," Ted yelled from the kitchen, not realizing that she had already spotted it.

The little farmhouse obviously reflected the personality of its owner. There was very little furniture in the various rooms of the house, and none of it matched. Some appeared to be in fairly bad condition as far as remaining paint or varnish. Conversely, other pieces seemed brand new. Stepping into the bathroom, Martha could not help but smile. Several dog-eared hunting magazines were lying on the floor beside the toilet. The one on top was almost two years old.

After using the facilities and washing up, she returned to the dining room, where she found the table neatly set. Ted was standing at the end of the small table like a good host, waiting for her to be seated before he took his seat across from her. He had even slipped on a rather stylish nylon wind suit over his rather outrageous attire that he had worn all afternoon. In addition to the ribs, Ted had placed two individual salads on the table to attempt to nutritionally balance what would otherwise appear to be a carnivorous binge. Their iced water was served in decorative quart fruit jars adorned with fancy handles.

They talked and ate long enough that the sun had set and near total darkness had surrounded the humble little house. The conversation bounced all around but usually remained tied to "what do you think about…" as well as a wide variety of personal stories.

Ted did most of the story telling, because he had visited so many interesting places and met so many memorable people. Well after the feeding frenzy had ceased, they continued to share. Ted finally said, "I need to put these ribs in the refrigerator and clear the table. Will you please excuse me?"

"Most certainly not. I will help you," Martha asserted as she rose to assist Ted in cleaning up the dining room.

"That is so kind. I would love to have your help," Ted graciously responded.

In just a few minutes, the table was clean and the leftovers were stored. Ted turned to Martha and said, "I promised you one more treat – if you are interested?"

Martha thought for a moment, not readily recalling what else Ted had promised to do or show her, but responded with a cautious, "Okay." She felt certain that his highly honorable behavior all day was not going to suddenly deviate into some unseemly compromise of her personal values.

As he walked to the outside door, Ted said, "Grab your jacket. You are in for a treat."

Only then did Martha remember their initial conversation, where Ted said that if it were clear, he would show her what stars really look like. Without reservation, she followed him into the yard, beyond the grill, toward the crest of the hill. Ted had stopped at the grill and waited for her because it was so dark, that he was concerned that she might trip over something on the way to the best viewing location. He gently took her hand and helped her away from the house.

The farther from the house they walked, the darker it seemed to be. It was as if the darkness was a solid object and the modest lights from the house could not penetrate it. "Let's sit right here," Ted suggested as he stopped walking. "It will be dark enough here."

Squatting first to check the ground for anything she did not really want to sit on, Martha then sat down and stretched her legs out in front of her. Slowly turning her eyes to the sky above her, she soon realized that giving in and lying down was definitely the best position for stargazing.

As amazing as the view had been in the daylight of the sprawling landscape below, the night sky above was equally spectacular. Even though she had grown up in the country, they had several security lights around the farm because of the chicken houses. Those lights had masked the true magnitude of the star-filled heavens. However, tonight there were so many stars that once her eyes became adjusted, the darkness actually retreated because of the uncountable pinpoints of lights that seemed to be working together to light the sky.

"If I did not know better, I would say that you have added some extra stars just for my viewing pleasure," Martha remarked playfully.

"Well, I did not add any. However, if you had asked and it was in my power, I would certainly try," Ted timidly admitted, testing the waters to see how Martha would react. He had truly enjoyed this day. For the first time, Ted had connected with someone that he wanted to spend time with. It was crazy. They had just met, but he just knew there was something special about this woman. However, he also knew that it would be even more important for her to be interested in him and that he must not do anything stupid to scare her off.

Martha glanced over at Ted, recognizing the sincerity and vulnerability of the comment as well as the veiled affection in his tone. Martha had thought from the first funny little dance that she saw Ted do beside the grill that this fellow is one carefree spirit. That attitude definitely struck a positive chord with her. "That is sweet. Thank you," she softly replied, letting Ted know that she was open to the idea of being more than common business partners.

Ted smiled. He knew Martha was someone he could call a friend. Over his life, there had been very few guys that he would have classified as a true friend and no woman had ever penetrated his defensive perimeter. Despite all this, he knew this just felt right.

"Do you ever wonder why God put so many stars in the sky?" Ted mused.

"Not really. I did not know there were so many until tonight," she replied, trying to avoid the issue of God and the idea that He had created them. Martha's parents never had time for God or church, and she was in college when Sam had "gotten saved." It had radically changed his life and Sam had even explained it to her. However, she had just opted to focus on her career. In her mind, that was a big enough challenge by itself.

"What do you believe about God, if you don't mind sharing?" Ted asked. The two things that you don't just come right out and ask about are politics and religion. He had broken the code, but there was no turning back now.

"I definitely believe there is a God. I am fairly convinced that He created the universe and everything in it. However, I have to admit I have a little trouble with believing that He is so loving and concerned about everyone when the whole world is at war and millions and millions of people are suffering and dying from a long list of horrible things. I have trouble seeing the 'goodness' when the 'badness' is so rampant and overwhelming."

Ted could not argue that point and simply chose to let the subject drop. He did not want to mess up almost as quickly as he had gotten started on this potential relationship. Conversation drifted to other topics and they laid side by side in the grass for over an hour.

Finally, Martha said, "I guess I better get home. I have a little drive ahead of me." As she sat up, a meteorite streaked across the sky. The shooting star and its brilliant tail following behind it remained visible for several seconds.

"I know it's corny, but we should make a wish on that shooting star before you go," Ted suggested.

Martha pondered the suggestion and then said, "Corny or not, I can always use a wish coming true. I'll let you make a wish for both of us."

Ted snickered at the thought and nodded that he would take care of the wish. Ted stood up as Martha did, grabbed her hand, and walked her back to the house. Once inside, she rounded up her various belongings and walked to the front door. Ted followed close behind.

"I have had a wonderful time, Ted," Martha began. "Thank you for the tour, the ribs, the star show, but mostly the great company."

Ted smiled from ear to ear. Wishes do come true.

Walking Martha on out to her truck, they shared an awkward moment where neither one was quite sure how to close the evening. Ted finally took charge and grabbed Martha's hand by her fingertips and gently kissed the back of her hand in a most gentlemanly manner. Martha then blew him a kiss as she sat down in the vehicle and followed it with a vigorous yet sincere wave.

By the time Martha got her work truck back to the university, her own vehicle out of the compound, and back to her apartment, it was almost midnight. She removed her pack and slowly climbed the stairs to her home. As she arrived at the door, she glanced toward the sky for one more look at the stars, but the lights of the city obscured all but the brightest one.

As she unlocked the door and stepped inside, she turned the light on. All of the familiar things were sitting exactly where she left them: piles of papers, stacks of magazines, shelves full of books. The clutter of her life seemed so extreme compared to the simplicity of Ted's home. Questions began to circle as to whether all of this "stuff" was really that important. In fact, what is really important in life, anyway?

Without further deliberation, Martha prepared for bed. It did not take long because she was quite tired. It had been a long but exciting day.

Chapter 40

Monday morning, the alarm clock rang much earlier than Martha was accustomed to. Sunlight was not visible above the horizon yet, a fact she verified by a quick peek through the window blinds. However an early start was essential. She had spent the weekend preparing for this dig: checking the equipment in the truck and pouring over the excavation records from similar sites. To her surprise there were several small caves throughout the Ozarks that had been scientifically excavated. While open sites have a very limited array of artifacts that are commonly recovered, caves and dry shelters can produce a diverse menagerie of objects. It is precisely this fact that has drawn so many people to pillage these dry sites in search of the rarest of artifacts: baskets, clothing, nets, and even mummified bodies of animals and people.

Martha had noted that Wolf Track Cave, as she had named it, was completely dry and that the potential existed for such delicate specimens to exist. She had to be fully prepared for every contingency. One other observation from her time in the cave: it did not appear that anyone had looted the cave. It was estimated that over ninety-five percent of the dry caves had been heavily vandalized if not destroyed. To have one that was untouched was verging on a miracle.

Rushing around the apartment, grabbing daily essentials of a lunch and water, Martha felt like she was out of control. "If I don't slow down, I WILL forget something important," she finally said to herself, so she walked into the kitchen. "I will fix some toast. That will give me a minute to stop and think. This is ridiculous."

Taking a deep breath, she dropped two slices of bread into the toaster and just stood there staring at the appliance. In just a few seconds, the handle popped up and she carefully removed them. As she ate, her mind became clear and focused. Going through her mental checklist one last time, she headed for the door with a large backpack full of supplies.

The weather report had predicted reasonable temperatures later in the day, but a cold north wind was promised. There was a chance of rain for Monday night, but she had to be prepared if it arrived early. The possibility of being cold and wet had further complicated her planning. She had to be properly dressed for being outside all day, regardless. The standard rule is to dress in layers in the winter so you can add and subtract them as needed and not needed. It was a bulky proposition, but better than being extremely uncomfortable or getting sick.

Walking to her truck, she noticed that the first light of morning was breaking. By the time she would get to Ted's and then to the site, the sun will be well into the sky. That would fully illuminate well beyond where she planned to investigate. The wind was already blowing briskly and the moisture in the air pushed the wind chill down to a point that she was beginning to reconsider this dig at all. However, in a few hours it would be warmer, and inside the cave the wind would not be so intense.

The drive over to the university did not take long. Although there were students on campus, few were stirring at sunrise. Martha transferred her belongings into her company truck and was soon on her way to Ted's.

The sun had climbed above the horizon before she pulled into Ted's yard. Ted already had the Jeep parked there so she could easily transfer her equipment into it, but he was apparently back in the house. Martha first placed a small sifting screen in the Jeep followed by her hand tools and other possible essentials crammed into a plastic bucket. Before she got the remainder of items moved to the Jeep, Ted appeared from around behind the house.

"Good morning, Doc!" Ted shouted as he approached. "I knew you would have some things to transport down to the site. I figured I would make that as easy as possible. I have already carried all the things that I thought we might need down there. I did that yesterday.

"Morning, Ted! I was wondering where you were. It sounds like you are ready to get started," Martha replied. "I feel like I am moving, but I have reduced the amount of gear that I usually take because of the logistics of this dig."

"I counted on that. That is why I carried what few things I wanted to provide down to the site beforehand," Ted explained.

"What have you taken down already?" Martha asked.

"Well, I took a couple of Coleman lanterns, two lawn chairs, and a roll of plastic. I thought it might be nice to have a place to sit down comfortably and the lanterns will provide light as well as heat. The plastic is useful for all kinds of things," Ted said.

"Those things will be quite useful. I think I have loaded everything else we may need. Are you ready to go?" Martha asked.

"I sure am," Ted answered enthusiastically. Ted turned and quickly returned to the house and locked the doors. "I don't figure that was necessary, but it just makes me feel less vulnerable." Descending from the porch again, he quickly climbed into the Jeep and started the engine. Martha was already settled into the passenger seat, waiting patiently.

Lurching across the yard, the Jeep rolled toward the trail that led down the hill. Martha had prepared herself as much as possible for the hair-raising ride, but now that it was at hand, the butterflies were fluttering. It reminded her far too much of those roller-coaster rides at the amusement park. That first drop was always the worst.

Knowing that Martha was uncomfortable with the ride, Ted took particular care to handle the vehicle safely. About halfway down, Martha relaxed her death-grip on the edge of the seat and actually began to loosen up and enjoy the adventure. Ted kept both eyes on the trail, but noticed the positive expression on her face. He smiled. It would be a great day.

Reaching the parking area, Ted eased to a stop and turned off the key. The stiff breeze whipping across the top of the mountain was substantially less at the base of the mountain. However, the trees were still swaying briskly and the cloud cover kept the temperature a little cooler than desired.

They began to gather the equipment and realized that even with the most proficient arrangement, there will be a need for at least two trips. Ted had already delivered the chairs, lanterns, and plastic to the cave. They each grabbed as much as they could carry and started up the step slope. It was a difficult climb without anything in their hand. It soon proved to be impossible with both hands full. They agreed to make a pile at the base of the hill and then shuttle things up to the bench above where they would make another pile before proceeding to the cave.

In just over thirty minutes, they had all of the gear delivered to the mouth of the cave. Ted unfolded the two chairs and offered one to Martha, who gladly accepted it.

"That was a chore," Ted remarked.

"I am glad I pared the amount of stuff that I usually bring down to what I knew I would truly need," Martha said. "All the extra stuff is in my truck in case we run into something unexpected."

After a brief rest, Martha got up and started unpacking the things that were needed to lay out a grid and produce an accurate map of the cave. A tree stood directly in front of the mouth of the cave. She took a spike and drove it into the base of the tree using a large rock. She had thought about bringing a hammer but she did not want to carry it up the mountain for just one usage. This *datum* would establish a permanent reference so that accurate measurements could be taken for all of the excavations that would be done today as well as in the future. Maintaining continuity is paramount in the understanding and interpretation of archeological deposits of any site, but especially in caves where everything is in such close association. Separating the distinct layers of materials is often very difficult.

Ted rose from his seat and asked, "What can I do to help?"

Rising from her task at the base of the tree, Martha said, "I need the long tape measure and my compass. We will use the tape to lay a baseline down the middle of the cave. Normally, we try to set up a dig along a north-south axis, but caves are best dug however they are naturally oriented. I will use the compass to determine the bearing of the baseline."

Ted pulled the orange tape measure from Martha's pack, handed her the compass, and the end of the tape, and then retreated into the cave as he unrolled it. When he had crawled as far as he could, he stopped and laid the tape on the ground. Martha had hooked the long tape measure on the spike and was studying the compass to determine the angle. Without a word, she picked up her clipboard and made a few notes in the margin of the graph paper where she would later draw a map of the cave.

Ted reappeared from the darkness and asked, "Why do you use metric tape measures?"

"All archeological work is done using the metric system. It is a base-ten system that is so much simpler than having to calculate things in fractions," Martha explained. She then handed a smaller retractable tape to Ted and said, "This *datum*-tree is about two meters from the mouth of the cave. Starting at the two-meter mark on the orange tape, measure over to the cave wall and tell me how far it is. Try to keep the small tape perpendicular to the long tape, if you can."

Martha pulled her chair over to the baseline tape and sat down. Ted squatted down facing her and straddling the long tape. Taking measurements both directions as he backed into the cave, Ted called the numbers to Martha, who carefully sketched the cave outline onto her graph paper.

With the map of the cave walls complete, Martha tied a string to the *datum* spike and stretched it along the orange tape. She chiseled an "X" at the distant end of the string to mark the far end of the baseline. Finally, she placed a bright pink pin flag at every meter along the string before rolling the long tape back up.

Using a small hand-held tape measure, she slowly worked her way from the mouth of the cave back to the rear, drawing the various rocks that were visible on the surface. Once the scaled drawing was complete, she documented the exact location of the pictograph in relation to the map of the cave floor.

Since numerous rocks littered the floor Martha decided to use colored pencils to designate whether the rocks were lying flat or at an angle. Secondly, she put an asterisk on each rock that obviously did not originate from the roof of the cave. While she was not certain about the potential significance of the angle of the rock's current orientation, she was certain that the few rocks that had not fallen from the ceiling must have been carried into the cave by someone.

As she continued to draw each rock, as well as color them, she noticed that her earlier observation was accurate. Basically, the only flat rocks were directly beneath the pictograph of the wolf track. Conversely, the distribution of non-roof rocks was totally random and provided no indication of function, use, or any significance at all. Therefore, focusing on the possible feature designated by the accumulation of flat rocks, Dr. Jefferson marked the perimeter with orange pin flags. The area was not so far back in the cave that adequate light would be a problem unless they had to dig fairly deep. Then, there would be serious issues concerning shadows and even being able to see obvious things which might be hidden in the soil.

Ted had taken a seat, while Martha diligently produced the detailed map. However, when she had the map completed to her satisfaction, she asked, "Ted, can you fire up one of those lanterns? I would like to see how much light they produce."

"Gladly," he responded and stood up. Three lanterns were lined up along the wall of the bluff just outside of the cave. In a few minutes, a lantern was hissing and glowing brightly. Ted carried it to Martha and sat it beside her. She was sitting on the cave floor staring at the oblong arrangement of orange flags. "Well, Doc, what are you thinking?"

"Well," she started and then paused, "these flat rocks are clustered in this one spot. It just does not look natural. Since it is directly below the rock art, it would suggest that there is some association between the two things. Lastly, the size and shape of these orange flags is almost perfect for a grave. The problem is that it is never this simple and straightforward. I am surely missing something that is really obvious or I am overly simplifying what I see. It just can't be this easy." Looking over her shoulder she added, "The only way to find out is to dig."

"I was hoping you were going to say that!" Ted exclaimed with such enthusiasm that Martha could not help but chuckle.

The lantern provided enough light to dispel the shadows but without creating a yellow glow that would overpower the natural white light from the sun. Additionally, it provided some much appreciated heat to keep their fingers from getting stiff and achy while they worked.

Martha pulled her trusty trowel from her pack and handed a similar one to Ted and said, "Let me show you how we are going to dig. If this is a burial site, we will need to proceed very slowly. There could be all kinds of objects in the grave fill or nothing at all. We will just have to take it slow and easy until we see what this is." Ted nodded that he understood.

Martha explained as she went. "We should work on one end first, rather than tackling the whole thing at once. That will provide a quicker assessment into the depth of this possible feature as well as provide a control sample. In open sites, burial pits are often easiest to identify by the profile that we leave across the middle."

With that explanation, Martha began to gently scrape the surface, delicately placing each rock that she encountered into a cloth bag. She planned to take all of the rocks back to the lab to determine if they were naturally occurring or not. Ted studied her technique for a few minutes, then began to scrape also. He had never participated in a real archeological excavation. He had seen them on television and had even stood beside the excavation units and watched others dig. This was a new and exhilarating experience.

The area where they were digging was only fifty centimeters by fifty centimeters. Martha had explained that they were only going to dig down five centimeters per level. At the bottom of each five-centimeter level, they would close up the artifact bag and draw in any unusual rocks or change of soil that they saw. Only after a level was completed and the paperwork wrapped up, could they begin on the next level.

Level one was completed without finding anything. Not a single artifact was observed even though the sack was half full of ordinary rocks as far as either one could tell. Level two produced the exact same results as level one. Ted's enthusiasm was not dampened, though. He just wished that they could dig faster and find out if there was anything down there.

Level three began with the same general assortment of small rocks which were dutifully tossed into the bag. Martha insisted that they keep the floor of the test unit level and Ted discovered that that was especially difficult to do, but he continued to try.

Then, in an instant, the intensity of their effort changed. Martha's trained trowel had encountered something that was neither rock nor soil!

Ted stopped and pulled the lantern closer. What was it that was hiding just beneath their feet? Martha ever so gently picked dirt away from the pliable object and said, "It feels like fabric of some sort, but I can't tell what. I will need to get a little more dirt away from it."

Martha pulled a piece of split river cane from her pack. It was about the size of a Popsicle stick but had been tapered to a point on one end. Martha explained that this soft digging tool would not damage any fragile object that might be encountered. Ever so slowly, she picked at the edge of the soft lump until she had reached the bottom of the third excavation level. Clearing the soil from around the object, she then said, "Let's get this level on down to the bottom and get the plan-view drawn, so we can see what this is. We will know when we get into the next level."

With as much haste as possible and without getting careless, they cleared the remainder of the soil and rock from the third level. Once again, no artifacts were found, but the strange cloth lump was very unique and highly unexpected. Martha had a pretty good idea what the lump would turn out to be, but with only a tiny portion of it exposed, she could not be certain. Only more excavation would confirm her suspicion.

Chapter 41

Ted was beside himself with anticipation but he did not dare rush Martha's highly methodical procedures. When the lump was brushed clean and photographs were taken, she said, "What do you think it is, Ted?"

"It looks like a piece of an old burlap bag to me, but I don't have any idea why there would be an old bag buried in this cave. I'm only guessing. What do you think it is?"

Martha looked up at Ted and then back into the excavation unit and said, "I think it is a blanket. As we go down with the next level, we are going to be looking for any evidence of a body. If my hunch is correct, this is an Indian burial. On rare occasions, in perfectly dry caves like this one, perishable items such as rope, clothing, moccasins, and even blankets have been found. With the level of preservation that I see in this blanket, there is an excellent chance that if there is a body inside, it will be very well preserved also."

"What do you mean by – well preserved?" Ted asked, his eyes now opened wide in an expression of complete surprise.

"There are several instances where complete human bodies have been recovered from perfectly dry caves. That means that they still have skin, internal organs, hair, and the clothes they were buried in. It takes an absolutely perfect set of circumstances to achieve this, but it is possible. However, there is a state law that says if we continue to dig and do actually identify a body, we then have to stop digging and call the county sheriff. The sheriff will come out and make a determination that the body is not part of a crime scene. We then call the State Historic Preservation Office and a local Native American representative to determine what course of action can be taken. It may be that we simply cover the body up and leave it buried right where it is, or it may be exhumed and reburied in a place the tribe calls a keep-safe cemetery."

"Oh, my goodness! That seems like a lot of complicated bureaucracy. What ever happened to the good ol' days when you just dug stuff up so you could learn more about the past?" Ted naïvely asked.

Martha sighed and began to explain. "Those days are gone, my friend. Archeologists don't just dig anymore. We have awakened to the reality that what we have been digging up all these years is the past of a group of people that live right here amongst us. Basically, we had ignored them and their feelings in our own quest to investigate the past and study their ancestors. For so long we treated their ancestors' remains like any other artifact. The truth is: this is the deceased relative of the very Indians who still live in this region. I had a Native American ask me one time how I would feel if he went down to where my grandparents are buried and just dug them up to look at their bones. It is a good question. Most people would be horrified at the thought. Is it any different for us to just decide for ourselves whether this person should be dug up or not? There has been a real awakening in the archeological community. While the process is terribly laden with seemingly silly requirements and regulations, the bottom line requires that the descendants be consulted before any bodies are disturbed. I think that part is good and reasonable."

Midway through Martha's lecture, Ted had sat down directly across the unit from where she sat. When she finished, he said, "So what do we do now?"

Martha smiled. "First, we don't know that we have a body at all – yet. I think it is a blanket but it might not be. We need to dig some more to find out. If we do indeed find a body, it will be necessary to expose it sufficiently for the sheriff to determine that it is not a modern burial or crime scene. People have been dying in the area since the Indians were forced out just like they did in Indian times. If the body is modern, there is no requirement to consult with the Indians at all. We simply need to continue to dig and see what this is before we jump to any premature conclusions. After all, it could be an old burlap feed sack!"

Ted and Martha shared a good laugh. She knew that she needed to lighten the mood before Ted left and called the sheriff.

Martha estimated that the area of flat stones outlined by the orange pin flags was roughly 150 centimeters long by fifty centimeters wide. The first test unit they opened was at one end of that area. Rather than taking the first unit any deeper just yet, Martha decided to take the middle unit down in five-centimeter increments as well.

The first level of unit two was almost identical to what they found in unit one. However, right at the bottom of level two, the mysterious fabric was once again encountered. As she exposed the highest part of the fabric-covered lump, the faint smell of tobacco wafted up in the dusty air. The smell seemed out of place since neither she nor Ted smoked. She quickly dismissed it as being her imagination or just a *latent* smell from the old fabric.

The biggest difference she observed was that it was not just a lump in the middle of the unit. It appeared to be getting wider as it extended deeper into the cave. In unit one, the lump of fabric had only been about twenty centimeters wide. In unit two, it was closer to forty. Delicate paint brushes were used to clean the powdery dirt and some sort of tiny fragments of vegetation that looked like dried and crumbly cedar boughs from the fabric. With each stroke the intricate patterns of a hand-woven blanket began to appear. One thing was obvious; it was not a burlap bag.

The first five centimeters of unit three were exactly like the previous two. However, the blanket was encountered almost immediately upon starting level two. At first, it was a lump in the center of the unit but as the soil was removed from around it, it did not take much imagination to see that this lump was caused by it being laid over someone's face and head. There was no doubt at this point – they had discovered the body of someone who had been buried in the cave.

Martha busily brushed the blanket as clean as possible as well as removing the soil from around the perimeter of the blanketed corpse. Ted lit the other two lanterns and placed them on opposite sides of the grave. When Martha decided that the scene was as clean as she could get it, she got her camera and began to take photographs. She shot general overviews to gain the relative association to the wall of the cave and the pictograph. She took close-ups of the beautifully decorated blanket as well as the ever-clearer indication of the body contained within. After almost fifty images had been taken, she stepped back from the hole and sat down in her chair. Ted made his way to his chair and sat down also.

"This is a find of incredible significance," Martha started. "I think we should stop right here and call Dr. Hodges. He really needs to see this. To my knowledge, no archeologist now living has ever excavated a mummy in Arkansas. All of the mummies from the Ozark Mountains were found back in the 1920s and 1930s. We have the notes from those old excavations, but no one has any actual experience in the matter. I'm not qualified to tackle this alone. I need a whole team of people with a variety of expertise if we are to recover this body without damaging it. There should be a textile expert, a physical anthropologist, and possibly a coroner."

Ted hated to interrupt but he just felt that he must. "Don't we need to call the sheriff first?"

Martha stopped and looked up. "You are absolutely right. Let's drive back up to the house and call Dr. Hodges AND the sheriff. We can eat lunch while we wait.

Ted extinguished the lanterns and placed them back outside the mouth of the cave. After that, they took a piece of plastic and cover the excavation gently just to be sure that the exposure to the high humidity of the air did not cause the blanket to start deteriorating. With the area secure, they made their way back along the bluff and down to the Jeep. Within a few minutes, they crested the mountain top and arrived safely back at the house. Martha had watched her cell phone reception as they climbed the hill and it was not until they got to the house that she was able to place a call.

"Dr. Hodges? This is Martha Jefferson. Do you have time to talk? I have a situation here at Ted Wilson's," Martha shouted into the phone as Ted killed the engine.

"Certainly. I have time. What is the matter, Dr. Jefferson?" Dr. Hodges replied.

"As I told you, Ted has a cave on his property and we started a test excavation at a suspicious location hoping to determine what the archeological evidence might be directly below some rock art. Well, we found a grave."

"Okay. What is the problem?" Dr. Hodges asked.

"We have not actually seen the body yet. What we have found is a blanket that has every indication of a body being wrapped inside it. The preservation on the blanket is excellent and from the weave and design, I am guessing it is prehistoric Indian. I think we have an excellent chance of recovering a mummy," she concluded.

The silence was brief but profound. "Oh, my goodness," Dr. Hodges finally uttered. "THAT is a BIG SITUATION! Let me think." After another span of silence he finished with, "Call the sheriff, like the law says, but don't unwrap it until I get there. I will bring Dr. Lilly, the physical anthropologist with me. I know he is home because I can see his car in his driveway just down the street. I am on my way."

Martha closed the phone and looked at Ted. "Do you have any leftover ribs? We are on hold until Dr. Hodges and the sheriff get here."

Ted chuckled and answered, "Sure do. Let's warm them up."

"If you would, please warm them for both of us and I will call the sheriff."

"Sure thing, Doc," Ted said as he got out of the Jeep and started to the house.

Martha pulled her address book from her pack and looked up the number of the sheriff's office, then dialed the number.

"Sheriff's Office. How may I direct your call?" said the receptionist.

"Hi. This is Dr. Jefferson from the university. I am an archeologist and I have been excavating on a site out in the county and have discovered a body. I am certain that it is the body of a prehistoric Indian, but the law requires that the sheriff come out and declare that it is, indeed, not part of some crime before I can proceed."

"Just a moment, let me connect you directly with Sheriff Brady."

After just a moment, the booming voice of the county sheriff rang through the receiver, "Hello, Dr. Jefferson. How are you today?"

"I am doing quite well, thanks, but I need your help," she began. For the next several minutes, Martha filled the sheriff in on the events leading to the discovery and the magnitude of what it could mean for science and the university.

"I will be there in about thirty minutes. I was tired of sitting in the office anyway," he replied. They talked for a few more minutes before she was finally able to bring the call to an end.

Martha closed the phone and proceeded to the house. The delicious smell of ribs greeted her as she stepped through the door.

"You know the routine. Make your self at home," Ted shouted from the kitchen. "Everything will ready in about three minutes." The familiar hum of the microwave oven could be heard in the background.

"That is just enough time to powder my nose," Martha answered as she made her way to the restroom at the end of the hall.

Chapter 42

The leftover ribs were an excellent substitution for the cold sandwich that she had prepared. It also provided an excellent diversion while they waited for the county sheriff and Dr. Hodges. Just as they finished clearing the dishes, the sound of a car door in the front yard told them that one of the expected visitors had arrived.

Ted opened the front door just as the sheriff was about to knock. "Good afternoon, officer," Ted said.

"Good afternoon, sir. Is Dr. Jefferson here?"

Martha stepped around Ted and onto the porch to shake his hand. "Hi, Sheriff Brady. I appreciate you coming out on such short notice."

"From your description, it sounds like this is a spectacular discovery. I am very interested to see what you have found whether it is a crime scene or not. I find archeology to be so fascinating," the sheriff remarked.

Ted stepped back and motioned for both of them to come inside. They would still have to wait for Dr. Hodges.

Sheriff Brady, Martha, and Ted made their way to the dining room where Martha pulled her drawings from earlier in the day out of her pack. She laid the maps on the table and began to point and explain the details on each map. Finally, she pulled her digital camera out and, although the tiny screen did not reveal adequate detail, it had captured some quite amazing images of the cave but especially of the blanket-covered body.

"Wow!" exclaimed the sheriff as he toggled through the photographs. "I have never seen anything like that before."

"Me either," Martha added.

About that time, a knock at the door announced that Dr. Hodges had arrived. Ted went to let him in while Martha and Sheriff Brady continued to look at the maps and drawings.

Dr. Hodges and Dr. Lilly soon crowded around the tiny camera screen. Aside from the sound of Martha's voice describing what each picture was and pointing to detail that was not readily apparent, the two older scientists only uttered an occasion grunt or gasp as they peered intently at the images.

Ted finally broke in and said, "It is already 2:00. If we don't get back down to the site, we are not going to have enough natural light to work by."

Martha nodded vigorously in agreement and quickly stashed her maps and camera as Ted led the visitors out to the Jeep. When all five were securely seated, Ted turned the Jeep back down the hill with the utmost care. He had never taken five people down the hill at the same time before. The extra weight made the vehicle a little more top-heavy than usual but they soon arrived at the base of the hill without incident.

Getting everyone up to the cave was interesting. Dr. Hodges and Dr. Lilly had been *cloistered* in the university for almost two decades. Neither one was in any shape to be climbing a mountain. While Martha led the way up the mountain, Ted and Sheriff Brady brought up the rear, occasionally lending a hand to push the elder scientists upward or stop their downward slide. Many brief rests were required before all five reached the ledge that led to the cave. Nevertheless, they all eventually arrived at the cave, where Ted promptly lit the three lanterns and carried them to the edge of the grave. Martha began carefully removing the plastic from the grave while the others looked on with *rapt* attention.

Martha looked up at Dr. Hodges as she removed the last layer of plastic. The expression on his face was pure delight. She glanced at Ted and smiled with great satisfaction.

"Oh, my!" Dr. Hodges exclaimed. "I can't believe my eyes!" Then, pulling his hands up to his face, he covered his mouth as the scene of the blanket-clad body soaked into his whirling mind. A thousand questions were racing around in his head. The urge to peek under the blanket was almost more than he could stand when he asked, "Have you found an edge of the blanket so that you can see what the condition of the body is?"

Martha was soaking in the silent praise for her amazing discovery. She said, "Yes, along this side the blanket appears to be tucked under the body a little. There are a few places where the original edge of the blanket is visible. However, the end of the blanket above the head is not tucked under. I believe that we may be able to access the body from this end," pointing at the head.

"Have you taken adequate photographs and are you ready to expose the body?" Dr. Hodges asked.

"I think that is our next step. We don't have ALL of the dirt away from the blanket yet, but we have enough dirt moved to allow at least a cursory peek inside," Martha answered.

Sheriff Brady nodded. From what he could see, it was not possible for him to determine whether the grave was recent or ancient. In fact, without seeing the body, it was not possible for him to even declare that it was a grave. Clearly, he would rely on the expertise of the scientists around him to make the call unless the body turned out to indeed be the victim of a recent crime.

Martha gingerly sat down at the head of the grave, and with the delicate touch of a brain surgeon, she began to pull the folds of the gathered blanket that was above the head area away from the head itself. The blanket was not stiff or exceptionally fragile. In fact, it was unsettling just how well preserved the fabric actually was. If the style and weave of the blanket were not clearly handmade with obvious Native American characteristics, it could pass for one that was only recently discarded.

The extremely dry conditions caused the powdery soil to become airborne the more she dislodged the blanket. Using a dry paintbrush, she removed as much sediment as possible, but the dust still fogged badly. With the last fold of the blanket pulled free, she separated the material until she found a corner. Ever so carefully, she began to lift the corner of the blanket-shroud, pulling it back. Then, grabbing a second corner, she pulled it the other direction until the cleft between the two portions was just about to part right over the face of the person buried there. Glancing up at the faces of the four men gathered around, she almost laughed to see the suspense etched across them. With one last pull, the person's head was exposed for the first time since his burial.

"He still has hair and skin!" Ted blurted out.

The exposed head and neck revealed the face of a young man with long black hair and a few facial whiskers. Although the skin was drawn tight against the skull, it retained most of the personal features that he would have had at death except that the skin was almost black. Martha explained, "That is a normal aspect of mummification and has nothing to do with the racial background of the individual. This appears to be a young man about fourteen to eighteen years old."

Dr. Lilly leaned in close and, using rubber gloves, very gently touched the face to see if the body was completely *desiccated*. This was vital information to have so that proper care and storage could be arranged. Any moisture at all would cause the process of decay to resume. This was most critical concerning the internal organs. They could be extremely valuable for scientific research.

Dr. Hodges squeezed in close just to get a better look. His expression was something between shock and elation.

Sheriff Brady leaned over Dr. Lilly and said, "How long do you think that person has been dead?"

"It is extremely hard to tell, but it takes hundreds of years for the skin to turn black and based on the high cheek bones and long black hair, I believe that our dearly departed is a prehistoric Indian," Dr. Lilly interjected.

"That is good enough for me," the sheriff replied as he stepped back to give the three scientists some room to work.

Ted had been standing speechless just staring at the whole scene. Then he said in a quiet tone, "I can't believe how many times I have sat and walked on this fellow when I would study that wolf track on the wall. I had no idea he was buried there. He was only a few inches below me. There was just no way to know …." His voice trailed off as he contemplated his past action in the cave.

"With confirmation that the body is that of a Native American, we need to contact the State Historic Preservation Office and the local tribal representative," Martha announced.

Dr. Hodges leaned back and said, "I called the Historic Preservation Office before I left home. They are faxing the required permit to the departmental headquarters. I also called the tribal representative and described what had been found. She said that since this was probably going to be a mummy and that it could be disturbed if left in place, she authorized us to remove it but she wanted to see it before she would say what kind of research the tribe might allow."

"Great. Well, I guess we have permission to remove it. Now, I am wondering how we will actually remove it from this cave, down to the Jeep, and up the mountain without destroying it ourselves. Ted, do you have any ideas?" Martha asked.

"The best idea I can offer is to build a wooden case and pack the body inside with bubble-wrap or something like that," Ted suggested.

"That sounds like a good plan. In order to get the body into a box like that, it will be necessary to remove some more dirt from beside the body so we can get the box down to the same level. That will minimize the lifting that will be needed. The greatest danger will be lifting it into the box," Dr. Lilly added.

Ted said, "I have some lumber stored in the barn that can be used to build a box. I could have it built and back down here by the time you guys get the hole enlarged."

Martha indicated to Ted what an excellent idea he had and that she would expand the hole while he worked on the box. A brief discussion of the size of the box quickly led to a consensus that the box should probably be assembled after the body is exhumed. The body could be placed on the board that would serve as the bottom of the makeshift coffin more easily without having to deal with the side boards. It was also felt that no lid should be needed either or that one could be added later. Ted agreed and wrote down a few notes to guide the construction project.

Sheriff Brady had been listening carefully, trying to figure out how he was going to excuse himself and get back up the mountain without climbing. "I like that idea. I can ride back up with Ted. This is all very interesting, but I should probably get back to town."

Martha laughed and stood up to shake the sheriff's hand. She thanked him for coming out and promised to file a full report with him as soon as possible.

"My pleasure, Dr. Jefferson. Call me anytime," Sheriff Brady concluded. Then, he and Ted started back to the Jeep, leaving the three scientists to their discussions and digging.

Dr. Hodges and Dr. Lilly stepped away from the grave to let Martha gain access to the area that should be excavated. Starting near the body and working her way out, she quickly exposed the edge of the grave fill. She knew this because the soil was somewhat more compacted outside the grave. Once outside the grave, she moved more quickly. Ted indicated that he would be back in about an hour. If all went well, it would be almost dark before they could get the body into the coffin. There was no way they would be able to remove it from the cave in the dark – even with lanterns. Conversely, she knew that it was to everyone's advantage to have Dr. Lilly's expertise on this effort and she hoped he would oversee the actual removal.

Once the area adjacent to the body was enlarged sufficiently, Martha focused her efforts on removing the remaining grave fill from the other sides. This would allow proper access for lifting the body so that the board could be slipped underneath. Martha wondered what might be found in the grave fill, so she collected several large samples for further analysis back in the lab.

With the blanket-wrapped body fully excavated, the exquisite detail of the blanket itself was clearly visible. It took all of her will to resist taking a peek inside the blanket. Her curiosity, as well as that of her two colleagues, was almost unbearable.

Just then, Dr. Hodges announced, "I hear the Jeep coming down the hill. Ted will be here soon."

"I will go down and help him carry the lumber up here. You guys have a seat. I will be right back," Martha said as she left the cave, making her way down to the makeshift parking area.

The cave clearly provided protection from the wind and the lanterns had provided a very welcome heat source. Now that she was back out in the open, the cold, damp wind stung her face, reminding her that it was not just the darkness that would certainly delay the removal of the body tonight. Her mind pondered the various issues and scenarios that would surely play out during the next twenty-four hours.

Ted was unloading the various components of the disassembled coffin. Martha walked up as he hoisted the lumber onto his shoulder. "Can I carry something?" she asked.

"Grab the cordless drill and that sack of sheet-rock screws. We will need them for assembling the coffin," Ted directed.

Although the wood was not heavy, it proved to be very *unwieldy*. However, with persistence, Ted managed to get all of it up the slope and into the cave. Martha stayed with him, offering encouragement and support as well as bringing the necessary tools. The sun was setting and the temperature was dropping. Without the lanterns, their mission would be halted for the day.

Minimal discussion was necessary as Ted placed the bottom of the would-be coffin into the hole beside the body. Dr. Lilly took several handfuls of dirt and began to cover the board. "This," he explained, "would provide a *malleable* surface on the board. It is not likely that the body would be lying perfectly flat. The dirt would be shifted on the board as needed to conform to the contour of the body and minimize damage."

Dr. Lilly and Dr. Hodges then positioned themselves on either side of the torso. Martha took charge of the head and shoulders. Ted gladly accepted the feet and lower legs. Each of them gently eased their respective hands under the bundle at evenly spaced intervals and on the count of three lifted it every so slightly. The tension and anxiety was extreme. No one dared to even breathe until the short distance was bridged and the blanket and body were resting securely on the board. It was surprising how light the wrapped body was.

Once moved, Dr. Lilly carefully adjusted the dirt under the body to form a solid support before stepping aside. Ted moved in with his drill and quickly secured the sides and ends onto the base. When he finished, Ted stood up and asked, "Martha, what is our next step?"

"I think that it is time to call it a day. Do you agree, Dr. Lilly?" Martha asked looking toward the distinguished scholar.

"Yes, I do. I think we should leave the coffin right there until morning. Can you come back and get it?" Dr. Lilly inquired.

"I am available. Ted, are you available to help me?" Martha inquired.

"No problem. I am flexible. That is a perk of being the boss," Ted answered with a snicker.

Dr. Hodges waded in and suggested, "There are always museum volunteers we could enlist to help as well. It will take more than two of you to get this box down to the Jeep, especially with the additional weight of that dirt in it."

"That's a good idea," Martha agreed. "Let's get things gathered up and go home."

While Martha picked up all of the equipment and stacked it deeper in the cave, Ted pulled several brass handles from his coat pocket and attached three to each of the long sides of the coffin. They would be essential in the morning.

By the time the Jeep reached the top of the mountain, it was dark. After a few parting words of thanks from Dr. Hodges, he and Dr. Lilly drove away. Martha and Ted made plans for resuming the project in the morning and then Martha, too, got in her museum truck and drove away.

Chapter 43

Martha was back to Ted's house by about 9:00. As she was driving back to town the night before, Sam had called just to talk. Martha had told her brother about the exciting discovery and the plans for the following morning. Sam immediately volunteered both himself and Jim. Although the actual discovery and excavation was complete, Sam was sure that Jim would be eager to help, too.

Martha led Jim and Sam to Ted's back yard. Ted already had the Jeep pointed downhill and ready to go. He joined the trio and proper introductions were made.

"So you are Martha's brother. It is so nice to meet you, Sam," Ted responded. "Is everyone ready to go?"

Soon the Jeep was once again picking its way down the slope. Martha had gotten more comfortable with the trip, having made it several times now. Jim and Sam were sitting silently in the back seat hanging on tightly. Martha glanced over her shoulder to see the expression on Sam's face. It brought a sharp smile across her face because she knew exactly what was going through his mind.

Arriving at the parking area, the four passengers disembarked and started the climb up to the cave with an ample supply of ropes of various sizes. Martha admitted to the group that she had slept fitfully because she was worried about something happening to the body. Ted quickly affirmed the same issue for himself.

Much to her relief, when they entered the cave, everything was exactly as they had left it. Ted had also brought several wooden support braces. He wanted to reinforce the coffin that he had hastily assembled the day before. Then he used the ropes to bind the coffin together as one last precaution.

Martha busied herself with repacking her portion of the field equipment. While she was not finished with all of the excavation that she felt the cave deserved, it was something that could be delayed until spring. She really wanted to investigate this mummified body first, and then decide what other course of action to pursue for additional excavations.

With the coffin structurally secure, it was time to carry it out of the cave. Gravity was going to make the task fairly simple because it would naturally be inclined to slide downhill. The challenge was to allow the descent to proceed at a controlled rate so the contents inside remained undamaged.

Once they carried the coffin along the ledge and arrived at the point where they normally climbed the hill, they sat the coffin down. Ted tied two ropes to the coffin. Martha grabbed one rope and Ted took the other. Jim and Sam started down the slope ahead of the coffin in an effort to minimize the bumping and jostling as it slid ever so slowly downhill. As Ted or Martha would reach the end of their rope, the one with the long rope would anchor the descent until the one with the shorter rope could work their way down to the coffin and tie off to a nearby tree. Jim and Sam continued to lift and divert the box away from a seemingly endless array of snags and hazards. However, with patience and persistence, they did finally reach the more gentle slopes of the ridge where the four of them once again picked it up and carried it to the Jeep.

The most difficult physical challenge of the ordeal was certainly behind them. However, getting the coffin secured to the Jeep while leaving room for all four live passengers was a new challenge. It was finally decided that Jim and Sam would take their place sitting normally on the back seat of the old open-top Jeep. The coffin would be laid across the vehicle in front of them, resting on the sides of the vehicle, effectively trapping Jim and Sam in the vehicle since the coffin would basically rest on their laps. Ted used the ropes, which had been utilized for slowing the coffin's slide down the hill, to bind the box to the Jeep.

"I think I could turn this Jeep over and that box would stay attached," Ted quipped.

"Probably so, but I don't want to find out," Martha countered.

"Amen," Jim added.

Ted started the old trustworthy metal beast and without further ado, it began the long crawl back up to the house. Even though the box did shift a little on the way up, Jim and Sam maintained a tight grip on it so that neither it nor they were ejected on the way.

Back at Martha's truck, Ted stopped the Jeep so the coffin could be easily transferred into the bed. With just one more trip to the bottom of the mountain and back up again, all of the equipment was successfully returned home as well. Martha sorted hers out and used it to stack around the coffin so it would not slide around during the drive back to the museum.

"Ted, I will deliver this to the museum as soon as we get back to town; however, we will not unwrap it until the tribal representative can be present. I will call you if you would like to be there," Martha offered.

"If I am in town, I would love to be there. Thank you," Ted replied.

They talked for a few more minutes before Martha finally decided that it was time to go. She, Jim, and Sam squeezed into the front of her pickup again. The drive to the museum was filled with talk about the discovery as well as the significance of it. Martha finally got around to asking what the guys remembered about the torches they had found as kids.

"Those torches were amazing," Jim said. "Sam said you were running some tests on them."

"One of them had a white residue in it. I sent that off to a lab and the preliminary report was that it was some sort of animal fat, probably turkey," Martha shared. "I am guessing that the turkey fat was smeared on it to help it burn slower or something. I really don't know why else it would have been there."

"It certainly sounds reasonable and logical. Did you get a date off of the torches?" Sam asked.

"Not yet. I have not heard from the lab. That will take several months to process," Martha answered. "Intuitively, I would estimate somewhere between 500 and 1,500 years old, but that is just a raw guess."

"Really!" Jim finally chimed in. "That is incredible that those artifacts laid in that cave for that long before we found them."

"It really is, but the dry conditions were a perfect environment for them to survive. There is no telling how much has been found through the centuries that has been lost forever. It is so sad," Martha concluded as she flipped on her blinker to indicate her intentions to access the street behind the museum.

Pulling the truck into the parking lot, she backed up to the loading dock that provided access to the lab. She had called Dr. Hodges enroute to inform him as to when the coffin and its contents would arrive. When she stepped out of the truck, Dr. Hodges and Dr. Lilly both stepped onto the loading dock. With ample help, Jim and Sam carefully slid the box out of truck until they could securely grab a handle on each side. Dr. Hodges and Dr. Lilly took the handles at the other end as it was delicately moved out from under the protective camper shell. With the four men literally serving as pall-bearers, Martha moved ahead and held the door open for them to enter the lab. Placing the box on the central table, Jim and Sam turned to leave.

"Thank you both for your help. I really appreciate it," Martha said as she gave Jim a big hug then turned and hugged Sam. "I'll see you guys later. I owe you."

Dr. Lilly glanced quizzically at Dr. Hodges. Dr. Hodges shrugged slightly. After they had left and Dr. Jefferson had returned to the exam table where the two senior scientists were standing, Dr. Hodges asked, "Who were your helpers?" He was sure that Martha knew the two men well. However, he was totally unaware of any man that she would have hugged with such open affection and then follow that with a promise to see them again. He also knew they were not members of the local archeological society.

"The shorter guy is my younger brother, Sam. The other guy is Jim Flagstone. They are local policemen now, but when they were kids they were part of that group that found those torches over on the Kings River. You know, the torches that you showed me a few weeks ago," Martha explained.

"Oh, my goodness! That's who that was. No wonder you seemed to know them so well," Dr. Hodges remarked sheepishly.

Martha just laughed. Her reputation for being totally focused on the science of archeology and the business of the museum was legendary on campus. Clearly Dr. Hodges had no idea that she was indeed a normal person on occasion.

The three colleagues gathered closely around the exam table and soon were enthralled in a deep discussion of textiles, burial customs, and the modern politics that set the boundaries for acceptable studies. They each expressed a definite hope that due to the uniqueness of this discovery, the tribes would grant enough latitude to at least properly document the discovery.

Dr. Hodges soon excused himself so he could make a phone call. Dr. Lilly stayed for a little while, examining the weave and decoration of the blanket-shroud. The light in the lab was certainly far better than the lanterns in the cave. After a little while, he too decided it was time to get back to his office.

Martha acquired some plastic sheeting and carefully covered the coffin and then tucked the edges underneath the box to ensure that no one bothered anything. After placing several signs on the plastic that boldly stated, "DO NOT TOUCH," Martha left the lab, too. It had been an eventful few days, and although it was still the middle of the afternoon, she felt exhausted.

After returning her work truck to the compound, Martha decided to just go home. The mail had run, but for once she was glad there was nothing of significance in it. Within twenty minutes, she had taken a shower, brushed her teeth, flopped into bed, and passed blissfully to sleep.

Chapter 44

The next several days around the museum passed in utter silence concerning the mummy. The tribal elders had not been able to get together to discuss the matter, so life pretty much got back to normal amongst the museum staff. Martha was actually relieved because it was the time of year when final semester exams were in full swing. That was stressful enough without dealing with the rigors of exploring and documenting the mummy. However, the flip side of the issue is that the holiday break would be a perfect time to devote uninterrupted time and effort into the analysis if permitted.

"Martha, are you in your office?" came the voice of Dr. Hodges from down the hall as he approached hastily.

Martha rose from her desk and met him at the doorway. "What's wrong?"

"Absolutely nothing! The tribal representative called and said that they want us to perform a thorough inspection of the body and the blanket to determine if this person is indeed related to them. They said that they would consider other tests but they wanted to get this determination first," Dr. Hodges declared excitedly. "When would you like to get started?"

The wheels of Martha's mind were spinning as she evaluated her class schedules and other obligations. "Today, I believe. I promised to call Ted so he could see the whole lab analysis. Whether he can make it or not, we should be able to get started after lunch."

"That will be fine. I have a meeting this afternoon, so I will not be able to be there, but Polly can help you. She is a good photographer. We should take very detailed photos of the whole process and all discoveries along the way."

Martha nodded affirmatively. She had seen some of Polly's handiwork in the various displays that adorned the many exhibits in the public hall of the museum. She would certainly be an asset. "I'll be sure to keep you informed."

Dr. Hodges turned to leave and Martha returned to her desk. Quickly picking up the phone, she dialed Ted's personal cell phone. Only his closest circle of friends and associates were privileged with that information. After three rings, the voice mail picked up and announced that Ted was out of the country on business and would not return for a few weeks. Martha left a brief message explaining the situation and hung up.

By the time she got off the phone, Polly was standing at the door. She had overheard Dr. Hodges. "I am ready to get started when you are, Dr. Jefferson," she announced in her perpetually chipper voice, holding her favorite camera up as if she needed to show evidence of her willingness to get started.

"We will begin right after lunch. Dr. Lilly would be a valuable asset to the team. I need to call him," Martha said, reaching for the phone.

"That sounds good," Polly agreed as she returned to her office to wrap up a few more tasks in preparation for being away from her desk all afternoon.

Martha called Dr. Lilly and explained the situation to him. He eagerly agreed to join the effort immediately after lunch. With no other arrangements to be made, Martha grabbed her coat and headed for the door. She wanted to get some lunch for herself and then get to the lab early. Most preparations could be done before the others arrived.

Her walk to the student center passed without her even noticing. Her mind was completely preoccupied with the afternoon's upcoming event. Mealtime passed with a similar degree of indifference. As she rose to return her tray to the kitchen, she suddenly realized that she did not even remember what she had just eaten. Looking down at the remnants and wrappers caused her to stop and think: "If I dug up this small pile of trash, would there be enough evidence to tell me what this meal consisted of? That thought was haunting, because the truth is, while there is evidence of some parts, other parts are completely unrepresented." How could she know what was missing if there was no evidence? Her mind jumped forward to the afternoon's task. She could certainly document what she sees, but how do you fill in the blanks for what you can't see? How can she draw conclusions from an incomplete picture or worse yet, from a puzzle with no box, no border, and no image on the majority of the pieces that she did have? A sense of futility and gross inadequacy washed over her as she sat down and stared at the trash on her tray. She had never contemplated this perspective before and it was terribly unnerving, especially in light of the tremendously important investigation that she was about to undertake.

Dropping her trash in the receptacle, she placed the plastic tray on top of the others that were already sitting there. Even that routine and virtually thoughtless act took on a whole new level of contemplation. "I have got to get out of here," she muttered to herself. "I am a good archeologist and I know what I am doing. It may not be possible to know everything, but any new thing we can learn is something we did not know before." By the time she reached the outside doors, she had her chin back up where it belonged and she marched confidently across campus.

Returning to the museum, she went straight down the hall and into the lab, which was located in the opposite wing of the museum from her office. She

257

needed to remove the protective plastic and ropes from the coffin. Within minutes the open-top box was once again illuminated by the bright lights in the ceiling of the lab. A chill ran down her back almost as if she had regret for coldly pulling the covers off a sleeping child.

Ted's design would permit her to simply use a screwdriver to remove the screws that secured the sides of the box to form the makeshift coffin. One by one, she backed the screws out. A battery operated driver would have greatly sped up the process, but Martha was not really in a hurry. As she freed each fastener from the wood, she carefully dropped it into her shirt pocket before moving to the next one. Just as she dropped the last screw into her now bulging pocket, she heard the growing sound of footsteps coming down the hall followed by the lab door being opened.

Martha stood up straight and turned to see Polly enter the lab. Smiling eagerly, Polly made her way through the maze of boxes and tables before stepping up to the table where the afternoon's project was lying. Polly had not just one camera but two hanging around her neck.

"I am ready, Dr. Jefferson!" Polly said quietly as if to not disturb the silence of the lab.

"There is no need to whisper, Polly. This fellow won't mind at all." Before the words completely cleared her lips, the lab door swung open again, and Dr. Lilly strolled in.

"Sorry I am late. The phone rang just as I was preparing to leave my office."

"No problem. Polly just arrived and I have only been here a few minutes myself," Martha reassured him. "All I have done so far is to remove the sides of the coffin, so we can get to the blanket and the mummy inside. Shall we get started?"

"Absolutely," Dr. Lilly interjected.

Dr. Lilly positioned himself on one side of the table while Martha got on the other. Polly dragged a step-stool up to the end of the table nearest to the mummy's head, then climbed the short ladder to gain a better vantage point for collecting some general photographs of the proceedings.

Dr. Lilly carefully freed the edge of the blanket that was tucked neatly under the edge of the body. Fine sediment filtered out of the cloth with each move, leaving a considerable amount of dirt collecting on the table around the body. With extreme care, he lifted the blanket slowly to be sure that nothing that might be stashed in the folds of the blanket, other than dirt, would be lost.

Martha slowly reached across and helped him pull the first layer of the blanket-shroud free. As she lifted, Dr. Lilly said, "Hold on. There is something here in the fold of the blanket."

Martha froze. She had no idea what that meant so she asked, "What does it look like?"

"It looks like a small bag. I can't tell what it is made of. The surface is a little cracked like old leather, but it is still intact. Polly, come around here and take a few pictures."

Curiosity was killing Martha. She wanted to see what Dr. Lilly had found, but she could not see around the blanket edge that she was holding up and she could not lay it down.

Polly busily snapped photos from various angles then stepped back. Dr. Lilly said, "Okay, Dr. Jefferson, pull the blanket on back."

Martha slowly and with the utmost care did just that, allowing it to rest on the table beside the mostly covered body. When she finally let go of the blanket, she quickly made her way around the table. Dr. Lilly's side of the body was still covered by the interior layer of the blanket. Lying near the bulge that was obviously caused by the mummy's arm was a small leather bag. The top of the bag was drawn tight by a leather cord. The blackened little bag was obviously placed with the body but it was not possible to determine what might be inside it.

Martha gently reached over and lifted the bag from its resting place. Despite the cracking visible on the outer surface, it was intact and from the feel, did contain something. Carefully loosening the cord, she coaxed the bag to open slightly despite its hardened texture. Dr. Lilly handed Martha a shallow cardboard artifact box so she could empty the contents into it.

Martha placed the box on the table and carefully laid the bag inside the shallow box. Ever so gently, she opened the bag and then using a pair of cotton-tipped tweezers, she gently eased the contents from the bag. Dr. Lilly craned his neck to see what special items might be revealed. Soon three small items: a bear claw, a piece of cloth, and a perfect little arrowhead were gingerly placed in a line beside the bag but still inside the safe confines of the box.

Martha examined the arrowhead first. "This is a Fresno point," Martha stated. "It was a common style in the last stages of the prehistoric time period in this region. That would put the date at somewhere between 1,500 and 1,700 A.D." Next, she picked up the claw and turned it over and over, then declared, "I am fairly certain that this is from a bear, but I will have to double check the comparative collections to be sure." Lastly, she picked up the piece of cloth and while it was apparently placed in the bag intentionally, there wasn't anything distinctive about it, so she placed it back into the box alongside the claw and the point. After returning the last item to the box, she moved the box to the adjacent table for additional analysis later.

Returning to her side of the table, Martha carefully pulled the upper layer of the blanket back and exposed the hidden edge. Easing it out from under the mummy, she carefully pulled the inner layer of the blanket loose. Dr. Lilly took the edge and began to carefully pull it toward himself. Inch by inch the second third of the blanket lifted free and exposed the mummified body underneath. Polly diligently snapped numerous photos of each stage of the unveiling.

In a few minutes the blanket was laid out flat on both sides of the mummified body and it was lying exposed for the first time in centuries. The body was clearly a young man and he was fully dressed in buckskin pants and shirt. Decorations were clearly visible on the garments but it would be necessary to do some cleaning before a complete analysis of the designs would be possible. Ultraviolet lights would probably be used to help document the faintest images. No other artifacts were found and essentially the analysis was complete for the moment. A full x-ray and *CAT scan* was planned and would be performed the next day at the local hospital.

Polly snapped pictures of every possible detail as well as from various angles. It was essential to document everything in as much detail as possible. Except for the x-ray and *CAT scan*, no other invasive investigation was planned until consultation with the tribe could be completed. It was feasible that this body would be transported to the hospital and then immediately to the tribe's burial grounds and it might never be seen again.

While it was completely understandable from a cultural perspective, the scientist in each of them longed to know more. An opportunity to do an autopsy on an American Indian mummy was almost unprecedented when preservation was so good. Dr. Lilly hung around for a little while, but soon excused himself for other obligations. Polly wrapped up the photography and headed to her desk to process the images. If there was anything wrong with the photos, she wanted to know it now so the shots could be retaken.

Soon the lab was quiet. The only sound was from her own breathing and the occasional vehicle passing in the distance. Martha pulled up a chair and sat down facing the mummified young man. A thousand questions raced through her mind: "Who are you? Where did you live? Who buried you? What does the symbol on the cave wall mean – if anything? What is the significance of the items in the little bag?" That growing sense of despair that she had felt in the cafeteria was creeping back into her mind. "How in the world do I answer these painfully simple questions?" she whispered to herself, not wanting to disturb the silence.

Martha sat there and stared at the silent and lifeless form. She wanted to believe that all the answers are, or once were, there. It was just a matter of understanding how to look, where to look, and how to interpret the evidence. Several hours passed before she finally rose from her place of contemplation.

The sun had gone down and the only thing holding the darkness at bay was the lights of the lab. Dr. Lilly suggested leaving the blanket beside the body and covering everything with plastic. Before he had left, they had carefully rolled the free portion of the blanket within a sheet of acid-free paper as a separation barrier within the roll. Rolling the blanket would prevent it from being creased or torn. It was still quite pliable but it was probably still hundreds of years old and extremely fragile.

Martha took a large sheet of black acid-free plastic and carefully draped it over the body and the neatly rolled blanket that was now lying adjacent to it. Securing the edges with several heavy reference books, she made sure that everything was covered up. Gathering her various belongings as well as her notebook where she had rapidly scribbled various thoughts and observations, she made her way to the door. Despite the abundant clutter in the room, her footsteps seemed to echo more than she had ever noticed before. Reaching the door, she started to turn out the lights but paused. One more look across the room confirmed that everything was in its place and it was safe to go home.

Darkness instantly engulfed the room when she hit the last light switch. Locking the door behind her, Martha quickly made her way down the hall and back to her office. As usual, her door was closed but not locked. The vacuum cleaner used by the overnight cleaning staff could be heard in the distance. She momentarily sat down at her desk. The light on her phone indicated that she had a voice mail.

After finding a pen and notepad, she checked the message. It was Ted. He was just wishing her luck and expressing his regret for not being able to attend the unveiling. What caught her attention the most was how he signed off. He ended with "God bless you."

The words caught her by surprise. She knew that Ted was a Christian by the conversation that they had shared in the past few weeks. He was not just a Christian in his words; he lived morally upright and was the kindest and gentlest man that she had ever met. The traits that she had seen for many years in her brother Sam were the same kind and considerate characteristics that she had seen in Ted. For a moment, her focus left the mummified boy and drifted over into the realm of spiritual considerations.

A brief search of her desk uncovered the little green book that she had found recently. Once again, she thumbed through it, stopping to read snippets from some pages that her eyes happened to lock onto. She closed the book and dropped it into her backpack. She was intrigued by the verses she read and determined to spend some time at home checking it out more carefully.

With no other reason to hang around the office, Martha gathered the other miscellaneous items and exited her office, closing the door behind her. The walk home passed in a blur. So many thoughts raced through her mind that when she arrived at her front door, she could not recall one detail about the journey.

Dinner passed almost as unnoticed. As she ate, she intently studied the photographs of Native Americans from the early 1800s. Several famous photographers had traveled extensively and photographed the Indians in their traditional attire as well as their ceremonial regalia. Many of these images have been published and serve as invaluable research sources. Occasionally setting her plate down, she would use a magnifying glass to get a better look at the specific detail of the decorations, especially on the more common attire. Not finding what she was hoping for, she would resume her obligatory meal and proceed to the next page. The thick book certainly would last longer than the food.

Glancing at the clock, she determined that it was time for bed. She would have to brief Dr. Hodges on the findings first thing in the morning. With her pre-bedtime routine completed, she slid between the sheets and immediately dropped off to sleep.

Chapter 45

Her first thought was, "this must be a dream" and even that seemed especially odd because she knew that it was one. She had never had a dream in which she was fully aware that it was a dream and that she could see herself actually in it.

She looked around and there were two Indian boys sitting at the base of a bluff. A commotion from the bluff drew all of their attention. A boy emerged from a small cave followed soon after by a second boy. The first boy joined the two that were waiting but the last boy went straight to the nearby creek. All of the boys were laughing. She was not sure but the one boy seemed to be washing something off.

The next thing she knew, the dream had jumped forward in time. The fourth boy was sitting in the mouth of a small cave. It was not the same cave but it looked strangely familiar. She could see his face clearly but she could not read any emotion on it. He was just sitting there, staring out into the forest beyond him. The next thing Martha saw was the boy lying motionless further back in the cave. The sun was dropping below the horizon and the dream-world was filled with darkness. Suddenly, she realized that the sun was up and that the three boys from the first part of the dream were placing stones on the spot where the boy had just been lying...

Buzz, Buzz, Buzz, Buzz, Buzz, Buzz. The alarm clock jolted her back to reality. With the hideously unpleasant noise silenced, Martha laid in bed staring at the ceiling. Her mind was spinning as she recalled the various stages of the dream. A few minutes passed before she threw the covers back and swung her feet onto the floor. She felt awful. The intensity of the dreams had robbed her of any rest that she should have gotten.

"That was a WIERD dream," she mumbled audibly even though there was no one there. She wanted to hear the sound of her own voice to settle her mind that she was indeed awake and that she was not going crazy. "I have no idea what I could have eaten to have generated such a strange dream," she continued. Walking into the bathroom, she began to prepare for work. The more she did, the less she thought about the dream until she finally dismissed it as just the product of an overactive imagination coupled with the challenge of finding answers to the mysteries of the mummy.

With a brief swing through the kitchen for a muffin that would substitute for real breakfast, she gathered her belongings and left the apartment. The cold north wind whipped through the leafless trees that lined the street. It was really too blustery to be walking but she simply enjoyed it regardless of the weather conditions.

Dr. Hodges was hanging around Polly's desk when Martha arrived. Polly had downloaded the photographs to her computer and burned three identical copies onto separate CD's. Dr. Hodges was holding all three.

"Good morning, Martha," Dr. Hodges exclaimed as she strolled up beside him. "Polly was telling me about the investigation and the little bag of items that was discovered. That is so exciting. Let's all sit down here at this work table and you can tell me what you observed and what you think."

Dr. Hodges, Martha, and Polly moved over to the eight-foot folding table in the middle of the office. It was surrounded by mismatched metal folding chairs and was the closest thing the museum had to a conference area. While multi-functional, it certainly was not fancy. Polly and Martha sat down on one side while Dr. Hodges sat across from them.

Martha recounted the series of events that transpired. Using her hands to demonstrate, she told about the way the blanket was doubled over the top of the body. She described the position of the little leather bag. Polly chimed in that the shots she took of that turned out very well. Martha then provided a synopsis of the various decorations, designs, and beadwork on the clothing.

"What was in the bag?" Dr. Hodges asked.

"There were three items in the bag: a bear claw, a piece of cloth, and a perfect Fresno-type arrow point," she replied. "It is a wild guess what the significance of these items might be, but apparently it was something the boy was carrying with him or whoever buried him placed it with the body as a grave offering. There is no way to tell which. The one good thing is that the point type is generally dateable to about 1,600 A.D. Last night I spent some time looking through the Catlin journals as well as the photos of others looking for any similarities in clothing style or decoration related to tribes from this general area. I knew it would not be a perfect match because he was documenting the American Indians over a hundred years later, but it was worth a look. I did not find anything that was very close at all."

Dr. Hodges listened intently. He hung on every word. His squinty eyes confirmed the degree of concentration that he was investing. As Martha had started her detailed descriptions, Dr. Hodges had leaned forward and propped his right elbow on the table, then used his right hand to rub his chin. It was clear that his mind was working diligently to process the information and possibly offer any sage wisdom to help solve the mystery. "What do you make of the piece of cloth?" He finally asked.

"It is strange. It is not your typical Native American weave. It really looks European. I will have to get it analyzed, but if it is European that would certainly fit the timetable of the arrow point. It could be a remnant of a trade good. I will follow up on that lead. That could have some very interesting ramifications," Martha concluded.

"So, what is the next move?" Dr. Hodges asked sitting back in his chair to indicate that he was satisfied with the progress and with the handling of the investigation.

"The mummy will be transported to the hospital and we will have an x-ray and *CAT scan* done. That will give us some basic internal information without having to perform any invasive procedure," she responded.

"Sounds good. Keep me informed!" Dr. Hodges rose from the table and proudly strolled out of the office and down the hall with all three *CD*'s firmly in his hand.

Polly looked after Dr. Hodges and then at Dr. Jefferson and said, "I'll burn you a copy of the pictures this morning."

"Thank you, Polly. I appreciate it," Martha politely replied. She then stood up and went to her office to make some preparations for the upcoming tests.

About an hour later, Martha stuck her head in Polly's office and said, "I am going to the lab. The ambulance from the hospital is on its way." Just as quickly, she turned and walked briskly down the hall to the lab. Everyone who worked in the lab had been instructed to stay completely away from the mummy. Martha was extremely concerned that something might happen to it and she had been making regular trips just to be sure it was undisturbed.

Entering the door, she glanced to the mummy and everything was exactly as she had left it. She released a deep sigh of relief. The last stage of the investigation would surely prove to be the most hazardous despite the hospital's assurance that they would be "extra careful."

Martha proceeded to the back door because the ambulance was already backing up to the loading dock. She held the door while the two technicians pushed the gurney inside. She led them to the table and proceeded to unwrap the mummy. In a few minutes, the body was once again exposed and ready to be moved. A soft new blanket was placed on the rigid gurney's surface and fluffed up so that the uneven bends and bulges of the mummy would be cushioned. It was critical that there would be no stress points on the body. Otherwise, it might simply break apart.

With the most extreme care, the three of them lifted the body and placed it on the waiting gurney, leaving the ancient blanket behind. The bunched-up gurney-blanket underneath was adjusted until the mummy was fully supported. The gurney had short side rails that were raised to ensure that the body did not slip during the ride to the hospital.

When the mummy was safely loaded Martha told the driver, "I will meet you at the hospital." She needed to take her own truck so she would have a way back, although she really wanted to accompany the precious cargo in person.

The driver, sensing her anxiety, replied with a smile, "We will wait until you arrive to unload the mummy."

Martha returned his smile with a beleaguered one of her own. "Thank you" was the sum of her reply.

Hours passed at the hospital as Martha went from department to department in the hospital getting the necessary paperwork finalized. The tests were finally completed and the data gathered. The x-ray showed absolutely nothing unusual. The *CAT scan* was equally inconclusive. Late in the afternoon, the ambulance returned to the museum, the mummy was once again securely laid on the lab table, and recovered for protection.

When everything was secure, Martha returned to her office and spent the next several hours writing up her findings and conclusions. Word of the mummy's discovery was beginning to filter out among the various professional archeologists in the region as well as some national scientific journals. The stack of phone messages grew each day.

Martha quickly thumbed through them. Only a couple of them were urgent. She picked up the phone and returned those calls. In each case, the caller had already left their office, so she simply left a message knowing that they would probably need to call her again tomorrow. Leaving the rest of the messages in her chair as she stood up, she moved toward the door, turned out the light, and left the office.

The walk home was brisk but still refreshing. There was something about walking across campus at twilight, but tonight her mind was full of questions. Much internal conflict was clouding her mind. She knew that there was so much more to life than what she was experiencing. Maybe she should talk to Sam. "He is certainly not the same person that he was when he was a kid," she said as she walked. "I'll talk to him – one of these days."

Chapter 46

Martha stepped up to the podium. She had gladly accepted the opportunity to speak to the National Association of Professional Archeologists. Their annual meeting is held every summer to enable archeologists from around the country to travel wherever the four-day symposium is held. It was a prestigious invitation for her to address this assembly.

"Esteemed colleagues and fellow scientists of the past: It was with great pleasure and *trepidation* that I agreed to present this paper to this revered association. As you have seen on the agenda, my paper will present the findings and conclusions related to the discovery of the very well preserved mummified remains of a proto-historic Indian boy recently recovered inside a cave in northwest Arkansas."

"The background on the discovery is simple. A landowner, who diligently protected the cave where the discovery was made, recognized that there was an odd stain on the wall of the cave. He finally contacted the University Museum director and I was given the task of evaluating it. In the proper light, it clearly resembles a paw print of a dog or a wolf, as you can see in the following series of images. Lighting was a challenge due to the remoteness of the cave and the image being well back from the opening. I apologize for how dark they appear." As she spoke, several images projected onto the screen behind where she stood.

"As we mapped the rock-fall present on the cave floor, an area immediately below the pictograph seemed to have an unnatural array of slabs that were all lying flat without overlapping. On a hunch, we laid out a test unit and carefully began to excavate. The blanket-wrapped body was first encountered about fifteen centimeters below the surface. It was fully excavated and removed to the Museum lab. *CAT scan* and x-ray imaging were both performed to assess the condition of the body as well as look for any *pathologies* or injuries. Nothing conclusive was observed from either test."

"The university's physical anthropologist, Dr. Lilly, conferred with the forensic pathologist and they agreed that the boy was about fifteen years old, seemingly in good health, and exhibited no signs of trauma that would explain his death. Their best guess is that he became ill from some virus or bacteria and died. Without doing any invasive testing, they were unable to be more specific than that. The local tribal council declined our request to allow additional tests."

"The body was dressed in buckskin pants and shirt. There was a modest amount of beadwork sewn onto the garment, clearly indicating that it was not his everyday attire. This appeared to be a special burial garment. The beads were perforated shells of local origin. In fact, the shells that were used are still commonly found in the streams of the area. That leads us to believe that he was probably living in this immediate vicinity, although, we have not found any nearby village that matches the associated time period. The common nature of the shells throughout the region does not preclude that this person was not a local resident and was actually just passing through. However, I believe that it is unlikely that a boy of this age would be out exploring in an uninhabited region of the country. I am certain that he was a local resident who was probably buried by his family."

"The only object found with the body was a small skin bag. It was clearly included as a grave offering. Inside the bag there were three objects. The first was a bear claw. The significance of this is debatable, but it is clearly something that was important to the boy or to the person or persons who buried him. The second item was a Fresno point. This small triangular arrow point is found throughout this region and has been found in radiocarbon context from about 1,700 A.D. There is no reason to believe that this point is not from that time period. It is also supposed that the burial was contemporary to the point. The third item was a piece of cloth. While immediately not viewed as being of much significance, it soon was revealed that the cloth is not of Native American manufacture. It was of a material and weave-style common to European technology. Whether it was made in Europe or by Euro-American settlers has not been determined yet. A microscopic analysis of pollen grains, trapped in the fabric, has not been completed as of this date. Regardless, the implications are clear. This individual or his family had encountered an early Euro-American explorer. I believe that this scrap of cloth is a symbol of that event. I also believe that it is possible that the illness which killed this young and otherwise healthy boy may have been directly related to that event. It is well documented that a tremendous die-off of native populations followed in the wake of these early explorers."

"There is so much to learn from the unwritten pages of history. The evidence that was found in this cave was profound and clearly told a story. It is so important for us to continue to search for the clues to the past and to correctly interpret the evidence we find. We should keep an open mind, embrace the facts, and then build on them to paint a portrait that has been lost for generations. The truth can be found in science and we should never allow ourselves to be governed by such weak-minded concepts as faith and religion. Thank you for your attention."

As Martha stepped back from the podium, the crowd rose to their feet with a resounding applause. Unseen by Martha, in the back of the room, Sam, Tammy, Jim, and Sarah stood silently. They had made the journey and wanted to surprise Martha with a big celebration following her keynote speech on that final evening of the conference. Jim looked at Sam. The tears welling up in his eyes were not from pride. Without a word, they slipped out of the raucous hall filled with self-enlightened scholars and into the truly majestic night. Far off in the distance, the soulful song of a dog could be heard as the full moon climbed higher into the heavens. Oh what truly divine mysteries await discovery, if we but close our eyes, contemplate the possibilities, and have faith.

"Jesus saith unto him, 'Thomas, because thou hast seen me, thou hast believed: blessed are they that have not seen, and yet have believed.' " John 20:29.

Glossary

back-strap: colloquial phrase referring to the meat along the backbone of a deer. See also: tenderloin

brownies: slang for Smallmouth Bass. It refers to the light brown coloration.

bluffshelter: Term for an archeological site at the base of a cliff where a natural overhang is present that provides a protected location of human habitation.

carbon-14: is a radioactive isotope of carbon. Its presence in organic materials is used extensively as the basis of the radiocarbon dating method of archeological samples.

CAT scan: It is a medical imaging method employing tomography where digital geometry processing is used to generate a three-dimensional image of the internals of an object from a large series of two-dimensional X-ray images taken around a single axis of rotation. The word "tomography" is derived from the Greek *tomos* (slice) and *graphein* (to write).

CD (short for compact disc): an optical disc used to store digital data, originally developed for storing digital audio.

chew the fat: colloquial phrase referring to casual conversation usually between men who are friends and neighbors.

cloistered: providing shelter from contact with the outside world.

countenance: facial expression that offers approval or sanction.

datum: a reference from which measurements are made.

denuded: to strip of all covering or surface layers, i.e. a tree with no leaves.

desiccated: to dry up or dehydrate.

dug out: colloquial phrase referring to the unscientific digging done by non-archeologists. It is usually done in a hasty, random manner that destroys the site in the hope of finding artifacts.

euphoric: a state of very intense happiness and feelings of well-being.

field dress: also called gutting, is a necessary step in preserving meat from deer harvested in the wild. Field dressing helps the overall quality of the meat. It also makes it considerably easier for a hunter to carry the deer from the woods.

269

floodplain: flat or nearly flat land adjacent to a stream or river that experiences occasional or periodic flooding.

frivolity: lacking seriousness and marked by unbecoming levity

intrepid: characterized by resolute fearlessness, fortitude, and endurance.

latent: present and capable of becoming though not now visible, obvious, or active.

malleable: having the capacity for adaptive change.

niche: a recessed place in the wall.

nocked: The end of the arrow that attaches to the string of a bow is called a nock. The act of placing the arrow onto the string is called "nocking the arrow."

pathologies: deviations from the normal that constitute evidence of a disease.

precipice: a significant vertical, or near vertical, rock exposure.

rapt: wholly absorbed or engrossed.

sinuous: a serpentine, wavy, or winding form

scrapes: during the breeding season, male deer will paw the ground until bare soil is exposed. Scents will be deposited in the bare spot by both bucks and does to attract a mate.

skittish: easily frightened.

spike buck: male deer with small antlers consisting of a pair of single points

stalactites: secondary mineral deposits hanging from the ceiling of limestone caves.

stalagmites: secondary mineral deposits that form on the floor of limestone caves usually directly below a stalactite.

tenderloin: the meat along the backbone of a deer.

trepidation: apprehension and nervous fear

unfurled: to open out from or unfold.

unwieldy: not easily managed, handled, or used.

About the Author:

John Riggs was born and raised in central Arkansas, graduated from Cabot High School, and then from the University of Arkansas in Fayetteville with a degree in anthropology. His lifelong interest in archeology was cultivated into a career with the U.S. Department of Agriculture – Natural Resources Conservation Service where he works as an archeologist. Another driving force in his life is his faith in God. Serving in various churches and ministries throughout his life has drawn him closer to God and molded his attitudes to be a caring and compassionate servant while continuing as a leader.

John's educational background in anthropology as well as a mission trip in 2004 to Zambia, Africa, solidified his call to serve in the African-American community. He now serves as an associate minister and Bible teacher in a rural African-American church near Carlisle, Arkansas with his loving and supportive wife, Cheri. You may contact John at jrzambia@yahoo.com.